THE
DUST BOWL
ORPHANS

BOOKS BY SUZETTE D. HARRISON

The Girl at the Back of the Bus

This Time Always

Basketball & Ballet

The Birthday Bid

The Art of Love

My Tired Telephone

My Joy

Taffy

When Perfect Ain't Possible

Living on the Edge of Respectability

THE
DUST BOWL
ORPHANS

SUZETTE D. HARRISON

FOREVER

NEW YORK   BOSTON

Forever
Hachette Book Group
1290 Avenue of the Americas, New York, NY 10104
read-forever.com
twitter.com/readforeverpub

Originally published by Bookouture, an imprint of Storyfire Ltd., in 2022
First Forever edition: December 2023

Forever is an imprint of Grand Central Publishing. The Forever name and
logo are trademarks of Hachette Book Group, Inc.

The publisher is not responsible for websites (or their content)
that are not owned by the publisher.

The Hachette Speakers Bureau provides a wide range of authors for
speaking events. To find out more, go to www.hachettespeakersbureau.com
or email HachetteSpeakers@hbgusa.com.

Forever books may be purchased in bulk for business, educational,
or promotional use. For information, please contact your local
bookseller or the Hachette Book Group Special Markets Department
at special.markets@hbgusa.com.

Library of Congress Control Number: 2023932070

ISBN: 9781538743232 (trade paperback)

Printed in the United States of America

LSC-C

Printing 1, 2023

This book is dedicated to my great grandparents,
Samuel "Papa" and Connie "Mama" Johnson Kelley,
whose journey from Oklahoma to California ensured our
family's continuance.
I am forever appreciative.

PROLOGUE
FAITH WILSON

April 14, 1935 "Black Sunday"
Wellston, Oklahoma

"Hope, hurry up! You gonna get us left collecting rocks from here to out west."

"I'm coming, Faye-Faye. Rock collecting takes time, so don't rush me."

My five-year-old baby sister was blissfully oblivious to the seriousness of our situation. I'd tried schooling her about Papa being on a devastating edge and Mama being mostly mute since our big sister, Charity, was fatally bit by a rattler and went home to heaven day before yesterday. She could see for herself our ten-year-old brother, Noah, was on the back of the mule cart, in our parents' care up ahead, after stepping on something jagged and rusty and might lose his foot for trying to save Charity. If she listened closely, Hope might even hear, floating on the arid wind, our brother's pitiful cries prompted by pain and tragedy.

But Hope was busy. The baby. Rock collecting and chasing dreams. I was fifteen and knew better than falsifying, but I'd fed Hope soft lies of grand adventures and golden glories awaiting us in California versus this dry, dust-bowl reality we were living. Or, rather, leaving.

We lost everything!

The farm. Our house. Church, friends, the school and Miss Bullocks, the best teacher I'd ever had. And most importantly, Charity.

Leaving my big sister in a grave was like seeing the sweetest pieces of me at the bottom of a dark well that sunlight couldn't reach and I couldn't possibly retrieve.

Charity, I pray those parts of me give you good company.

I didn't bother drying the fresh tears rushing down my face. Instead, I bent over, hands on my knees, letting tears fall, wishing they were plentiful enough to water this parched place. Maybe if I cried long and hard enough grass would grow again, crops would reappear. If my tears possessed such magic I'd weep until time rolled backward, allowing me to grab Charity so we'd all escape death lurking in the mouths of rattlesnakes and merciless black blizzards.

We'd been haunted by hard times. Drought. Sizzling temperatures with little reprieve. And frequent dust storms so vast and relentless that they were called black blizzards because of their choking, swelling plumes of dark, sooty soil and pillaging ferocity. Land that once bloomed with plenty had become stubbornly barren, mocking our labor and refusing to bear fruit or render a means of sustainable living. Now, dire circumstances had my family, like so many others, fleeing Oklahoma with little more than pain and precious memories.

I looked back not merely to make sure Hope had stopped her rock scavenging and was coming along like I'd asked her to, but for one last glimpse of the only home I'd ever known.

We'd been walking so long trying to connect with Route 66 that our homestead wasn't much more than a figment of my imagination in the far distance. Even so, my mind easily painted euphoric pictures of what was once ours. I wanted to tarry there enchanted by the past like a desert mirage. Instead, I fussed at my baby sister. Her playful curiosity had us lagging too far behind our family.

"Hope Ann Wilson, if you don't get your narrow butt up here..."

Her eyes bugged before she took to yelling, "I'm telling Mama you said a bad word."

"I didn't. Now hurry up before I say something that might send me to hell."

"Ooo, Faye-Faye, you did it again."

I was too hot, tired, and hungry—and my heart was too busy hurting—to tell her one word could have multiple meanings, that I'd meant that place of fire and brimstone and wasn't cussing like Papa sometimes did when he didn't know we were listening. Needing to get down the road, I enticed Hope with something she loved nearly as much as rocks. "Wanna piggyback ride?"

That terminated her rock collecting, brought her running.

I squatted down allowing her to hop up, taking on her weight despite my weariness. She wrapped her arms about my neck and for a moment I felt deceptive giddiness in her sweet closeness. As if we were playing on an ordinary day. Entertaining the youngest and keeping her out of trouble. Except now I was the oldest, Charity was gone, and elusive pleasure was short-lived. Our reality was uncertainty and a long, dusty road ahead.

Five minutes into walking with Hope on my back, she shrieked with five-year-old abandon.

"Look, Faye-Faye!" She pointed out a façade of a house set

far back from the road. It was deserted and had clearly outlived its heyday. Only two of its walls remained, and those were riddled with holes and nearly stripped, exposing its private insides like a cheap lady of the evening selling her business.

"It might have treasure." My baby sister scrambled free, heading that way before I could protest. "I'ma find something Charity might like when she wakes up," she sang, demonstrating her limited understanding of death's finality.

"Hope, come back here. *Please.*" I faulted myself for making a game of sneaking onto properties abandoned by folks escaping Oklahoma's miseries, telling Hope that we were pirates in search of booty. Sometimes we came away with something. A cracked pot. Cooking utensils. Or a scrap of fabric. That find had been her favorite. We'd taken the wad of material home to Mama, who decided it wasn't good for much besides crafting a doll for her youngest. Now, she was skipping toward that house like our family and California weren't waiting.

I opened my mouth to command Hope's return, but words took a back seat as something eerie skittered down my spine and left me shivering. I tried to shake it off only to notice the sky. It was absent of rain clouds, yet steadily darkening. My ears caught the sound of a low, deep wind, like how Papa hummed when working the fields. Suddenly, it was the only sound, as if creation had bowed to its symphony. That's when I knew. A black blizzard was coming.

I glanced over my shoulder, slowly and hesitantly, as if something inside sensed the magnitude of the monstrosity and meant to spare my soul from the terrorizing reality.

Terror is too tender a word. *Horror* is too pretty. If I had the ability to descend into Hades and come back again, that evil voyage could never inspire an accurate description of the wall of black swirling dust rampaging in the not-too-distant northeast.

Always be at the ready.

Papa taught us that lesson, but black blizzards hammered it

in. Those dry phenomena could come out of nowhere without warning signs in advance. Slow. Low. Or so fast and furious you couldn't prepare yourself. This was one of those, making it impossible for me to catch my breath.

It was opaque. Massive. Like some frenetic demon devilishly dancing a macabre jig. It appeared to be moving faster, more ferociously than any black blizzard I'd experienced. It plumed so high, spread so wide it had no beginning or end, blotting out the sun as if this was Egypt in Moses's day and the final plague was here. I stood nightmarishly transfixed; head craned to take in its mercilessness until hearing my name like a long-lost salvation song in the distance.

"Faith!"

Papa's frantic bellow snatched me back from my hypnotic trance. I looked away from that chilling tempest to see my father, racing toward me as if capable of saving me from that black blizzard's consumption. But he couldn't and we both knew it.

"Run, Faith!"

I obeyed his instructions reaching me through the roar of the storm.

Terrorized by dust and destruction, I took off running, screaming loud enough to resurrect Charity. *"Hope!"*

My baby sister stood in the shadow of that dilapidated house, wide eyes riveted on the storm, rivers of urine running down her legs. She was impaled by fear. Frozen.

I wanted to scream her into action but dust caught up with me. It filled my mouth, coated my tongue, and stung my eyes, obscuring my ability to see.

Dear Jesus, please!

Disoriented and confused, I tripped over God knows what and landed flat on my face, hurting myself in the process. I took to crawling, desperately trying to reach my youngest sibling. Coughing, wheezing, I managed to fight my way back onto my feet and took off running toward her, stumbling blindly. I cried, screamed, dared to pray that those raging waves of angry earth would part like the Red Sea and let me reach my mama's baby. I'd already lost Charity. I was the oldest now, and reaching Hope was *my* responsibility. Even if I died trying.

ONE

FAITH

Thursday April 11, 1935
Three Days Before "Black Sunday"

"Faye-Faye, how come you won't play with me?"

Hot, tired, vexed, and hungry I sat on the front steps ignoring Hope's whining. I loved my baby sister to pieces but sometimes she was a talented nuisance. "Go'n somewhere, Hope Ann. I don't feel like being bothered."

The fabric doll Mama made, Miss Rainy Day, dangling from one hand, Hope plopped her five-year-old self on the steps beside me, her lanky legs bare, ashy. "Why you so grumpy?"

'Cause we might have to leave.

I didn't tell her that. I wasn't even supposed to know myself.

That's what you get for sticking your big nose in grown folks' business, Faith Joy Wilson.

It wasn't intentional. I'd simply followed the blast of Papa's rifle, praying his hunting had produced something. Roast rabbit would be wonderful, but my belly felt so caved in that I'd take a squirrel. A possum. Even a rat if one happened across Papa's path. Mama was that kind of cook: she could make ugly things taste as if God had made them pretty. Plus, I was sick of shrunken potatoes, dandelion greens, and brined tumbleweed. And Hope's incessant singing.

"*A tisket . . . a tasket . . . a green and yellow basket . . .*"

Hope's singing to that dusty doll of hers had me propping my elbows on my knees, head in my hands, exasperated. My baby sister was sweetly innocent, but right then her naivety felt ignorant.

"*. . . I wrote a letter . . . to my love . . .*"

"You can't write." It was mean of me, but I wanted her to hush up and let me think.

"I can so! I write my name and a whole buncha other words. Miss Bullocks says my printing is pretty, so . . ." She punctuated her sentence by sticking out her tongue at me. "Come on, Miss Rainy Day. Let's not sit by Ol' Grumpy. We might catch cooties."

I felt bad for hurting her feelings as she stomped into the house with that ugly, cornhusk-stuffed wannabe doll Mama made that Hope named as if it were a talisman capable of coaxing severely needed storm clouds into the sky again. I typically tolerated, even enjoyed, Hope's company but, like she had said, I was grumpy, sitting, thinking. I was a mess after following the resonating blast of Papa's rifle only to see he hadn't been hunting. He'd had to shoot our last cow, Tillie, ending her starvation and misery.

"Tomas, honey, that's the last of the milk. We can't stay here." Mama tried rationalizing with my father.

I'd taken advantage of the fact that my parents' backs were to me as I approached the pasture, and scurried into the barn before my presence was detected. In our home, meddling in adult business was prohibited, but fear and curiosity had prompted my transgressing. I needed to know if Papa would finally capitulate to Mama's constant urgings, or if his dedication to Granny—who'd died last year—would win. Plus, I wanted to be near Tillie in her final farewell.

"Mae, I can't leave this place. You *know* that."

Leaving versus staying had become my parents' cyclical disagreement. They waited until we were in bed and presumed asleep before discussing tense, adult things. Charity and I had taken to lying awake in the dark, listening. No matter how Mama cajoled or cried for us to do like many of our neighbors and leave Oklahoma, my father wouldn't budge, even when she reminded him that his sisters had left days ago. The middle of seven children and the only boy born to his parents, Papa felt obligated, wearing his sonship like a crown and burden. Particularly, in matters pertaining to his father.

Tomas Senior hadn't been an Exoduster fleeing the bitter south after the Civil War ended and the country tried to rebuild itself through Reconstruction; or a freeman bravely joining the nation's wild push toward westward expansion. The Negro slave of a Cherokee master, my paternal grandfather was forced to travel that devastating Trail of Tears that dispossessed thousands of Cherokees, Seminole, Creek, Choctaw, and Chickasaw. Unlike the Indian nations whose land was lost, appropriated by the U.S. government and reallocated to white men, Granddad—the enslaved—had long been dispossessed of his ancestors' original birthplace and native language. Yet, the government's rabid campaign to diminish and limit Indians' landowning wound up being a twist of fate to his benefit. When his master was ordered to allot segments of land to his enslaved bondsmen in this new Oklahoma territory, Granddad received a parcel that became his children's birthright and legacy. It wasn't Reconstruction's promise of forty acres and a mule, but the magnitude of that inheritance became even more important after Granddad disappeared when Papa was twelve. Papa religiously drilled these facts into me and my siblings. He was famous for lining us up after supper, half-smoked cigarette behind his ear, requiring our recitation of family history like participants in an Easter pageant.

Don't not one of you better ever forget this land holds our blood and spirit.

Hiding in the barn and eavesdropping, I witnessed Papa's rigid insistence.

"Mae, my mother did everything necessary for this land after my father had to disappear. I can't dishonor that. I have the deed. I'm not leaving."

Mama had tenderly suggested a temporary absence; we would come home when the rains returned and life was back to normal.

"It don't work that way." Papa's tone had been strong, strident when voicing concerns about squatters and other land pirates known for staking false claims in an owner's absence. "I'm the protector of this homestead. My place is here."

Mama sent her pleading in a different direction, citing the few potatoes and yams in the cellar, our having nothing of value left to barter thanks to drought and high temperatures that had parched the land and caused crop failure for years. The little that was left was decimated by black blizzards. We were farmers without produce or product. That meant we had no income, and my parents were gradually forced to sell or trade our possessions to maintain a meager existence. Papa had even sold the family car last year, leaving us with the wagon and Morris the mule as transportation.

"Tomas, I know this farm's important to you. To us. I don't negate that. But right now, conditions aren't favorable and I'm at my wits' end." Mama's voice grew gentle as she unnecessarily detailed our predicament. No crops. Dwindling food. Canning tumbleweeds, eating cornmeal mush and root vegetables with old bacon grease. Frayed clothing and worn-down shoes. Farm equipment broken by the dry, unyielding earth. Our livestock

sold, eaten, or dead. Endless days of dust choking the air, impact-
ing visibility, and coating our skin and hair—leaving us wheezing, our eyes swollen and watery. She'd even reminded him that
our family friends the Kelleys and the Browns were headed
west Sunday. "There's room on that mule train. Traveling in
numbers'll keep us safe—"

"Dammit, woman! Are you listening?" Papa never cussed or
raised his voice at Mama. His doing so left me stifling a gasp.
"My father killed a man over this land!"

My eyes grew big at a revelation that had never factored into
our required Easter pageant-like recitations.

"Tomas, I know that—"

"Well, you ain't acting like it."

"Maybe you're too close to that fact to think straight, Tomas
Wilson! We *have* to leave Wellston. If we stopover in New Mexico like the Browns, we can return easily. We don't have to go
clear to California."

"Is that what this really is, Mae? You wanna go back to California and your family despite them disowning you for marrying me?"

Mama was silent before continuing. "Mother can help us
until we're back on our feet."

I peeked through the slats of the barn to find my parents
facing each other, squared off in battle. Theirs was an unfamiliar positioning. I was accustomed to their interactions being
warm, playful, loving, and sweet. Not confrontational and
frightening.

"I said what I said, Mae. I'm done arguing. Reverend Coulter
wants everyone to meet at church tonight to pray for rain. We'll
do *that* . . . but we're not leaving." Having had his say, Papa
walked off, leaving Mama to watch his proud, angry gait as he
stalked across a pasture that was once verdant and green but had
become a dusty, brown sea.

"Faith Joy Wilson, come on out of there." Mama's

summoning me was startling. I was unsure when or how my mother detected my presence but she had. I shamefully obeyed her instructions. "How much of that did you hear?" She stood, arms across her breasts, looking miffed enough to whack my backside with a switch.

I spoke with my head hung low. "A lot. I'm sorry, Mama."

"Sorry shoulda kept you outta grown folks' affairs." She stared hard at me. "If I catch you doing it again you will suffer the repercussions of your actions. And don't you dare repeat a thing. That was between your daddy and me. Am I clear?"

"Yes, ma'am."

She stared me down a moment, solidifying her threat. "Go next door and ask Miz Dorsey if we can borrow their saw." The fact that ours had gone mysteriously missing last month wouldn't keep Mama from doing what needed to be done. Her focus was on the horde of flies swarming Tillie's dead, open eyes, and her blood being greedily sucked up by the ground that was thirsty, dry.

The thought of Tillie being butchered and served on our table made me want to upchuck the bowl of "poor-mouthed cereal" we'd had for breakfast. It wasn't the bacon, eggs, grits, and Mama's fluffy-as-clouds biscuits enjoyed once upon a time when food was plentiful; but popcorn in milk was a welcome break from root vegetables and bacon grease. Even stringy beef would be a delicacy. But I couldn't eat Tillie. Not because she was emaciated and her flesh would be tough, but because I'd raised her from a calf. Yet, I knew better than to disobey my mother. Even if "next door" was a quarter mile down the road. "Yes, ma'am."

"And bring your brother home. He's been over there playing long enough."

That's how I'd come to intercept news not meant for my ears, leaving me short-tempered with Hope and sulking on the stoop instead of doing as my mother had asked. We'd had so many dust devils that month that school became sporadic. Storms turned daytime skies into midnight. Once, we'd even had to shelter in the schoolhouse overnight versus stumbling home with little visibility. After that, families still sending children to school opted to suspend lessons. Thus, our being home on a Thursday with Noah at the Dorseys' playing.

"Faith, why you sitting there looking like you lost something?"

I glanced up to see Charity, a basket of laundry in her arms, smelling and looking fresh despite working. Sometimes I forgot she was only eleven months older than me. She was Mama's replica: beautiful, slim but curvy, the color of warm honey with melted butter mixed in. She'd inherited Mama's freckled nose, wavy black hair, and finesse at the piano. My sister was a near woman. Sophisticated. Me? I was tomboy-tough with wild, coarse hair and Papa's deep-brown skin. Differences aside, my big sister was my best friend.

"What's wrong, Faye-Faye?"

"Nothing! And stop calling me that. My name is Faith." Seeing Mama in the distance headed in our direction, I jumped up, knowing I should've been on my way to the Dorseys'. "I'll be back."

"Where you going?"

"To get something for Mama." Best friend or not, I didn't need my sister in my business. We shared a room, a bed, and a triangular relationship. I liked Dallas Dorsey. He liked Charity. Charity could care less about the situation but if she knew where I was going and tagged along, I wouldn't get a lick of Dallas's attention.

"Something like what, from where?"

"Shouldn't you be hanging that laundry on the line?"

She'd abandoned her basket on the front stoop to fall in step with me despite my not needing her company. "It'll keep. So, where're *we* going, Faith Wilson?"

"None of your big-nosed business."

Her laughter was mischievous. "Must have something to do with Dallas."

That singsong teasing made me want to punch her in her neck. I ignored her, instead. When my silence got too heavy for us both, she started singing a little ditty Mama made up and liked to play before times got hard and her upright piano was sold for living money.

There's Faith, there's Hope, there's Charity,
My angels from above,
But Brother Noah built a boat,
And saved them from a flood.

Hope giggled every time we sang it, as if delighted that her name was within the lyrics. But I wasn't Hope. I wasn't amused and my face must've reflected that.

"Faith Joy, why you so sour-acting?"

"Because! Mama's badgering Papa to leave and I wanna stay." Our land had changed from a lush beauty to something dry, cracked, and unlovely. Yet, it held my most precious memories. Swimming in the creek before drought dried it up. Eating peaches picked for canning purposes. Laying in the field and cloud-watching, or chasing June bugs and butterflies. Caring for the livestock we'd had to sell or eat. Farming. Climbing trees. Family picnics and homemade ice cream. The land was our dynasty and legacy. We couldn't leave. "Charity, did Granddad really kill somebody?"

My sister didn't respond, but her nose turning red told me she knew something.

"Charity, you knew that about Granddad and didn't *tell* me?"

"Why're you hollering?"

"Because you're a musty-armpit-having, two-faced wench."

"Take that back!"

When my sister pushed my shoulder, I returned the gesture harder than she had, sending her off-balance. "We're supposed to tell each other everything, and you kept that from me?"

"Maybe that's because you're an immature baby who didn't deserve to know. Granddad killed his former master's son when they got into it over the man's tryna reroute water from our land. That's why Granddad had to hightail it outta Oklahoma and can't come back." She laughed as if proud of knowing something I didn't. "Guess what else? There's a reason Aunt Leola looks different. Granny had to do what she *had* to, to keep this place. Yes, even *that*," she emphasized when my eyes grew big.

Hands on my hips, I rejected her explanation of why our youngest aunt looked more Native than Colored. "Charity Lynn Wilson, you're full of devil piss." I flounced about angrily, heading back home. "Go to the Dorseys' by your lying-lipped self."

"I'm not lying! God's my witness, so stop acting salty and come on here. Don't you wanna see *Dallllllassss?*"

She laughed when I held up an angry fist in response.

"Just go get Noah and borrow the saw, you heathen." Her continued laughter left me screaming, "*I hope you fall into that dry creek and crack your crazy head!*" I stomped off, mad, wondering how long she'd kept secrets when we were supposedly best friends. By the time I re-entered our yard, I was only slightly less vexed.

"Faith Joy, you haven't been to the Dorseys' like I asked?"

"No, ma'am. Charity wanted to stretch her legs so we swapped," I informed my mother while hurrying to retrieve the laundry basket my sister had abandoned. Mama looked at me like she knew I was falsifying, but went about her business saying nothing, leaving me to hang clothes to dry. I did so, fussing beneath my breath about having a "two-faced, fish-headed fool" for a big sister.

Finishing my task, I decided to check on Tillie and ensure turkey buzzards or coyotes hadn't gotten to her yet. I picked up a thick stick to ward them off, just in case. I was halfway to the pasture when I saw Noah running or, rather, hobbling oddly. He was coming the back way where our property connected with the Dorseys'. It was a shortcut that we weren't supposed to take, thanks to a dangerous ravine, and the occasional rattler or cottonmouth.

"Why's he hobbling?" Shielding my eyes, I squinted at my brother who, seeing me, started waving frantically, yelling.

"Faith, go get Papa!"

A cold sensation rolled through me. *Where's Charity?* As I ran toward him, I screamed the thought aloud. Closing in on my little brother, I saw blood dripping through the shoe on his left foot and tears streaming down his dusty cheeks. "Noah, what happened?" I tried grabbing him about the waist to help him walk, but he pushed me off.

"Go get Papa. Charity's bit!"

I turned, screaming for my father, only to see him already rushing toward us. Noah barely finished conveying the horrifying facts before Papa was running toward Charity, leaving me to help my brother toward the house while hollering, *"Mama!"*

Everything was a whirlwind after that. Mama leaving me to tend Noah while racing the same direction Papa had. Hope crying and clinging to me. Our parents returning, Charity cradled against Papa's strong chest, her skin pale beyond belief. Mama cutting Charity's leg—already swelling and funny-colored where she'd been bitten not once, but twice—to extricate venom. Papa going in search of Doc Mason only to learn he was in Tulsa, far from reach. Me, huddling in the corner with Noah and Hope, fearfully keeping vigil as neighbors arrived and church members made a ring about our house outside. There were prayers and poultices. Hymns and chants. Homemade remedies and even the Native medicine man. All in the name of saving Charity.

Heaven heard our cries that night and showed mercy. Until the dark of morning.

I'd forced my eyes open so long, but had apparently dozed off only to be awakened by Mama's heart-shattering screams. I squeezed Noah and Hope to me, instantly knowing my best friend and big sister was no longer among the living.

Papa was broken yet stoic; my younger siblings cried oceans. Me? My devastation was complete. I was living but lifeless. If my whole soul was ripped in shreds, Mama's never existed. She wailed, screamed, and moaned as if her spirit had fled. Refusing to release her firstborn, it took four neighbor women to pry Mama's arms from around Charity's cooling flesh.

"We should've left!"

Mama's shattering accusation floated on the warm wind as my beautiful sister was lowered into the hard earth the following day.

"My baby's all alone in that ground, Jesus."

They were the last words I heard my mother speak before she became still and mute as a statue, leaving neighbors to help pack our meager belongings and load them onto the mule cart for our, now imminent, California departure. But Mama was wrong. My sister wasn't alone. I'd hidden Mama's tin of family photos wrapped in cheesecloth in the ground next to Charity when no one was looking so my sister would always have us with her.

Once everything was packed, Papa said goodbyes on our behalf, and we were prepared to leave. Except Mama refused to go without Charity. Mama's not speaking didn't keep her from fighting, wrestling.

"Mae, ain't nothing here for us but death." Papa's voice was thin, depleted.

My parents' reversal of opinion wasn't lost on me, but I said nothing. I merely helped Papa coax my wild, wailing mother away from my sister's grave and onto the back of the cart where Noah—foot swollen twice its size—waited.

"We'll come back when the land heals." With the property deed wrapped in cheesecloth and strapped about his chest, Papa led our mule from the yard without looking back. By then it was late Sunday and the Browns and Kelleys were far ahead. That's how *the* black blizzard of all blizzards found us traveling and exposed out there on that road, my baby sister frozen in terror as urine flowed down her legs, me fighting to get to her before death did.

TWO

ZOE EDWARDS

**Current Day
Oakland, California**

"Zo-Zo, what inspired your exhibition, again?"

I elected not to recount the number of times my cousin Natasha had posed that question since the initial conception of my upcoming exhibition. Either she was senile at thirty-nine or doing her usual my-mind-is-on-my-money routine and chit-chatting arbitrarily. I was tempted to make a smart-ass quip about her faulty retention, but why bother when she wouldn't remember it? Plus, it was spring, my favorite season of the year. The air was clear, my flight had been uneventful, Friday was a day away and I was back home in the bosom of my family. I was in a wonderful mood with patience for Natasha's forgetfulness. "Ever heard of Dorothea Lange?"

"Dorothy who?"

"*Dorothea* Lange. She's a photographer from the 1930s who

chronicled the Dust Bowl and the Great Depression." I held up a picture on my phone for her to view.

Driving, she glanced away from the road, briefly. "Nope. I know zero about that worn-out-looking white woman."

That had me snickering. "This isn't Lange. It's Florence Thompson," I explained of the woman featured in Lange's *Migrant Mother*, a 1936 photo that became the icon of the era, the plight of the people, and their poverty. It was haunting. Moving. A tight shot of Thompson, appearing distressed and desperate while seated with three of her seven children, cast her in a Madonna-like light that sympathizers couldn't dismiss. Within days of it appearing in periodicals, relief agencies delivered provisions to the California migrant camp where Thompson was located.

"Ditto for Florence," my cousin chimed while signaling left and changing lanes. "She's not in my wheelhouse and doesn't ring a bell."

"That's because you're an unenlightened cow."

Our shared laughter bounced about before Natasha clapped back. "Listen, chick, you're the only art curator in this car. If I quizzed you on dividends and yields, would you pass?"

"Absolutely not."

A highly successful financial investment adviser, my cousin had an amazing brain: a numerical, computational machine. She had little patience for the intricacies of non-numerical, non-fiscal things apart from music. Since childhood she'd been a math whiz but, like many in our family, she was also musically gifted and could have easily succeeded as a professional pianist. She'd armed herself with a double major in Music and Business only to discover she didn't care for the competitive nature of the entertainment industry, or the uncertainty of gigs, and opted for stability and something solid and went back to college to earn her MBA in finance.

"Exactly, Zo-Zo. So, stop schooling me as if artsy-fartsy stuff is important to me."

"It should be."

"Why the hell for? I'm not hanging pictures of that white woman on my walls. She looks beat, like she needs birth control or protein."

Her craziness left me laughing loudly. "You're ridonculous." Unbuckling my seatbelt, I grabbed my portfolio from the back seat and waited until she stopped at a red light to display several pictures. "Notice the differences?"

Her gaze glided over photographs juxtaposed side-by-side— those by Dorothea Lange versus JeShaun Halsey's—as I provided brief details on each collection.

"Yeah . . . the differences are clear. Lange focused her lens primarily on pale Americans. Halsey brought the neck bones and collard greens."

We were too busy laughing to notice the signal light had changed, prompting the driver behind us to blast their horn with obvious annoyance. Natasha offered an apologetic wave only to morph that into a middle finger in full-mast when the driver honked loudly again.

I lowered her hand. "Tasha, you can't be flipping folks off. This is Oakland. I'm not tryna get shot."

She snickered while driving away. "You haven't visited in a minute. Look around, chick. Oakland's a gentrified oasis. Like somebody poured powdered sugar over its residents. Case in point." She thrust an arm across my face to indicate a young blonde pedaling a bicycle complete with a basket bearing flowers and a loaf of what was probably artisanal bread. "Check out her happy ass. Just rolling down the street all smiley. Like this didn't used to be the 'hood before the powers that be priced brown folks out tryna turn it into Snowflake City."

Grinning at my cousin's lunacy, I silently observed my surroundings. I'd left Oakland ten years ago for Vince Edwards and Boston. Even then, the ethnic composition of the area was undergoing slight changes. Now, those changes were definite. This side of Oakland had been consumed, assimilated.

"All I know is, Everett & Jones still better be in business."

"Chil', don't get it twisted. That barbecue classic ain't going nowhere. Especially now that colonizers are always up in there relieving their tastebuds with our cuisine."

"Greedy colonizers got good sense." We both laughed. "Anyhoo... for the fifty-eleventh time, I give Lange big credit for those moments in which she aimed her lens on us but, otherwise, the *near* absence of blackness in photos from that era is what fanned my interest."

Our family had migrated from Oklahoma during the same time period that Lange's *Migrant Mother* was taken. My grandmother—whose parents migrated when she was just an infant—had shared stories passed down to her of the journey to the Golden State as well as those of other African-Americans. My grandfather was far less forthcoming. Granddad was older than Granny and remembered the journey firsthand. Having lost too much on that perilous trek, for him, it was a closed, taboo subject. Yet, in the work of photojournalists an African-American presence was often minimized, becoming yet another instance in which we were woefully, erroneously omitted from mainstream narratives. After reading an article celebrating the eightieth anniversary of Steinbeck's *The Grapes of Wrath* that also praised Lange's contributions to the opus of "Okies," something flared up inside of me, leading me to not merely challenge the white gaze and its selective blindness, but to celebrate and highlight the plight and survival of Black families who'd migrated west in search of improved opportunities; the lives of those more affected but less known due to the egregious limitations of poverty and racism. In a world obsessed with documentation, I didn't want us to be erased because of a lack of it.

When a recent surgery failed to fully restore my grandfather's declining eyesight, I became possessed by an inexplicable need to validate his journey, to present him a gift, a visual testament affirming his experience before his sight failed completely. I'd spent the past few years researching and creating this celebratory collection. The search had been arduous but unearthing oral histories, photographs, and pieces such as JeShaun Halsey's left me grateful and giddy.

Right then, after nothing save some pitiful inflight snacks, rather than giddy I was hungry. "I'll be hyper starving when I finish, so save your appetite for Everett & Jones. My treat," I advised, closing my portfolio before checking my phone for the time. My flight had been delayed. Thanks to a late arrival I'd had to forego settling into my lodging and head straight to the museum. "I appreciate you picking me up from the airport so I wouldn't have to deal with Uber or Lyft."

"Anything for my favorite cousin. Plus, I needed to see for myself that you're okay." She reached over and squeezed my hand, conveying support in my valley of crisis.

I silently returned the gesture, not wanting to think about Vince or the divorce papers in my suitcase.

"So, these photos should be of interest to me because . . ."

I smiled, appreciating my cousin's redirecting the conversation away from pain and back to my passion. "I'll show you when we get to the museum."

"I wasn't planning on coming in. I was going to kick you out at the curb and keep it moving. And why're you lodging at some old tired hotel instead of posting up with me, Zoe?"

"I love my sanity."

"Whatever, heffa. I hope that hotel's deep in the ghetto and overrun with rat-size roaches and geriatric hookers smelling like corned beef and broccoli."

I laughed heartily. "First of all, it's not a hotel. It's an Airbnb." A soror who'd recently purchased a quaint two-story, Cape Cod–styled cottage overlooking the marina offered use of it to our sorority cohort at a steep discount that I truly appreciated. "Secondly, Tasha, I swear you're doofus."

"Maybe, but you're smiling instead of crying over your trifling, hopefully soon-to-be ex-ho-of-a-husband. For that, you can thank me with cash or cookies."

"Estelle, these are *a-MAY-zing*." Seated beside my mentor and former boss—who now served as director of Oakland's multicultural museum—I leaned over a massive table, enthralled. The composites in my portfolio paled in comparison to the full-size images of JeShaun Halsey's *The Forgotten Okies* collection, pieces he'd been gifted and that had become our central installment.

"Can't you feel the brilliance?"

Nodding reverently, I expressed my appreciation at securing Halsey's pieces when an artist had withdrawn at the last minute. Thank God that artist—a colleague and friend of Halsey's with knowledge of his private collection—had referred me to him. I'd sat on pins and needles until he'd accepted my invitation. Feeling an indelible sense of rightness at his inclusion, I ran a white-gloved finger along the edges of the canvas nearest me, feeling utterly captivated by its subject. "How could anyone deny this child?"

"Sheer ignorance. Racism," Estelle offered. "Jim Crow-ism."

WHITES EAT FIRST. COLOREDS NEXT.

That stark command dominated a makeshift sign floating above the head of an African-American boy with huge brown eyes, standing near the entrance of a relief tent. He might have been seven or eight, yet his unflinching gaze was uncanny, direct. As if he'd seen other lifetimes, and the one he was experiencing wasn't his preference. His clothing was shabby, unkempt. Dust coated his skin like undeniable proof that he'd been a part of this particular piece of American history. He was frail, nearly gaunt, yet those eyes were beautifully arresting. The image of this precious urchin was but one photo from JeShaun Halsey's overlooked group of Black Okies.

"Zoe, I'm interested in the audience's reaction when learning that this sign, this segregated 1935 quasi-internment camp, was run by a highly respected relief organization yet in existence."

Moving to the next piece, I agreed, glad that I hadn't given up on this project despite my employer's lukewarm reception. When I'd pitched the idea several years ago it was met with interest that quickly fizzled thanks to Clarice Ritenour, the busybody head docent whose insanely rich family had been in Boston for centuries and proudly claimed Paul Revere as a main branch in their family tree. Miss Clarice took umbrage with "any art too primitive" and unapologetically used her husband's being a board member and her position as the museum's most prominent and generous donor to her advantage. A proud member of the Daughters of the American Revolution, she dictated museum business from behind the scenes, wielding power like some invisible deity. Her affair with the museum's director—a man two decades her junior—was a poorly kept secret so I wasn't shocked, just pissed at his shelving my project the day after my proposal was submitted. His "Sorry, Zoe, but it doesn't resonate the sensibilities of East Coast residents, and is too narrow in scope and non-inclusive of *white* migrants" sideline regret cloaked in budgetary risks and other racial-toned nonsense was BS that had Clarice Ritenour written all over it. The expenditures fit within the museum's annual budget and were well under cost in comparison with a colleague's recent project; plus, West Coast connected or not, Boston had a sizable African-American and diverse population that patronized the arts and we both knew that. Clarice made it a point to explain the decision to me a few days later, as if someone had died and crowned her Queen of Museum Things.

"The world needs unifying art, not that which separates or celebrates *yours* alone. I'm sure you understand, dear."

That reverse discrimination–sounding sentiment left me wanting to tell her to take her pinched-lipped, vegan-eating, OWL (Old White Lady) ass to England to sip tea with the queen. Except I actually admired Her Majesty and didn't want her subjected to a siddity socialite who lived for liposuction, plastic surgery, and seaweed. Instead, I focused on something my grandfather always said.

One monkey don't stop no show.

Clarice might've successfully shelved that Boston project, but she didn't own the globe. And I owned my space. Unapologetically. I'd studied hard, paid my dues, and wanted to reap the harvests like any other hardworking woman with a dream. Unfortunately, there'd always be folks like Clarice Ritenour who felt the need to keep me in my place and come for me.

I refused to give in, to see the dominant retain center stage, as if only Caucasians existed in that historic westbound migration. As if the primary existing body of work wasn't already drastically focused by a narrowing lens. The Head Hoot Clarice—as staff called her, making a play on that whole OWL concept—didn't do a thing except light a fire beneath me. I *would* highlight through art that phenomenon of African-Americans migrating farther west in search of hope during and after the Great Depression. Artistic benevolence aside, at the heart was my tribute to my grandparents and unknown ancestors. Pissed but determined, I'd vented to Estelle.

Zoe, you can do this with or without them.

Her encouragement was duly noted and received. I'd completed projects as a junior curator on loan to other museums as well as juggled multiple exhibitions before, but this time was personal and I couldn't relinquish my vision. For days

I'd planned, plotted, prayed, and consumed copious quanti-
ties of my neighbor's homemade chocolate chip cookies while
flushing out ideas to curate the exhibition independent of my
employer, and emailed Estelle a proposal that weekend. I practically held my breath until receiving her enthusiastic "yes!" Since
then, I'd run full speed into the project as if commissioned by
heaven.

Without question, juggling my work at my Boston site with
this independent project in Oakland stretched me at both ends.
Not to mention, I was co-creator of an upcoming Juneteenth
art festival in Cambridge in conjunction with a group of Har-
vard students. All "starving" artists, they were enthusiastic
but admittedly some were jaded after confronting the limiting
beliefs of others, marginalization, exotification, or lukewarm
receptions. Entering this ten-artist collaborative had been my
way of stretching myself, trying something different. It wasn't
merely about padding my resumé but preparing myself for
life as an independent curator. I valued the experience. Net-
working and building lasting relationships. My profession's
cultural landscape had evolved over the years, but was still a
work in progress and overwhelmingly rich, white, and cliqu-
ish. I needed art to not only be increasingly accessible to a
population that looked like me, but to reflect people of color's
sensibilities.

Technology was a blessing, allowing me to handle much
of my work remotely via phone appointments, Zoom meetings,
email correspondence, and virtual viewings. Some travel had
been necessary for archival research and to visit artists' studios.
Thankfully, I had more than sufficient sick leave and vacation
time to accommodate my being in California. With this particular exhibition mere weeks away, I chose to be onsite for the actual
installation. As we moved into final production, my excitement
increased daily.

"Estelle, wait until viewers discover these photos were taken right here in the Golden State and not somewhere down in the 'racist, wicked' South. They'll be clutching their West Coast pearls and gasping in shock."

"Ah, California: the utopia of make-believe liberalism," Estelle commented. As she pushed tendrils of graying red hair behind one ear, her smile turned impish. "Don't you love using art as a stickpin to bust arrogant, ideological bubbles?"

"Absolutely." It was one of the reasons I loved curating. Art forms could be subtle or intense, based on color, lighting, composition, or placement guided by visionary creatives. But as an African-American woman, I loved that art offered a non-threatening, deceptively innocuous means of examining—even challenging—social norms and conditions. "I can't believe Halsey's grandmother sat on these so long."

A nationally acclaimed photographer, JeShaun Halsey was a low-key celebrity. Low-key because despite immense success, he was elusive. He avoided the limelight, allowing the indisputable genius of his work to inhabit center stage. His images were bold, sometimes controversial. But always contemporary. These pieces given to him by his grandmother were absolute opposites, throwbacks to a bygone era and that natural phenomenon—the Dust Bowl—from which African-Americans were, too often, woefully and erroneously omitted.

"We have heaven to thank that his grandmother found that camera during their migratory trip and started snapping pictures." Estelle waved a hand toward the collection that would grace the museum as part of my *Black Life in a Distressed West* exhibition over the next several months.

I sat back, feeling as if I were viewing the photos for the first time. Some were rough. Subjects were often unfocused while others were startlingly clear. Compiled, they created an incredible collection that was arresting in its raw honesty and inescapable realism. "Her work rivals Lange's and Ernest Lowe's in capturing African-American life in early California."

"Missus Halsey may've had a different experience, or even a career *if* . . ." Estelle's sentiment didn't require finishing. We both understood the exclusions and impositions caused by racism. Any ambitions for a career in photography that Miss Halsey may have had had likely been short-lived thanks to a curt rejection after entering a contest decades ago. Her photos were returned with a "Dear Entrant, thank you but no thanks" missive wrongfully reducing her work to unneeded and amateurish. "Jerks," Estelle griped before brightening suddenly. "I have a surprise for you."

"What is it?"

"The thing about surprises is revealing them in advance defeats the purpose." We laughed as my mentor, a woman who'd graciously guided me even while challenging and demanding excellence from me, looped her arm about mine and led us away from the collection and toward her office. "You'll find out in forty or fifty minutes."

"Fair enough. Thanks for accommodating me in all of this."

"Zoe, of all the independent exhibitions you've done so far, this is your best. It's personal and that places you as a living subject easily able to communicate passion with every intimate breath."

I smiled when she squeezed my arm, affectionately.

Estelle and I had flip-flopped geographically. She was a Bostonian now on the West Coast, and I was a Californian residing in her native city. We'd worked together prior to her relocation, during her term as curator at my Boston-based museum. I'd followed Vince east in his pursuit to further his sportscaster career, and was blessed to land a junior curator position under Estelle. I valued our professional relationship and felt providence had positioned us as it had, allowing me to come full circle in hosting this exhibition in my native land. My family had migrated to California during the Great Depression and this showing honored them. I'd had no idea during the initial planning phase that the timing would prove divine, and that this Bay Area sojourn would not only allow this experience with family, but would grant me an escape from marital mess, if only temporarily.

"I'm thrilled your grandparents agreed to be photographed as living legends."

Plopping onto the spare chair in Estelle's office, I accepted the bottled water she pulled from a mini fridge and took a long, satisfying sip. "I'm amazed that Granddad did."

Granny was the loquacious one who loved sharing stories of life long before I was born. My grandfather, however, withdrew into himself whenever the subject of his past was broached. I grew up knowing mere fragments and shadows of his life story. There were matters—like details and names—that Granddad held close to his chest as if afraid that by sharing them they'd vanish. Apparently, his siblings and mother died when he was young, resulting in a childhood so tumultuous that it was sealed off and something he simply didn't discuss. I didn't fully understand the secrecy. That didn't prevent my honoring his privacy or respecting the fact that he was from a generation of men who didn't necessarily divulge everything. I knew I was taking a chance in even inviting him to be photographed on opening night and attributed his acquiescence to the fact that he was nearing his mid-nineties and had decided there was value in leaving something for posterity. Granddad's sight had deteriorated to the point that he was legally blind despite cataract surgery. Large images were easy enough, but the more intricate details of the art pieces might be lost on him; yet it was my way of honoring and celebrating my grandparents' journey, as well as their origins. Granddad was a sensitive spirit and, whatever minutiae he couldn't see, his soul would intuit.

. . .

"It's perfect, Estelle." We'd been at it for over an hour. We'd reviewed my schedule for training time with docents and confirmed the elementary schools attending a special "Artists of Tomorrow" seminar I'd concocted. I loved children, and being able to share this work with the next generation upped my usual surge of excitement. I knew jet lag would catch up with me soon, but right then I was loving the sample materials based on my write-ups of the collection—the minimalistic yet eye-catching design of the catalogs and labels. "I'd like to—"

A knock on the door interrupted.

"Hold that thought, Zoe. I think your surprise is here. Come in."

"Hello . . . oh, pardon my intrusion."

Due to his demanding schedule, we'd only spoken via phone, but that deep, resonant voice was immediately recognizable. Glancing over my shoulder, I smiled at the man entering Estelle's office, the one and only JeShaun Halsey. I knew him on sight because, though a rarity for him, he'd been a panelist at an art symposium I'd attended years ago. Plus, I'd haunted his website when researching his work once he'd accepted my invitation to participate, and included his headshot in the exhibition promotions and literature.

That headshot didn't do him full justice. This man is luscious.

I evicted that thought from my mind as Estelle vacated her chair to greet him, clasping his large hands in both of hers and offering a warm greeting. "It's a pleasure, Mister Halsey."

"Likewise. And JeShaun is fine. Actually, I prefer Shaun."

"Shaun it is. Can I get you something to drink? Oh . . . wait . . . meet my esteemed colleague. No, actually, you've already met."

I could've laughed at Estelle's uncharacteristic gushing and rushing, but I didn't blame her. The man was incredible enough to have easily enjoyed a profession in front of the camera. Slightly over six feet with skin like melted dark chocolate, full lips framed by a goatee, intense eyes, and a physique a professional athlete might envy, Shaun Halsey was *everything*. Since that long-ago symposium he'd allowed his hair to grow into locs which were intricately designed in a manbun atop his head. Which, incidentally, I typically disliked.

But this bun is yum.

"Shaun, Zoe Edwards, the exceptional woman who has come from the other side of the globe to curate this extraordinary exhibition."

I laughed at Estelle's exaggeration and stood to welcome the world-renowned photographer when my cell chimed an incoming text. I made the mistake of looking down at it.

Sign the papers already, Z. Enough damn game-playing.

I suppressed the cocktail of anger and loathing triggered by Vince's callousness and focused on Shaun. We'd talked often enough by phone that seeing him felt comfortable. "It's so nice to finally meet in person." Something warm shot up my arm as I placed my hand in his.

"I know you." His furrowed brows and intense stare were puzzling as he gripped my hand, scanning my being as if I were an unbelievable phantom or long-awaited apparition.

"Pardon?"

"I know you," he repeated with quiet, unmistakable intensity, "beyond our phone conversations . . ."

I hadn't interfaced with him at that long-ago symposium and had, since then, only communicated via phone. His intense stare was disconcerting and I found myself dismissing a shiver. "I must have a familiar face."

He shook his head slowly as if in a trance. "No . . . that's not it."

I extracted my hand, telling myself I had nothing to fear, as if only ugly men were psychotic.

"I'm sure it'll come to you," Estelle inserted, drawing Shaun further into the room, offering him the one remaining chair, and navigating the discussion elsewhere.

The afternoon proved pleasant. Discussing art was a passion, and Shaun Halsey's laid-back humility made conversation easy. I loved hearing behind-the-scenes information about the pieces he'd donated to the exhibition and what his grandmother called her "one-minute hobby."

"My grandparents came here as teens and eventually had eleven children to feed. How Nana Sam found a free moment to learn to operate a camera, let alone photograph anything, was nothing short of amazing." According to Shaun, his grandmother had enjoyed her hobby until the demands of being the young mother of a growing brood made it an impractical whim. Even so, when Shaun demonstrated an interest in the craft—despite her work being rejected—she'd encouraged him, even gifting him the bulk of her photographs. "If not for my grandmother, I might not have pursued what my father worried might be an act in futility. To this day, she's one of my biggest cheerleaders." He glanced at his watch. "And on that note, I need to jet. I've taken up enough of your time. I had business nearby and just wanted to pop in and thank you in person for including my grandmother's work in the exhibition."

We'd been so engaged in conversation that I was surprised to see an hour had passed since his arrival. I stood with Estelle, prepared to shake his hand in farewell. Instead, I stood there, his prisoner again.

"I *swear* I know you."

A funny sensation shimmied over my skin, leaving goosebumps in its wake as he held my hand and made that declaration. "Perhaps we met in another life," I offered, jokingly.

The seriousness of his conviction apparently kept him from smiling as he released my hand and shook Estelle's. When he'd exited, I looked at my mentor only to find her grinning.

"What?" I crossed my arms and waited for her to voice whatever notions were running through her head.

"Nothing. Except you might have an admirer."

For some crazy reason my mind switched to Vince and how I used to admire and love him, but no longer did. His serial betrayals had destroyed our union and I needed to be free of him. So why was part of me dragging slow feet as if divorce was an ultimate failure best avoided? Perhaps, I was being petty by holding on and denying him what he wanted, which was to live free of me.

Let him go, Zo. You've already lost too much to this marriage. Mostly Jaelen.

"Zoe? Are you okay?" Concern etched Estelle's face.

I grabbed my purse while checking my texts, and gingerly laid thoughts of Jaelen in that safe place in my heart where I kept them. "I'm good, but starving. Those little pretzels on that plane made me hangry. Natasha's on her way. Let's go eat."

It was barely eight o'clock when Natasha dropped me off at my Airbnb, but jet lag and a meal of barbecued ribs, hot links, candied yams, sweet tea, cornbread and collard greens put me in a food coma. After doing my armpits a favor and taking a shower, I'd slipped into my oversized Wakanda Forever sleep tee and fallen into bed. When my cell phone buzzed hours later, I was dreaming of the caramel cake I'd declined at the restaurant as if my mother hadn't taught me good sense. "Yes?" I answered, irritated that my food fantasy was being interrupted.

"Zoe Edwards, please."

"Speaking."

"Zoe, sorry for the late call, but—"

"Who's this?" I asked despite a warm sensation caused by that sexy, recognizable voice.

"Shaun Halsey."

I rolled onto my back and talked through a yawn. "Hi Shaun, how can I help you?" Of course, he had my number from previous phone discussions, but it was deep, dark night and too late for random, casual calls.

"I need to see you. Please."

"It's after midnight," I advised, checking the time.

"I know, and I apologize for disturbing your sleep, but you have to see this."

The urgency in his voice had me sitting up, turning on the bedside lamp, and launching my calendar app. "I have some free time in the morning between—"

"I'm here. At the marina. Don't be mad at Estelle for telling me your location. I coaxed it out of her. But she didn't give me the actual address of your unit."

Mildly vexed, I pulled my phone away from my ear to see a missed call from Estelle as well as a text.

Z., Halsey asked your location. Sounded like an emergency. Don't hate me.

Evidently, I'd been so sound asleep that I'd missed her attempts to connect.

I pushed back the covers with a sigh. "Give me five minutes. I'll meet you in the parking area."

"Do you mind my coming in?" He added when I hesitated, "I promise it's strictly business."

"Fine." I confirmed the unit number while quickly slipping back into my bra and jeans, before texting Natasha what was going on in case I came up missing.

Fine ass men can *be crazy. Not just the ugly.*

Moments later, I was opening the front door to my unexpected guest.

He rushed in, removing his jacket and talking fast. "Is there a flat surface I can spread these on?" He'd tossed his jacket on an armchair and was already unzipping a leather portfolio.

I removed my laptop and miscellaneous items from the table by the window, caught up by his energy and whatever the mystery was. "How about here?"

"Perfect." He quickly, yet reverently, laid out several eight-by-ten black-and-white images. "You have to see these. I didn't submit them for the exhibition because they were in storage and I actually forgot about them until seeing you in person this afternoon." Perhaps instinctively, he grabbed my hand when he'd finished and pulled me beside him, introducing me to my own reflection captured in multiple photographs.

Air gushed out of me and my hand shook as I slowly retrieved the photo closest to me: a black-and-white picture of two teenaged boys on the side of the road circa 1930s. The dryness of a surrounding field and the condition of their clothing, their persons, and the run-down automobile they leaned against with smoke escaping from beneath its raised hood could easily situate them as migrants within that white Oklahoma wave, the antithesis of my *Black Life* collection. The penned in "Okies" in a bottom corner confirmed that. Yet, these details felt insignificant as I stood speechless, my gaze filled with the image of two Black children holding hands and positioned near them.

The youngest might have been five or six, and her face was partially hidden as she pressed herself against the side of an older girl who appeared to be in her mid-teens. They were poorly clothed—forlorn-looking—and the hem of the older child's simple dress was uneven, as if it had been torn intentionally. The cloak of sorrow draping her was so palpable that my heart ached, but even that sensation was nearly lost on me. My whole self was absorbed with the face of the teen.

Shaun's quiet tone echoed my mystified state. "Zoe, I wasn't making it up when I said I've seen you before."

He had. I was there in the palm of my hand.

It was my heart-shaped face looking back at me with its almond eyes, dimpled chin, thick eyebrows, and the roundish nose with its slightly turned-up tip. Seeing those photos was like gazing into a mirror and viewing myself in another life, another time. Yet, it was unmistakably me. Zoe.

Speechless and trembling, I stared at that photo, possessed by the impossible thought that I was this young lady's reincarnation. Or, perhaps, she was me.

THREE

FAITH

I will never know why we survived. But we did. And I didn't immediately thank the good Lord for it. I was terrified. Bewildered. Alone with Hope. Fifteen and filled with grief over Charity. But clearly heaven had plans that didn't include our being consumed by that smothering, monstrous mother of all black blizzards that separated us from our family and left us in what felt like the middle of nowhere.

How I got to Hope through all that choking, blinding dust that knocked me to the ground with its ferociousness is a miracle I can't forget. And a matter that still haunts my nightmares. Trembling, crying, screaming her name until I heard her frail response in that tempest, I somehow reached my baby sister. Grabbing her, we crawled into that hollowed-out house with its two hole-riddled walls. Buffered by raging dust and detritus, I clung to my sister and she to me as we fought through the storm, together crawling on hands and knees.

Lord, please let us find the cellar!

Oklahoma homes were built with underground holding places for root vegetables and shelter from tornadoes. It was the only thing I could think of that might provide our saving grace. I fought with everything in me to get there. For Hope's sake.

Instinct didn't guide me. Angels did. I felt something leading me until my hand grazed that latch within minutes of searching. I yanked upward with every ounce of strength I had left. *"Go, Hope, get in!"*

The dust storm had darkened the sky, turning Wellston's day into night. We didn't have the benefit of candles or light. Feeling about, I realized the ladder that could have lowered us into the cellar wasn't there. I had no way of knowing how deep the drop was. Still, I lowered my baby sister into its bowels, before flinging myself in as well. Landing on my right side, I grunted from the impact that left me bruised and winded as the cellar door crashed shut.

"Faith?" Hope rarely called me anything but Faye-Faye. Her voice trembled with terror, yanking me from my pain.

"I'm right here." I groped the darkness until our hands connected and I could pull her safely against me. Her tears wet my chest as I held her fiercely.

"Faye-Faye, I . . . want . . . Mama."

I did too, but I kept that to myself and pretended to be brave just to stay sane. "As soon as this black blizzard stops, we'll go up. Mama and Papa'll be waiting for us."

"And Noah? And Charity?"

The cellar was pitch-black; still, I closed my eyes to grief's ever-present specter.

I should've been in that casket, Charity. Forgive me.

If I hadn't been acting mad and moody, I would've been the one at the Dorseys' borrowing that saw and bringing Noah home like Mama instructed. We knew that back pasture was forbidden. Why Charity chose to come home that way I'd never know. Still, I blamed myself and didn't explain again to Hope that our big sister was in heaven because of me. Instead, I did the thing I always found soothing. I began to sing.

Mama's parents sent her to Fisk University to further her education as a classically trained pianist. She married Papa instead, a sin which my grandparents never forgave. Charity inherited Mama's musical gift and had played piano since she was six. Even Noah could pick out a tune on the keys. Not me. What I'd been given was singing.

The irony hit me as I sang a hymn about the light of God's blessed sunshine touching all mankind. We were sequestered at the bottom of a cellar where darkness, root vegetables, and rodents waited. And I had the bald-faced audacity to sing about the sun, wanting its reassuring warmth, despite the horrifying howl of a black blizzard above.

Hope didn't object to my song choice. Snuggled in my arms, her crying lessened and she gradually quieted as I sang as if the universe would bow to my melodies and right itself miraculously. The longer that storm blew, the louder I sang. As if miracles might truly happen. As if, when that devil of dust departed, we'd climb from that cellar only to be greeted by green grass, fresh skies, flowing creeks. Noah. Our parents. And Charity. Gloriously beautiful. Living and breathing.

I don't know how long we sat that way, but eventually Hope fell asleep, leaving me alone. Feeling empty. With her weight on my lap, I managed to scoot in different directions until I found a cellar wall at my back. I leaned into it, needing its anchoring strength.

Don't worry. Papa's coming.

The thought that my father was out there in that storm, searching, was both soothing and frightening. I couldn't stomach the idea of Papa being hurt and hoped he'd hadn't been swept up; and that he, Mama, and Noah were together, safe. But I also knew Papa was the kind of man who wouldn't let this storm take us from him. He was tall, slim; muscles hardened by years of farming. Determined in nature. Even, sometimes, obstinate. That grit would let him wait out this storm for his two remaining daughters. ·

A skittering sound on the other side of the cellar redirected my thoughts. "Oh God . . ."

I was a farm girl and not necessarily afraid of rodents. That didn't mean I wanted to be in a dark cellar with them. *If that's what I'd heard.*

What if it's a snake?

Horrible pictures of Charity helpless at the bottom of a deep ditch full of rattlers commandeered my imagination. My foot went to bobbing, and I started humming to keep myself from imagining my sister like that, and to stave off the fear of whatever was there in the dark.

Time passed and my legs grew numb with Hope on my lap. Her underwear was still damp from when she'd wet herself on seeing that blizzard, and the smell of urine was prevalent. Preferring her and her pissy scent to a lonely alternative, I wiggled and resituated myself into a more comfortable position. That resulted in Hope's stirring, whimpering in her sleep, so I forced myself to stay still.

I'm unsure how long we stayed that way. Could've been five minutes or five hours. The longer I sat, the heavier I felt. I hadn't rested much since Charity was bit, and wasn't sure if I'd even slept since Mama's shattering scream alerted me that my sister was dead. There in the dark sorrow was an exhausting weight, draining.

I'm so sorry, Charity. Forgive me.

My last words to my sister were ugly. I was ashamed and wished I could take back their nasty energy. We had our sibling squabbles, but never stayed mad at each other and always made up. Now, I had no such opportunity and could only pray my sister wouldn't hold my stupidity against me.

Charity's fair. Forgiving.

I consoled myself to keep a mountain of guilt from crushing my chest. Yes, we both had Papa's temper, but we also had Mama's gentleness to balance it. Having our own social circles didn't keep Charity and me from being best friends and loving each other fiercely. When folks liked to point out our differences—that I was dark and tomboy-tough while Charity was bright and girly—we pitied their ignorance and remained devoted. We shared a room, a bed, sometimes clothing, and whispered secrets. I brushed her hair. She braided mine. We were Mama's "bookend twins," uniquely two of a kind. Now, she was gone and I was at the bottom of the world, my heart crushed to dust.

If I'da gone and borrowed that saw like Mama told me to, Charity, you'd be here with Hope and me.

I felt a wail rise up in me to rival any storm that ever was. Only the thought of scaring Hope awake allowed me to stifle it. Biting my lip, I swallowed an agonizing scream, leaned my head back against that wall and wept quietly, bitterly. I cried so long I drifted off only to dream of snakes and black blizzards. I jerked awake, but fatigue was real and I wound up in a vicious game of nodding off and startling awake until exhaustion won and I slept for only God knows how long.

Awaking, I was temporarily disoriented, not knowing where I was until Hope murmured something in her sleep and I felt her weight pressed against me. In the dark, time felt foreign. My stomach growled and my body was stiff, indicating I'd sat in that position longer than I'd guessed. I panicked, praying I hadn't missed my father's rescue attempts. What if he'd called my name and I hadn't heard him? I listened for sounds above only to hear silence. Not Papa. Or the storm.

"It's over?"

Sitting with my own company and Hope's soft breathing, my whispered words seemed loud and jarring as I strained to hear the outside world. Sweet silence answered in return.

Thank You, Lord.

That evil dust devil was done.

I wanted to raise my hands and do a little dance like Miz Dorsey did in church when hit by the Spirit. I gently shook Hope, instead.

"Wake up, Baby Girl. Papa's looking for us. We have to go."

Her voice was groggy as she stretched awake. "Good 'cause I'm hungry and I have to pee."

Peeing when you saw that storm didn't drain you dry?

"Can you hold it until we get outside?"

"I guess."

"Good girl." I started to ease her from my lap only for her to scream. "What's wrong?"

"You're gonna leave me!"

"No, I'm not. I was only standing up."

"Okay, but hold my hand when you do."

Clutching my sister in one arm, I braced the wall with my free hand to push myself into a standing position. I placed her on her feet and gripped her hand as she'd asked. "See. I'm here."

"I can't see nothing, Faye-Faye. I don't like it this dark."

"I know, Hope. Wanna help me find the ladder so we can get outta here?"

"Yes . . . but don't let go of me."

I gently squeezed her hand in a reassuring gesture as I cautiously moved a foot back and forth in front of me like one of those white sticks blind people walked with. Feeling nothing, I tried remembering the distance from where I'd fallen into the cellar and the wall, intent on getting beneath that cellar door.

"Faye-Faye, I can't wait no more. I gotta pee."

I sighed when her complaint messed up my concentration. "Fine. Go ahead."

"Right here?"

"Yes."

"But we might step in it."

I rolled my eyes, irritated. "Let's back up to the wall again."

Clutching my hand, she followed my lead, slowly walking backward, counting.

Six baby steps.

I cataloged that fact.

"Okay. Keep your back against the wall and move sideways like a crab. Only small steps. Go to the left. And count out loud," I added, making a game and lightening our predicament.

"One . . . two . . . three . . ." She'd counted to ten before we reached the corner as I'd intended.

"Good counting, Hope! You can go here. Just squat with your legs wide. Don't sit." I had no idea what was on that floor and didn't want her contaminated.

"I'm finished, Faye-Faye," she announced as the sound of her personal stream ceased. "I need something to wipe with."

"Stay squatted . . . drip-dry yourself."

"Okay." A scampering sound elsewhere in the cellar terminated that. "Faye-Faye!"

"Fine, Hope." I bent down and pulled my dress up to my mouth. Gripping the hem with my teeth, I ripped away a strip and handed it to my sister. "Here. Use this."

"Do I gotta put these pee-pee panties back on?"

"No, Hope, leave 'em off. We'll clean you up once we get outside and get some fresh undies from our things on the cart." I reached for and found her hand. "Let's count our way back."

She proudly counted our return to where we'd started. "Now, count six forward." Once in position, I looked up, hoping to see something. Slivers of sunlight. Gray skies. Anything. But it was so dark above I feared more time had passed than I thought and that night had actually fallen.

Or maybe the door is covered with a world of black dust.

That set fear racing around my heart like some crazy, hopping frog.

Sometimes these black blizzards stacked mounds of dust so high they reached or even covered our windows, obscuring sight. One time a dust mountain reached the roof of the Kelleys' house. Papa and our neighbor men had to help Mister Kelley dig his way back inside. We never knew when a black blizzard was coming or what damage it would leave when it finished. And this one had been the mother of all monsters.

God, please, don't let that door be covered over. Don't let us be trapped.

"Hope, we gotta find the ladder." I heard the fear in my voice but prayed my sister hadn't.

"How we gonna find something, Faye-Faye, when we can't even see?"

"Use your feet." I explained what I'd done just moments ago. "Slide your feet slowly. Be careful."

"Okay, but don't let my hand go."

"I have to, Hope. We need to spread out."

"Then I'm not doing it." Even my baby sister had inherited our father's stubbornness.

I thought for a moment, knowing the faster we found the ladder the faster we could get back to our family.

Your dress.

My mother was adamant about us being neat and clean in the presence of others. Even when times turned hard, money became lean, and our wardrobe was on constant repeat, we went to church with our aging clothing pristine. Thankfully, the old dress I'd put on that morning was longish in length. I'd already ripped it so Hope could dry herself. I'd rip it again, knowing Mama would understand. If she was even present. Since lowering Charity to her final resting place, I questioned my mother's awareness.

I made quick work of tearing away three more strips measuring the full circumference of the hem. Knotting them together, I tied one end about Hope's wrist and the other about mine. "There. We won't get separated in the dark. Now, do like I said. Feel with your feet. Not your hands."

We worked in tandem to find the ladder, moving in one direction and then the other, all the while counting steps in my head so I'd know how to relocate that space beneath what I hoped was the cellar door.

Our efforts produced nothing, and I felt panic worming its way up in me when Hope bumped into something, causing whatever it was to crash to the floor with a dull thud.

"Ouch! I hit my toe on some ol' crate or something."

"Stay there!" I followed the fabric binding us together to where Hope was. My heart danced as I discovered it wasn't just one crate, but a whole mess of them. The kind we used to collect vegetables on market day. "Help me stack these like a pyramid."

"You mean like in Egypt?"

We'd recently had a lesson about Moses and the Children of Israel in Sunday School, complete with illustrations. Hope was proudly demonstrating the fact that she'd paid attention. "Exactly!"

It was slow, tedious work in the dark, but together we piled those crates upside down on top of each other, forming a rectangular bottom of nine, working our way up from there with Hope handing them to me, and me stepping onto that base and steadily stacking, lifting crates until they reached above my head.

"Come on up to the first tier and stay there. Do *not* move. Understand?"

"Okay, Faye-Faye." Hope's voice was small and I knew she was scared, but she obeyed as I undid the binding about my wrist to complete the last stack, praying it was high enough for me to reach the ceiling and that our makeshift ladder wouldn't crash.

Feeling with my hands, I did my best to make sure the crates were flush against each other and as centered as possible in their pyramid structure. Carefully, I tested its sturdiness before leaving Hope there on the lowest tier and attempting a slow, cautious ascent. I approached our pyramid as if it were stairs, using my hands to guide me in the dark on one tier before mounting the next. I managed the first two easily enough, but on the next I wobbled and held my breath while slowly balancing again. By the time I reached the top my heart was beating hard in my chest, but I felt like somebody's prized gladiator when my fingers brushed the ceiling.

Those long arms look like spider legs.

Papa liked to tease me for being long-limbed like him, but right then I thanked God for it and the fact that I could reach the top, and that we'd succeeded in structuring our pyramid beneath the cellar door.

Triumph was short-lived. "I can't open it." Something was on top of the door, forcing it closed. *Dust.*

"Try again, Faye-Faye. You can do it."

Standing atop the highest crates, I wanted to put my shoulder to the wood and heave against it but mine was a precarious perch that didn't offer leverage. Excess force could send me toppling down and breaking something I needed. An arm. A leg. My crazy head. "I gotta find something to push with..."

There had to be something in that cellar that could help. A broom. A rake handle. *Something.*

I started my way back down but was arrested by a sound. Muffled. Distant.

"Faye—"

I shushed Hope in order to concentrate. When I heard it again, I took to screaming. *"Papa, we're down here!"*

"Yay, Papa's coming!" In her excitement, my sister jumped up and down, causing the pyramid to wobble.

"Hope, stop."

She obeyed. I sat. We both screamed, repeatedly, in an

effort to guide our father to us and were rewarded moments later with the sound of a nearby voice answering in response.

"Hold on!"

Hope giggled. "Papa sounds funny."

I smiled in my relief. "We probably do, too. Like underground gophers. Or bunnies."

We both fell silent at scraping sounds overhead. It went on a long time, an indication of just how high that dust must've been.

"We're coming . . ."

I coughed when dust fell through the door slats and into my face. But I welcomed it, if it meant freedom from our dark hole that was starting to turn cold.

"*Got it.*"

Within moments of that triumphant declaration, the door swung open and I was blinded by a shining light. I assumed it was the sun until, after being pulled up and out by two pairs of hands, my eyes slowly adjusted only to discover that it was nighttime and the world was black.

"You okay, miss?"

Squinting and blinking rapidly from flurries of dust stinging my eyes, I found it hard to focus on the boy before me; but based on the hazy outline of his size, he couldn't have been much older than me. Realizing he was white, the age similarity suddenly failed to be comforting.

"Micah, look at this!" A bigger, older-sounding boy loomed beside him. He was equally white, and his voice was less kind as he held the lantern near my face before directing it into the cellar. "Lord-a-mercy, there's another one down there?" His laughter was unfriendly. "Little brother, looks like it's our night for coon rescue."

FOUR

ZOE

"Who is she?"

I glanced away from the photograph to my cousin seated beside me on the bed and shook my head. "I've no idea."

"That's brilliant, Zo-Zo. You spent infinite hours researching materials for your exhibit and never came across these pictures?"

"Clearly I didn't, Natasha." Missus Halsey wasn't a professional photojournalist; rather, in her words, a one-minute hobbyist. "These were private photos, not part of a public collection."

Staring at the photograph she held, I was extremely thankful for the idea to host this *Black Life in a Distressed West* showcase despite my director's lack of support and any uncertainty I may have experienced.

Since earning a Master's in Fine Art and starting my career, I'd dealt with veiled racism, being mistaken for the administrative assistant and even asked why I was present at meetings and functions, or what middle school art program I represented. I'd been employed at two different museums since graduation and, without fail, I'd primarily been assigned to projects showcasing people of color and relegated to the background in assisting, subordinate positions whenever mainstream artists were featured. Never the lead. Just some supporting actress. As if I were incapable of curating Warhol, Rockwell, Picasso, O'Keeffe, Michelangelo, or Monet. My skills were too often overlooked or marginalized. And working with OWL docents like Clarice Ritenour who acted as if I was hired solely because of Affirmative Action was enough to make me want to come out swinging. I'd felt pigeonholed despite my pushing back, fighting to secure equity for my abilities. In some instances, the ish got so real and wrong that Vince jokingly called me the "Curator of Negroes and Lesser Things." I never laughed, finding nothing funny.

Relocating to Boston and working with Estelle had been a desperately needed breath of fresh air. She saw me, believed in me, opened doors, and granted opportunities. After her move to northern California, she'd remained a mentor and supporter, even cheering me on in a recent conversation when I'd mentioned toying with the idea of becoming an independent freelance curator. My soon-to-be ex, on the other hand, pronounced the idea as crazy.

You don't go out on your own at your age.

I was a few months away from forty, not the grave, seated in an Airbnb, immobilized by a likeness of myself from the distant past. Though purchased as a place of rest, my sorority sister had turned one of her unit's bedrooms into an office, complete with a printer that had enabled me to scan the photos before Shaun's departure last night. Or rather, this morning. We'd been so immersed in discussion that it was after one a.m. when he left, leaving me intrigued and frustrated.

"So, dude doesn't know when or where his grandmother took these?"

"Not precisely, just that it was likely during his grandparents' westward migration in the mid-thirties." I stood and stretched the kinks from my back. After Shaun left last night, I'd been so enthralled with my other self that I'd barely slept. I'd sat in bed staring at copies of Shaun's photos, asking questions and concocting scenarios.

Who was the young girl? What was her name? Who was the little girl with her? And why were they with those white teens? And, more importantly, what tragedy had befallen them to imprint her lovely face with such all-consuming sorrow and misery?

After hours of mental wrangling, I'd drifted off to sleep only to be awakened by Natasha's calling in response to my "SOS just in case I come up missing" text. Now, I was hungry and could use a long soak in the tub.

"Missus Halsey usually included details on the back of her photos, but for some reason she didn't with these."

The photographs Shaun had spread across the table last night were the same, simply taken from different angles as if the photographer had been in motion with each frame.

"I can't put my finger on it but she reminds me of someone . . . other than you," Natasha murmured, perplexed and frowning at the photo before brightening again. "Well, Cuzzo, we have a mystery that needs solving. Does dude intend to ask his grand-mother about these?"

I padded to the windows and pushed open the curtains to welcome in the California sun. "That's where the gumbo thickens. Missus Halsey has dementia. He's visiting her soon. Hopefully it'll be on a good day and she'll remember something."

"Cool. Cuzzo, this is eerie. It's like you walked this earth before you got here. I think she's a relative."

I leaned against the window, watching the tethered boats in the marina resting on the gentle ripples of the bay. Its shimmer-ing surface was hypnotic. "That's my thought as well."

"What if she's kin to Aunt Gladys?"

I looked at Natasha and nodded, wondering if this was a gift I could give my mother.

I was in middle school when Mama learned she was adopted. Since then, she'd invested an enormous amount of time and resources attempting to locate her biological parents. My maternal grandparents were marvelous, but Mama had natural curiosities and questions she needed answered. Unfortunately, the few leads she'd found resulted in dead ends and she'd abandoned the search a few years back. Walking over to the table where copies of the photos lay, I picked up another one taken at a different angle and wondered if I was looking at my biological grandmother.

Something in her eyes reminds me of Mama.

"I want to find out for sure before saying anything to Mama about it." She'd gone through enough emotional upheavals and disappointments trying to locate missing pieces of herself. I was not interested in giving false hope before having concrete evidence.

"When is dude getting back to you?"

I laughed through a yawn. "His name isn't 'dude,' Natasha. It's Shaun."

"And I should care because?"

"Because he's our type. Tall. Dark. And finger-licking fantabulous."

She stopped eyeing a photo and looked at me. "And you didn't think to call and invite me to see these pictures last night *while* he was here?"

"Why? So you could cuss me out for disturbing your beauty rest?"

"You're right. There's that."

We both laughed.

"If you're at the gallery on opening night I'll introduce you." Even as I made the offer something odd pinged through me, like maybe I didn't want to introduce Shaun to any woman, not even my favorite cousin.

She shook her head. "No, thanks. I don't do snobbish men dressed in all black and dripping egotism. And he's probably gay to begin with."

"Aren't you Miss Politically Incorrect."

"Honey, I have too many curves to be kicking it with some photographer dude accustomed to snapping shots of skinny-ass chicks in need of ten plates of Granny's neck bones and hot water cornbread." She laid the photo on the bed as we laughed. "I'm just saying. I'm out here living single and have zero tolerance for having my heart played with by some uptight ignoramus."

My cell phone rang before I could respond. "Speaking of ignoramuses . . ."

"Vince?"

I nodded, knowing by the ringtone that it was him.

Natasha snorted and grabbed her wallet. "I'm going to the corner coffee shop to get us something to eat while you talk to your cone-headed he-ho. I'll be back."

My cousin was a mess, but I appreciated her allowing me a private moment.

No telling what foolishness this man is calling with.

"Good morning." I didn't believe in messy breakups and answered as pleasantly as possible.

Vince, on the other hand, operated from a different code book. "Why the hell is my lawyer still waiting on those m-f'ing divorce papers? You forget how to sign your name, or something? Quit playing simple-minded games and let's get this over with, Z."

Moments like these made me wonder why I'd ever found His Dumbness attractive. Yes, he was physically appealing, professionally driven, and gave off good vibes when we first met. Experience proved those vibes were counterfeit.

Subterfuge and deceit were his strong suit and my soul had the wounds to prove it.

"I'm countering the terms. My attorney will update yours ASAP."

His laugh was hostile, brittle. "You sat back and took the ish, now you wanna flex?"

He was semi-right, but his arrogant ass didn't need to know that. "Call it what you want—"

"I already called it. You found out how I roll years ago, and still you stayed and dealt with it. Now that I want something different you went and grew some balls and want to dictate?"

Irritated at being called on the carpet, my jaw twitched. "I want the brownstone, and half of our investment portfolio. The rest? Do what you want with it."

He laughed that dry laugh again. "Just damn, Z. You might as well take everything."

Our brownstone in Boston's Jamaica Plain had nearly tripled in value since we purchased it six years ago as newly-weds; and the investments we'd made with Natasha's *savoir faire* and guidance had yielded solid dividends and returns. Outside of that, we held very little tangible property together. Despite earning a good salary, Vince had a mindset of seize the day by spending now rather than saving for a future that was too far distant, resulting in his personal net worth being not so impressive. My approach differed. I wasn't rich, but after discovering his infidelity, I'd established separate banking accounts, worked hard to increase my savings, and made sure my retirement investments and portfolio were healthy. The unhealthy behavior of which I was guilty was holding on to a man who wasn't good for me.

"I'm sorry you see this as my taking everything."

"I'm sorry you see me as some sort of bank, Zoe."

Gritting my teeth in annoyance, I opened the sliding glass door that led to a second-floor balcony and stepped outside, allowing the California sunshine to kiss my skin. "Is my being properly compensated after suffering your ho'ish ways too much to ask?"

"Really, Z.? Fine. While I'm compensating you, who plans to compensate me for the son you couldn't carry?" It was one of the lowest blows he could ever strike. Yet, he did because he was a despicable sub-human.

I disconnected to avoid exploding all over Vince and his need to trigger me. I'd worked too hard, intentionally dealing with my grief through years of therapy, to let the inhumane flippancy of a jackass like my estranged mate sabotage my healing.

Release his ignorance, Zoe. It's not for you to carry.

I closed my eyes and engaged in deep-breathing exercises to re-center my inner equilibrium and avoid being crushed by a high wall of emotions.

"Sometimes I'm close to hating him." And I didn't only because my life couldn't afford poisonous bitterness. That didn't mean I'd never fantasized about some apocalyptic curse or condition striking him, his tropical fish, and that parrot. Cockatoo. Whatever that damn exotic winged creature he'd paid three thousand dollars for and gifted himself last Christmas was.

Zoe, you're more mature than this.

I reminded myself of that fact while yanking my purse from the closet and scrounging through it hoping it held my secret stash. Praising God it did, I slipped my fix between my lips and was ready to puff up only to realize I didn't have my lighter.

Damn.

I checked the desk, hoping to find some suitable flame source as the front door opened and Natasha mounted the stairs. I was the kind of mad that I didn't care about being caught and stood in the middle of the floor, a challenge on my face, one hand on a hip.

"Oh, hell naw!" Natasha took one look at the cigarette

clenched between my lips, walked over, and snatched it. "You and Virginia Slims are no longer friends."

"Return that!"

"Not even. Since when're you smoking again?"

I'd quit after learning I was pregnant, but resumed after trauma wrecked my existence only to quit again a year later when detoxing all things vile and Vince. "I'm not. I keep a backup for stank ugly moments."

"I've been gone a whole ten minutes. Precisely what trauma have you experienced since I left?"

I snorted disdainfully. "Did you forget who called before you exited?"

"Oh . . . yeah." She looked at me before shaking her head. "Naw, not even Satan's seed merits cancer and nicotine. Here. Take this."

Accepting the caramel frappé and apple-carrot muffin she offered, I watched her crush my guilty fix beneath her sneakered foot and drop the mangled mess in the garbage. Deprived but appreciative, I headed for the balcony with Natasha on my heels, recounting to her the phone conversation I'd just had. Discussing the stupidity of Vince Edwards was softer than the low-handed stab to the soul he'd attempted to deliver, or the goading he'd tried to accomplish. I'd rather go to hell and stare Satan in the face than to permit anyone—*especially* Vince—to misuse, tarnish, or otherwise manipulate the sacredness of my deceased son, Jaelen.

FIVE

FAITH

The world as I knew it had vanished. Papa. Mama. Noah. They were nowhere, and there was nothing except the dark night, two white boys, and their parents eyeing me and Hope as if we were some strange breed of purple possum fallen from a mystical tree.

"You have no notion where your parents are?"

I shook my head, too afraid to speak. The man who'd introduced himself as John Owenslee was intimidating. Not because of size or any gruffness in his tone, but because he was white. And religious. In the short time since Hope and I were pulled from that cellar and introduced to him and his wife, Miz Lucy, it seemed like he'd quoted more verses than Reverend Coulter did in a month of Sundays. His being a scripture-lover didn't grant me any consolation or peace. White folks had used the Bible to justify their actions and guilt the enslaved since before slavery. Pat you on the head one moment, beat, molest, or sell you off the next, and still preach Jesus with their last breath. Bible-loving didn't make a white person less of a threat. Miz Lucy on the other hand: her I could deal with. Her thin lips were set in a clear, hard line of dislike and annoyance. She wasn't deceptive.

"Husband, we ain't got time for this. We're behind schedule enough as is. Standing here tryna get something sounding like good sense from nigras ain't helping our progress one bit."

"Wife, what did our dear Lord say in the scriptures?" John Owenslee didn't wait for a response. " 'I will not leave you as orphans; I will come to you.' We have come. God sent us to aid these orphans."

Orphans?

I wanted to kick him in his skinny shin for calling us that ugly thing. Hope and I had people. We were lost, but loved. Hadn't Papa run into that storm for us? I bit my lip to keep from crying at the thought that Mama and Papa were out here in the dark night worried and distraught.

"We ain't got much of nothing, Husband, so give 'em a little and let's move on."

" 'Whoever is generous to the poor lends to the Lord, and he will repay him for his deed.' Proverbs nineteen, verse seven."

There he was, again, using scripture for classifying. Now, according to him, we were pitiful and poor. Glancing at that run-down jalopy of a truck of his and his ragtag looking sons and missus, I wanted to tell John Owenslee he didn't look wealthy. That truck was loud and stinky, shooting exhaust like toots from a horse's back end. But I had home-training and knew to avoid disrespectful behavior. Plus, I was terrified—me and Hope were out there alone with white folks. If I said or did one wrong thing, we could wind up dead, damaged, or missing. I kept my mouth shut and prayed Papa would burst through the dark night and rescue us. Until that happened, I had to move sensibly.

As the adults continued their Bible-scented argument of whether or not they should help us, I eyed their sons. Micah, the one about my age and size, seemed mellow enough, perhaps even kind. But that oldest one, Henry, I didn't like. He had snake eyes and thin lips like his mother, except he plastered on a mean smile. I didn't care for the way he stared at me, especially my breasts. I was still growing into my full-woman silhouette, but was already top-heavy like the women on Papa's side of the family. That had me clutching Hope in front of me, shielding my upper body.

"They can ride as far as the first station. After that, God bless 'em." Miz Lucy's pronouncement got my attention.

"That's fine for now, Wife, but we'll let the Lord decide what's next. Sons, go do your business and get these lanterns back where they belong."

"Yes, Pa."

Apparently, the Owenslees had stopped to relieve personal needs. Tired of riding so long, Micah and Henry had used the opportunity to stretch their legs and ventured farther from their family's truck than they should have, only to stumble on a new discovery: us.

"Faye-Faye, I'm hungry."

I squatted down and turned Hope toward me, answering her whisper with mine. "Me too, Baby Girl. We'll get something to eat as soon as we find Papa and Mama. Okay?" I smiled when she nodded, thankful that she was cooperating versus acting spoiled. Patience and waiting weren't Hope's strong suit or preference, being the youngest, with the benefit of three older siblings who doted on her and too often gave into her whims.

She has two *older siblings.*

My mind was still molding itself around the fact that Charity was gone, and I had to bite my lip as an image of her playing the piano suddenly surfaced. She'd cried when Papa had to sell that thing in order to buy food and household sundries. He'd held her as she'd wept, promising to buy a bigger piano once life got better. Life never did. Now, Charity was dead.

"Why y'all standing there instead of getting up here?" Henry Owenslee startled me.

I'd told myself to stay alert and there I was thinking on Charity. Mister and Miz Owenslee had seated themselves up front, and Henry and Micah were climbing aboard that truck bed with its high sides made of wood slats.

"Thank you, but we'll be fine."

Miz Lucy's laugh was disdainful. "You slow in the head? Look around, gal. Ain't nothing but dust mounds and gnats out here. We're doing this for the Lord, not y'all, so get in the back and hurry up about it."

"Yes, ma'am." I didn't want to be on that truck with them no matter what Jesus said, but her sharp command left no room for argument. I helped Hope aboard before scrambling up beside her and holding her close when she sat on my lap and burrowed her head in my neck. Her little body trembled as if cold, but the night was warm and I knew it was fear.

I'm scared, too, Baby Girl.

I felt like a mad misfit, but I refused to be called anybody's orphan. We had people and getting back to them was where I put my concentration. I tried scanning the night in hopes of finding something familiar just to feel half normal. But it was pitch-black. I was unsure how long we'd slept in that cellar or what time it was, and I could no longer remember how close we'd gotten to Route 66 before that monster blizzard blew in, separating us from our world of love.

Lord, please, help us get to Route 66 and find Mama and Papa waiting on us.

That's where we were supposed to connect with the Kelleys and the Browns, our neighbor families traveling the same direction. Maybe if the highway was a simple thing none of this would've happened. We could've been straight on the route and in a better position without having to walk miles just to connect with it. But no, our town, Wellston, had to be difficult.

I wasn't but a little kid, maybe five or six, when Route 66 was first designed to run through Wellston and head toward Edmond. All I remember is folks being excited about the traffic the highway would feed through town, hopefully bringing tourists and their money with them. But the government got involved and rerouted the road. Despite our town fighting back, that original road got renamed The Loop, and the government did what they did, like some fickle-minded god redirecting rivers, and took Route 66 from us. Wellston lost the road war and the tourists. Now, we were what we had been: a small, one-horse town that used to be good for farming. Thoughts of the bountiful, fresh foods our land used to yield set my stomach rumbling.

"Y'all lend them nigras some of that hardtack and salt pork." He must've had magic ears to detect my stomach's rumbling over the rickety racket that truck was making, but Mister John's voice shot into the night as if he'd heard my belly protesting.

Micah, the younger boy, moved to do as his father instructed. Both he and his brother sat at the top of the truck bed near the cab, leaving me and Hope at its tail end. We sat separated by the meager mountain of their family's possessions, as if those goods were the demarcations maintaining white and Colored sections.

"Don't give 'em too much. Just enough." That snake-eyed Henry held up a lantern for his brother's benefit.

Micah approached, leaning over that meager mountain with dry cracker-like bread and dehydrated pork, offering some to Hope then me.

I hated hardtack. It was a mockery of good times when Mama had baked light, fluffy bread with yeast. But my parents didn't raise fools so I accepted with a quiet "thank you."

"Why was y'all out there in that cellar?"

I didn't feel like answering questions and asked one instead. "Do you know what time it is?"

Micah shook his head. "Not really. We left home in Claremore early today and stopped off in Tulsa to say goodbye to relatives. By the time we left there it was 'round midnight." He went on about his mother trying to convince his father to stay the night rather than getting on the road in the dark, but Mister Owenslee had a promise of a job waiting in California and couldn't arrive late.

I barely heard any of that because my heart had nearly stopped. Tulsa was an hour away from Wellston. If it was midnight then, it had to be one o'clock in the morning by now. That meant it was Monday and no longer Sunday. If that was the case, we'd been trapped in that cellar for hours, and Papa's not finding us in that time could only mean one thing: he was dead.

"I don't like this, Faye-Faye." Hope's voice was soft as she held up the hardtack, still I was glad Micah had returned to his place up front so as not to hear her complaint.

"It's all we have for now, sweetie, so please eat it. Okay?" When she nodded, I stared into the night, those dry rations in the palm of my hand, not eating. My hunger had disappeared with the notion that my father lay lifeless somewhere—Mama half mute and Noah with an injured foot on the back of a mule cart, alone and defenseless.

What if something happened to all *of them?*

My mind couldn't take that. It was enough to drive me crazy like Mad Mister Purefoy who sat in front of the general store talking to George Washington and Abraham Lincoln. I didn't want to be that kind of insane so I did what I did to calm myself in crisis: I sang. Or, rather, I hummed. Just enough for Hope to hear as she settled against me, finishing her makeshift meal. Her dress had dried, but I still caught a hint of urine when she shifted periodically. That didn't keep me from humming. Other than Hope, my voice was the only familiar thing available to me; so, I hummed until my throat felt about as dry as Oklahoma had become.

"Your humming is practically as pretty as the rest of you."

Henry Owenslee's voice was quiet, but still reached my ears. It brought my humming to an end. I didn't like that white boy and didn't want his attention.

"Faye-Faye, wake up."

Hope's shaking my shoulder had me jerking awake and rubbing sleep from my eyes. I felt strange and out of the ordinary, like I'd slept wrong or had a nightmare. My behind ached. So did my back; and I couldn't figure out why Hope wasn't in her bed instead of sleeping on my lap. Glancing about at our surroundings dropped me square in the center of our ordeal; but seeing those two white boys curled up asleep made me want to hop off that truck and run in the opposite direction.

"Are we in California yet, Faye-Faye? Are Papa and Mama and Noah coming to get us?"

"Shhh, 'fore you wake everybody." Shushing Hope was the best I could do, considering I had no answer to her heartbreaking questions and could only pray our parents would find us soon.

It had been so dark last night and the road so treacherous with newly formed dust mounds that Mister Owenslee had pulled over to wait until daybreak after the truck nearly got stuck in one of them. We'd slept on what we supposed was the side of the road; now my baby sister had shaken me awake only for me to see the truck was back in motion. From what I could tell, Hope and I were the only ones awake besides Mister Owenslee. I took advantage of that fact to scope out those boys of his. I had to put Hope off of my lap and raise up on my knees to peek over their piled-up possessions to do it.

I'd only seen them by lantern-light, but in the dawn of day Henry and Micah Owenslee looked like destitute urchins, curled up on their sides asleep, their light-brown hair dusty and dirty. Their faces were a filthy mess, and their clothes weren't much better. Hope might've smelled like pee, but they were rank and musty. Clearly, black blizzards didn't discriminate. Nature considered us equals and had inflicted her destruction on whites as well. Micah's suddenly stirring in his sleep sent me back to the rear of the truck where I should've been.

The moment I sat, Hope was trying to climb on my lap, which I prevented. "Baby Girl, my legs are tired." And my knees were sore and scraped from falling when running to save her from that storm. "Can you sit on your own bottom?"

"I'm gonna get splinters."

Her whining had me remembering we'd left her soiled underwear in that cellar. Mama would pitch a fit if she knew I had my baby sister sitting there in her natural business.

I looked at the Owenslees' things hoping to find something I could fashion into underwear. Seeing a sliver of cheesecloth protruding from underneath a jar, I thanked the Lord. Quietly as I could, I tugged at the fabric, trying to free it without waking anyone.

Hope frowned at my crazy smile when I succeeded. "What's that for?"

"You. Lift up on your knees." When she did, I shielded her by repositioning myself, back against that pile, and worked the fabric beneath her body and between her lanky legs. "Hold the front part against your stomach." As she complied, I took the corner edges of the back and tied them together about her belly. "There."

"You made me a diaper!"

"*Shhh*. It's not," I hissed. "It's underwear, so sit down and say nothing."

She sat back, mad; bottom lip poking out, arms crossed over her skinny chest. I would've laughed in a brighter time, and if that voice hadn't slithered through the dawn.

"You plan on paying for that cheesecloth, gal?"

I glanced backward to see Henry on the opposite side of his family's property, glaring down at me. I opened my mouth but dread kept words from forming. I simply engaged in a staring war with him until Henry slowly grinned.

"You can pay for it in coins or kisses. You choose, but you paying."

"Good morning, all God's children. 'This is the day the Lord has made. Let us rejoice and be glad in it. For the Lord is good and His mercies endure forever.'" Mister Owenslee's morning salutation and scripture recitation kept me from having to answer Henry.

"Morning, Pa. Morning, Ma."

From the corner of my eye, I could see Miz Lucy up front, waking, moving.

"What's your name anyhow?"

Henry had my attention again. For some strange reason I felt like keeping my real name to myself, so I gave him Hope's derivative. "Faye."

"What about her?" He lifted his bony chin in my sister's direction.

"Baby Girl."

His expression said he didn't believe me, but I didn't care as I scooted back against the tail end of the truck bed into my original position.

"Henry, wake your brother. We're never lazy. Get 'im up so we can pray."

The truck slowed and Henry obeyed his father's instructions. Next thing I knew, we were told to hop down and join the Owenslee family standing there forming a circle and holding hands.

That was foreign to me. Not the praying, but the being ordered to join hands with them.

I wasn't nowhere near comfortable doing it.

Growing up in Wellston, Coloreds and whites got along good enough provided we stayed on our side of town and carefully followed race codes. The general store was the central hub and whenever we visited, we knew to wait until white customers were served even if we'd arrived first. We couldn't try on nothing and there were limits on how many of us could be on the premises. One time when the crops were real good and Papa wanted to treat us to some nice steaks with the extra he'd made, he was told no. Steaks were reserved for white folks. He was welcome to go to the end of the counter near the back door and choose from "nice ends, scraps, and chitlins." When on the wooden walkway in front of the store we knew to stand aside or step onto the dirt road whenever whites neared, allowing them to pass. As if they deserved deference. I recalled Charity and me sneaking out of bed to eavesdrop on grown folks gathered in our yard one night, grief-stricken over Mister Purefoy's wife, son, and daughter-in-law being lynched for asking how to sign up for voting. Which is how and why Mister Purefoy lost his mind and keeps company and counsel with dead presidents. Now, suddenly, I was supposed to stand there in God's good morning holding a white hand and praying?

Lord, don't let me wind up with a noose around my neck swinging from a tree limb because I touched them.

Gripping Hope's hand with my left, I barely grazed Micah's with my right as his father prayed a long-winded prayer outlining the causes of black blizzards. Years of drought. Increased temperatures. Strong wind erosion. Poor farming practices and over-tilling black top soil. Economic depression. White farmers "laying up with Injun women."

I opened an eye and peeked at him. Other than liking Dallas Dorsey from a distance, I'd never had a boyfriend and couldn't imagine heaven being so outdone by anyone's romance that it would scorch everything under the Oklahoma sun because of it.

When Mister Owenslee finished his long, loopy prayer we found private places to relieve ourselves before heading on. It was slow going with all the dirt mounds left from the storm reconfiguring the road. By the time we pulled into the petrol station, I was starved, frantic. For the entire ride, my focus was fixed on the countryside in search of my family, the Browns or the Kelleys. There was nothing, no sign of them, as if no Wilson beyond Hope or me ever existed. If the moon fell to earth shattering in irreparable pieces, I'd know its devastation. That's how I felt then.

"Y'all go 'round back and handle yourselves."

"Yes, ma'am." I was slow-moving when taking Hope's hand and heading for the Colored outhouse as Miz Lucy went to the filling station's ladies' room. We didn't have separate women and men's facilities; all Colored folks had to use the same privy. Nothing more than a woodshed with a hole in the ground, that thing looked and smelled demonic. Yet, that's not what had me close to crying. I was moving slow and biting my lip to keep from bursting into tears because that paltry stream of customers at the station didn't include many brown faces like mine and, certainly, none that I recognized. My people weren't here.

"Faye-Faye, I'm not going in there."

Even at a distance that Colored outhouse stank like the dickens.

"Let's go in the field." I preferred taking my chances in the weeds than stepping a foot inside that thing.

I can't wait to find Mama and Papa and get to California.

I hated that Jim Crow ignorance let others treat us like nobodies because of the color of our skin. "Here, Hope." I'd snuck some stuffing from a cushion on the Owenslees' truck so we could clean ourselves. When finished, we found the Colored "water fountain," a pipe sticking up from the ground, and washed our hands and took a drink before heading back only to bump into a young woman with a camera around her neck, a baby on her hip, and two kids clinging to her dress. She apologized for our collision while I stood mouth hanging open, and probably looking stupid, staring at the prettiest, smoothest, darkest skin I'd ever seen.

"You okay, honey?"

I offered a respectful "yes, ma'am" despite her only looking a year or so older than me.

"Watch where y'all walking, now, and have a good day." Her smile was sweet as she moved on.

She'd only gone a few yards when I ran after her.

"Excuse me, please." Catching up, my words came out in a rush as I described my family in detail, giving my parents' names, and asking if she'd seen them on the road or anywhere.

"No, I haven't. Are y'all out here by y'all selves?"

Before I could answer, a truck in only slighter better condition than the Owenslees' rolled up, filled to the brim with Colored folks and their belongings—migrants like us, going somewhere.

"Samuella, we gotta get going." A good-looking boy about Dallas Dorsey's age leaned down from the truck bed and helped the children clinging to the woman's skirt aboard before reaching for the baby, his motions swift yet protective, leaving me to conclude maybe he was her husband.

"Sweet Pea, I'm coming. I just wanna know if these girls're okay. Who y'all out here with? What's your name?"

"Faye! Baby Girl! Come on here." Henry's yell interrupted us, as well as provided an answer.

"Y'all with *them*?" It was "Sweet Pea" this time doing the questioning. "I'll say . . ." he added as if mystified when I nodded. He reached for Miss Samuella to help her up without further comment.

"Hold on. Can I take y'all's picture?" She lifted that camera to her face just as Henry started yelling again for us to get over there like we were his possessions.

"Sorry, but we gotta go." Hope's hand in my mine, I moved toward Henry and Micah, who were leaning against the side of their truck sharing a bottle of pop; the truck hood up and steam lifting toward the day. When we got there, I did the same: pressed my back against that conveyance, letting it take my woes and weight. I wanted to be on that truck with Samuella and Sweet Pea, seemingly loaded down with everyone and everything. Not knowing where they were headed didn't keep me from wishing there was room for Hope and me. There wasn't, so I simply stared as it neared and Miss Samuella snapped pictures.

"What the blastedness is she doing?" Henry's voice was curious, disdainful.

"She got one of those picture-makers." Micah sounded intrigued.

Downing the last of their pop, Henry hurled the bottle at them. Thankfully, he missed and it shattered on hard-packed dirt. "Get on 'way from here with that soul-snatcher."

His laughter at my back, I took off running after that truck. "Miss Samuella, I'm Faith Wilson! That's Micah and Henry Owenslee. I don't know if they're letting us ride all the way, but they're headed for Los Angeles, same as my family. If you come across my parents, *please* tell 'em you saw us."

Her promise to do so was like honey. I swallowed its soothing as I returned to Hope who was busy eating the jerky meat Micah had given her.

"How close're we to Route 66?" I asked.

Henry laughed that mocking laugh again. "Gal, we *done* been on it. We're nearly in Texas."

I stared at him, wishing he was fibbing while realizing the stretch of road, this filling station was unfamiliar. My heart raced. Air gushed from my lips in a thin stream. I started shaking inside, livid at Papa for not finding me.

SIX

ZOE

The rest of the day was a busy blur, for which I was thankful. Immersing myself in gallery duties and formalities for my upcoming *Black Life* exhibition provided a welcome escape from my situation with Vince and his viciousness. His jab earlier that morning at my inability to carry our son full-term was cruelty personified, lower than Hades. I knew better than to bite the bait. Doing so would take me down a hellacious rabbit hole from which there was no easy exit. I'd be inundated with not only sorrow, but hate that my soul couldn't afford.

Stay clean of Vince.

I turned to prayer, meditation, and ambient music to pull myself away from the edge and re-center. Thank God for the sweet touch of Spirit. It allowed me to face the afternoon without rancor and I arrived at the museum ready. Determined.

I was in my element and loved getting lost in reviewing the photos that would be showcased, as well as fine-tuning then practicing aloud my introductory speech for opening night and the VIP reception to which donors, top-tier members, and other notables were invited. That also required a tasting with the museum's caterer to which my greedy self did not object. I had to reschedule a session with the docents when a local radio-show host called with a last-minute interview request. The exhibition had already had several write-ups in Bay Area newspapers, but any added publicity was a godsend so I hustled my hips over to the station for a rousing conversation. By the time that was finished, I was running on pure adrenaline.

"Zoe, you sure you don't want to call it quits for the day?"

"No, Estelle. Why?"

"You've only yawned ten thousand times."

I smiled at her exaggeration while rubbing my tired eyes. "I'm good. It's just jet lag."

And the fact that I met an ancestor in a photograph.

I was still overwhelmed by the discovery and the unanswered questions it raised. Seeing a near mirror-perfect image of myself, captured in a different era and in a body that wasn't mine, was eerie yet stimulating. I couldn't shake the sense that we were, indeed, blood-related. Connected. Yet, detached at some point in the past. Not knowing her name, I'd dubbed her Miss Me, and the notion that she could be a relative of Mama's left me determined to uncover her identity.

"By the way, I apologize for telling Shaun where you were staying, but it sounded urgent. Did he reach you?"

"No worries. And, yes, we connected and worked out the issue." I hadn't divulged Shaun's late-night visit or what it entailed. I trusted Estelle, but until I knew exactly what I was dealing with I chose to keep the issue private. Besides, if Miss Me was biologically related to my mother, I wanted Mama to be the first to know. "I'm glad we got Alexander Morgan and his trio to play opening night."

It was my way of rerouting the conversation, but I was genuinely thrilled. A native son of northern California, the young, up-and-coming artist was a musical phenom helping to preserve the art of old jazz standards while serving them to a new generation in his unique way. He'd just returned from a European tour and we were delighted to have him.

"He definitely has cross-generational appeal," Estelle commented, pushing her glasses onto her head and shoving away from the conference-room table where I'd been sitting for the past few hours handling social media posts, emailing marketing promos, and dealing with other pressing exhibit-related business as a result of the administrative assistant going home sick.

"That he does. My grandparents will definitely enjoy. Speaking of . . ." I glanced at my phone to see a text from Natasha that she was waiting out front. We were headed to our paternal grandparents' home in Richmond. I couldn't wait to see them and whatever family members stopped by for Granny's Friday Night Fish Fry. It was a holdover from Granny's life as a girl who'd grown up in California but maintained southern roots. It was one southern tradition we didn't mind continuing. "I guess I *will* be calling it quits."

"I have a few more items on my agenda before I head out. You're running at full speed these next few weeks, so kick up your heels this weekend." Estelle added a little back-kick for effect before leaving.

Laughing, I responded to Natasha's text, packed my belongings, and cleaned my workspace. Minutes later, my cousin and I were on the freeway with its Friday evening, bumper-to-bumper traffic. By the time we reached our grandparents' my stomach was demanding to be fed, but first I had to run the family obstacle course of cousins, uncles, and aunts whom I hadn't seen since my last visit.

I endured the typical intrusive, family-tossed questions: "Honey, how's your career; are you still with *him;* are you ever moving back here, and has your behind spread?" I took no offense (despite being seven pounds lighter), grateful to be loved and missed. And all of that before I could even get to my grand-parents. When I did, I found Granny seated at the kitchen table calling out orders like a general. Ten years Granddad's junior with severe arthritis in her knees, we'd long ago commanded Granny to stay off her feet and let us do the cooking with her overseeing, making sure we strictly followed her recipes.

"Who's this cute thing coming in my kitchen?"

"Your *favorite* grandbaby," I sang, sashaying happily across the floor and ignoring my cousins' protests. My grandparents had a way of loving their brood of twenty-two grands so fiercely that we each swore we were the favorite and only. I kissed her on the lips like I always did before hugging her tightly. "How's my duchess?"

"Grand and fabulous." Granny regally waved a hand as if the queen of her own island. "Whatcha bring me from Boston?"

I did a slow spin before striking a pose. "Me."

She sucked her teeth, waved a hand dismissively. "You, I've seen. I'm talking about something sweet."

Poking my tongue at my laughing cousins, I reached into my leather messenger bag slung across my body and pulled out a king-sized box of Junior Mints. They were my grandmother's favorite and she claimed they tasted better when I shipped them, seeing as how there was a factory in Cambridge. "You mean these?"

She accepted her gift with a smile and said *sotto voce*, "Don't tell them, but you *are* my favorite."

"This I know. On that note, let me go greet Granddad then I'll be back so you can get in my personal business, nosey woman." I jumped away when Granny snatched a towel from the table to whack my "fresh-mouthed" behind and walked off, laughing and—beyond arms' reach—switching my tail end, teas-ingly, while heading in search of Granddad.

As if compensating for his compromised vision, his hearing

was keen and—despite the noise of family—he called out before I even entered the den where he sat in his favorite easy chair in front of the TV. "Here comes Zoe Noelle with her magical bells and angel tails."

"And there's the duke to my duchess." After kissing my father's oldest brother on the cheek, I headed for my grandfather, grinning at the silly rhyme he'd sung since I was a child. Whenever I questioned what an angel tail was he'd say if I had to ask, I wasn't flying high enough. "Granddad, how'd you know it was me?"

"I felt my earth moving."

I knelt beside his chair to complete our ritual greeting. Eyes closed, I pressed my forehead against his as he cupped my face in strong hands that were rough from years of farming California's Central Valley. But his touch was love.

"I've missed you, young man."

"I've missed you too, old woman. You gotta boyfriend yet?"

I laughed. "No. Are you applying for the role?"

"What kinda benefits it come with?"

I sat back on my haunches and pulled his special treat from my satchel: a pecan roll. A neighbor two doors down from me—the one guilty of supplying me with endless homemade chocolate chip cookies—had recently waded into entrepreneurial waters with her confectionary delights. I loved supporting Black-owned businesses. Granddad loved pecan rolls. It was a double-win. *If* he liked it. Unwrapping the candy, I waved it beneath his nose.

He grinned and snatched it from my hand. "I might be half-blind, but I'm quick."

"And disrespectful," I teased as my cell rang. I glanced at the caller ID and saw it was Shaun Halsey, who'd promised to call if he came across any new information. "Hold on a second, Mister Handsome. Hey, Shaun."

"Hi, Zoe, I apologize for the last-minute call, but are you free tomorrow?"

"I'd planned on spending time with my parents. Why?"

"My grandmother has a vague recollection of that photo, so I'm driving down to Sacramento. It could be a stretch, but perhaps seeing you could help a memory fall into place."

"I'll meet you there. What time and where?"

SEVEN

FAITH

What should've been a three-day journey took five and a half and was the longest in my life with Mister John pulling over for prayer service before each mangy meal and driving as if getting anywhere too fast was a sin. In every patience-sapping prayer ordeal, I silently petitioned heaven that the day wouldn't end without Hope and me finding our family. I'd been diligent about questioning the Colored folks we encountered at filling stations and stops along the way if they'd seen our people, but discovered nothing. When one family invited us to join them, I was tempted but they were headed for Colorado not Los Angeles. I clung to the hope that Papa had stuck to his plan of remaining with the Browns and Kelleys as far as the state line before selling our things and Morris our mule, and purchasing train tickets with the proceeds so we could get to California quickly and leave behind Oklahoma's misery. Once the Owenslees got there, I planned to haunt that LA train station until I discovered *something*. Arriving and finding Papa waiting at that station was my daily fantasy.

If left to Miz Lucy, we might not have been included in the journey. She was inclined to be free of us at that first filling station where we'd encountered Miss Samuella, leaving my baby sister and me there to wait on some magical manifestation of our parents versus our being her burden.

"Husband, we barely have enough and California's a long way off. We can't starve to death out here on account of taking on someone else's problem." Every time she complained and canvassed to leave us on the road, Micah would plead our case, begging his mother's grace, and Mister Owenslee preached.

" 'The ravens brought him bread and meat in the morning and bread and meat in the evening, and he drank from the brook.' Wife, we are like the Prophet Elijah. God provides for us."

I wasn't sure why Mister John insisted on taking us along. Other than quoting scripture justifying our presence, he acted as if we were nonexistent. That left us being an eyesore to his wife, and a curiosity to his kids. I wound up liking Micah. He talked nonstop and asked ten thousand questions, but he was kind and mild-mannered enough that I overlooked his loquaciousness. Henry on the other hand was rough, gruff, with nothing nice about him except his harmonica. We were two days in when he suddenly pulled it from his pocket as if just remembering it existed. It shocked me, hearing that ornery white boy playing that mouth harp like he had a Colored musician hiding inside of him. He was so gifted I forgot where I was and who I was with and started humming. Next thing I knew, words were floating from my lips, making music.

"Amazing grace, how sweet the sound, that saved a wretch like me..."

When I reached that part about being lost but found, my heart hurt wishing for reunion and an opportunity to run into Mama's arms and give her all of my love. I'd even hug my annoying little brother, as well as forgive Papa. After all, it wasn't his fault he'd been up against nature and failed.

"You sing real pretty." Micah's compliment pulled me back to the present and I hushed.

"I was about to say the same thing," Henry barked as if mad that his brother had. "Micah, with you on the guitar and her singing we could go 'round performing at churches and make a pretty penny. How's that sound, Faye-Faye?"

I hated Henry calling me by my nickname and gave him the evil eye. "You don't sing in church for money." *Idiot*, I silently added.

He grinned his snake grin. "Then we'll hit the juke joints and speakeasies."

I sucked my teeth. "One: I'm too young. Two: I was raised better than to step foot in such places. Three: have you ever heard of a mixed-race band existing, let alone performing anywhere?"

"Race-mixing is good for *some* things."

I didn't like his suggestiveness and was glad he was on the other side of their possession pile separating Colored from white. Unlike Henry, Micah had crossed the divide and was seated with his back against the opposite side of the truck, facing us as if our mingling was of no consequence.

"I bet you could make a living just by singing, Faye. Your voice is that kind of pretty."

Performing professionally wasn't something I'd ever considered so I simply stared at Micah without comment, but it did get me to thinking about the life I'd expected before black blizzards sabotaged my existence. I'd assumed I'd further my education like Mama wanted. I'd get a certificate or degree, marry, have babies, and sing in church on Sundays. Mama always told me and Charity to go farther than she did and actually finish college, but sometimes it was hard dreaming in a world where Colored folks were limited.

"Thanks, Micah, but that's not for me."

"Sure, it is. You sing *way* better than a lot of folks on the radio. Just consider it."

I sat a moment before playfully responding, "No . . . I think I'll head for Hollywood once we get to LA so I can be the next Hattie McDaniel, Nina Mae McKinney, or Fredi Washington."

"Who're they?"

"Only some of *the* finest Colored actresses ever." Mama and Papa never took us to picture shows so I'd only read about them in magazines, but I still puffed up as if an authority. "I bet they're rich, wear fancy clothes, and have lots of boyfriends."

"Is that what you want?"

I sobered and rubbed Hope's head laid on my lap as she napped. "Only thing I want right now is to find my folks."

Micah was quiet a moment before continuing. "Faye, you still ain't said why we found y'all out there by yourselves in that cellar."

I glanced across the pile at Henry. I'd found out he was only eighteen, but liked to exaggerate that fact by treating us like babies. Thankfully, he was doing it then, ignoring us and playing his harmonica as if we were of no interest. Still, I lowered my voice when answering Micah so he wouldn't hear. "We were tryna stay safe." I closed my eyes against nightmarish memories of that black blizzard bearing down on us before opening them again. "That's it."

Micah nodded soberly. "Well, I'm glad we found y'all."

"How did you? I know y'all was taking a personal break, but why so far off the road?"

Micah peeked at his brother the same as I had before leaning forward, whispering, "Don't say nothing to Henry, but I saw something and followed it."

"What kind of something?"

"Don't laugh . . . but it was a girl all by herself. I swear on a stack of Bibles," he added, cutting me off when I opened my mouth in question. He raced to explain having the lantern and being farther ahead of Henry and seeing her despite the deep darkness. "It was kinda creepy. She never said or did nothing, just stood there, right about where we found y'all."

That had me frowning. "What did she look like?"

"She was Colored, about your age, maybe older. A little skinnier than you with lighter skin. It's funny 'cause with all that black dust and dirt out there her dress looked brand new and in perfect condition. I remember 'cause it was sparkling white with big pink roses down the left side. And a blue sash at the waist," he quickly added.

My mouth hung open at Micah's describing Mama's dress that Charity was buried in. Except it hadn't been perfect, just Mama's favorite. I leaned toward him. "Describe her hair."

He looked into the air, mouth twisted to one side. "I don't know . . . I guess like when y'all girls take yours braids and wrap 'em 'round your head like pretend crowns. I couldn't get close enough to see her face 'fore she ran off. That's when I heard y'all."

I sat back shivering in silent amazement, recalling how Miz Dorsey styled Charity's hair in a braided crown for her burial because Mama had been too distraught to do it.

Charity, you were there?

That's when I recalled feeling as if somebody had helped me and Hope work our way through the blizzard to that cellar and thinking it was angels when all along it was our big sister. Instead of relaxing in heaven enjoying Jesus, she'd hung around earth long enough to bring us help. I wanted to cry so badly, but held onto my tears to shed them in the sweet quiet of night when it was just Hope and me, alone, on our side.

As nice as it was having a friendly someone in Micah to chat with, I never forgot my mission to keep Hope safe, or our color differences, knowing that things could change on a dime because those differences were dangerous. If Hope wasn't right next to me, she was always in eyesight and arms' reach. When it came to Mister and Miz Owenslee, we stayed as quiet as we could to avoid getting left behind for being burdensome. I tried offering help with our pitiful meals, but Miz Lucy always shooed me away, saying my assistance wasn't required to serve pickled fruit, cornmeal mush, or roasted potatoes. She was the queen of her kitchen, even out there in nowhere.

Our traveling assumed a pattern. Prayers three times a day. Meals so terrible I made myself be grateful. Henry on the harmonica or being obnoxious and acting funny whenever Micah spent too much time talking to me. Micah chatting up a storm or wishing his guitar hadn't been sold like Mama's piano. Hope and me largely staying to ourselves, nearly blending into that pile of possessions as if invisibility offered safety. Mister John pulling off the road at night to sleep except the one night he stopped at a house and the occupants let the Owenslees rest on their enclosed back porch while we remained on the truck. We all stank. We were dirty. I wanted some of Mama's home-made soap and a creek of water, badly. My behind ached from sitting so long every day. I was grouchy and scared and as anxious to be as free of the Owenslees as Miz Lucy wanted to be of us. The morning we rolled into San Bernardino, California, as the sun rose, I wanted to run down the road in my natural business screaming, "Hallelujah, Thank You, Jesus!" I wasn't Moses, but we'd made the Exodus.

Mister Owenslee was so moved by our safe arrival that that morning's prayer lasted long as a tent revival. That man just about prayed every scripture pertaining to Canaan and a milk and honey Promised Land, Joshua taking Jericho, and the ten plagues of Egypt. Other than their connection to Moses and our obvious Oklahoma exodus, I wasn't sure why the plagues were mentioned. It went on so long that I opened an eye to peek at him only to see Micah across the circle doing the same. When we saw each other looking, I crossed my eyes and stuck my tongue out which led to his having to suppress his loud laugh by raising his hands and pretending he'd been touched by heaven. The notion of the Holy Ghost settling on his son stirred Mister John up. That man hopped around so wildly, praising God, that Miz Lucy had to calm him down.

Welcome to California where the sun shines on the sane and insane just the same.

I grinned, thinking that was something Charity would've said.

After a paltry breakfast we cleaned up in a creek running alongside the road before hopping back onto the truck and heading for the Owenslees' destination. The thought of finally arriving in Los Angeles had me so giddy I didn't even mind Henry.

"You sure you don't wanna form a musical trio? We'd be original."

I didn't bother denying him *again*. I was too busy wondering why Mister John was slowing down and pulling over when we'd just resumed traveling. His "Wife, I believe the Lord is leading us here" had all four of us in the back lifting up and looking through the truck's side slats. Henry even stood despite the truck's rocking dangerously down a rutted, dirt road.

"Pa, what we doing, sir?"

"Following the Spirit, son. Looks like we've found a migrant camp, and I sense there're sinning souls here crying out for God's deliverance. We need to help them find Him."

"Husband, we can't stay long. You got that factory job waiting. If you don't hurry up and get there, they gonna wind up giving that job to one of them Mexicans."

" 'Why are you fearful, o ye of little faith?' Wife, the job will be safe." Mister Owenslee continued up that road into what appeared to be a camp of vagabonds and hobos. There were countless cars and trucks in varying conditions; some with, some without wheels. Others were half-hidden beneath sheets, offering the families living in them a measure of privacy in these makeshift homesteads filled with some of the most desperate-looking folks under heaven.

Good Jesus.

My family had fallen prey to hard times, had never been rich by any stretch of the imagination, and didn't have fancy conveniences like electricity or indoor plumbing; but the folks milling about early that morning looked like they'd never even heard of enough and life had become too heavy. Most of their faces were hard, lean, and lacking joy or any good feeling that might've softened their edges. Even the kids stood there staring at us with blank expressions like miniature versions of the lifeless-looking adults about them.

"Faye-Faye, is this Los Angeles?" My baby sister held tightly to my hand, staring back at the kids staring at us.

"I sure hope not."

Mister Owenslee slowed to a stop not far from a man seated atop an upturned bucket with a dry stalk of something hanging from his mouth. "Good morning, brother. What is this encampment that the good Lord has blessed us to stumble upon?"

The man stood and approached the truck before answering. "Just a few farmers and folks waiting on work. Been hoping them Farm Security Administration folks would come through here, but them Spics and Filipinos keep getting to 'em first and taking our jobs like they's white men."

"That's a terrible occurrence."

"Sho is! Them damn FSA fools say there's too many of us coming in here from Texas and Arkansas for jobs. But we know we cain't get nothing 'cause them Filipinos and Spics undercuts us by taking lower wages."

I wasn't sure what "Spics" were but the way the man spat it out I figured it was a group of people he didn't care too much about.

"Hell, plus these dumb Okies keep pouring in here near 'bout every damn day overrunning the place. Y'all ain't from Oklahoma, is you?"

"Yessir, we are."

"Well . . . ain't meant no harm. We just hungry and tired of waiting, is all."

" 'But they that wait upon the Lord shall renew their strength; they shall mount up with wings as eagles; they shall run, and not be weary; and they shall walk, and not faint.' So says the Book of Isaiah. Amen, brother?"

"Amen, but if some eagle mount up and come anywhere near here, I'm putting his ass in a skillet like fried chicken."

Hope giggled at that but immediately quieted when the man looked in our direction.

His voice hardened. "They with you?"

"They're looking for their parents," Miz Lucy offered.

"Ain't no niggers here, ma'am." He hiked his thumb to the right. "They's up the road at the Colored camp. Now *that's* who they need to be turning back at the border instead of us white men. There's plenty cotton down South for niggers to pick. Why the hell come all the way to California to do it?" He didn't wait for a response. "Bet they'd stay their black asses down home if they saw these border police rounding up Spics and shipping 'em back to Mexico. These border patrols is God sent. Plus, I hear them lawmakers is working on some kinda ree-pat-tree-ay-shun something or other to send Filipinos back where they come from. That oughta help some."

"One can hope," Mister Owenslee commented while looking about. "How many folks you think are camped here?"

The man sank grubby fingers in his oily hair and scratched. "Near 'bout fifty or sixty."

"Wife, that's a big catch for the Lord. We can't leave till we cast the net. Sons, we're setting up an early-morning prayer vigil."

Next thing I knew, Henry and Micah had hopped down from the back, Miz Lucy exited the front cab with Bible in hand, and my sister and I were instructed to prepare ourselves for sacred service. I had no idea what that entailed so I simply helped Hope down from the truck and stood aside as the Owenslees worked like a well-oiled machine intent on reclaiming Jesus's lost sheep. Mister John climbed up and stood in the truck bed summoning "all God's precious children" while Henry pulled out his harmonica for a rousing rendition of "Bringing in the Sheaves" as Miz Lucy and Micah sang.

"Come to the living waters, children. Come and drink. The Lord is visiting you today."

As Mister John made his appeal, I looked in the direction the greasy-haired man had pointed, wishing I could kick him in the teeth for referring to Colored folks as "niggers" before heading in the direction of the Colored camp. Even if it took all day on foot, I was determined to find it. My parents might've passed through, or miracle of miracles, they could be waiting there on us before heading to Los Angeles.

I bent and whispered in my sister's ear. "Hope, we gotta go."

"Okay, but where?"

Before I could answer a horn started blaring annoyingly, repeatedly. We turned to see Mister John on the truck bed reaching through his open window, blaring that horn like a trumpet in Zion.

"Come, children. Don't keep the Lord waiting!"

Taking Hope's hand, I eased us backward as folks responded to Mister John's call. Some seemed curious, others irritated at being awakened. Several ignored him altogether.

As he talked, we walked. I didn't mean to be rude and not tell the Owenslees "thank you" for transporting us safely, but I was so fixed on finding that Colored camp that manners seemed insignificant. Leading Hope toward the road, I froze when Mister John shouted at us.

"You Colored gals, come on back here! The Lord has need of you in this service."

I turned to see Henry still playing, Miz Lucy and Micah still singing. And too many sets of white eyes on us for me to continue exiting. A white man had commanded. Obedience was expected. Slowly, I returned to where Mister John was quoting scripture, all the while hoping whatever he wanted wouldn't be long or laborious.

"Come gal, sing for the Creator. Lift His praises. Let His children know His goodness."

The man had been more aware of me than I thought and had actually heard my voice. That didn't mean I wanted to sing in front of all those unfriendly looking folks.

I glanced at Henry for musical help. He merely shrugged. It was Micah who whispered, " 'There is a Fountain Filled with Blood.' " We sang that in church every first Sunday before communion. I started singing, thinking the quicker I did, the quicker we could disappear. Instead, the usual happened. I closed my eyes and got caught up in the majesty of melody.

Music was oxygen and life to me. It took me out of myself and elevated my being. It was humbling. Filling. With Henry's accompaniment, I melted into the song, becoming one with it, singing until my spirit was content. When I finished and the last note of that harmonica faded into the air, my eyes snapped open. Seeing myself seemingly surrounded by a sea of white folks was a jolt to my senses. There were no Colored hands raised in praise, or shouts of exultation, or ushers fanning folks caught up in the Spirit. No Reverend Coulter collecting his tears in a handkerchief. Just dead silence.

"This is the God we serve!" Mister John thundered. "He can take a simple nothing of a nigra and fill her mouth with intelligent melodies that prove His existence. 'Then the Lord opened the donkey's mouth, and it said to Balaam, "What have I done to you to make you beat me these three times?" ' The

Creator uses the least of creation. Even donkeys and Coloreds. So why not come to Him, O white brothers and sisters, on whom He's ready to pour out blessings?"

The fifteen or more people moving toward Mister John enabled Hope and me to ease away unseen. Debased. I was so hot over the ugly way that man had tarnished me and my music that I was shaking.

"How dare he compare me to a donkey!"

"It's okay, Faye-Faye. Don't cry."

I wasn't aware of my tears until hearing Hope's gentle comfort. I glanced down at her, hoping she hadn't understood our being belittled, how Mister John compared us to animals. "I hate them for acting like God's stupid enough to waste time making inferior stuff. They use something as silly as skin that ain't nothing but a body covering to make themselves feel better. It must be miserable being so ignorant and arrogant!"

"Faye-Faye, Mama doesn't like us saying 'hate.' "

That diminished my flaring up somewhat and fueled my determination to get where we were going. "Come on, Baby Girl, we gotta find that Colored camp."

We'd been walking several minutes without success when a group of mocking voices rang out not far behind us. I knew without looking back that they were white. And hostile.

"Hey, niggers, where y'all headed?"

"Hope, keep walking. Whatever you do, do *not* turn around." Clutching her hand, I increased our pace while scouring the ground for what Papa called an "equalizer." With Charity and me being the oldest, expected to protect ourselves and our younger siblings, Papa taught us to do whatever was necessary.

If ever outnumbered, you find yourself something to even things out. A stick. A brick. I don't care what the weapon is, but give yourself an equal chance to come out of whatever danger you're in.

"Gal, you hear us talking to you?"

I did what I told Hope not to. I glanced back and saw three girls and a boy, all around my age, running toward us. I recognized them as having been among that camp crowd we'd just left. They were mean and hungry-looking. Seeing the hot hatred in their expressions, I picked up a thick stick and pushed Hope behind me as I turned to face them. "We don't want no trouble so just move on."

The biggest girl reached us first. Clearly the leader of their ragtag team, she might've been cute at one point in life but just then her unmasked meanness eradicated her delightfulness. She was practically in my face, snarling.

"Singing and being with that preacher man won't ever make you good enough to tell us what to do."

"Yeah, plus you don't sing all that great," the solitary boy in the band added. "You sounded like a wounded octopus."

Their ragtag group found that supremely funny and laughed uproariously as the bandleader stepped even closer. "I'm the one who sings 'round the campfire every night. And here you come. Tryna compete for Ezra's attention."

I had no clue who Ezra was and didn't care to meet him. "We're not looking for trouble."

"You shoulda thought about that, nigger singer, before doing what you did."

When that girl poked her nasty finger in my chest, I made myself take a deep breath while considering this threat. The three minions had spread out, encircling us. Hope was still behind me and had wrapped her arms about my waist, pressing against my back, afraid. I had to be cautious with only a stick as defense.

"I don't know him, but I'm sure Ezra's interests—"

I nearly saw stars when that girl hauled back and hit me in the mouth. Hope screamed.

The ragamuffins laughed as the jilted singer spat, "Keep Ezra's name off your ugly nigger lips!"

Livid, I wanted to slap her into next week but knew better than escalating that nonsense and would've walked away outraged, pride bruised, lip throbbing, if another girl hadn't touched my sibling.

"Looka here! This little darkie done peed on herself."

Hope was suddenly snatched away from me, and I whirled in time to see her being viciously shoved to the ground as if an inconsequential non-entity. I didn't think. I did what Papa taught me. I equalized the situation. Except I didn't use that stick. I swung my fist with the fury and force of all my grief and heartache and smashed it into the face of Hope's assailant.

The impact was so solid it reverberated up my arm as she stumbled backward, clutching her nose and howling loudly, as the rest of us fell into stunned silence.

"Oh, God . . ." Leader Girl's voice trembled with amazement and shock when seeing that bloody fountain seeping through her accomplice's fingers.

Knowing better than to linger a moment more, I snatched Hope from the ground and forced her into a run.

"Y'all niggers get back here."

We ran like our feet had wings and our lives depended on them, which they did. Our assailants might've been peer-aged, but adults would inevitably enter the fray. For white folks, my laying hands on a white girl was sacrilegious and liable to get me lynched. Running and wanting my mama, I begged heaven for divine intervention only to be waylaid by a rifle-wielding white man.

EIGHT
ZOE

I adored multiple art forms. Particularly music. I was a hard-core nineties R&B fan. Mint Condition. Sade. The Fugees. TLC. Boyz II Men. I was also quick to groove to gospel, pop, and select country on occasion. Having accepted Shaun's invitation to rideshare, I found his musical tastes proved more eclectic than mine. Weekend traffic was heavy and we'd been en route to Sacramento for over an hour and already Cole Porter, Bonnie Raitt, Carlos Santana, Charles Mingus, Salt-N-Pepa, and the Red Hot Chili Peppers had joined our journey via his stereo. His conversational skills were equally fluid as rhythmic beats and electrified voices became the background of our effortless discussion.

"What brought you to art, Zoe?"

We'd tackled topics from the weather to travel and food preferences; as well as those triplet taboos of religion, race, and politics. I'd been his enthralled audience as he credited (his grandmother aside) the inestimable Gordon Parks—*Life* magazine's first African-American staff photographer and writer—as the inspiration for his foray in photography. He admired Parks, a self-taught renaissance man, for using his lens over a six-decade-long career to document life in the United States from the 1940s forward, highlighting disparities and inequities with boldness and artistic beauty. Now, he'd turned the spotlight on me to share what had inspired my chosen career.

"Remember me saying my family's heavily into music?"

He nodded.

"Well, my grandfather was, or is, a member of a gospel quartet."

"Really? I love those old school harmonies."

"They weren't bigtime or anything, and never recorded, but like I said, I grew up immersed in music and thought that was my career path."

"Do you play? Or sing?"

"Now, that's the thing!" I angled toward him, warming to the subject. "Nearly everyone in my family can perform in some musical capacity. Except a handful that includes me. My thing was songwriting. And before you ask, no, I never wrote anything any superstar has ever sung. My skills weren't that kind of fabulous." The deep notes of his quiet chuckle made my toes tingle. "Anyhow, my dad sent me to a summer songwriting camp when I was twelve and the program included a field trip to a small, local museum." I'd been enthralled by its Harlem Jazz exhibition and asked the curator countless questions about the incredible images of musical legends. I was swept up by her knowledge and passion that seemingly breathed life into the subjects, animating them for me—visually, mentally. I'd asked how she knew so much and she'd laughed before explaining that extensive research was part of her job. "It was more than a cerebral thing. This might sound off, but it was like she *became* them and their stories."

He nodded appreciatively. "When you honor your subject, you can easily take on their essence."

He gets it.

Vince never did and would move our conversations onto other topics when I discussed art and he felt in over his head.

"I talked my parents into taking me back to that gallery and introduced them to the curator, Missus Jeffries, who invited me to apply for their junior docent program. I worked weekends and summers until graduating high school. And that, kind sir, is that."

"Impressive. Unfair question, but who're your favorites?"

Shame on him for asking, but he had. That led to my gushing like a geyser the wonders of Augusta Savage, Archibald Motley, and Ernie Barnes. Henry Ossawa Tanner. Elizabeth Catlett. Edmonia Lewis. Lois Mailou Jones. Kehinde Wiley, and Thomas Blackshear.

"You like multiple art forms but only Black artists," he commented when I quieted and took a much-needed breath. He glanced away from the road to look at me. "Every artist you mentioned is of African descent."

I was pleased by his knowledge. "I greatly admire the work of non-Black artists, but the mainstream gets enough admiration so you won't find me listing them."

Our joint laughter slowly faded into comfortable silence. Shaun was easy to talk to, a fascinating individual, and a fantastic listener who made me feel in the company of an old friend.

"Any children?"

He was divorced with a seventeen-year-old daughter and already knew I was separated. It was a logical question, but one I wished could be avoided. Looking out my window, I inhaled deeply. "I had a son. Jaelen. He was born eight weeks premature . . . and didn't make it."

My little guy was a fighter, but underdeveloped lungs, in addition to other problems and conditions, led to his death five days after his birth. It had been a hard pregnancy and I was on bedrest for most of it; but I'd undergo it again if it meant even two more minutes with my beautiful angel of innocence. Three years had passed since I lost him and even with therapy, meditation, and mindfulness exercises sometimes the hurt could sneak up on me, feeling as fresh as if my son's death just happened.

Focused on the passing terrain, I was surprised to feel the gentle press of warm flesh, and turned to find Shaun's hand covering mine.

"You have my sincere condolences."

I looked at him, thinking how he was the opposite of Vince.

Initially, my husband and I clung together in the aftermath of our devastation, but our baby wasn't gone a month before Vince started in with the blame games, citing my age, when my contracting PID, or Pelvic Inflammatory Disease—the condition that led to our child's being born premature—was in fact his doing. While pregnant with Jaelen several routine tests came back with abnormal readings. I'd developed gestational diabetes and elevated blood pressure that resulted in my pregnancy being high risk. That, in turn, resulted in my obstetrician electing not to subject me to additional, potentially harmful probing. It wasn't until after my son was born that we discovered I had PID, a condition contracted through sexually transmitted disease. That's how I learned about Vince's first affair—the one he started two months before I conceived.

I am lovely and more than enough.

Affirmations were part of my healing process. Mentally reciting that favorite, I pushed aside thoughts of Vince's whoremongering ways and reached for the warmth of Shaun's tender sentiment. "Thank you. I appreciate that."

He gently squeezed my hand before releasing it.

We rode in companionable silence, traveling northbound on I-5 toward our destination with the sounds of music between us. We'd come up the back way, taking I-580 from the Bay through Tracy, and were now in that long stretch of country playing host to herds of cattle moseying through fields bordering the interstate.

I laughed at a memory. "My grandparents had a small farm when we were kids and I used to call the cows 'dogs' and bark at them, and be mad when they didn't bark back."

Shaun cracked up laughing. "Is there a need to revisit *Sesame Street* and relearn your species, Miss Zoe?"

I swatted his arm playfully. "Whatever, Shaun. I wasn't even three."

"That's quite a defense."

"It is and I'm sticking with it." When nearing Elk Grove, I remarked on how it had changed, courtesy of the housing boom of the early 2000s and folks fleeing metro Sacramento and the Bay Area for idyllic suburban bliss.

"It's an enclave of metropolitan diversity now, but Elk Grove used to be a sundown town."

He had my interest. "Are you serious?"

Shaun lowered the stereo volume as if his words held importance, and they did. "Back in the day, persons looking like you and me knew better than to—as my grandfather used to say—be brown and in town when the sun went down. Elk Grove was known for its KKK presence. That white-hooded vigilante violence aside, quiet as it's kept, the area including Sacramento was big on restrictive covenants."

"Keep it white, keep it right." I shook my head, thinking on that old practice of forbidding persons purchasing a home from ever, in future, selling that home to African-Americans. Such agreements—written into a contract or implied—were upheld and enforced by real estate entities and neighborhood associations. "The more things change, the more they stay the same." People of color were no longer legally restricted from purchasing where we wanted. That didn't mean we weren't generations behind, trying to catch up on a playing field that wasn't level, or required to do more than others to ensure a seat at the table. We could protest and fight back when under attack. But attacks happened. Racism was still pervasive, just slick in its manifestations.

"Zoe, are you sure I can't pour you a drink?"

Shaun's mother was an attractive woman about my height with a southern sense of hospitality and kindness. I smiled at her despite being on the edge of my seat. Literally. Shaun had gone inside to get his grandmother while we sat on the back patio enjoying the spring weather.

"No, ma'am, but thank you. And thank you so much for allowing me into your home."

"My son's friends are always welcome. I'm sorry my husband's out fishing and not here to greet you, but I'll leave the pitcher and glasses on the table in case you change your mind about this fresh-squeezed lemonade."

I started to respond only to see Shaun exiting the house pushing an elderly woman in a wheelchair. He'd said his grandmother was in her upper nineties and suffering from dementia, but her smile and eyes were bright, clear. And that *skin*. Smooth. Dark. It shone like black porcelain.

Nervously, I stood to greet her as Shaun steered her near. "Hello, Missus Halsey. It's a pleasure to meet you."

"Nana Sam, this is Zoe, the friend I told you about."

She shook her head and frowned. "Ain't no Zoes here."

I glanced at Shaun but he was exchanging looks with his mother as she came to the rescue.

"Mama Sam, remember I explained this morning that Shaun was bringing his friend Zoe because she needs your help?" She stroked her mother-in-law's hand in a soothing fashion only for Nana Sam to snatch her hand away angrily.

"I done told y'all already. Zoe ain't here!"

Her insistence prompted Shaun to lower on his haunches beside her. "Nana Sam, who *is* here?"

Slowly, the angry lines on her forehead relaxed and she smiled that brilliant, carefree smile while reaching out to me in a beckoning fashion. "Come here."

God is my witness, a jolt of energy surged through my body when our hands connected.

"Baby Girl, it's been a long, *long* time. Thank God, you finally made it to California."

"Nana, who's Baby Girl?"

She slapped Shaun's arm. "She is, silly. Push me closer so we can have a drink."

I sat, heart pounding, wanting to snatch the Xeroxed photos from my bag and jump feet-first into whatever revelations she might offer. But I knew better than to overwhelm or scare her. It was best to let her set the pace. I didn't want the lemonade she had Shaun's mother pour for me, but I sipped it just the same. Anything to keep Nana Sam relaxed and talking.

"When'd you get to California, Baby Girl?" Her smile made her seem young, vibrant.

"A while ago." I was two months shy of forty and born in the state, so it wasn't a lie exactly.

"How was the journey and where'd y'all wind up?"

"It was rough." My mother had had to have an emergency cesarean section with me. No lie again. "And we decided on Oakland."

"Oakland? I thought y'all was headed for Los Angeles?"

I shared a look with Shaun, feeling as if I'd been gifted a nugget from the past. "We were. Just me and . . ." I let the sentence dangle, hoping she would finish it.

She laughed heartily. "Honey, you younger than me but like they say, the first things to fail are your titties and your memory."

"Mama Sam." Shaun's mother looked aghast as he coughed to keep from laughing.

"Oh hush, Verdean. You always was prissy." Nana Sam returned her attention to me. "Now, lemme think . . . it was you and . . ." She frowned in concentration before brightening suddenly. "Faye! Just the two of you. No . . . Wait . . . there was others. White boys, if I remember correctly."

When I reached for my bag, Shaun nodded in agreement. I extracted the photos and laid them on the table in front of her. "Is this us?"

She studied them a long moment. "My, my, y'all Owensbey girls were so sad. Just heartbreaking. I wanted to take y'all with us, but there wasn't any room. I hope you forgive me."

"Yes, ma'am, of course. Do you remember taking these pictures?"

Caught in her memories, Nana Sam ignored the question, pointing at the teen girl in the photo instead. "Baby Girl, that's you. That itty bitty thing hiding in your skirt is Faye." Her finger shifted to the males. "I don't know which was which, but one of 'em was Micah and the other Harvey or Henry or something. Do you remember, Sweet Pea?"

Despite the sorrow flashing lightning-quick across Shaun's countenance, he lifted his grandmother's hands and kissed them. "No, Samuella, I don't."

She patted his face affectionately. "I have my bad days, too, baby. When're we going fishing?"

Shaun's mother stood as if on cue. "Zoe, I apologize but my mother-in-law has reached her limits."

"No apologies necessary. I thank you again for allowing my visit."

Shaun stood as his mother moved behind the wheelchair, but she declined his help. "I'll take Mama Sam back inside. You sit and enjoy a drink with Zoe."

I waited until the women were indoors before sitting back

with a long, audible sigh. "Oh. My. Goodness. She *remembered*."
I stared at Shaun, amazed by the intricacies of memory and the
dynamics of the human brain.

"She did. Your doppelgänger is Baby Girl Owensbey," he
commented, sitting across from me. "I'm sure that's a nickname,
but it's better than nothing."

I agreed. "And theirs is an unusual last name, especially for
African-Americans." Hopefully, that would work in my favor,
narrowing down the misses and producing hits leading to this
lost ancestor. My mind was racing with next steps and I even
fantasized a glorious moment of being able to tell my mother I'd
found the biological link she needed. "I can't wait to dive into
this research."

"I'm glad Nana could help." The sad note in his voice wasn't
lost on me.

I quietly questioned, "Do you mind my asking who Sweet
Pea is?"

He stroked the goatee framing his full lips before responding. "My grandfather. He passed eight years ago, but I favor
Grandpa so much that sometimes Nana thinks I'm him."

I reached over and gently rubbed his hand. "We have that in
common. We both favor people from Nana Sam's past."

NINE

FAITH

Happiness at seeing Henry Owenslee wasn't an emotion I'd ever imagined feeling until he arrived on the scene, rifle at the ready. That angry band of white kids had caught up with Hope and me and would've tried their best to beat us into the dust, but a horn blast intervened. Seeing that truck barreling our way, I snatched my sister aside as it skidded to a stop, effectively separating our feuding factions.

"What the blasted hell's going on?" When Henry hopped down from the cab, I was amazed that he was driving instead of Mister John, but more amazed by the rifle he held.

"That nigger hit my friend!" Leader Girl was livid as Micah exited the passenger's side looking scared, mystified.

Henry glanced at me before approaching the bloody-nosed girl who'd slammed Hope to the ground. "Are you all right? Lemme see."

"Is it broken?" Micah was instantly beside him, taking the rifle Henry pushed into his hands in order to examine that girl's nose like he had a doctor's license.

"I ain't sure, but might be." Henry glared at me. "It's already bruised and swelling."

"Faye, what happened?" Micah's frantic question set off that band of bullies.

They were gesticulating and talking simultaneously, twisting the truth so viciously that even Hope piped up in my defense. I put a hand over her mouth, knowing silence was best as that group lied and exaggerated about minding their business and my attacking them. Henry was crazy enough to hear truth in fiction. Red in the face, he stalked toward us and backhanded me so fiercely that I fell against the hood of the truck, stunned.

That brought all jabbering to an end, plunging the day in silence.

"How dare you lay hands on God's property!"

I didn't care that he was bigger or heavier than me. I'd had enough of white folks touching me that day in violent ways and was about to slam a foot in Henry's privates even if it resulted in my meeting up with Charity. Except there was Hope, crying, needing me. And Henry's fervent but quiet hissing.

"Be still, Faith." His calling me by my right name cut through, tethered my rage. "Do exactly as I say." Grabbing my arm, he marched me to that circle of violators and roughly pushed me onto my knees and started talking to heaven so vociferously he might as well have been Mister Owenslee. He begged the Creator's forgiveness for my "heathenish ignorance," and prayed my soul would be spared damnation and come to Jesus. He got to rebuking demons of violence and waywardness so hard I almost expected to feel spirits flying out of me. "Repent, dark child. You've touched God's anointed and must beg His mercy."

When I stayed silent, Henry squeezed the back of my neck, commanding I repent. I wanted nothing more than my parents' sudden appearance. I wanted to run into Papa's embrace and be taken away from hurt and humiliation, to scrape white folks from my existence. But seeing Hope in my peripheral view, crying and scared, I did what I had to.

"I'm sorry."

"Say it louder so that heaven hears."

Throwing my head back, I screamed the words at the sky as if I meant them and I did. I was sorry for all the happenings that had me there in the middle of nowhere with dusty white folks, no better than me, bent on their ways and insisting on their empty superiority.

Satisfied with my cry, Henry wrapped up his prayer and yanked me to my feet while addressing the girl holding her bloodied nose and quietly sniffling. "Sister, is there anything you want to say to this wretched soul?"

"Yes. This!"

I had to slide down inside myself when that girl spit in my face. I went down deep to the place where music lived and hummed inwardly to keep from exploding into wildness as my eyes filled with molten tears.

"You wait till my big brothers see what you did to my nose. When they get through with you, you ain't gonna be good for nothing 'cept a prayer or a rope."

"I got one better," Henry interjected. "Where's the nearest sheriff? Let the law deal with this infidel so you and your family keep yourselves pure and holy."

"Up a ways, almost to the next town." Leader Girl's eyes glittered with glee at the idea of my being handed over to the authorities.

"Thank you, sister." Henry marched me to the back of the truck and all but threw me on. Hope instantly climbed aboard, holding onto me, wet and smelling like urine, crying quietly. "Y'all wanna hop on so I can take you back to camp before we head to the sheriff?"

"We ain't getting on no truck with pissy niggers in it," the boy in the band decided.

Henry clapped him on the shoulder before climbing into the cab and urging Micah to hurry up. "If y'all need to find us you know where we'll be. Ah, shoot!" His exclamation was accompanied by the sound of the truck engine grinding pitifully.

"What's wrong?" Micah sounded slightly panicked.

"We outta gas. Y'all think you can get someone back at the camp to come help?" Henry thanked the gang when they assured him they would as they walked off in that direction. "Are they gone? You see 'em still?"

When Micah confirmed the group were specks in the distance, Henry started that truck without incident.

Next thing I knew, Hope and I were holding on as that jalopy took off at a speed I didn't know it was capable of. I wasn't sure what Henry was up to but as the countryside flew by, I did my best to spot that Colored camp. If it was out there tucked back from the road somewhere, I missed it with that boy driving like Satan was after him. He maintained that hard pace for so long, that truck rattling mightily in response, I thought it might fall apart and was relieved when he pulled off the road into a thick grove. Disgusted and disturbed, it wasn't until then that I realized I'd never seen Henry drive before and that Mister and Miz Owenslee were missing.

My nerves were rattled and that truck had barely stopped before I hopped down, bringing Hope with me, and took off. I had to get away from white folks, especially these Owenslees. I was walking fast, dragging Hope along, determined to find a way to reach LA. I'd heard about hobos, and hitchhiking. If I couldn't find the railroad and hop a train, I'd pray up a kind Colored person who'd take us the final distance. I was money-less but didn't care the cost. I was ready to steal, connive, lie, or whatever was necessary to get to my family, people who loved me.

"Faye, wait!"

Hearing those Owenslee boys running to catch up, I grabbed the first thing I saw: an old rusty can with the jagged-edged lid still attached, and turned it on them.

Henry jumped back when I slashed at him. "Hey, now, wait a minute! We ain't here to cause you no harm."

"You can't go out there. What if that girl got her brothers and you run into them?"

I didn't care about Micah's pleading. What caught my attention was Henry's expression. That boy had never shown himself to be anything except torment and aggravation. I was confused by his looking shamefaced, repentant.

"Sorry about what happened back there." His voice was meek. "But it was the only thing I could do right then. Come on. I ain't here to hurt you none. Put the can down," he gently coaxed, adding when I didn't, "hell or high water, we're gonna get you to your people. I promise."

Hope's pulling on my arm, saying she didn't want us to be out there by ourselves, cut through my mind and I felt myself capitulating as fire and anger slowly ebbed out of me. Exhausted, afraid, and hungry, I chose a familiar enemy versus Hope and me being alone in unknown territory. When I tossed that can aside, both those boys grinned. I opened my mouth to give them a piece of my mind only to scream when a body popped upright on the back of the truck.

"Praise you, Jesus!"

It was Mister John. He hollered and fell back flat, leaving me staring and wondering why I hadn't seen him until then.

"Notice the mound's a bit bigger? Folks started giving us stuff after Pa's sermon. He and Ma were so moved by their generosity despite their needs that they caught the holy vapors," Micah offered as if privy to my thoughts. "Ma's back there, too. On our side of the pile. It took a couple of men to help us lift them, but we got 'em up there as comfortably as we could."

"That's why I'm driving . . . even though I lost my license,"

Henry added, explaining they'd noticed our absence and wanted to make sure we'd made it to the Colored camp. Instead, they'd encountered our ruckus in the road. Now, we were fleeing like fugitives.

"Think we oughta hide back here a while, Henry?"

"Naw, little brother, we've been on the road long enough to have lost 'em. Plus, we're almost to LA. We oughta be okay. Baby Girl, come on. I ain't gonna let nobody hurt you."

Hope stunned me by taking Henry's outstretched hand and heading toward the truck while gesturing for me to follow. "Come on, Faye-Faye."

Tired of feeling alone and afraid, when Micah touched my shoulder, I let myself be steered toward whatever was next on this journey.

Los Angeles was much more than I'd expected. Bigger. Brighter. Faster. There were long streets, a plethora of people, and buildings that made me crane my neck to see their heights. Noisy. Busy. Fascinating and frightening. Most of it was strange; some of it was pretty. There were plenty of orange and palm trees, but I never saw Fredi Washington or Hattie McDaniel. The thought of finding the train station and my parents possessed my focus, leaving me breathless with excitement. But I had to curtail my enthusiasm while the Owenslees navigated to Mister John's new job site. His holy stupor had lasted longer than Miz Lucy's, but his snoring was proof that after driving from Oklahoma his wasn't merely a heavenly touch. The man was sleepy. When he finished with his employer, behind the wheel again, he headed for a residential district. Not the train station.

We wound up at some old spinster relative of theirs who made it painfully clear our Oklahoma dirt—especially Hope's urine smell—wasn't welcome in her home. "Leave it out yonder in the yard."

After the Owenslees bathed and changed, Hope and I were given a cube of homemade soap, fabric scraps, and ordered to do the same. We took turns playing lookout while the other quickly scrubbed in that outdoor tin tub surrounded by a wooden enclosure, only to put on the same soiled clothes we'd been wearing since leaving Wellston. She protested, but I made Hope another "diaper," before wetting our hair and undoing and redoing our plaits as best as I could without a comb or Mama's hair pomade. Mama would've objected to us looking such a mess, particularly me with my mangled dress hem, but at least we were clean.

"Y'all come on and eat so we can unload this truck."

Hope swiftly obeyed Miz Lucy's clipped instructions, but I held back, wondering when we could leave. It was far past lunchtime and my stomach screamed its emptiness; still, I needed to find that station and scolded myself for getting caught up in the sights and sounds of Los Angeles instead of paying attention to the street names and all the twists and turns that led us here. That information would've made it easier to backtrack to the business district. Bothered by my oversight, I slowly ate the hot, buttered biscuit with a slice of fried scrapple sandwiched in between, thankful for something besides salt pork and hardtack.

I'd barely finished before Miz Lucy had us setting up their belongings. The process would've been quick and lickety-split, except that old spinster relative wasn't satisfied with anything we did. I lost count of the times she made us place and resituate the Owenslees' property, or discarded their things not to *her* liking. Irascible and difficult to please, by the time things met her approval night had fallen.

Supper had been served and Hope was on the back porch with Micah playing some game involving sticks and rocks while I sat on the empty truck bed, moping and discouraged. It was too dark to try to find our way to the station. We had no choice but to spend our first night in California with the Owenslees. Stretching out across the truck bed, I counted the stars, wondering if my family was looking at them. Telling myself not to get upset, I started humming. Before long, I was singing "Twinkle Twinkle Little Star."

"That girl back there was upset for good reason. You sing like you came from heaven."

Hushing abruptly, I hurried into a seated position, mad that I hadn't heard Henry sneaking up on me like a cat in the night. With the truck parked away from the porch there wasn't much light, but it was enough to see his crooked grin and that glittering snake gaze locked on me.

"Mind if I sit?"

"It's y'all's truck. No need to ask my permission." Not wanting to be anywhere near him, I scooted toward the tailgate intending to exit as he sat, only to find his sudden hold about my wrist.

"Don't leave, Faith. Sit with me. Please."

I snatched my hand from his grasp, but some soft thing in his voice caught my attention. It was humble, pleading. Nothing like the always staring, flippant-lipped, never-minding-his-own-business boy I'd ridden from Oklahoma with. "What do you want and how do you know my name?" I couldn't recall Hope calling me anything but Faye-Faye in his presence.

"You been singing some 'Faith, Hope, and Charity' song off and on since we found y'all. I figure your little sister calls you by a nickname. That makes you Faith. You slipped up once and called Baby Girl, Hope. That's two outta three. Is there a Charity?"

I jumped off the tailgate and would've run away except Henry blocked my path.

"Whoa. Hold on. I apologize for upsetting you. Wasn't nothing meant by it. It was just a question."

Staring at him in the dark, I was suddenly back on that road protecting my sister from that band of ruffians, reliving his hitting me like I was some kind of devil seed. I wanted to slap the white off his face, and inflict on him what it felt like to be alone, scared, humiliated.

"You didn't have to hit me." I was too stubborn to cry; that didn't mean tears weren't pooling.

"I didn't like it one bit but yes, Faith, hitting you was necessary." He was quiet a long time. "If I didn't do what I did, those kids woulda never quit. Even worse, they woulda run back to camp and next thing you know you'da been facing a swarm of vicious, outraged folks."

I ignored the truth in that. "You made me apologize when I wasn't the one in the wrong. If Micah was being hurt, wouldn't you fight back?"

"Of course! Faith, you ain't wrong for protecting yourself or your loved ones, but—"

"*But nothing.* I ain't never been hit by no white person. I didn't come to California to start living that experience. Just get away from me." I pushed past him.

Again, he blocked my leaving. "Listen, instead of being so damned hot-headed! You saw your folks out there picking cotton today? Might be a different state, but ain't too much changed."

I glared at him while recalling being shocked to see a group of "my people" picking cotton, sacks draped across their backs, as we drove through a stretch of fields before reaching Los Angeles.

"All I'm saying, Faith, is stay careful. Hate ain't confined to no part of the world. Just like you came here, so did a bunch of southern Crackers." He lowered his voice, seeing he had my attention. "This might be California, but y'all still Colored and race hate ain't stayed back home."

I plopped onto the tailgate, slightly deflated and wishing the world wasn't this way. "I'm sure hate got to California long before this set of Crackers did." I closed my eyes and gently kneaded my forehead only to feel Henry sit beside me. Opening my eyes, I spoke without looking his way. "Hate been on this earth since Cain killed Abel."

"It ain't gotta be like that . . . at least not between us."

When he took my hand, I felt wary and suspicious but remained silent.

"I'm sorry life is what it is. And I'm sorry for smacking you."

I flinched when he raised a hand only to be surprised by his gently stroking my cheek.

"I like you too much to cause you pain, Faye-Faye. Let's leave today in the past. Okay?"

I studied him as best I could in the dark night with nothing but fragments of porch light. He'd bathed, washed his hair, and was clean and fresh-smelling. Out there, those hazel-colored eyes didn't seem so mean. Sitting all quiet and kind, he was a different person. "Okay," I cautiously agreed.

His smile was bright. "Let's start fresh." He extended a hand. "Hi, I'm Henry Owenslee and I'm here to be your friend."

I shook his hand. "Faith Wilson."

His grip tightened when I tried removing my hand from his. "Any boy ever tell you how pretty you is?"

That confused me. Charity was the one made in Mama's image: slim, bright-skinned, and feminine. I was a tomboy who'd choose dungarees before a dress, and had no qualms about running wild outside or tumbling in the grass. "No."

"Shame on 'em for being stupid." Henry stroked my hands while staring like he wanted to see deep inside of me. "Does that mean you ain't been kissed?"

I'd kissed Lester Rollins on the cheek after church one Sunday simply because Charity and our friend Helen Kelley dared me. The only boy I'd ever *wanted* to really kiss was Dallas

Dorsey but he was too stuck on Charity to know I existed. "That ain't your business."

Henry's laughter was loud yet so warm and welcoming it startled me. "I'm taking that as a 'no,' Faye-Faye. You ain't been kissed. Would you like to be . . . by me?"

I frowned and snatched my hand free. "You're crazy."

"Maybe. But I was serious when I said I like you." He stroked my face again. "You sing real nice. I play decent enough, and Micah's a guitar genius. God led us to you and your sister for a reason. I think He wants us to be together. Musically. To prove harmony between our people is possible. Let's test what that's like . . . with a simple, friendly kiss."

That glittery-eyed boy wasn't the snake, but the snake charmer. Shame on me for being somebody's silly two-legged thing, letting his slippery invitation enchant me. His oily offer eased through the hard hurt I was carrying. I'd never been apart from my family, and was starved for my parents' hugs and love; the safety of Papa's strength, the sweetness of Mama's touch. I even missed Noah's loud, rough-and-tumble antics. Maybe deprivation had made me a little dizzy, but days without my family felt like decades and after all Hope and I had been through I wanted something soft. Even if it was a deceptive mirage.

Helen Kelley said kissing's nice. And easy.

Our friend was the same age as Charity and nobody's loose woman, but Helen had two full-on-the-lip kisses under her belt that I didn't. That made her the expert.

"Whatcha say? Wanna solidify this new friendship?" Tucking a finger beneath my chin, Henry moved quickly, touching his lips to mine, causing me to jerk back as if burned by fire.

"What're you doing?"

"Relax, Faith. You're a long way from home, here in this new city with just your little sister. That can be dangerous." His voice gradually quieted to a whisper. "How you gonna survive without someone like me looking out for your needs? God sent you to me, Faith, so do this for Hope, if not yourself, and please the Almighty."

My thoughts were so busy swimming the river of uncertainty and fear his words elicited that I barely felt his lips press against mine in a gentle manner meant to disarm resistance. That didn't keep me from stiffening or wondering what on earth I was doing. Something deep inside hollered for me to run away from this thing that could land me in a whole new heap of problems, but Henry had locked his arms around me so tightly I could barely breathe. I felt myself panicking.

Pretend he's Dallas.

Imagining that it was Dallas holding me was calming. That—and Henry's hint that my cooperation could help keep Hope safe—sent my mind drifting elsewhere, allowing my tension to ease. I felt myself relaxing for the first time since losing Charity. And my family. Unfortunately for me, my relaxing accelerated the strange thing that was happening. Henry's lips stayed on mine so long that new sensations wormed their way into the midst and I felt foreign. Like a rose blooming, its petals opening. I sensed myself surrendering. Too easily. To unfamiliar things. It was confusing. Terrifying. My heart raced and my body tingled, alarmingly. I needed to breathe.

I gulped in air only for my mouth to open. That left me tasting Henry's lips. He tasted like our dinner of turnip greens and black-eyed peas.

And something sweet?

It was deceitful. Intoxicating.

When he increased his hold about me, I didn't resist. Instead, I let myself drift and touch the fringes of a sweet illusion that was suddenly interrupted by a bright light crudely thrust in our faces.

" 'O wicked generation of young, aimless infidels! Flee fornication!' " Mister Owenslee's roar sent Henry and me springing apart and barely escaping the leather belt his raving father swung while spitting scripture as if bullets. " 'Do you not know that your body is a temple of the Holy Ghost? You are not your own. You were bought at a price. Therefore, glorify God with your body.' " He ended his holy tirade by bringing that belt down on the tailgate with a resounding thud. Thankfully, he missed us.

Miz Lucy appeared, pulling Henry away as if I was some kind of contaminant while her husband walked in circles firing off verses against immorality before falling on his knees, wailing.

"Holy Father, spare my son and punish him not. Don't send him to the pit for kissing a nigra 'for the lips of the adulterous woman drip honey, and her speech is smoother than oil.' Like Adam, he has been beguiled." With that, he started sobbing. "Enchantress, what did you do to my child?"

When Miz Lucy lunged at me, Henry caught her about the waist. "Ma, she ain't did nothing. It was my doing."

I nearly felt her slap against his face.

"You know better than entertaining iniquity. You kissed this gal and ain't virginal now. *You're filthy!*" Falling to her knees, she joined her husband's weeping.

Backing away, I hugged Hope when she ran to me, and simply stared at Henry. My gaze shifted to Micah as he slowly approached, finding on his face a look of bewilderment and betrayal as the four of us stood in a frozen, uncertain tableau until the Owenslees exhausted their sorrow. Slowly, Mister John stood and helped his wife to her feet.

"You two go indoors." He pointed at his sons before pointing at us, his voice all hollowed out. "Y'all have a seat on the porch. Don't go nowhere. You'll hear from me after I've heard from God."

I waited for Mister and Miz Owenslee, clutching each other

and weeping, to precede me before climbing the porch with Hope as instructed. Before going inside, Miz Lucy turned and spat "Jezebel!" at me as I sat with Hope on my lap, wondering if the train station was within walking distance and if we could find our way in the dark, only to recall Henry talking about this place being dangerous. I was willing to take a chance by myself, but I couldn't with my baby sister. We'd leave in the morning. For now, I'd endure Mister John's holy lecture.

A half hour or more passed before I heard a vocal commotion indoors. The words weren't clear, but the Owenslees were going at it. Ten minutes later, Hope and I hopped up when they came outside with Henry in tow.

Mister John looked my way but not directly at me. "I've heard from God."

A red-and-puffy-eyed Miz Lucy started whimpering.

" 'If a woman puts away her husband and is married to another, she commits adultery.' You joined yourself to our son. If we send you away and you entangle yourself elsewhere, we'll all be guilty of contributing to your adulterous iniquity. Further-more, we are subject to the Almighty. In the Bible days of old, He wed Hosea, a mighty prophet, to Gomer, a lowly prostitute. If God used a prophet to save a prostitute, maybe He's using Henry to save the souls of a Colored gal and her kin. So go wash up. My wife will lend you something. Henry." He waved his son forward. "The license is on its way. Make yourselves ready. Soon as it gets here, y'all getting married."

TEN
ZOE

"Baby Girl" Owensbey: age, approximately fifteen or sixteen.
Faye Owensbey: age, five or six; lighter complexion but looks like
Baby Girl enough to be her sister.
Destination: Los Angeles.
Others in pic: Micah and Harvey/Henry. Unknown surname.
Year: 1935.

Those notes were all I had. Yet, they filled me with an incredible sense of adventure, mystery, and even purpose. As if I'd been chosen to locate this precious, missing familial link. I didn't take that lightly. One who honored her ancestors, I felt humble to have been invited into their lives through a picture. I wasn't merely obligated to do this; I was delighted.

I'd learned from Shaun that his family had migrated from Tennessee to California in the spring of 1935 and that Nana Sam had taken that photo at some point during the journey. He wasn't sure who'd written "Okies" on it, and although I was clear that the term was coined because the largest number of Dust Bowl migrants came from Oklahoma, that massive influx included people from Missouri, Texas, and Arkansas. Still, I was stubborn enough to consider it a divine sign that Baby Girl and Faye were from Oklahoma, the strawberry state—a fruit my grandfather relished. The researcher in me started there, hoping it was their place of origin.

"I'm coming up with *nothing*." I sank my hands in my hair, pulling in frustration.

"Whoa, chick, your hair is"—Natasha snapped her fingers—"that short as it is. Keep pulling and see if brain damage doesn't happen."

I smirked at my cousin's quip. My hair was short by choice and I loved it. I'd had too much hair all my life and had made the big chop—*à la* Toni Braxton—shortly after finding out about Vince's second round of infidelity. I did it then out of heartbreak, being bewildered at still loving him, and out of spite because he liked long-haired women. It took me weeks to get accustomed to the short sassiness, but I fell in love with its ease and how it accentuated and framed my face. It also helped me to stop hiding behind my massive hair—as if hair could truly hide pain. Crazy as it may sound, the boldness that chop required helped me harness courage enough to separate from Vince. That was the *real* blessing and benefit.

"Whatever, Tasha. Just pour me another merlot and be silent."

"There's a one-glass limit up in here. I don't do alcoholics."

We were seated in Natasha's breakfast nook, snacking on leftover mini cornbread muffins from our earlier Sunday dinner at my parents'. Mama was watching her weight *and* Daddy's and had "only" served a southern fried chicken strip salad the way I loved it with grape tomatoes, black olives, shredded cheese, cucumbers, diced beets, green onion, crumbled bacon, sliced boiled egg, and avocado. I'd freely indulged in the mini cornbread muffins and sweet tea served on the side, not to mention a dessert of Mama's make-you-wanna-slap-somebody homemade peach hand pies. Baked, of course, not fried. I'd had to unbutton my jeans when finished, but justified my gluttony by telling myself dinner had been salad.

"Whatever, wine police. Get to pouring."

Doing whatever she was doing on her iPad, my cousin took her absentminded time complying. "Zo-Zo, these social media trolls are so ignorant. They're actually arguing over whose behind is better, J-Lo's or Beyoncé's. Chil', please! Y'all better recognize that Serena Williams–Janet Jackson situation. Now, that's a whole other kinda azz-a-matazz celebration."

I snickered slightly, too involved in my research to really laugh. My brief time with Shaun's Nana Sam had been a god-send. I didn't walk away with loads of information, but enough to start the process. Not to mention the time I'd spent with Shaun was pleasant. Recalling how upsetting Granddad's declining eyesight had been, I empathized with Shaun's sadness at Nana Sam's calling him Sweet Pea. Accepting a loved one's decline wasn't easy, but I appreciated Shaun allowing himself that moment before readjusting his equilibrium.

Truthfully, there was much I appreciated about the man. Being with him held the comfort of chilling with an old friend. I loved his personality and his vibe, and had enjoyed our time together and appreciated his introducing me to his family, helping me obtain clues I needed—so much so that I'd kissed him when returning to my lodging last night after our Sacramento drive. It was only on the cheek, and just an expression of my appreciation and excitement. Yet, its feeling so nice highlighted the fact that it had been too long since I'd enjoyed romantic intimacy.

"Doggone it! You're telling me there's not one damned Owensbey in the whole state?" I sat back, pushing my reading glasses onto my head and telling myself not to be discouraged by the lack of data on my laptop screen. Remembering how a college professor had repeatedly insisted that finding an ending required starting at the beginning, I'd been searching for Owensbeys in Oklahoma for over an hour. The process might've been weird, but I went with it, knowing that Oklahoma was much smaller than California and might provide a place of origin from which to fan out. My hope was finding Owensbeys there who could possibly prove a connection to Owensbeys here. Unfortunately, my methods produced nothing.

"It's a strange name, Zo-Zo." Busy scrolling her iPad, Natasha sounded distracted. "Are you spelling it correctly?"

"I hope so." I opened a new browser tab and searched for residents, last name Owensbeys, in Arkansas, Missouri, Texas. The results were nearly instantaneous. Nothing. Zilch. That left me with California and, more specifically, Los Angeles. Nervous energy had me holding my breath as I copied the name in the search engine and pressed enter, praying for success. "Damn!"

"Cuzzo, first you want more wine, now you're cussing and hitting my tabletop like you've lost your mind. If you can't do this research like a sane woman, hire an investigator. And when did you start wearing glasses?"

I took them off. "They're for reading and computer use. It's a 'your fortieth birthday is months away' hazard."

"Speaking of, Shaun's grandmother is elderly. Age alone can scramble the memory, but add dementia on top of that and . . ." She shrugged rather than finish. "Maybe she got the last name twisted, or maybe you're spelling it incorrectly. Try spelling it with 'l-a-y' at the end."

I followed her suggestion and came up empty-handed. "Owensbey." I repeated the name aloud several times only to stop and straighten suddenly when hearing Nana Sam's pronunciation in my head and realizing West Coast living hadn't erased her Southern accent. That might've distorted the ending. "What if it's Owensby?"

"Zoe, you talking to yourself or me? If me, I'm not really listening."

"Hush up, nut." I was prepared to try census records if this new tactic failed, but it didn't. "*Bam.* Tasha, look!" I angled my laptop in her direction. "There're nearly a hundred people in the state with that last name."

"Yay! Guess who gets to contact each and every one of them?"

"Listen, buzzkill, at least the mystery door is open," I sang in my excitement.

"What if that door's a Pandora's box best left shut?" We stared at each other a moment before she placed a hand on my arm. "Boo, I know you want to do this for Aunt Gladys, but your mother was adopted for a reason. What if her birth family isn't down for this?"

"I don't have dreams of some sappy family reunion, Tasha. I'm clear that this may not have a happy resolution, but I also know better than to refuse the opportunity to discover something about a possible ancestor." I reached for that now ever-present photograph with its relentless haunting, racking my brain, trying to recall if there were photos even remotely similar in family photos albums, only to come up with nothing. "I won't be intrusive or disrespectful, but if unearthing her means finding pieces of my mother or even me, then any possible rejection is worth the risk." Picking up another photograph, I backed away from the table and padded down Natasha's hallway to position myself in front of a mounted, decorative mirror.

I'd scanned the Xerox copy from Shaun and manipulated it via Photoshop, isolating Baby Girl Miss Me and resizing her solitary image into an eight-by-ten photograph. I held that likeness next to mine in the mirror. I was old enough to be her mother, but she could have easily been me in my teens and I was, once more, arrested by our uncanny similarities. We were built the same. Heavy-breasted, little in the middle, with curvy hips. Except, having never fully lost the weight from my pregnancy with Jaelen, I was a size twelve to her possible six.

Gently pressing that picture against my chest, I closed my eyes and whispered a prayer, pausing between each sentence in case her essence chose to respond. "Who are you? What is your real name? I need your help finding you . . . *if* that's what you want. And I believe it is."

Natasha's scream interrupted anything my spirit may have received. "Oh. My. *God.* Zoe, have you seen this?"

I sighed dramatically, irritated at the interruption. "What is it?" I headed toward the kitchen and nearly collided with my cousin rushing in my direction.

"Look at this ish!" She stopped beside me, iPad in hand, indicating a social media post that already had thousands of likes and hundreds of comments despite being posted an hour ago.

My stomach dropped as I silently read an announcement posted by the network that employed my estranged husband.

Congratulations and warmest wishes on your pending addition, sportscaster Vince Edwards and fiancée Jillian Masters.

A snapshot of Vince standing behind his "fiancée" with his arms around her waist, his hands cradling her early trimester baby bump rounded out the ludicrousness.

"*What the . . . !* Who the hell is Jillian and how the hell is this mofo engaged to someone when we're still legally married?" I was livid and ready to open a crate, not a can, of whip ass and go in on him. "I can't even!" I yelled and stormed off, teeth clenched.

"Come on, Zo-Zo. Breathe. Please." I must've looked real off for Natasha to be playing the calming role when typically, she would've been cussing and plotting death to the demon seed with me.

"Tasha, this is so . . ."

She finished for me when I didn't. "Wrong. I know, Boo. It is. Absolutely. Don't worry. Karma is a beeyotch. He'll get his."

I failed to squash an onslaught of tears accompanied by a mournful, unrecognizable sound I didn't realize was erupting from my mouth until my cousin embraced me. I felt bad accepting her comfort, knowing she was mistaken. These tears weren't about Vince, but his happily pregnant Jillian.

I returned to my Airbnb shortly thereafter, drained and tired. Natasha had tried to convince me to stay the night, but I needed alone time to process that life was beyond my control and I was being left behind. Again.

When my son died less than a week after his birth, it was as if a mountain had crushed my chest, flattening my existence. It hurt to breathe and, initially, I didn't want to be here. Not without Jaelen. I'd leaned on Vince and still got lost in a maze of grief, and took what felt like forever to make my way back to a place where living was acceptable. But then I'd discovered my spouse wasn't only unfaithful; his whoredom had infected me with the condition that prevented my baby from living. If my family hadn't helped rescue me from myself, rage and hate would've pushed me over the edge.

"This is why his trifling ass has been hounding me to sign those divorce papers?" I'd ignored Vince's texting me three times yesterday while I was with Shaun, demanding my cooperation. Standing on the balcony overlooking the marina, I couldn't ignore the truth that my marriage was dead. I was a May baby, but loved bodies of water so much that I should've been a Pisces. Right then, the majestic peace of the Pacific Ocean's tributary was lost on me as I viewed that social media announcement on my cell phone. "Look at this ish. Whoever heard of a Black woman named Jillian? She looks like a Barbie dipped in weak, watery chocolate."

Stop it, Zoe. You're behaving like what you detest: a bitter woman.

I commanded myself away from a ragged ledge and struggled to make an internal course correct. I'd had much practice, thanks to Vince.

After his first affair, I'd pieced my broken heart together and accepted his Oscar-worthy repentance and crocodile tears. Plus, I was pregnant and stayed, desiring that normalized institution of an intact, nuclear family. When discovering that second affair, I'd actually packed, intent on returning to California. That had unleashed more crocodile tears and more "Baby, I love you and can't do without you." I'd given him an ultimatum of marriage counseling despite his remorse stage and being on his best behavior. Coming home on time. Being attentive. The gifts I never wanted. His acting apologetic. He'd attended three whole sessions when a woman named Crystal emailed me selfies of herself and Vince hugged up on a Florida beach. I was a fool for thinking he'd had two affairs when, really, he'd had twice as many. Crystal had outed him to me only after discovering she wasn't his sole side-chick. I put him out and filed for legal separation, crushed that my husband's affairs were nearly equal to the number of years we'd been married.

"Beware, Jillian. He's a chronic cheater, incapable of change."

Sliding my cell into my pocket, I closed my eyes and tilted my face to the California night sky, remembering Natasha's gentle question once my weeping over this newest bit of traitorous news had subsided.

When is this divorce gonna be over with?

I inhaled deeply, ashamed to admit vindictiveness and denying Vince the freedom he wanted had fueled my dragging my feet, prolonging the inevitable. Initially. The other, more weighted, truth I couldn't bring myself to admit had everything to do with my precious baby, Jaelen.

After a long, hot shower I consoled myself with my drug of choice: two of Mama's homemade peach hand pies. I went to bed, stomach stuffed, soft jazz streaming from my laptop, and cool night air flowing through the open balcony door. Maybe it was the rich dessert too close to bedtime, or the upheaval of the evening; either way, I had deep, crazy dreams, the threads of which I couldn't recall when waking up in the middle of the night to use the restroom, but still sensed nonetheless. Only the dream that visited after I'd fallen back to sleep stayed with me.

I was dressed in a silver, vintage gown and long satin gloves, on the stage of an old night club, singing my heart out to a small, intimate crowd. My voice was rich, velvety, and utterly unique, holding the audience captive. Just when I realized the woman on stage couldn't be me, *Zoe*; that singing was not my gift or ability, the dream shifted and I was at a farmhouse surrounded by incredibly lush, green grass and verdant fields bearing crops in abundance. The place was cocooned in a palpable peace and the young female seated on the porch and the infant in her arms were the only persons present.

Faye?

Even in my sleep I called her name, recognizing her as the little girl in the picture half-hidden by my look-alike's skirt. Except she was an older, teenaged version of herself. Her hair was braided and wrapped about her head like a lovely halo. Her white dress with flowers on one side nearly glowed. When she invited me forward with gentle hand movements, I eased toward her only to hear myself singing again. That's when I appeared behind the seated girl's chair in that silver gown. Rather, my look-alike Baby Girl Miss Me did. I knew it was she and not me because she sang in a flawless voice, richer than all the pearls in the world, as she placed her hands on Faye's shoulders, lovingly. Holding the baby in one arm, the teenaged Faye reached up with a free hand and smiled back at Miss Me. The two clasped hands, and the look of affection they exchanged was so pure that I felt its energy as the baby squirmed, emitting a soft sound that reverberated throughout my being. I was pulled forward by some powerful, indestructible string but my heart hesitated in disbelief seeing, in Faye's arms, Jaelen, my newborn son—beautiful, healthy, perfect.

I woke up shaken and wrestling to capture whatever it was the seated young woman had said to me before awakening. I had to take several deep, meditative breaths before the shadow of the words resurfaced in my hearing. Reaching for my phone with shaky hands, I wondered what 1 Corinthians 13:13 had to do with anything. Typing it into a browser, the results were immediate, granting me various translations. I stuck with King James since that was the version I'd grown up with.

"*And now abideth faith, hope, charity, these three; but the greatest of these is charity.*" I read the passage aloud several times hoping for clarity, only to lay there frustrated.

Launching my photo app, I touched the snapshot of that eight-by-ten of Baby Girl Miss Me. "Thank you for visiting me in a dream . . . and for escorting me to a place where I could see my beautiful son. But I don't know what I'm supposed to take away from this scripture. Please help my understanding."

Closing my eyes, I took long breaths to quiet myself, to welcome stillness. Several minutes in, my spirit intuited one message.

Faith.

A soft smile kissed my lips. I may not have cracked the case like a detective yet, but my ancestor had come to encourage me to have faith, to trust and believe that things would work out. Hugging myself, I drifted to sleep with the song she'd sung wafting richly, thankful for seeing my lovely son again, and certain I was on track to finding my missing ancestor.

ELEVEN

FAITH

There weren't enough verses in God's Good Book to make me want to marry Henry Owenslee. I didn't care what fire and brimstone his father preached behind us kissing. I disliked Henry, and dismissed fairy tales of his liking me. I came to California to find my family, not be bundled up with some evil-eyed Okie.

"It ain't good for the two of you to be alone. I can take care of you and Hope." Henry's parents being indoors—still weeping in between praying in tongues while preparing for this farce of a wedding—permitted his sneaking back outside, talking nonsense aimed at being persuasive.

I held Hope, gently stroking her hair and humming her favorite lullaby as her head lay against my chest. I was suspicious, unsure what that boy had up his sleeve other than wanting to make money with his playing and my singing. I was disinterested in all of it. "I'm only fifteen. That's too young to marry you or any other body." Even as the words left my lips, I remembered Granny had been married with one child and another on the way at my age. A chill ran through me while considering the likely, other half of Henry's agenda: doing what folks did that *led* to conception. That left me desperately trying another tactic and stating the obvious. "Besides, how you gonna take care of us when you can't take care of yourself? You ain't even gotta job."

"Pa says the folks who hired him need more white workers and less of them Mexicans. I'll get on easy enough. We can stay here at Auntie's. Renting her back room ain't gonna cost much, and you can help around the house. Won't be no time before I save up enough to replace Micah's guitar. Once we start performing, we'll be bringing money in hand over fist. I'll be our manager and even if we have to cut into Micah's share, I'll make sure we have more than we need for us and our responsibilities... our doing like God commanded and being fruitful and multiplying."

I cringed, hearing him confirm my suspicions about his lustful agenda. "You can't cut your brother's earnings down like that, not to mention race-mixed marriages are frowned on."

"I can do whatever the hell I need to get what I want. And mind you, this is California, not Oklahoma. They ain't as God-fearing here as back home so I'm sure race-mixing is okay. Plus, this gotta happen so we don't sin. The Good Book says it's better to marry than to burn."

I wasn't nowhere near burning for Henry and hated that he had it all worked out in his hard head, leaning up against the porch railing looking like he actually wanted this while I wasn't agreeing to any of it. Not my singing with him, and certainly nobody's wedding or the bedroom business that came with it. I sat there, hugging Hope, trying to figure a way out, knowing I couldn't just walk off into the night. Maybe if I was alone, I might've tried. I may have taken my chances and left right then to find that bus station and my parents. But I wasn't alone, and my sister didn't deserve to suffer our wandering unknown dangerous roads in the dark.

"I'll help you look for your folks." He offered that ray of

sunshine as if privy to my thoughts. "But until that happens, I'll take care of you and Hope *only* if we're joined in holy matrimony before the eyes of the Almighty."

"This is stupid! Y'all so darned religious that one little kiss—"

Henry snatched something from his back pocket and threw it at me before I could finish. "Consider it a warning from heaven." He stalked into the house, leaving me staring at a folded-up newspaper page laying at my feet, a big red circle drawn around an article of obvious interest.

I didn't want to pick it up, but curiosity won and I found myself tentatively holding the edges of that newspaper page as if it were a living thing capable of biting me.

"What's s-l-a-i-n mean, Faye-Faye?" Hope sat up, wanting to prove her reading skills. Her sweet little voice spelling part of that headline made it more gruesome.

"It's just a word, Baby Girl." I crumpled the page too late. I'd read enough of the article about a girl my age being found murdered two days ago here in Los Angeles to make me want to vomit. This new dazzling, dizzying city was intimidating and overwhelming enough as it was, without the murder of an innocent being thrown into the mix. It left me cold, restless. My foot started bobbing as I wondered if something so horrific could happen to me on these big city streets.

My eyes widened when my imagination decided I hadn't been tortured enough and treated me to a vision of the lifeless body of a Colored girl sprawled on the ground, blood soaking the concrete. Except she was too small to be me. *"Oh God . . ."*

"What's wrong, Faye-Faye?"

My baby sister caressed my face soothingly, but I could only shake my head in distress, realizing that imagined corpse was closer to her size than mine. My ripping that paper into shreds did nothing to eradicate that terrifying image from my mind as the screen door opened and the Owenslees poured somberly into the night.

Dressed in their passable best, the adults and even Micah looked a frightful mess with scowls of displeasure draping their faces. Only Henry seemed somewhere near happy as his old aunt pressed a dress into my hands.

"Go'n around the side of the house and put it on."

The foul stench of mothballs hit my nostrils hard. Even so, the smell was comparatively sweeter than the sight of this high-neck, mutton-sleeve-having velvet and lace eyesore looking like it had escaped the wardrobe of some mistress on a plantation deep in the Antebellum south. It's only saving grace was the dress was ankle, versus floor, length.

You don't have to wear it.

I looked from Mister to Miz Owenslee, ready to beg their pardon for my perceived offense only to encounter sullen, merciless expressions. Surrounded by those white faces, I felt their presence seemed suddenly ominous, like failing to comply could turn the situation treacherous. Just the same, I opened my mouth to plead my case, but thoughts of that newspaper article and my baby sister stole my words away. I didn't know Los Angeles, and needed it to not consume either of us. My shoulders sagged and I was left with no other way except taking Hope's hand and heading to the side of the house to change into a dress that might as well have been a shroud.

By the time I returned, some liquored-up license man smelling like moonshine and stale sweat was positioned at the ready, slightly tottering on drunken feet, a Bible in hand. "Come, child. No one will hurt you. You're safe here. I'm Henry's great-uncle. Welcome to the clan."

Drunk or not, the genuine kindness in his voice poked holes in my resistance so that unwillingness slowly seeped from me, joining the viscous pool of confusion and fear about my feet. I felt heavy. Lonely. Outnumbered and unable to think clearly.

Sighing, nearly crying inside, I gave in. If this was the only way to save Hope from ever being somebody's concrete cadaver, so be it.

In that moment, I wished I'd never met these religious zealots wanting to bamboozle me and overturn my existence behind some stupid little kiss. Yet, I swallowed my pride while becoming Henry's bride, feeling like a shadow of myself standing there hearing scriptures concerning a wife's obedience and submission.

Charity, this isn't it.

It wasn't the plan I had shared with my big sister of us finding brothers to fall in love with and marry in a double ceremony. I didn't have many dreams, but that one was definite and I blamed Henry that it would never happen. The harder truth was that even if I could escape this fiasco intact, there was no Charity to share that dream with.

My big sister will never have love or marriage.

My tears poured, knowing neither of us would know a union like our parents', filled with laughter, warm looks, and tender kisses. I stared ahead, silently crying and refusing to let that vile lie cross my lips when asked to say, "I Do." I merely nodded. And just like that, I was wedded and my world imploded, sucking me down into deep darkness.

It felt like light would never grace me again. If there was a blessing in it, it was that that sad mockery of a ceremony was straight to the point, without thrills or frills. No flowers, no cake, no happy guests, or congratulations. No Papa smiling proudly, or Mama getting watery-eyed at me wearing her wedding gown. There was just the Owenslees with Miz Lucy calling me names unsuitable for Christian tongues and crying on the sidelines, shrieking periodically about my taking her boy away and that I would never be welcome in *her* family. Thankfully, when that drunk uncle pronounced us man and wife, Miz Lucy passed out, which shut her mouth.

Seeing her unconscious form sagging in her husband's arms, I wanted to pinch her awake and yell that *I* was the one deprived of breath. And options. I was parentless, fifteen, and limited in my choices, mothering my beautiful little sister who was daily reverting to babyish ways that I'd have to deal with. Sucking her thumb. Wetting herself. I could tolerate that. What I couldn't handle was being a penniless stranger in a new land, helplessly controlled by, and at the mercies and machinations of, *them*, knitted together with Henry under heaven. Being caught by this whirlwind was nowhere near celestial.

I'd rather face that mother of all black blizzards again than be with him.

"Sign and date, April nineteenth, right here," Uncle Drunk instructed, words slurred behind a hiccup.

I couldn't take that pen. Signing a marriage certificate would make it all too real.

"Wait, now. It's after midnight. That makes it the twentieth," he corrected himself.

"Faye-Faye, April twentieth is your birthday."

I stared at my baby sister, feeling exceptionally lost and caught, as if I was wearing boots made from boulders and unable to run. I was possibly orphaned, married, and no longer fifteen?

If this is life at sixteen, Lord forgive me, but I ain't sure I wanna see seventeen.

"I'll take the pen, Uncle. I'm the man of this marriage. I should sign first." Henry quickly signed the certificate as if rushing toward something. Smiling at me, he whispered in my ear, "I know how to get what I want. Me and you 'bout to have some fun."

When he extended that pen to me, I ran down the steps to the side of the house, trying to reach the shadows before regurgitating.

. . .

"Faye-Faye, Mama's gonna be mad you got married before Colored college."

This union wasn't a celebratory occasion. It rippled with the same kind of joylessness I imagined Abraham must've felt when doing his duty by God, making ready to sacrifice Isaac. Now that the deed was done and the Owenslees had retired indoors, it was quiet as my baby sister and I snuggled together on the enclosed back porch atop the pallet Old Spinster Aunt provided that was only slightly better than sleeping upright in the back of the Owenslees' truck.

"Yes, I know, Hope. I mixed things up."

Our mother had preached college before marriage so long to her children that it was a song and litany. I knew Mama loved us with her whole self but sometimes—particularly after black blizzards started ruining things—I'd find her staring at nothing, a sadness rolling off of her that I couldn't name but somehow tied to her marrying and having babies before finishing her education. Maybe that's because whenever I asked her what was wrong, she pasted on a brave face and kissed my head while quietly stating, "Get your higher learning *then* your love," before she walked off. We'd never met Mama's parents because they didn't want anything to do with her or us on account of her quitting college to marry Papa. Unlike Mama's parents, mine weren't well off. We were farmers. That tempered any excitement I might've had about advanced education. Until then. Laying on that back porch, my baby sister snuggled against me, I latched onto the notion of college and other inconceivable fantasies, stubbornly trying to escape the idiocy I'd just committed. More than missing out on Colored college, what I'd done would devastate and enrage my parents.

It's not a real marriage. It's just something to keep me and Hope safe and together.

It was what Papa had taught: a balancing rod, an equalizer.

Or that spelling word Miss Bullocks gave on our last test: a *transaction*. Not love, and certainly not romance.

"Faye-Faye, why's Micah mad at you?"

Hope had always been an inquisitive little thing who didn't miss much, but I was surprised by this particular perceptiveness, especially given how wild the night had been and Miz Lucy's fainting theatrics. When she came to, Micah had helped her indoors, glaring at me as if he wished I was dead. "I guess Micah feels like his mother, that I took something away from him."

"When we find Papa, Mama, and Noah will Charity be with them, or is she still in Wellston?"

I sighed quietly, drained by the night and the past week of my life, and Hope's questions jumping topics. "Charity doesn't live on earth with us anymore, sweetheart."

"She's an angel now?"

"Mmm-hmm." It wasn't the purest truth, but I was too tired to articulate my understanding of eternity. Besides, Hope's perspective was as good as mine and if not a bona fide angel, our big sister was certainly somewhere in the heavenlies.

"You're married. Are you and Henry having babies?"

"Go to sleep, Baby Girl. Enough talking." I kissed my sister's cheek and wrapped my arms around her, vowing never to be close enough to Henry for those types of possibilities . . . only to hear the porch creak.

"Y'all awake?"

I sprang upright to see Henry slinking to a porch chair, wondering if he was part cat with those funny-colored eyes and his ability to sneak up on me. "What do you want?"

Gaze on me while talking to Hope, he didn't answer my question. "Baby Girl, come here."

Hope slipped from my arms before I could react. Micah was her favorite of the two. He was kind, patient, told funny stories, and shared his food with her during our voyage when he thought no one was looking. But since our encounter with that band of hooligans, Henry had laid on the niceness so thickly and reconfigured his hitting me into a gallant rescue thing that Hope, in her innocence, looked at him as if he were heroic.

"There's a nice hunk of honey cornbread and a glass of milk waiting on you at the kitchen table. Stay in there, eat it all, and don't come back till I come get you. Understand?"

Thanks to the extreme scantiness of food during our westward journey, he'd barely finished before Hope was headed for the kitchen. That left me alone with Henry looking at me like a starving, dying man eyeing his last meal. He might've only been the second boy I'd ever kissed, but Mama had schooled me and Charity in married folks' private bedroom business. My blood chilled, knowing that's why he was there and what he wanted. Heart racing as he moved toward me, I blurted a half-truth without thinking. "I'm on my monthly."

That stopped him, immediately.

My body had been sending signals since earlier that day that my monthly visitor was making ready its appearance. No actual flow had started yet, but Henry didn't need to know that. I couldn't care less what that marriage certificate said. He wasn't my husband, and I regretted what we'd done. He wasn't Adam. I wasn't Eve. And he never needed to *know* me.

I couldn't recall the whole verse in my rattled state, still I did like Mister Owenslee and used the Bible to my advantage. " 'If a man lies with a woman having her sickness, and uncovers her nakedness . . .' "

Slowly, reluctantly, Henry mumbled its conclusion, something about the offending couple being isolated and cut off from their tribe, their nation. "How long before it's finished?"

"Ten to twelve days." I was stacking up lies in heaven while testing Henry's intelligence. He was a boy without sisters and I prayed he didn't know better.

His mean, jagged stare translated bitter disappointment.

"It's my wedding night and I was ready for this. I'll wait till you're clean 'cause the Good Book says that's best, but when we come together you gonna do extra and make up for what I missed." That said, he stomped indoors, letting the screen door shut angrily.

Not if God helps me.

I nervously chewed the skin around my thumbnail, unable to relax until Hope came back, cornbread crumbs on her lips, needing her presence like a protective shield. I was the older sibling and didn't like that notion one bit. Feeling upside down and inside out, I stayed awake while she slept, determined to think my way out of marital predicaments even if I stayed awake all night to do it.

Clearly, I dozed off and was jarred awake by the sound of the screen door clapping shut. I sat up in the pale light of dawn, afraid Henry had come to claim his husbandly rights despite what I'd said. I inhaled, relieved, when seeing Micah.

"I brought y'all some breakfast." He placed a small dish of warm cornbread near my feet and backed away.

"Micah, I'm sorry you're mad at me, but I didn't mean to take your brother from you." He was the closest thing I'd had to a friend since leaving Wellston, and I didn't like hurting him. Plus, I needed things to be right between us in case I needed his help with Henry.

His hurt was clear when he glanced at me before nonchalantly shrugging. "Ma told me to give you this."

I grabbed the folded sheet of paper he placed near the plate as he clomped down the porch steps. His leaving like that left me sad as I unfolded Miz Lucy's note. Every word was legible, including the scripture that started it; still, it took me a moment to fully comprehend.

Give to everyone what you owe them: If you owe taxes, pay taxes; if revenue, then revenue . . .

That was followed by a "Lend to the Lord" list of expenses Hope and I had accumulated on our Oklahoma to California journey that the Lord apparently had no intention of repaying. Transportation. Cheesecloth. Meals. Water. Lodging. Each item included an amount that was tallied at the bottom in huge red print. Marked "due immediately," we owed the Owenslees a whopping fifteen dollars and forty-two cents! That was over fifteen hundred pieces of penny candy. Or one hundred and fifty-plus jars of Mama's peach preserves. Or, in a good year, half an acre of corn. I'd never had more than two or three dollars in my hands at any given moment in my existence. Now, I owed five times as much?

Oh God, I don't have a cent to pay this.

I thought I'd whispered my despair only to hear a mocking response.

"Guess you'll be getting up from there and looking for work like the rest of us."

I lowered the note to find Henry near the back door, looking flat and unhappy about the eyes despite the mocking lift of his lips as he settled a newsboy-style cap on his head.

"I'm heading over with Pa to his job, hoping to get on. As for you, Ma was Christian enough to remind me that all ablebodied beings living here need to contribute money for the family. She specifically mentioned indisposed wives unable to do their duty." He hawked something up from his throat and spat it over the railing into the morning. "Know what else she said? Females' monthly issues last five days, not ten."

My heart dropped, knowing my falsehood could no longer serve me, but I offered neither repentance nor apology.

"I was fixin' to tell Ma you should stay here and help, but seeing as how you ain't as indisposed as long as you claimed to be, you coming with me."

"Where're we going?" I disliked the quiver in my voice and

pushed my shoulders back, my head up, in a brave counter-balance.

"If me and Micah don't get on with Pa, we'll look into some money-making of our own. We'll drop you off in the Colored neighborhood first so you can find work." He paused to scratch the back of his head before looking into the distance. "You and me might be joined on paper, but I can't support you like a real wife *until* . . ." His unfinished sentence dangled like a dagger in the air. "That should've happened last night, but I guess you can't control nature." He refocused on me. "Baby Girl can stay here, but you need to come on."

"I gotta wash up first." I'd been so discombobulated over last night's wedding that I'd failed to change back into my clothing and was still wearing Aunt Spinster's mistress-of-the-plantation madness. I eased away from Hope so as not to wake her when standing and frantically searching for my dress.

"This whatcha looking for?"

I turned to see Henry holding my garment as if pulled from his back pocket. "Yes."

When I stepped forward to retrieve it, he balled it tightly and stuffed my dress down the front of his pants.

"Give that back!"

He came toward me, menacingly. "Who you yelling at?"

My body tightened into fight mode, but I softened my tone. "I need that. Please." It was filthy, wrinkled, and I'd destroyed its hem in that cellar to tie Hope and me together. It had seen better days, but it was mine and I wanted it.

"Why you so bent outta shape over this raggedy mess?"

"My mother made it."

I could tell by the way he stood there, head cocked to the side and staring just above my head, lips twisted to one side, that my sentiment was lost on him.

"Wear what you got on so it reminds you you're *my* wife,

and that I don't take kindly to lies. Or if you're bold enough to take your dress . . . reach in and get it."

We exchanged angry glares until he spat into the day again and sauntered down the steps.

I hate him.

Seething inside, I wasted no time shaking Hope awake and putting her shoes on despite her being sleepy, slow-moving.

"I'm tired. I don't wanna wake up yet."

"I know, Baby Girl. Here. Take this." I gave her one of the cornbread squares before rolling up our pallet to store in a corner, determined to get my dress. It might've been meaningless and worthless to Henry but—other than Hope—it was the only thing I had from home. I slipped on my shoes, grabbed the remaining cornbread and Hope's hand, hurried down the steps and onto the truck, knowing better than to leave my baby sister anywhere I wasn't.

"We'll see you in a few hours if we don't find nothing. If we do, we'll be back around supper time. Either way, we'll pick you up here. Good luck finding employment."

With that, Henry sauntered into the small corner store in front of which Hope and I were being left to search for work. I felt like a fish out of water, in need of help and oxygen.

I glanced at Mister Owenslee, humming hymns from the passenger seat, completely oblivious to my sister and me. Only Micah remained, but we were no longer speaking. Even if we were, it didn't matter. Not only was Micah in the same boat I was, needing a job, after last night I wasn't sure he still considered me a friend.

"It's just me and you, Baby Girl."

"What're we doing, Faye-Faye?"

"Playing a game called Let's See How Much Money We Can Make." I didn't want her worried when I had enough worry for us both. I'd had chores on the farm, but this was a real city. I couldn't imagine many folks needing help collecting eggs, slopping hogs, milking cows, or feeding chickens. I surveyed the assembled women waiting for work like me and realized my skills were woefully limited. They were workers for hire, these women in the Colored district we'd happened across on a long stretch of street named Central Avenue. We called them "day workers" back home in Wellston; folks hiring themselves out, hoping to earn wages on a daily basis after regular work disappeared or was slim to none, thanks to the Great Depression. I'd heard Papa and Mama discussing such things, lamenting how tough times were and how tight money was since some 1929 stock market debacle. That was six years ago and thanks to black blizzards, things hadn't gotten better. The economy was so bad that white folks had taken to putting Colored folks out, taking over the jobs we once had. Now, there I was with Hope, feeling ill-placed and praying for work despite current conditions.

"Ooo, Faye-Faye, a penny!" Hope released my hand and rushed across the pavement to pick up a copper coin glinting in the morning light. She returned, holding it triumphantly for my viewing.

"Look at you! We just started the game and you're already winning." I gave her a victory kiss before instructing her to put her win in her pocket even as I felt a presence behind us. Turning, I found Micah.

"You'll be okay out here." He might not have felt charitable toward me but, obeying his father's instructions to go inside and hurry Henry along, he'd paused to offer a vote of confidence.

I simply nodded and moved to let him pass only to rethink it. "Micah . . . are we still friends?"

His voice was quiet as if to prevent his father overhearing. "My brother's my brother, so it don't feel right saying this, but he ain't the right kind of person to be a good husband. You gonna need to be careful 'round Henry. The way he hit you in front of those kids yesterday? That wasn't no accident." He fell silent a moment before continuing. "And he's the kind to have more than one girlfriend. I wish you'da kissed me instead of him."

He abruptly hurried indoors, leaving me with my mouth hanging open.

Micah likes me the way I liked Dallas Dorsey?

I was still stunned when Micah returned and rushed past me with Henry not far behind. He stopped in front of us, his mean spirit enough to blot out the sunshine. "Baby Girl, did I see you pick up something?"

Hope was giddy with her discovery and held it up. "Yep. A penny. Now, I can buy some candy!"

"It's better safe with me." Henry pocketed Hope's coin and patted her head as if she were a loyal pet, focusing on me and ignoring the fact that taking Hope's penny had left her crestfallen. "Come to think of it, Faith, that's a damn good idea. You'll be turning all your earnings over to me."

"Why in the world would I do that?"

He stepped closer, breathing angrily. "Because I'm the husband." Obviously, in his mind, that explained everything. "You can keep a dime for every dollar you make. That's ten percent. Like reverse tithing." He laughed uproariously. "Speaking of what you owe me"—his voice lowered—"I forgive your ignorance. A girl who ain't been kissed can't be expected to be nobody's expert on women's monthly issues. Or maybe you ain't too good at math. Either way, with your monthly lasting five days not ten, you have God to thank that you get to be with me sooner than expected." He grinned like I should praise heaven. "Being new to kissing, I imagine you're untouched and ignorant to your wifely duties?"

I pulled Hope closer instead of answering.

"Well, ain't no need for worrying." His voice oozed oil, warmed by the subject. "Y'all Colored gals gotta natural knack for carnal things."

I was too shocked by his brazen insult to speak.

He softened his tone and smiled magnanimously. "No need for shyness, but seeing how you are, a friend back home told me California got places where customers pay for relations and girls like you learn to please their husbands. Gimme a couple of days and I'll find one near here."

His words were so completely terrifying and degrading they left me shaking. I changed the subject to avoid removing my shoe and whacking him in the head. "I need my dress." I wasn't sure where he'd put it, but it was no longer an obscene bulge in his pants.

"Henry, come on before you make Pa late for his job," Micah called.

"Hold on, son. Don't go getting in married folks' affairs," their father paused his hymn-singing long enough to caution.

Neither redirected Henry's attention. He was fixated on me like nothing else existed. "You're a smart Colored gal with big bosoms and nice hips. Betcha when we find that pleasure school, you'll learn quick. If you *really* please me, I'll repay Ma what you owe." He pulled something from his shirt pocket and tossed it at me. It was a sleeve from my dress. "I imagine, seeing as how your mammy made it, that you want the rest back?"

I offered a defiant, "Yes."

"Guess you'll do *whatever* you need to get it." He leaned down, whispering in my ear, "I heard y'all Colored gals're like sweet, juicy peaches between the legs. You can forget the niceness I woulda had on our wedding night. After making me wait five days, I'ma enjoy busting your peach wide open."

He strolled away whistling and adjusting the front of his britches.

"Five days, *Missus* Owenslee. Let the countdown begin."

I would've torn that corner store down to its foundation just to break bricks on his back if I had strength like Samson in the Old Testament. Instead, I stood there percolating in rage and dread as Henry drove off, his threat drifting across the day, leaving me so rattled it took Hope to bring me back to our surroundings.

"Faye-Faye, that nice lady in the pink dress looks like Miss Bullocks."

I turned to see a woman who favored our teacher eyeing us, her ice-cream-pink dress a sweet calling card that made her stand out from the crowd of women wearing sensible navy or black. "She sure does, Baby Girl," I commented quietly, offhandedly, noticing the sympathy coating the woman's pretty face and the hint of sadness in her bright brown gaze that made me wonder if she'd somehow overheard the low-down, disgusting things Henry said.

The very notion of someone witnessing my degradation left me feeling unsanitary and less than. "Come on, Hope." I took my sister's hand and turned away, hiding my shame and wondering how on God's good earth I'd gotten myself into this mess. I was so caught up in misery it took me a moment to admit I was in the midst of too much competition. Huddling with Hope against the storefront, I counted ten women waiting on the sidewalk for work. They looked able, confident. Not desperate like me.

I bet they never did nothing as ignorant as making a mockery of holy matrimony, or getting tangled up with a snake-eyed stranger they didn't exactly like or even trust.

They looked too capable to be duped or caught up in my brand of shenanigans. A few were dressed as domestics; others like professionals with brown fingers agile enough to type like the wind. This uncertain economy hadn't crushed their spirits. It might've pulled on them, but their backs were still strong, their hips still smooth and feminine. They had ready dispositions. Any bosses coming in search of help would choose them over me, and I'd wind up ending the day the way I started it: penniless.

"Faye-Faye, are Mama and Papa meeting us here?"

Hope's question was like water on fire, dousing sorrow and redirecting my attention.

"Oh God, we gotta get to that train station!" That's where salvation waited. With our parents. Not here in the midst of capable women for whom I was no competition. And certainly not in marriage to Henry Owenslee.

Let the countdown begin.

His words were a lustful threat with nothing nice on the tail end, issued by a rough-n-ready boy acting like a man too eager to push my "peach" in. Without love. Or gentleness. Hardness never factored into the whispered conversations Charity and I had about what "it" would be like. Horror never drifted through the bedroom wall we shared with our parents who waited until they thought we were fast asleep before *being together*. Even their muffled sounds rippled with peace and other things I didn't understand. But I never felt as if their intimate life caused my mother shame.

"I'm sorry, Baby Girl, I can't do it."

"Do what, Faye-Faye?"

Her hand in mine, I was too busy moving toward that wave of waiting women to reply. I approached the woman closest to us: the one in the pink dress who favored Miss Bullocks. She was Mama's height, my color, and smelled comforting. Like strawberries and cream. "Excuse me, please. How far is the train station?"

She eyed us with open curiosity before responding in a musical voice. "Which one? Central or La Grande?"

That knocked the wind out of me. It made sense that a city as large as Los Angeles would have more than one depot. The fact that I hadn't considered that left me feeling countrified, backward. I pushed down panic and did my best to recall con-versations concerning our train travel but, with Charity's pass-ing, things had been quick, chaotic, and I'd only caught snatches of Papa's discussion with Mister Brown and Mister Kelley. I wanted to drop onto that sidewalk beneath a warm California sun and cry for my ignorance.

"Which one has trains coming in from Oklahoma?"

"Both I believe, but this is Central Avenue here so you're closer to it. Just stay on Central and head to Fifth. It'll take you, maybe, thirty minutes."

"What about La Grande? How far is that?"

"Depends on how you get there. By cab? Twenty, twenty-five minutes. By bus? Quite a bit longer, depending on the number of stops."

"How long if we walk?"

Her laugh was quick, sharp. "Honey, you really don't want to do that."

"Can you point me in its direction?" I politely insisted.

Her face grew serious. "Those white boys who dropped you off couldn't have taken you there?" She made a funny sound in the back of her throat when I shook my head. "Are you afraid of them?"

Her genuine concern had me fighting back tears. "Just the directions please . . ."

She sighed, realizing further discussion wasn't forthcoming. "Can you read?"

I wasn't sure why she asked that. Maybe because my voice wasn't California-smooth like hers and came out my mouth twanging like the old, deep South. Or because I looked like something from last century in Old Aunt Spinster's makeshift "wedding" dress. But I needed her help and couldn't be offended. "Yes, ma'am, I can."

"Like I said, Central is closest so start with that." She rummaged through her pocketbook until finding a small notepad and pen. She took her time writing before tearing away the paper and handing it to me. "I don't know every twist and turn to get to La Grande, but that's the gist of it. The closer you get to La Grande ask someone for help if needed." She glanced from me to Hope. "It's rather far. You sure you want to walk?"

I nodded.

"Well, your legs're younger than mine." She dug in her purse again. "Here. That's all I have, but you probably need it." Handing me a nickel, she told me not to lose it. "Don't let nobody bother either of you. Stay close together. Can I ask why getting to the station's so important?"

She had the type of kindness that tempted me to lay my troubles at her feet. Charity being taken by venom. My childhood home consumed by black blizzards. My lost family. But Papa had taught us to always try to fix our own problems before burdening someone else with them, so I swallowed sorrow and uncertainty like a sugarless cup of rancid coffee and simply thanked her before steering Hope in the direction of Central and Fifth.

We'd barely gone a block before I wanted to run back to the strawberries and cream lady to upchuck my story just to grant my insides some breathing space. But glancing back, I saw her climbing into the rear seat of a white lady's car. Clearly, she'd found work for the day.

Who wouldn't want to hire a butterfly like her?

That thought in mind, I returned my attention to where we were headed only to hear a horrific horn blast. I'd stepped into the street without paying attention and was staring down the face of an automobile. It seemed to be moving twice as fast as our old car could, and we might've been flattened underneath its wheels if not for strong arms pulling Hope and me to safety.

"Whoa now, little ladies! Watch where you going."

I looked up into the worried eyes of an older Colored

gentleman dressed as if headed to work involving manual labor. "Thank you, sir, we're sorry."

He nodded and headed off, reminding us to be careful.

Lord, I can't even walk down a street without nearly killing us.

I felt small and deficient but I *had* to get us to that station and the safety of Tomas and Mae P. Wilson. Our parents.

TWELVE

ZOE

It was Wednesday. I'd been in California less than a week and already my proverbial candle was burning at both ends. The art lover in me welcomed the flame and fuel of my upcoming exhibition—being engrossed in necessary minutiae, dotting i's and crossing t's to ensure the success of the project. It was demanding as well as exhilarating, providing familiar adrenaline surges. Yet, within the mix was a unique energy. Someone or something beyond me was present and invested, lending spirit and leading me toward outcomes of success. The experience was uncanny, leaving me curious; but that didn't prevent me from welcoming its phenomenon versus doing my normal and questioning it to death. It was a divine source that I sensed was specific to this exhibition.

Leaving the gallery at the end of each day, I felt it wane—sometimes leaving me so exhausted that it was an effort mustering energy to spend time with family. My mind was moving in too many directions. Work was its own world of wants; now I was equally immersed in finding Baby Girl Miss Me while my personal life experienced paralysis. Being with

Vince was as joyful as buying tampons, yet divorce papers sat in my suitcase, begging attention. I had subzero interest in navigating the elaborate labyrinth of foolery constructed by the man I'd married. Telling myself I needed to preserve my sanity and focus on the exhibit, I pushed Vince to the back-burner, ignoring his calls, texts, and threats. Avoidance wasn't my norm and postponing the inevitable was ignorant, but right then it was all I was willing to give.

Remarkably, energy resurged each night when turning to Baby Girl Miss Me and what became our sacred time. I adored my family, but having a quiet place to rest was heavenly, strategic. Certainly, I'd spend a night or two with Natasha and my parents before returning to Boston, but solitude during these weeks leading up to the exhibition in order to center myself and my energies was imperative. I valued the serenity, the presence of the marina outside my window, and what became my nighttime ritual. Showered and changed into PJs, I'd listen to ambient music or meditate. When centered and calm, I'd launch the app on my phone to be greeted by photos of Baby Girl Miss Me. Her image was my companion and guide as I resumed my research to find evidence of our familial connection. But again, I had to find the little one in the picture first. Without Faye—who I now presumed to be Baby Girl's little sister—I couldn't locate my doppelgänger ancestor.

Admittedly, for myriad reasons, it was slow progress, even vexing in some aspects. I'd found no Faye Owensbys, but I'd called the two White Pages listings I'd discovered with a first initial "F" only to come up disappointed. One F. Owensby turned out to be a forty-something-year-old named Frank, and the other was a very talkative Freda. Neither were African-American and had no knowledge of a Faye in their family tree. That left me re-examining the gathered data, forming new questions, and deducing possibilities.

Was little sister Faye yet living, or deceased? If alive, my best guesstimate was that she was in her late eighties, early nineties. Did she reside with children, on her own, or in an assisted care facility? Was she still in the LA area, or had she relocated within the state or elsewhere? I used modern technology to my advantage in researching census and property records; even cemetery plots and obituaries online. When that produced more misses than hits, I created an account with a highly touted ancestry research platform to build out my family tree only to come back to the fact that with my mother's unknown biological origins too many vital links were missing. My frustration and disappointment were mounting, but I'd experienced clarity enough to realize little sister Faye might have married and perhaps her last name was no longer Owensby. I acknowledged that very real possibility, knowing that if that was the case, I was chasing rabbits in the wind.

It was Wednesday night, well past ten. I was tired. Still Granddad's homily had me smiling. He used it on me as a child when I was struggling with or being stubborn about something.

Zoe Noelle, you chasing rabbits in the wind. Go sit down. Breathe. Think. Then try again.

I was always outdone by Granddad's not helping me solve whatever my issue, especially if it was homework, only to feel a sense of triumph whenever resolution occurred. As an adult, I'd reflect on those moments and appreciated my grandfather's way of teaching me to problem-solve and trust my instincts.

Ready to do as Granddad suggested—take a break and breathe before resuming this searching-for-a-Faye-in-haystacks business—I eyed my laptop beside me, exhausted by the mere idea of searching marriage licenses just as my cell phone rang. I answered with a smile when seeing Shaun H. on the ID screen. "Well, hello, Mister World Famous Photographer. It's after one a.m. in New York. Why're you still awake, and how goes it?"

"I can't complain. And I'm awake because East Coast time

hasn't caught up with me. My body's moving on a California clock."

I suppressed a naughty thought involving the ways I'd like to see his body move. "How's the photo shoot?" I listened with genuine interest as he conveyed technical difficulties he'd encountered that had caused delays.

"Thankfully, it wasn't major and we were able to regroup and get back on track. I'm still in line to finish tomorrow and be home this weekend. How's your research? Any progress?"

I sighed airily. "Not really. Thus far, all roads lead to dead ends."

"It's unfortunate nothing has panned out, Zoe, but hopefully you can approach it as a weeding process. You're walking through weeds right now but maybe that good harvest is ahead. Don't give up before you get it."

"I was chasing rabbits, now I'm on my way to carrots?"

"Pardon?"

I laughed at his confusion. "Nothing. Don't mind me. I'm a little loopy." A yawn spilled out of me, proving my state of being.

"Exhausted?"

"Yes," I admitted before taking a satisfying drink of water and rolling my shoulders backward and forward, trying to alleviate tension. My spirit might've been exhilarated but these nightly searches after a full day were physically taxing. "You know what I need besides Faye Owensby? A massage."

"Really? Hold that thought."

Grabbing an open box of snack crackers, I plunged my hand in only to think better of it. I'd been overindulging in Granny's and my mother's rich cooking this visit. If I didn't mind myself, I'd wind up finding the seven pounds I'd recently lost and taking them back to Boston. Congratulating myself for my selfcontrol, I lifted my cell at the sound of an incoming text.

It'd better not be Quasimodo, aka Vince.

"What's this?" My inquiry was an absentminded murmur while accessing a website link Shaun just texted, leading me to a wellness salon. "Oh my! I'm relaxing just looking at this."

"It's my sister's gig. Tell her I sent you. Better yet . . . enjoy some relaxation on me. My treat."

"Thanks, Shaun, but I can't let you do that."

"It's a friend thing, Zoe. No strings. Plus, didn't you just say you need a massage?"

"I did, but you can't sponsor it." We weren't teenagers texting, calling relentlessly, yet we'd softly fallen into a comfortable pattern of communication. I enjoyed our conversations, appreciated hearing from him, and sent thoughts of well-being into the universe when I didn't. I told myself ours was an "artists of a feather flock together" situation; but even I didn't believe that okey-doke completely. God knew I wasn't in the market for a man. That didn't prevent my intuiting what I believed to be a mutual attraction. I wasn't a random woman but if Shaun Halsey offered me a nuclear night of nasty, I'd probably be butt naked, legs spread before he finished the invitation. "I appreciate you, Shaun, but no. I've got this."

He was quiet a moment before clearing his throat. "Forgive me if this sounds insulting, but are you of that pool of sistas who say they want to be showered with affection and attention, but dislike a man doing anything for them as if their self-sufficiency or strength are insulted?"

My "Why you coming for me, Mister Halsey?" had us both laughing. "And no, I'm not a member of any such sista pool. I'm unique," I teased.

"You absolutely are, Zoe, and you intrigue me."

The deep and sexy way he uttered that sentiment shot an errant thrill from my belly to my private spaces that hadn't entertained a man in more than a minute.

"I'm not incapable of accepting your kindness. It's just a bit generous," I offered, focusing on practicalities versus the warmth floating through my being. "I'm all about support-ing Black-owned businesses so I'll gladly pay for this self-indulgence."

"To be honest, Zoe, and the fact that my grandmother thought you were your possible ancestor aside, you put a smile on her face and gave me a glimpse of Nana that I haven't seen in a long time. Consider this my way of saying thanks." His voice flowed with sincerity. "Plus, like you, I'm all for supporting our businesses, and the owner's my baby sis, so it's a triple win."

The chime of another incoming text diverted my attention. Shaun had sent a screenshot of his text to his sister advising who I was and that I would be contacting her to make an appoint-ment for which he was paying.

"Ooo, that's dirty, Shaun Halsey."

The velvety smoothness of his laugh stroked that fluttery sensation inside of me, again; left me wondering if I was declin-ing his generosity because I was more attracted to him than I cared to admit. Other than the drive to and from Sacramento, we hadn't spent additional time together. Subsequent, occasional communication had been via email and text. Just the same, odd though it might seem, our conversations had proved open and substantive enough to further this new connection that could easily lead to friendship. I was fine with friendship. Despite no longer loving him, I was technically married to Vince and was disinterested in bringing another man into our mess. Even if Shaun and I weren't about romance, the openness he triggered in me might have been the universe's way of letting me know there was goodness waiting, that it was okay to move on, release my toxic marriage.

"Fine. Let me demonstrate that I wasn't raised by wolves and simply say thank you."

"You're welcome," he said after chuckling, "and on that note I'm headed to bed."

Can I come with?

"Sweet dreams and I truly appreciate your kindness. Let me know a good night for dinner when you get back. And that's on *me*. It's my thanks for this blessing," I gushed in an attempt to side-step the salaciousness of my unspoken sentiment.

"I'd call you competitive except I'd like to avoid an argument." We chuckled at his remark. "Don't stop researching, Zoe. Something will break loose. Just keep the faith."

I shivered as we exchanged good nights, feeling that now familiar jolt of energy generated by the one word that had become my rallying cry and homing device. *Faith.*

Sliding my cell onto the nightstand, I ruminated on my consulting the Bible since that initial prompting to visit 1 Corinthians 13:13, and how often I'd landed on verses pertaining to faith. They proved timely, encouraging. Clearly, heaven intended to keep me from losing heart midway or giving up on divine discovery.

It'll be Mama's birthday gift.

My mother's birthday was in August. That gave me five months to track down something solid. Hoping to gift her a link to her lineage that she could forever treasure, I found myself humming an unfamiliar tune only to realize it was the song Baby Girl Miss Me sang in that dream. The lyrics had faded from memory and back into the dream, but the tune was unmistakable and enveloped me in peace.

Busy as I was at the gallery, it took me several days to get around to contacting Shaun's sister. When I did it was like finding a new friend. She was as personable as her brother, and her website did her establishment little justice. Modest in size, it was an oasis of tranquility that enveloped me and Natasha the moment we walked in. I'd invited my cousin as a way of thanking her for how supportive she'd been. Submitting to the magic of those massages, we left feeling like queens but not before Natasha signed up for spa membership with its perks and benefits.

"Zo-Zo, I am *so* glad you suggested using Lyft."

We sat in the rear of the rideshare en route to my parents', eyes closed, heads back. We were light, floaty, utterly relaxed. "Mmm-hmm," was the best I could do. I wanted nothing more than to sleep for days. Instead, I found myself ignoring an incoming call from my estranged husband.

"Is that the beast?"

I grinned at Natasha's labeling. "Yep, and he can enjoy my non-responsiveness." I refused to sabotage my peace and let the phone go unanswered, even when he called again a minute later, prompting me to silence all notifications. My efforts to preserve peace were clearly effective. The next thing I knew the driver was waking me with, "Excuse me, miss. We're here."

I straightened my posture and glanced at my dozing cousin. We'd both fallen asleep as an aftermath of magic masseuse hands. "Tasha?" Grinning at her mumbled response, I unbuckled both of our seatbelts and thanked the driver while pulling my cousin from the car.

"Oh my God, I'm too relaxed to walk. Carry me, Zoe."

"Girl, please. I have one spine and I need it," I quipped, as we headed up the walkway. Disinterested in finding my folks engaged in any funny business, I gave the doorbell my signature triplicate press before unlocking the door and walking in. "Mama? Daddy? Y'all home, and are you decent?"

I followed my mother's laughter to find her and my father in the den snacking on popcorn and watching one of their favorite films. "We're always decent. We just engage in a little something every now and then not intended for juvenile audiences."

"Spare us the gory details." I feigned disgust before kissing my parents and wiggling myself in between them.

"Who's 'us'?" Daddy asked, draping an arm about my shoulder.

"Tasha's with me. She stopped off in the bathroom."

"Good thing your mama and I got dressed after taking care of business, huh, Baby?"

I snickered when my father reached across me to bump fists with my mother. "You two need Jesus."

"Maybe, but what we don't need is Viagra."

"Daddy, *please.*" I made a face as if ingesting disgusting medicine as my father laughed.

"Hey, Unc. Hi, Auntie Gladys." Entering the room, Natasha kissed my mother and plopped herself on my father's lap. A semi-retired postmaster, my dad was the cool uncle my cousins came to when needing advice or a listening ear. He was very much like Granddad—playful but full of wisdom. Both Natasha and I were only children and had spent so much time together we'd grown up like sisters. I was accustomed to sharing my parents with her, but this sitting on Daddy's lap at her age wasn't what his knees needed.

I pushed her off. "Sit your behind on the sofa like you got good sense."

"You ain't gotta get violent." She reached across Daddy and popped my ear.

Mama swatted us both on the legs, laughing, when I popped Natasha back like we were ten instead of staring forty in the face. "You two be still and let us enjoy our movie."

My parents had watched *The Color Purple* so often they'd memorized practically every line. Still, I complied. Thirty minutes later, I chuckled on hearing my father's light snore. He wasn't the only one out for the count. Mama and Natasha were dozing as well. That left me in the company of Shug Avery and Miss Celie, while glancing back and forth between my parents in assessment, amazed by genetics.

All my life I'd been told I was my father's spitting image. Now, Baby Girl Miss Me had inserted a new connective essence and presence into my existence. Turning to my mother, I wanted to wake her, to ask for access to whatever data she'd compiled when searching for her biological family, but she seemed so peaceful, her head propped against a sofa pillow, that I chose not to. Plus, I had nothing concrete and had to avoid giving her false hope that might increase a sense of alienation or rejection.

I'm going after the truth.

I was suddenly gripped by the notion that this trip home wasn't merely about the exhibition. Divine intervention was at work as well. I blame that for what I did next. Easing from the sofa, I tip-toed from the den and headed to the spare bedroom-cum-office. Sitting at the desk, I opened my mother's laptop only to stop.

Z., what're you doing? You cannot intrude in matters not concerning you.

I silenced that flash of conscience by asserting that this thing most definitely did concern me. It was my face in that picture and I owed it to my mother and myself to reconnect our dangling roots. Ignoring the guilty twinge at invading her privacy, I typed a password, hoping to unlock my mother's computer.

"*Yes.*" I celebrated Mama's consistency. She still used the same password she had for years: ZoeN0524. My name, middle initial, and birthday. Telling myself I'd bypass personal items and focus solely on my hunt for pertinent clues, I prayed that something would advance my search. An executive administrator for UC Berkeley's Biology department, Mama was meticulous and her laptop reflected that fact. All folders were alphabetized, organized, but offered nothing revelatory or even remotely relevant.

"Dammit." I'd hit another wall and was sick of dealing with dead ends. If something didn't shake loose soon, I'd be forced to bring Mama into my quest. Her search had been unsuccessful, but that didn't mean a clue didn't exist. Working in tandem, perhaps we'd find it.

Stay zen, Zoe.

My massage had been magical. Intent on maintaining its effects, I closed the laptop and considered the room's comforting familiarity. Other than fresh paint and two new plush chairs, the room hadn't changed much over the years. It functioned as an office, yet was warm, welcoming. Walls and curios showcased my parents' career awards, Mama's bric-a-brac and plethora of plants, and framed family photographs. I loved old photos with their sense of history and timelessness, their ability to capture then and now in visual storytelling. Seeing one of my favorites of me as a baby on the desk, I picked it up and was instantly hit with a surreal sense of my mother's experience, her being adopted and the mystery of unknown origins.

"I've gotta find *something*." Determination and compassion surged through me, accelerating my snooping. I hopped up, intent on searching every possible place in hopes that Mama had printed and stored her research somewhere accessible. Desk drawers. File folders. Bookshelves. The closet. I even got on the floor to look underneath the desk as if Mama had taped papers there. Clearly, I'd seen one spy movie too many.

"Get your crazy self up." My knees cracked in protest as I did. "That's what you get."

Research was a significant part of my role as a curator but after searching every inch of that room and coming up empty-handed, I slumped back onto the chair, hating to admit that perhaps I was in over my head. I had work back home in Boston, my Oakland exhibition, and the student collaborative. I was an organized multitasker and could easily manage my duties, including the requisite social aspects. I did the cocktail parties, the schmoozing before galas, and had made a name for myself within the art community. True, too often I was ethnically out-numbered, or like Granny said, a fly in the buttermilk—a cultural representative. Curating an exhibition was intense. I'd added to its demands this chase for a phantom relative, not to mention a divorce that needed to happen. Kneading my brow with a twinge of exasperation, I wondered if hiring a private investigator might be the better course of action.

"Let a professional have at it." I tended to be competitive and hated the idea of giving in but I clearly needed to stay in my lane and do as Shaun and Natasha had suggested, which was to simply keep the faith, *and* let an investigator have all this head-ache. Sighing in submission, I fingered a picture of Daddy and Natasha's father, my Uncle Ulysses, on a fishing bank holding up a fresh catch. "Talk about competitive." I smiled, remember-ing how they'd walk in the door fussing about who had the best catch when returning from their annual two-day fishing trips. Mama and Aunt Eva, Uncle Uly's wife, would ignore their animated shenanigans, clean and filet the catch, and fry it up—leaving Daddy and Uncle Uly to their antics.

Cry your tears in your beer 'cause you can't never out-catch me, U-Leeee.

That might as well have been the dinner blessing seeing as how Daddy said it every time we indulged in their prized filets, over-emphasizing his younger brother's nickname.

"U-Lee . . ." An inexplicable shiver skittered down my spine as I stared at that picture, repeating Daddy's play on my uncle's name. I suddenly had the sensation that something was in front of me that I hadn't seen.

Breathe. Think. Then try again.

My grandfather's wisdom spooled through me so powerfully that I jerked upright in my seat as a name slowly slipped across my lips. "Owens*lee?*"

Heart pattering, I snatched open Mama's laptop and

launched my chosen site, wondering if maybe, just maybe, I'd been searching for the wrong name all this time. In my excitement, I forgot all about my reverse search method, and started with California versus Oklahoma. My fingers flew across that keyboard, typing in my search criteria. Pressing enter, I closed my eyes and held my breath before daring to peek. I pumped a fist in the air and let my feet do a happy dance as results populated the screen. Finding fewer than one hundred persons in California with the last name Owenslee wasn't disappointing. I viewed it as a fortuitous narrowing down and honing in on possibilities. I was ready and willing to contact each one if necessary.

"Where are you, baby sister Faye?" Scrolling the list, I found three persons with first names beginning with "F." None were Faye. I called just the same, and probably sounded like a Grade A idiot leaving messages about looking for a long-lost relative. It didn't matter. I was desperate.

By the time I finished, my body was humming with adrenaline. Maybe an attempt to exhaust some of it, or just plain human interest, incited me to keep scrolling the list until the name Henry Owenslee jumped out at me. I had zero need to access my notes. Nana Sam's naming the boys in the picture with Baby Girl and Faye—"Micah, Harvey or Henry"—was crystal clear in my memory. What if Owenslee was *their* last name, not Baby Girl Miss Me and Faye's? I dialed, fingers shaking, only to receive a recorded greeting.

You've reached the Owenslees. Please leave a message. The voice was female, Southern, elderly.

"Hello, my name is Zoe Edwards. I'm curating a museum exhibition in northern California involving native Oklahomans who migrated here during the Dust Bowl era. It's been brought to my attention that Mister Owenslee may have been part of that wave. If he's available, I'd love to speak with him." Providing my phone number and email address, I thanked them, and disconnected without questioning my using a professional versus a personal approach. Something cautioned me not to spook them off; plus, she might've been napping, but I didn't want Mama accidentally overhearing anything and becoming suspicious.

Pocketing my phone, I looked for a Harvey and Micah Owenslee just in case this Henry was a bust but found nothing. That didn't keep me from feeling appreciative. "God, thanks for this. Please let it lead to something."

I was back at my lodging and ready for bed when my phone rang. Seeing the number I'd dialed earlier, I answered immediately. "Zoe Edwards speaking."

"Yes . . . hello . . . Miss Edwards, this is Gregory Owenslee returning your call. I'm the grandson of Henry Owenslee. My grandmother says you left a message wanting to speak with him?"

"Yes, sir, I did." I repeated the information about my upcoming exhibition. "I promise not to take up too much of his time, but I'd love to schedule an appointment at his convenience."

"I see." His voice was suddenly somber. "Unfortunately, Miss Edwards, my grandfather passed away last month."

My heart dropped, and my hope wavered. "I'm so sorry to hear that. You and your family have my sincere condolences."

"Thank you. I just thought it best that I inform you about my grandfather in case you want to look for someone else to interview."

"Actually, I *am* looking for someone else." Confessing my interest wasn't solely exhibition-related, my words rushed like a river. "I'm trying to find a relative who may have come from Oklahoma to California in the 1930s. I have little to go on, but she and her older sister traveled with a family, possibly named Owenslee. Her name was Faye and—"

"Did you say *Faith*?"

I hadn't, but elusive truths shifted and fell into place: my hearing "faith" at the tail end of my Jaelen and Baby Girl Miss Me dream. The faith-centered verses I'd read lately. How the very essence of the word continued to deeply resonate within me. Except now, maybe, faith wasn't mere encouragement, but the name of my ancestor's younger sibling.

THIRTEEN

FAITH

"Faye-Faye, this city's big and scary."

We should've done nothing except hurry to Central Station like the lady in the pink dress said, but the longer we walked, the more Hope and I wound up distracted by new sights and sounds until we were barely moving. There was a hustle-bustle energy that felt too massive for the morning. Clearly, California rolled into its days hot and ready. There was much to see and the scenery seemed to constantly change. From nice sections in what appeared to be a Colored community, to wide streets and even wider boulevards with big buildings. We gawked as if in some exotic place, fascinating people and the strangeness about us impeding our progress. Yellow taxis, their drivers stopping and letting people in before zipping off God knew where. Boys in short pants hawked newspapers on corners. More cars flooded the streets than we'd ever seen. A man outside a restaurant shouted into a bullhorn, pleading with pedestrians to come in. Two Colored men in suits and bowties called me "sister" and offered some weird-sounding greeting before asking if we wanted to buy a pie made from beans. There were food smells from diners, restaurants, and corner stands. Some scents were like home, others foreign. We saw stores, hotels, and people in a hurry. There were so many churches I decided Los Angeles must've been holy. No matter that some things seemed frayed about the edges, like testaments to the Depression; compared to Wellston, the city had a touch of shine and I felt drawn to its tarnished gleam like metal to a magnet despite feeling overwhelmed.

"I know, Baby Girl. Here. Climb on." I bent to give Hope a piggyback ride so she'd feel safe, less intimidated.

Despite myriad distractions and an enormous sense of urgency, what wasn't lost on me was the way Colored folks moved amid humanity. Unlike back home, they didn't lower their eyes and step off sidewalks when white people approached. Colored folks kept their position, showing no interest in treating white skin like some kind of royalty card requiring obsequiousness. I smiled, liking the idea of owning my space versus side-stepping to whiteness.

"Faye-Faye, I'm almost hungry again."

The walk felt long. What should've taken twenty minutes had to have been three times that amount with our walking wide-eyed in wonderment. Thankfully, our journey was without incident other than a begging man dressed in rags, and passing a scary wino lost in liquor and talking nonsense. I was still hesitant after that earlier incident of walking into the street without paying attention and made myself hyper vigilant when crossing streets, especially at the corners where white-gloved officers blew whistles and rapidly motioned us from one side of the block to the next. It all felt so tense and terrifying that I wanted to ball up in a safe corner and hide.

"Do we gots more cornbread?"

"Say it right, Baby Girl, like Miss Bullocks taught you, or I can't answer."

"Do we *have* any?" She over-emphasized her correction.

"Good girl . . . but no, we ate it all." I offered soothing

promises of food waiting on us with our parents, ignoring the rumbling of my stomach. That little cornbread square from earlier hadn't done a thing except make me hungry. Still, we needed to get where we were going. "The train station can't be too much farther. We'll be there soon."

There were so many more sights. More sounds. Our surroundings were so incredibly different to anything I'd grown up with that I wished Charity were there to share it, despite all things not being glorious. Like the winos and the begging man. Their scariness kept me moving, constantly praying we were headed in the right direction and wouldn't wind up lost in that big city.

"We shoulda been there by now." I was beginning to feel anxious, as if our destination would never be reached and we'd be left forever searching. The California sun had heated up. My feet were beginning to ache, Hope felt heavy on my back, and Old Spinster Aunt's dress was itchy and made my armpits sweat. I was edging toward scared irritability, ready to take a break when a train whistle sounded in the distance.

"Faye-Faye, I see it!"

The excitement in Hope's voice was fresh water on dry land. My woes were forgotten as I hurried us along those lengthy Los Angeles blocks toward the train station, so like an oasis, only to stop when it fully came into view. It was so vast, I lowered Hope to the ground and held her hand just to allow myself to take it all in. *"Good God . . ."*

Never had I seen so many people in one place. Entering and exiting that station, their swell had to be as wide, brisk, and noisy as an ocean. It seemed as if heaven had taken all of creation and dumped them in front of us. Hope's squeezing my hand and easing behind my leg indicated she felt as swallowed up as I did. I wasn't sure how we were supposed to find anyone or anything in that human hive of activity, and simply stood there before reminding myself that that crowd might be the only thing standing between me and my family.

"Stay close to me, Baby Girl." I bent so we were eye to eye. "And do *not* let go of my hand." Her grip was lock-tight as I took a deep breath before cautiously moving toward what I prayed was divine reunion.

We made slow progress navigating that human ocean. It was loud, dense, and strange with the occasional sound of people speaking words other than English. I did my best to keep us from getting swept up by staying on the fringes. But when someone jostled us so hard that I lost Hope's hand momentarily, I whirled about and snatched my sister up and put her on my hip to avoid any further accidental separations. She sniffled a bit as I kissed her head wedged in the crook of my neck. "I've got you, Baby Girl. You're okay."

People stood in long lines at ticket counters, above which were large boards with so much information it might as well have been shorthand. Realizing it had to do with departures and arrivals, I did my best to make sense of it and searched for incoming trains from home. I spent futile minutes in that pursuit only to remember Papa had planned to sell our mule at the border of New Mexico. Had they boarded there, or Oklahoma proper? And did it make a difference in this search for their arrival? Altering my search didn't prove any better when I realized I had no idea which train my family might have arrived on. I moved away, looking for the waiting area instead.

We found it easily. An absence of signs indicating *Coloreds* or *Whites Only* proved puzzling until we saw the configuration of humans. Posted signs may have been missing but folks were separated in designated pockets as if naturally divided by skin. I hurried toward the Colored section at the back, desperately seeking out my parents only to feel as if the bottom of the world was missing when they didn't magically appear.

"Where's Papa?" Hope's mumbled question vibrated against my ear.

Unable—or maybe unwilling—to speak defeat, I shook my head while making my way to a corner. I sat on a bench with Hope on my lap, forcing my eyes wide, afraid to blink. If we waited all day and night, so be it. Come hell or high water, our parents would find us or we'd find them.

We spent that day at the train station, sitting, watching. Waiting. Praying and willing Tomas and Mae P. Wilson to appear. By late afternoon I wondered if our parents ever would. My spirit was starting to sag but Hope and I remained vigilantly in place just the same, crossing our legs and defying our bladders, afraid a restroom trip might result in our missing them. Only when we were on the verge of accidents did we rush to relieve ourselves before hurrying back to our seats where we became living fixtures set on discovery.

Throughout the day we watched travelers come and go. I made a game of counting them and concocting stories about their destinations whenever Hope became fidgety and irritable. "I bet she's headed to China to visit mystical pandas." I pointed to a white woman in a blue-and-yellow dress with pale skin that seemed even paler thanks to her very black hair and bright crimson lipstick.

"Can trains get to China from California?"

"Yep," I falsified, spinning a fantastical tale of magical railroads high in the sky.

"Nuh-uh, Faye-Faye, trains can't fly!"

"They can, too! But only at night. When good little children like you are sound asleep, the tracks grow gossamer wings kissed by fairies. The trains're silent as mice and float into the air, all glittery and filled with chocolate and delicious things, and their whistles are sweet as a lullaby." As if to demonstrate, I hugged my sister and hummed softly before segueing into our signature song, "Faith, Hope, and Charity," my voice fading on "Brother Noah built a boat . . ."

"I hope Noah's foot is better. I miss my big brother," Hope mumbled around the thumb stuck in her mouth. She removed it when her belly rumbled. "Faye-Faye, my tummy's noisy. I *really* wanna eat, please."

I had hunger to thank for derailing Hope from further fretting. She'd had a crying spell earlier when Papa and Mama didn't readily appear, and I'd hurried to silence and soothe her when her distress drew unwanted attention by playing hand games, singing "Oh Mary Mack" so many times my throat took to aching.

Now, glancing at the large, vestibule clock, I was taken aback by the many hours that had passed since. Not knowing how long our vigil would be I'd coaxed, coddled, and pleaded with Hope to wait, but my baby sister was finished with delays and distractions. My rumbling belly testified I was just as hungry. Still, I didn't want to move and possibly miss our parents, or exhaust the only money we had: the nickel the kind-faced woman had given us.

Dear Lord, let it be enough.

"Come on. Let's find some supper." I held Hope's hand and started forward, only to feel her pull back. Our being jostled and separated by the crowd earlier that day, resulting in a split-second separation, left her hesitant. I bent down so she could scramble onto my back before heading toward the exit and halting enough to get my bearings and follow the food smells.

With our choices limited to what five cents could get, we found ourselves in line at a wheeled cart shaded by a tall umbrella and boasting a "Louisiana Dogs" hand-painted sign. The cart was managed by a freckle-faced, copper-haired Colored man selling long, fat, delicious-smelling sausages snuggled in warm, thick bread. "You want the tiger or the tame?

Spicy or mild, Miss?" he clarified, when I stood there looking uncertain.

"Mild, please." It was a safer choice since Hope couldn't handle spicy heat. "Thank you." Accepting our food, I hesitated. "Excuse me . . . can you help us?" I described our parents and asked if he'd seen them, thinking perhaps his position on the sidewalk and interaction with customers granted some special advantage.

"Can't say I have. If you don't know what time their train comes in, check at a ticket window. Better yet, ask the porters if they've seen 'em. They're the *real* eyes and ears of the station."

I'd watched the red-capped porters, Colored men, carting luggage and bustling about with soldier-like precision and efficiency throughout the day. "Thank you, sir, I will once we eat."

"Can we sit in the shade, Faye-Faye?"

Again, I was surprised at how far and fast the day had progressed. Morning had long ago eased into afternoon; now, early evening danced in the wings. Still, the sun was bold, the air warm. Finding a shady space away from foot traffic but with a clear view of the station entrance, Hope and I sat not far from a magnificent water fountain whose gurgling spray kissed us with its mist.

Breaking our meal, I said grace before giving my sister the larger share. With its bold flavors, that Louisiana Dog ate like a feast. I blessed the musical-voiced woman we'd encountered that morning for her nickel-giving kindness yet again.

"You think we're eating somebody's pet?"

I frowned at my baby sister's question. "What?"

"I can't read the big word on that man's cart, but the second is d-o-g and that spells dog. If we're eating somebody's pet, God I'm sorry but, it's the best-tasting dog on the farm."

I hadn't laughed since Charity passed, but Hope's comments had laughter bubbling out of me. "It's just a food name, Baby Girl. We're not pet killers."

"Oh, okay. Can we get some water, Faye-Faye? That dog made me thirsty."

Holding hands, we headed back into the station for the drinking fountains I'd found confusing because of their lack of signage indicating if they were for us or them. Back home, Jim Crow would've had *Coloreds* and *White Only* markers posted on all kind of public spaces and conveniences. Clearly, California's segregated places were overseen by a more civil and sophisticated racial attendant: Sir James Crow, not Jim. Make no mistake: signs might've been absent but there was certainly separation. Just as we had found the Colored folks' waiting area at the rear, I knew the fountain we were supposed to drink from thanks to its run-down, less than cared-for condition.

At least it's functional, I thought, hoisting Hope for a drink.

That was when I saw him.

He stood in the distance, cap in hand, scowling and scoping his surroundings in search of us. Henry Owenslee's sudden presence had my heart pounding, made my throat nearly seize.

He must've gone back to that corner and, not finding us there, come here. But I ain't going back with him.

I couldn't. I wasn't too young to understand that there wasn't one good thing waiting on me in a life with Henry. Lowering Hope to her feet, I grabbed her hand and took off walking fast in the opposite direction, weaving in and out of crowds, determined to go undetected.

"Faye-Faye, I wasn't finished!"

"Shhh!" I hissed my sister into silence. Mama had taught us to be thankful so I wasn't an ingrate and appreciated the Owenslees for seeing us safely to California, but that didn't give them the right to decide my life. I didn't want to be married, and I didn't want babies. At least not with Henry. Thinking on him and his snake-eyed meanness, the way he looked at me as if already undressed, not to mention his hitting me, the only existence I pictured with him was one boiled in misery. And scary prayer services lasting to eternity. Laundry. Cooking. No Colored college. Being hated and mistreated by Miz Lucy. And having to fend off Henry to avoid baby-making. Back home I'd never given Papa or Mama much trouble and did my best to be obedient, but Henry wasn't my parent and I couldn't stomach the idea of being treated like less than. True, I was stubborn and didn't want to be told what to do or how to do it, but there was deep-rooted disharmony between us that was more than slave plantations and history. The generations hadn't changed much since then, and I'd seen enough racial injustices in Wellston to never want a white man.

"*Faith!*"

We didn't have anywhere else to go so it might've been stupid of me, but Henry suddenly yelling my name had me clutching Hope's hand and outright running. The restroom was the only destination I could think of. I meant to race there and hide, but hearing Henry behind us hollering for Micah and knowing they'd both be in pursuit, I shot down the first corridor we came to. It was narrow, absent of people, and lined with doors. Panicked by the dim possibilities of what pursued me, I tried the first doorknob and the second. Both were locked. That left me racing to the next, swinging the door wide and pushing Hope into the darkness. I managed to squeeze into that space that was nothing but a broom closet crowded with brooms and cleaning equipment.

"That was Henry! Why're we running off instead of going home with him?"

"*Shhh, Baby Girl, please.*" My jagged whisper seemed too big for our tight confines. I didn't care to be in there with funny cleaning smells, but I welcomed the darkness that swallowed my distress. How could Hope consider sleeping on a back porch pallet at Old Spinster Aunt's worthy of the word "home"? Home was Papa, Mama, Charity, and Noah; Granny, aunties, uncles, and cousins. Friends. Reverend Coulter. Miss Bullocks teaching every grade in our one-room schoolhouse. Laundry on the line. Mama on the piano and Papa telling stories at bedtime. Hot buttered bread, fried catfish, singing in the choir, June bugs, warm hugs, and pure love. That wasn't what a back-porch life promised. It scared me to think Hope was little enough to forget what we'd had and who she was. "We gotta stay and look for our family. Going with Henry won't let that happen."

That was enough to silence her as we hid in the dark. Several minutes passed before she quietly asked, "How much more we gotta stay in here?"

I'd been carefully listening, tensing whenever noises drew near; holding my breath and exhaling when the door wasn't yanked open. I reached for Hope's hand in the dark before answering. "Only a little while longer."

Just long enough to make sure those Owenslees leave.

I felt bad for hiding from Micah, but my freedom was more important. He'd simply have to forgive my trespasses.

As I was hiding in that closet, it wasn't lost on me that we were in a dark space again, same as we'd been in that cellar when a gruesome black blizzard separated us from our beloveds. Only then, I'd welcomed being helped from the bowels of darkness by strangers. Now, I was preserving myself from being something I couldn't be.

You're escaping them but if you can't find your parents, you're going nowhere to nothing.

Tired of standing in the dark, I eased down onto the floor and sat with my back against the wall in between buckets and mops only to feel weighted, petrified by the impossible notion of not reuniting with my parents. The idea of living without those I loved hurt so bad I rejected it.

But what if that happens? Do I have options, alternatives?

I tried not to entertain the thought, but it forced itself on me, made me fearfully consider other kin. I reflected on the fact that, fleeing drought and dusty destruction, Papa's sisters had left for California, some with hopes of finding my long-lost grandfather who'd fled here after killing that man in self-defense over our land. Having disappeared before I was born, Granddad was little more than a specter or legend; someone spoken of in hushed whispers. His whereabouts were a mystery and, until last week, I'd been ignorant of the very reasons for his leaving. For all I knew, he could have a new family and identity. He might have disconnected himself from his past and could consider me an unwelcome reminder of things best left forgotten.

What then?

Los Angeles was too enormous for me to go door to door looking for a phantom grandfather, or my aunts and their families who'd departed only days before us and most likely weren't situated yet. I didn't even have phone numbers or addresses to locate them. The only other persons who came to mind were Mama's parents. But if they'd disown their only child for leaving college—forfeiting becoming a concert pianist able to uplift the race—just to marry my father, I didn't imagine Hope and I would be too welcome. That left me feeling helpless. Limited.

"Faye-Faye, I thought I liked California, but now I don't know if I wanna be here."

My sister's hand still in mine, I pulled her down beside me, understanding her sentiment. "It'll get better. I promise." I offered optimism I didn't really feel as my mind rolled back to that notion of options and alternatives. I didn't like its relentlessness and found myself wrestling with an unthinkable "what if."

What if you can't find anyone?

Releasing Hope's hand, I drew my knees up and wrapped my arms around my legs as my eyes filled with hot tears. I didn't want such vile, frightening thoughts and buried my face in my arms as if doing so could keep ugliness at bay, but it didn't. Unable to escape, I let my tears soak into the scratchy fabric of Old Aunt Spinster's dress and—feeling that fighting wouldn't do me any good—relaxed some of my stubbornness. Just enough to consider who and what I was, and what I might be dealing with. I was a farmer's daughter, but by virtue of Mama's experience, I'd existed with the vague inkling of Colored college. I couldn't get there without my parents. Not unless I kept my grades up in hope of a scholarship. But even if that happened and I graduated, what then? If I was lucky, I could become somebody's secretary instead of a domestic, or maybe be employed by a cleaning service, or cook in a restaurant kitchen. Would it be enough to keep me and Hope until we reconnected with Papa and Mama?

Stop thinking stupid thoughts!

I wasn't ready for life without my family, and knew God was too good to let that happen. Still, I tossed a prayer toward heaven that the Almighty would keep us from becoming orphans.

Life can be sneaky sometimes, so be ready to make other plans and pivot on a dime.

That was something Mama said every now and again, but I heard her voice so clearly right then that my head jerked up, and I searched the darkness as if she was there. Of course, she wasn't and I was forced to slowly inhale in an effort to calm myself, knowing Mama was right about the sneakiness of life. I'd never thought I'd see Charity being lowered into the ground before she'd lived fully. Or my whole family leaving Oklahoma the way we did, and getting separated. I swiped away fresh tears, wishing Mama was there to hold me. Instead, I silently asked her if she was trying to tell me something. Ignorance wasn't to my benefit, but I didn't relish Mama's warning words or their possibly foreshadowing unseen things that might be ahead.

Can't nothing keep me from family. Mama, I'ma find you!

I'd fought my way through a black blizzard to get to my baby sister. I rode on the back of a truck with folks I didn't know, like, or love just to get across the West. Was accosted by and survived a gang of white hoodlums. I'd entered unholy matrimony against my will, and was ready to work when dropped off on the streets of this city with my limited skills. I'd been able to do such things not because I was brave but because I was a Wilson. Being a Wilson made me determined.

I'll wait a few more minutes to make sure Henry and Micah are gone, then we're heading for La Grande.

Coming to Central Station had been logical because it was closest to where we were dropped off, but apparently it was the wrong choice. I'd do like the Louisiana Dog man suggested and find a porter to inquire about my parents. And if they hadn't been seen, I'd move on. My only hope was endurance for the journey to the other train station. Getting here had made my feet hurt and my legs were tired.

It's gonna be okay. You have train station options.

I grinned and leaned my head back against the wall as Hope snuggled against my side, knowing everything was going to be just fine.

"Lemme put these things away, get home, and clean up. I'll meet you at the Downbeat."

Disoriented, I jerked awake at the sound of a man's voice only to smell the cleaning scents about me and remember where I was. I was immediately annoyed with myself for nodding off when I should've been preparing our escape.

"Sounds good, Solomon. See you there." I knew by the smooth intonation and rhythm that the speakers were Colored men. And far too close for comfort.

When footsteps neared the door, I jumped up, snatching Hope with me. My ear was pressed against the door, listening for movement, when it was suddenly opened by a wide man in a janitor's uniform. Despite his size, he stumbled backward as I tumbled into him, his brown face bathed in shock at our unexpected presence.

"What the hell?"

"We're so sorry, sir! We didn't mean to do nothing wrong." Hope's hand in mine, I took off and was halfway down the corridor before he recovered.

"Y'all ain't got no business hiding back here!"

I apologized again, my words trailing behind me like the wind. This was California and I wasn't familiar with its laws, but I found myself outrunning the crazy fear of being snatched up and put in jail. All because of nodding off in a broom closet. It wasn't until that corridor emptied us into an outlet that I realized we'd headed in the opposite direction from which we'd entered and were at the rear of the station.

"Thank You, Jesus."

At least back here we could avoid Henry and Micah if they were still searching. I prayed they'd gotten tired and given up as we scurried out a nearby exit only to stop. I wanted to take back that "thank you" I'd just given the Lord when we were greeted by the descending dusk of Los Angeles.

"God, no . . ."

I couldn't have slept that long. I had no urge to use the restroom and my behind wasn't numb. Still, the evidence of passing time confronted me in nighttime shadows. I heard, but was unable to answer, Hope questioning what was wrong. I was too struck by the truth that night had caught us unaware, that I was on the darkening streets of a huge, new city, alone with Hope, and had absolutely nowhere to go.

FOURTEEN

ZOE

Without question, I had negative time to spare with the exhibition swiftly approaching. Still, there I was, three days after speaking with Gregory Owenslee, exiting an Uber after an hour-long flight, rushing toward our designated meeting place—a café not too far from LAX—as if time bowed at my feet and was subject to my whims. I was pressed for answers. Obviously, so was Gregory Owenslee who had been scheduled to travel to Sacramento on business week after next. He felt there were matters best discussed in person and we planned to meet then. But when he had casually mentioned a cancellation in his schedule today, I suggested this earlier opportunity. Assuring him it wasn't an inconvenience, I gladly gave up my Saturday and booked a flight, praying our encounter would somehow provide a pivotal link in my search for Baby Girl Miss Me. Besides, I relished this quick break from an absolute immersion in all things exhibition and considered it a worthwhile investment in my mother's happiness.

Make sure you meet in a public place.

Natasha's caution wasn't necessary. My need for answers didn't authorize my being reckless or at Gregory Owenslee's mercy if he turned out to be unhinged. Hopefully, his aura would immediately indicate if he was off or not.

"Good morning. Table for one?"

Greeted by a smiling hostess, I was informing her I was meeting someone when a man at a table near the rear stood and waved, grabbing my attention. "I see my party."

Clearly intent on doing her duty, the hostess escorted me in the gentleman's direction.

I extended a hand in greeting. "Mister Owenslee?" We'd texted one another that morning, indicating what we were wearing to make recognition easy. The hazel-eyed, brown-haired man in his mid-fifties, sporting a green-and-white checkered shirt and blue jeans, fit the expected description.

"Good morning, Miss Edwards." Tall and solid, he offered a firm handshake. "Have a seat. Please." He exhibited old school chivalry when holding my chair for me.

"Thank you. I hope you haven't been waiting long."

"I haven't, but even if I had, the importance makes it worth it. Why don't we order before broaching our discussion? Conversations like this are best served with coffee."

"Agreed." I consulted the menu, deciding that, so far, he was sane and there were no red flags.

Moments later we'd placed our orders and sat sipping cucumber and mint iced water.

I wasted no time diving in. "Thank you again for meeting me today, Mister Owenslee."

"Call me Gregory, or Greg. You're sure I can't reimburse you or contribute to the cost of your airfare? I know firsthand how expensive last-minute flights can be, Miss Edwards."

I'd secured a same-day round trip ticket on a discount travel site at a reasonable price, but the economics were secondary. I somehow sensed he was testing me. "Thank you, but no. And call me Zoe."

"Absolutely. Zoe, I don't wish to be offensive, but what is your motivation in this?"

I appreciated his directness and explained again, as I had during our initial conversation, my search for a possible missing ancestor.

"And you have no other hidden agenda now that my grandfather has passed?"

That confirmed my earlier sense of being tested. "Mister—"

"Gregory," he reminded.

I nodded. "Gregory, I'm not a casket-chaser and solely wish to connect missing dots in my family tree. I am without any ulterior *or* monetary motives."

He began speaking only to fall silent when our server appeared with my peppermint tea, his coffee, and a promise that our food would be ready soon. He waited until we were alone before continuing. "I apologize if that was offensive, but my grandfather's death hasn't been easy on my family. Henry Owenslee was a hard man raised the old school way, but he was my grandmother's rock and she's having a hard time without him. So, I admit to being overly cautious." He paused to stir creamer and three packets of artificial sweetener into his cup before staring at me as if weighing whether or not I was trustworthy. "Are your grandparents living, Zoe, and do you share a loving relationship with them?"

"Yes, and yes."

"Then you understand my hesitation." He blew against the steam rising from his cup before taking a cautious sip and exhaling slowly. "My grandmother's up in years. She hasn't been in the best of health lately, and seems to be rapidly declining since Grandpa's passing." Grief briefly registered on his face. "I'm the oldest grandchild and very protective. I've no idea how much time Grandma Martha has left on this earth, but she's a phenomenal woman and I wouldn't blink twice at doing whatever necessary to keep her content in her last days. That includes barring her from anything or anyone I consider dangerous."

I added honey to my tea and enjoyed its peppermint warmth before responding. "Sounds like our love of our grandmothers runs along parallel lines." I leaned toward him. "I'm an educated, church-going, law-abiding citizen, but mess with my grandparents?" I sat back. "I promise you I'll lose my religion."

He chuckled heartily. "Let's pray life never comes to that."

"Amen."

His smile slowly faded and he shook his head as if disgusted. "You'd be amazed by the crackpots coming out of the woodwork wanting something since Grandpa Henry passed. If it isn't charities or churches asking for donations in the name of our 'beloved deceased,' it's distant relatives—some we didn't even know existed—calling for handouts. It's gotten so bad we've instructed my grandmother to let all calls go to the answering machine." His disgust gave way to a half-smile. "Yesterday, a cousin five times removed requested two thousand dollars to help pay the taxidermist for preserving her pet possum."

I rapidly stirred my tea and pressed my lips together in an effort to keep from laughing.

"It's redneck ludicrousness. And it's okay to laugh, Zoe. God knows I did."

I let loose with an unladylike snort that caused us both to chuckle.

Our shared mirth seemed to clear the air. When he continued, he'd visibly relaxed and his frankness indicated he'd decided I was trustworthy.

"Folks would think Grandpa Henry was wealthy with all the kooks coming out the closet. He wasn't poor, but rich he wasn't. He was a veteran who served his country, and retired after working fifty-plus years at the same factory. Whatever his net worth, it's to be protected for Grandma Martha, my mother, and her siblings. But, again, I apologize for lumping you in with crackpots trying to hone in on Grandpa's pension." His smile was sheepish.

"It's water under the bridge," I offered as our server arrived with my turkey-bacon omelet and cranberry-orange scone with a ramekin of lemon curd, and Gregory's ham and spinach quiche.

He surprised me by saying grace, and we enjoyed a few moments eating in silence before I posed a question.

"How long were your grandparents married?"

"Grandpa passed two weeks before their seventy-eighth wedding anniversary."

I nearly dropped my fork. *"Seventy-eighth?"* I'd barely made six with Vince. "What a blessing!"

"Indeed, especially since Grandpa wasn't the easiest person on earth." He chuckled lightly. "Our family's running joke is Grandma Martha has two halos. Between that and keeping Grandpa supplied with her pecan pie, she managed that man just fine." All traces of laughter fled; his face grew serious. "They were both old school in that their relationship wasn't overly demonstrative, yet I never doubted my grandparents' mutual devotion. Now, there's this . . ."

He passed a napkin over his mouth before grabbing the leather satchel I'd noticed atop the chair beside him. Unlatching it, he reached inside and extracted a three-ring binder that he placed in his lap, propped against his chest, as if protecting invaluable content. "When you see this, you'll better understand my previous concern. There's no way around it," he added as if to himself while opening the binder and extracting two documents in plastic-sheet protectors. "Plus, we need answers."

I accepted the documents when he turned them for me to read and forgot all about my breakfast. I skimmed them quickly and glanced up at Gregory, only to slowly read them again.

They were marriage certificates: one dated April 1935 and the other July 1940. Henry Richard Owenslee was listed as the groom on both; but the names of the women differed. The latter bride was Martha Sue Rutherford. The bride on the first certificate? Faith Joy, conceivably the younger sister of my ancestor. "Wait. This doesn't make sense."

"My sentiments exactly. My grandfather having multiple marriages—and a secret one at that—has thrown my family into a tailspin. Maybe he and Faith married, perhaps rashly, thought better of it, and terminated it quickly?" he rushed in a hopeful, almost pleading tone.

I didn't correct Gregory's misunderstanding of my outburst. If Henry Owenslee and Faith Joy were married in 1935, that meant the *older* sister, my look-alike, whom I'd dubbed Baby Girl Miss Me was actually *Faith*. Not the other way around. In hindsight, the younger sibling being nicknamed Baby Girl made perfect sense. Not only had Nana Sam erroneously offered the name Faye, but she'd mixed up which sister was which as well.

Perusing that marriage certificate, I felt a sweet clarity settle into place as I softly affirmed her identity. "Faith. Joy." Like music, her names flowed from my mouth as my fingers trailed over the paper, coming to rest on her signature—further proof of her existence, a tangible witness that left me feeling emotional. Connected. Gregory sat quietly, respecting the moment until, with a long calm exhale, I relaxed in my chair and looked at him. "What was her last name?"

He shook his head. "I'm clueless and hoped you could help with that."

"I wish I could, but can't," I murmured while fingering that plastic sleeve with the same care I'd show any museum artifact. The paper seemed ancient, yet intact except for the space where Faith's surname should have been. The only distinctive marking was a partial, capital "V." The rest was illegible, as if water damage or age had greedily devoured it. I breathed through the disappointment by embracing the fact that I'd been gifted another step in this voyage. "Do you mind my having a copy?"

"I figured you'd want one," he allowed as I returned the documents. "I'll check with my family to make sure they don't object . . . but I'm still trying to understand all of this. You're certain you've never met, or don't otherwise know, the Faith on this marriage license?"

I confirmed that.

He massaged his brow as if warding off a headache. "Can I tell you how we came across this certificate?"

"Please do."

"My mother is my grandparents' oldest child, and has power of attorney for them."

I listened as he explained his mother's sorting out her deceased father's business the prior week, and coming across an old family Bible in the process. "Grandpa had a trunk in the attic that held his prized possessions. Mom had me bring it down so she could go through it." Inside were his grandfather's military uniform and tags, old albums, and other memorabilia. Including a Bible between the pages of which was Henry and Faith's marriage license.

"Calling us floored *and* confused would be the understatement of the century, Zoe. The family's still in an uproar over this."

"I can only imagine. Was your grandmother able to offer any clarity?"

"We haven't approached her with it. My mother and her siblings never heard of another marriage and assume Grandma Martha knows nothing of it either. Whether she does or not, considering the state of her health, we're reluctant to broach the subject and cause her possible distress. Doing so would be a last-ditch effort on our part if nothing else pans out."

I understood them not wanting to upset their matriarch, but I also wanted answers.

Our server appeared, seemingly out of nowhere, to ensure we had everything we needed, interrupting our conversation. When he left, Gregory immediately continued.

"We've researched county records and found zilch." He unknowingly answered my unasked question. "Nineteen thirty-five was a lifetime ago so either the records are lost or were never on file." He shrugged. "I was starting to give up and then you called."

"I have nothing enlightening to offer . . . only this." Retrieving my messenger bag draped across the back of my chair, I withdrew that photograph of four young people from eons ago, kept safe in my portfolio, and handed it to him. "Can you identify any of them?" The lightness of his eyes was the same as the boys' in the photograph; still, I wanted confirmation.

Taking the photo, he sank back as if the wind had been knocked out of him. A bevy of emotions swept over his face. His eyes watered; his mouth hung open. A moment passed before he spoke again. When he did, his voice was thick. "That's my grandfather and his younger brother."

I sat silently as he snatched a napkin from the table to staunch the onset of tears.

He studied the picture at length. "He was a good-looking son of a gun, but even here his hard edge was clear. This photo is amazing." He looked at me. "Where'd you get this?"

I gave him an abridged version of Nana Sam's photo coming to me via her grandson, JeShaun Halsey, and her identifying its subjects. "I never knew this photograph existed. Now, I'm consumed by it."

Gregory's focus returned to the photo. I saw the moment his

gaze shifted from his grandfather to where Faith Joy and Baby Girl were positioned.

His gaze narrowed before widening and darting toward me. He stared while uttering, "Your resemblance to Faith is uncanny. It's like you're her, but here and now, in a different time of her life. Were you unnerved when first seeing this?"

"Incredibly." I tended to be a private person who didn't readily divulge personal business, and might not have shared as much under normal circumstances. But that photograph and our forebears connected us, which allowed me ease in sharing my mother's story.

Gregory swallowed a bite of quiche before asking, "So . . . you believe Faith is a missing link in your mother's biological lineage?"

"I do, and thank you for giving me a new piece to this puzzle. May I ask you something? Were you surprised when meeting me, and when seeing Faith in this photo, to know we're African-American?" I gathered from the way he set his fork on his plate and sat chewing his bottom lip that he was cautiously formulating a response.

"Excuse my language but, *hell yes.*"

Our quiet laughter floated gently.

"I'm not defending him or making excuses, Zoe, but my grandfather was born and raised in the deep South at a time when social inequities were not just part of hard hearts, but—as you know—upheld legally. He was an old school Bible-thumping, outspoken Oklahoman with politically incorrect views. So, yes, learning that he was married to an African-American woman is mind-boggling."

Downing the last of my tea, I stared at a point in the distance. "Interracial unions couldn't have been easy back then. Maybe race contributed to the dissolution of Henry and Faith's marriage." I refocused on Gregory when he agreed. "Your search of county records didn't produce proof of this marriage, but what about a divorce decree?"

"That was equally non-existent and, in a way, more important."

My brow lifted. "You want the divorce decree in order to con- firm that your grandfather wasn't married when he exchanged vows with your grandmother, I assume."

He slowly nodded while eyeing the photo. "She was a lovely girl and I can understand why my grandfather was attracted to her, but I'd hate to discover he was a bigamist, and that my grandparents' union—not to mention their offspring—was illegitimate."

We sat silently a moment before I muttered my thoughts aloud. "I wonder if we'd have better success looking for birth records? What if Faith and Henry had children?"

"If they did, we could have common relatives somewhere."

"And possible heirs who could lay claim to an inheritance?"

He cleared his throat and looked away before sighing. "All of this is a lot to swallow, but it could be that my family and I will have to prepare for that possibility."

I put myself in his place and wondered how I'd feel if some unknown person popped up claiming to be my sibling resulting from either of my parents having other relationships. "Gregory, thank you."

"For?"

"I value that you're wrestling with this discovery, yet you've approached me in a protective mode versus being hostile. I appreciate that."

"My being antagonistic won't help either of us. I prefer to partner in piecing this thing together, rather than treating you like an enemy."

"Same, but other than those photographs, I essentially have nothing to offer. What about your grandfather's brother? Can he shed light on the matter?"

"I don't have a relationship with my great-uncle." He shifted in his seat uncomfortably. "I know it's him in this photo only because of another picture I found at the bottom of Grandpa's chest. Whatever happened between them, my grandfather and his brother were estranged long before I was born. We weren't allowed to ask questions or say my great-uncle's name in his presence. As far as Grandpa was concerned, he never existed."

I was disappointed, but could relate seeing as how my grandfather had tucked his early days in some secret place. I pierced my scone with my fork, feeling opportunity slip away. "So, you've never met him?"

His eyes sparkled as he held up a corrective finger. "Not yet but, thanks to Mom, I plan on correcting that." Apparently, his mother had inherited her father's stubbornness gene and was all about family. When her father passed, she felt his brother had a right to know. With the help of relatives, she'd located and reached out to him. "He didn't attend the funeral, but he did send Grandma a nice bouquet and his condolences. I've spoken to him on the phone. He reminds me of Grandpa, but on the gentler, kinder spectrum."

I leaned toward him. "Do you think he'd be willing to talk to us about this marriage?"

Gregory grinned. "I hope so and intend to contact him. Hold on please," he cautioned when I started wiggling like a happy kid at Christmas. "Uncle Micah is in Arizona visiting one of his daughters. *And*, he doesn't have a cell phone. Which is why I haven't discussed this with him yet. I'll do my best to track down his daughter's number. If I can't, our getting answers may be delayed until he returns."

I sat at the airport waiting on my departing flight, absent-mindedly people-watching while processing my meeting with

Gregory Owenslee. He was kind. Direct. He'd been honest about his family struggling with the appearance of this marriage certificate linking Henry Owenslee to a woman other than their matriarch. I prayed he'd approach any revelations his uncle provided with fairness.

I wish him good success in tracking down his cousin's contact . . . and with whatever comes next, I thought while watching a little girl chase down a small, runaway ball and scamper back to a woman I presumed was her mother. I smiled at her cuteness while wondering why Miss Faith Me married Henry Owenslee. By all accounts, he sounded like a difficult person. Even racist. How in the world did their marriage come about? Were they in love? What led to their separation, and did they actually divorce?

I had many questions and zero answers. Just the same, Miss Faith Me became even more substantive. She wasn't a mere phantom figure caught in a picture, but a young woman with definite, defining experiences. And I wanted to know more about her, and them.

Something hitting the side of my foot brought my thoughts out of yesterday. Seeing a Hot Wheels car resting against my shoe, I looked up to find a little Latino boy standing several feet away, looking uncertain. He was a cutie patootie with his huge brown eyes, dark curly hair, and angelic face.

I picked up the toy, wondering if my son would've had tiny cars like this, if he had lived. I'd endured a season where the mere sound of a baby crying or the sight of a child could reduce me to an avalanche of tears, even jealousy and resentment.

Grief and healing are works in progress, and each day they can look different. Just be open to however they manifest.

I thought on my therapist's words as I extended the toy to the child with a soft, reassuring smile, and waited as he glanced at his mother for permission.

"It's okay," she assured.

He approached, hesitantly, grabbed the car from my hand and raced back to hop onto his mother's lap.

"He's shy," she offered apologetically. "What do you say, *mi hijo*?"

"Thank you." His voice was so small, sweet.

"You're welcome." I exchanged a smile with his mother only for a tender pain to hit between my breasts when realizing he was around the same age my son would have been. I averted my gaze and took a deep, calming breath as other children came into focus. The girl who'd chased her ball. A set of twins twirling in the aisle, exerting energy, falling down laughing. There were little people seemingly all about me. Seeing them brought me joy. And soft sadness.

I'd been a mother once, but never again.

I dabbed an unexpected tear forming in the corner of my eye.

I miss Jaelen.

FIFTEEN

FAITH

Outside of marrying Henry, that first night in Los Angeles was the worst experience of my whole existence. Being out there alone with my baby sister was beyond frightening and I had to fight the urge to break down crying. Clearly, I'd done something to upset heaven. Trouble was stalking me to no end, but I couldn't figure out what I'd done so I could repent and get on God's good side again.

Walking down a wide boulevard, I let Hope ride on my back as if she weighed nothing despite my exhaustion; partly because she was equally tired, but also because her warmth gave me stability. Her arms about my neck were anchoring, helping me feel connected to myself, family. My sanity. I was all Hope had and couldn't afford to go crazy. I needed all my good sense to keep us safe, and to face whatever came next on this tempestuous journey. I'd learned about Odysseus and his odyssey last year when Miss Bullocks made it assigned reading for the upper grades. I'd found it thrilling, adventurous. But God knew I didn't want to be wandering those Los Angeles streets nobody's decade like the king of Ithaca.

Ain't nothing mythical in this.

Carrying Hope, it was all too real. Her rumbling belly reminded me that hours had passed since we'd shared that Louisiana Dog. I prayed she wouldn't ask for something I didn't have to give. We had neither means, nor money and that was enough to make me consider desperate deeds so my sister wouldn't suffer behind my foolishness. She must've been too scared out there to utter one hungry complaint; she merely burrowed her head against my back and tightened her arms about my neck. I hurried along knowing we needed to eat, but focused on the larger need: a safe place to sleep.

There's an easy fix. You can go back.

Back to Old Aunt Spinster's house. And Henry.

Maybe I'd have more sorrow than joy, and a marriage that wouldn't amount to much. No freedom. Singing when, where, and whatever I was commanded—like how Mister Owenslee had demanded at the migrant camp. I'd never get to become my own woman, winding up dry as Miz Lucy, haggard, stiff, and unloving. So much sacrifice was attached to turning back but, out there quaking in my shoes on those big city streets, I wondered if I should've stayed and prayed for someone to hire me on that corner today so I could earn desperately needed money. I could've paid Miz Lucy's list of debts, and even stomached sleeping on the back porch on a hard pallet and being treated with contempt.

That's better than this.

My steps slowed and I turned about, ready to return the way we'd come. God knew what kind of humiliating treatment I'd face for running off, but if humbling myself to the Owenslees' twistedness was what it took to keep my baby sister fed and safe, then I'd willingly eat crow all day.

But I'd be married to Henry.

He ain't the right kind of person to be a good husband.

Micah's dismal words rolled through my head, worse than bad omens. Henry's being inclined toward violence. His multiple girlfriends. That wasn't Micah trying to shine a bad light on his brother. He was warning me and I had good reason to believe him.

"You done stepped in a cow patty, Faith," I quietly lamented.

"Huh, Faye-Faye?"

"Nothing, Baby Girl. Just talking to myself . . ."

"Papa said that's ok to do unless you answer back."

I was too lost over being fool enough to let Henry kiss me to even smile at Papa's humor. But kissing was one thing. Laying up under Henry letting him "bust" me open, and surrendering my "peach" whenever, however he wanted left me with a vision of myself: tears streaming, vacant-eyed, head turned away from his thrusting into me, feeling more lost and used than I'd ever dreamed. That alone had me reversing my direction *yet again* and heading wherever the night sky led.

I glanced up, remembering tales of the North Star guiding slaves to freedom but, despite my trying, I couldn't find it. I had to trust my own feet and, after the mistakes I'd made, that wasn't easy. Still, my only option was forward. I had to outrun Henry and keep him in the past. I didn't want to be like Granny, doing what she had to, conceiving Aunt Leola, to save our land.

Mama said each generation should do better than the last.

I didn't have land to keep and didn't want a cruel husband or his beige babies to remind me of my stupidity. That was enough to keep my feet moving in a forward direction.

That strange city was stranger by night. Shadows loomed thick, threatening. Sounds were sharp, disturbing. A group of mangy alley cats knocking over a garbage can brought me close to screaming. I quickened my pace when hearing men laughing in the distance, feeling desperate enough to even consider finding the police. Except Papa had taught us to avoid the law at all costs. Back in Wellston, Sheriff Dodd headed up the Klan, wearing a badge by day and the Klan's white hood by night. He rarely lifted a finger if and when Colored folks came to him with complaints, brushing things under the rug, minimizing whatever the grievance. He'd even jailed Old Mister Purefoy when he'd gotten confused and wandered into the white side of town, calling him a threat to Wellston's white women. Someone said Mister Purefoy called Sheriff Dodd a liar. Maybe that's why he left jail five days later with a broken jaw and two black eyes, his injuries reminding Colored folks, yet again, that the law did more harm than good. I had to figure this out on my own no matter the fear choking me, leaving me breathing heavily. Getting off of those streets became my desperate need.

Find the Lord's house.

Mama and Papa had raised us to be God-fearing Christians who found fortitude worshipping in the company of fellow congregants. Our pastor Reverend Coulter loved referring to our small, clapboard edifice as God's holy residence. He preached it so often that Charity and I laughingly called our church a Hallelujah Hotel, "where angels checked in and devils went to hell." If the Almighty didn't mind dwelling in a man-made temple, I certainly couldn't take issue with it. Locating a church where we could hide for the night became my sole objective.

Sadly, all around us were businesses, most of which were closed for the evening. Others didn't look inviting. There were no sanctuaries for stray Colored girls seeking parents, and I knew I had to try something different. Leaving that main thoroughfare, I veered in another direction, carefully noting the street signs so I would be able to find my way back. I strung the street names together in a singsong chant, making Hope sing it with me so I wouldn't forget.

The longer we walked, the darker it became, the less confident I felt. I was ready to concede defeat, admit I'd made a mistake and hightail it back the other way until I noticed a tiny knot of people ahead, outside a small building, bustling about as if shutting down whatever it was they'd been doing.

That building was something other than a house of God, but I thanked the Lord just the same, hurrying toward that handful of folks busily cleaning, boxing canned food, and folding tables that had been in use. I wasn't sure what the "FSRC" printed on a large sign over the door meant, or why the scene brought to mind a newspaper article Miss Bullocks read in class last year, featuring a picture of a long line of hungry-looking people needing assistance. Its heading read *"Will FDR's New Deal Dent the Depression?"* These folks here were on the giving end of whatever charitable work had been in action. Papa was proud and had taught us not to beg or accept handouts; but he was also known to say that hard times made desperate measures okay. Why he didn't listen to his own advice and get us out of Oklahoma before Charity died I wasn't sure and pushed the thought to the corner of my mind as I approached a big-busted, stern-looking woman with wild blonde hair escaping a bun at the back of her neck who seemed to be in charge, based on the bossy way she ordered others about.

"Excuse me—"

"We're finished for the evening. You'll have to come back tomorrow morning," she barked before I finished. "And when you do, go to the left side of the building. That's where we serve Coloreds."

"Yes, ma'am." There was that California Sir James versus Jim Crow again; serving us on the side versus at the back of the building. "What's FSRC?"

"Young lady, I don't have time to educate you on the Federal Surplus Relief Corporation or the wonderful work we do. Simply thank President Roosevelt for his foresight in getting surplus food from farmers all across the country into the hands of the needy . . . like you." That said, she marched inside, slamming and locking the door behind herself and her crew.

I did a truly sophisticated thing and stuck my tongue out at that woman and her high-falutin' ways before heading to the left side of the building, deciding Hope and I would return in the morning for whatever their food distribution.

Provided we don't get murdered first.

Our day had been safe enough but there in the dark, thoughts of that dead girl in the newspaper Henry had tossed at me yesterday suddenly swarmed my mind. I didn't come all the way from Oklahoma to be a victim of God knew what. Maybe I'd been too hot-headed and hasty in abandoning the Owenslees. Perhaps I needed to eat crow, make my way back to them and do whatever they wanted. Weren't they the lesser of two evils, a tolerable concession until I found my parents?

"Faye-Faye, I don't wanna sound like a big baby, but I'm hungry. And I gotta potty."

Hope's lament didn't only interrupt that defeated thinking, it coincided with a sudden sensation. Warm. Wet. Between my legs. "Oh, Lord . . ."

"What's wrong?"

"Nothing. I just need the restroom, same as you." Setting her on her feet, I held Hope's hand as we walked along the "Colored" side of the building, thinking how Mama often reminded us that God didn't like ugly and wasn't fond of fools or falsehoods. Obviously, my body felt a need to make an honest human of me after my falsifying that I was already, fully on my monthly to avoid transacting married business with Henry.

My actual flow was beginning.

I tried not to cry, thinking on how Mama made tea of raspberry leaves, ginger root, and cinnamon for me and Charity whenever we got our monthly; or how she'd rub our temples and press certain places on the bottoms of our feet if achiness got out of hand. Avoiding tears and longing, I rounded the building only to stop immediately when seeing the same folks who'd been up front back here, headed to one of two cars in the parking area. Snatching Hope back with me, I stepped out of view.

"See you in the morning, Pete." That strident voice was easily recognizable as Miss High Falutin's. "And don't be late. Colored folks get up bright and early only when it comes to getting something free."

I disliked the crackling laughter of Miss High Falutin' and her cronies. Clearly, they didn't know squat about Papa and Mama greeting each day before dawn six days a week, except Sundays.

"Yes, ma'am. I'll be here to open the building at seven like always," a male voice promised as doors closed and a car drove away.

I peeked around the corner of the building and found an old, bent-over man—Pete, presumably—shuffling toward a large bin, bags of trash in hand. When he swung both, missed, and refuse rocketed into the air before smashing to the ground, he stood, fists balled at his waist, as if garbage could pick itself up. Taking advantage of his back being toward us as he complained and cussed, I cautioned Hope with a silencing finger at my lips while inching around the corner to the rear door of the small building, intent on getting in and out undetected before he'd finished righting his mess.

We easily found a restroom just big enough for us both. I let Hope go first before making her turn around and close her eyes while I handled my business, wishing I'd borrowed a few coins from Central Station's fountain. I'd have paid it back, eventually; but right then I needed money for monthly sundries, and was forced to do the best I could with what was at my fingertips.

"You finished?"

I answered Hope's quiet question while washing my hands and making her do the same before cautiously exiting the washroom only to be plunged in darkness as the lights went out. I put a hand over Hope's mouth to muffle her alarm, and stood there listening, trying to determine what was happening. The answer was immediate as the sound of a key turning a lock filled the space. I stood like a statue, afraid Old Pete would remember something he'd left behind and return only to find the surprise of a lifetime. I didn't want to be accused of trespassing and have the law called. They wouldn't care about our merely needing the facilities and accidentally being locked in. They'd separate me from my sister, and put us in a home for wayward children. That horrifying thought left me barely breathing until I heard that remaining car in the lot drive away.

We were locked and alone inside the FSRC building.

Air rushed out of me in relief as I stood there, allowing my eyes to adjust to the darkness.

"Faye-Faye, are we stuck here?"

Reaching the back exit, I turned the lock, hoping we hadn't lost our freedom. I didn't want a repeat of that black blizzard cellar, or the containment felt in that mad midnight marriage. Hearing the lock freely click, I answered my sister. "No, we're not." Hand on the doorknob, I was ready to face the night again only to wonder if God had meant for us to be here. If so, it was a gift from heaven I could gladly accept. "Come on . . ."

I felt like some kind of sneaky burglar, creeping back down the hall and into the room it connected with. I left the lights off, not wanting to alert any passersby that we were inside. Instead, I focused on the shadowy outline of objects. A long table. No chairs. A sink and counter. Apparently, we'd entered a small kitchen.

Lord, let it have something for us.

"Stay by me and don't touch anything." Sounding like Mama giving Hope the same instructions she gave us whenever we went shopping, I carefully made our way to the table, on top of which were several boxes. "Look, Baby Girl!"

"What is it?"

I wanted to squeal a praise toward heaven as my eyes adjusted to the dark and found food packed inside those boxes. Apples. Corn. Sweet potatoes. Tomatoes. A few loaves of bread, and what seemed to be jars of pickled okra. Clearly, it was food for FSRC distribution. I grabbed an armful while thanking the Lord and FDR.

Franklin Delano Roosevelt, you're all right by me.

Hope and I sat, backs against the wall, greedily eating our presidentially ordered, government-issued goodies in the dark. It didn't matter that everything was raw. I shucked corn, cleaned those tomatoes with my dress, and ate as if Mama had cooked her best. We even copied the Louisiana Dog man and ate pickled okra bedded in slices of bread before finishing everything off with apples for dessert.

"Faye-Faye, my tummy hurts."

I rubbed my sister's tight little belly. We hadn't eaten so much since before black blizzards gobbled our crops and decimated our livestock. We'd been gluttonous.

If Reverend Coulter were here, he'd rebuke us.

I grinned, remembering how Charity and I would snicker behind our hands whenever the pastor preached against excess, our private joke being that if our beloved reverend found a mirror, he'd have to rebuke his belly for looking twelve months pregnant.

"I know something that'll make you feel better, Baby Girl."

"What?"

"It's a surprise, but you can help gather the husk."

We made a game of finding our discarded husks and corn silk, piling them on my lap. Hope giggled frequently, wanting to know what I was doing.

"Patience is a virtue, Miss Nosey Rosey," I teased. In the dark my task wasn't easy, but I let my hands guide me, using corn silk for hair and binding, and husks for stuffing until finished. "There!" I placed my creation in Hope's hands.

"What's this?"

"Your brand-new Miss Rainy Day." It might've been a poor substitute for the doll Mama had made from fabric found during one of Hope's and my excursions, but it was all that I had in that moment.

Hope's response was a sharp intake of breath. Her voice was excited. "What did you use to make it?"

"The sleeve from my dress." The remainder of which was in Henry's possession. "Now, Mama's with us until we find everyone again."

My sister threw her arms about my neck in a tight embrace. *"Thank you, Faye-Faye!"*

"You're welcome, baby." I kissed her forehead as she sat beside me playing with and singing to her new companion—glad the piece of my dress Henry had thrown at me could be transformed into something sweet.

I grinned, thinking how, come morning light and visibility, Hope's new doll would probably look like, as my big sister would say, "an undignified mass of madness."

My smile faded.

Charity, I wish you were here with us. With me.

I disliked snakes before Charity was bit; now I loathed them. Evil things had me missing my sister and her sunshine-and-satin ways that brightened any room and lightened the darkest of days. I wanted her to be here, to be the oldest again, telling me with all her bossiness what we were going to do and how we'd find our parents. I'd give the world to see her, laugh with her, even fuss and feud with one another. All my wishing couldn't bring my big sister back to earth, so I simply licked the tears sliding down my cheeks into my mouth like a salty tribute.

"There's Faith, there's Hope, there's Charity . . ."

Singing our song's opening refrain, I closed my eyes as

Hope leaned against me, doll cradled in her arms. Moments later she was asleep, leaving me awake with the sounds of my humming and the steady ticking of a wall-mounted clock for company.

You have to get gone by seven, when that man Pete is expected.

The clock wasn't visible in the dark, but I promised myself we'd leave before that trash-thrower arrived, and knew I needed to stay awake to make sure that happened. Intentions were one thing; reality was something other. I was tuckered-out tired and wound up in a tug-of-war of nodding off and jerking awake until sleep ultimately triumphed. Next thing I knew, a rooster was crowing and I was jumping out of bed to run and milk Tillie, while fussing at Charity to get her lazy bones in gear. She merely flopped onto her side, pulling the covers over her head. The smell of ham, biscuits and Mama's buttery grits enveloped me in goodness, encouraging me to hurry about my business. The sooner Tillie was relieved, the quicker I could sit at the breakfast table and lose myself in deliciousness. I was out the door before Charity was out of bed and was halfway to the barn when Henry appeared in the distance, whistling and carrying an overflowing milk pail. Seeing me, he set down the pail and slowly unzipped his pants, smiling lasciviously and exposing himself to me as countless snakes came out of nowhere, wrapping about my feet. I screamed, only for the hard, cold floor beneath my bottom to impress itself on me. I jerked awake and gazed about the strange, dim place where we'd slept and realized I'd lost myself in a dream.

I breathed a sigh of relief that there was no Henry, only for an agonizing, bone-deep sorrow to squeeze my insides. There was no Charity. And I was still without my family.

Papa, why didn't you fight that blizzard to get to me?

Deep inside, I knew Papa did all he could and would've given his life for us if necessary. He'd likely scoured that landscape in his search, leaving broken-hearted and defeated only when it was clear Hope and I wouldn't manifest. That didn't keep me from acting accusatory. I was cold. Cranky. Cramping from my monthly, missing Charity, and highly disturbed by Henry appearing in my sleep. It's shameful to admit, but I let my mixed up and uncharitable feelings roll out onto my little sister, and was less than gentle when rousing her awake and marching her to the restroom. It was ten to seven, according to the clock on the wall; we had to hurry before Pete appeared.

"Why're you being so ornery?"

Ignoring the hurt in Hope's voice, I hurried us from the ladies' room and through the building like two brown mice, pausing only to grab a handful of apples before scurrying out the back and into the morning, feeling lost, in need of a bath, and abandoned. I secured the door as best I could without a key, imagining that man being mystified by the fact that the door wasn't locked the way he'd left it. I'd cleaned behind us as best I could, but traces of our presence were surely evident enough to become an unsolvable mystery for Miss High Falutin'.

Rodents can take the blame.

Pocketing fruit while fast-walking through the parking area, I pushed two apples at my sister as if she was a burden. "Take these and hurry up about it."

She walked alongside me, arms crossed over her chest, refusing breakfast. "Don't be so mean, Faye-Faye."

"Just hush up and take 'em." I shoved them in her pocket.

"I don't like you, Ol' Grumpy. I'm going back with Micah and Henry." She flounced about in the opposite direction, taking that shambles of a doll with her. In daylight, Miss Rainy Day looked like she'd been made in the dark by an eyeless person with two fingers, no thumbs, arthritis, *and* rickets.

"See you later, alligator."

Glancing over my shoulder, I saw Hope had stopped to face me, eyes narrowed, bottom lip poked out before yelling, "You're a musty meanie and I don't like you, Faye-Faye. And I don't like sleeping in closets. Or kitchens. I want my bed, Mama, and flapjacks!"

"So do I, Hope, but do you see me acting like a whiny baby?"

"Take that back."

"If the shoe fits that makes you it." That had her mad enough to throw an apple at me. Picking it up, I wiped it on my sleeve, bit it, and kept moving. "That's one less for you. One more for me."

Shocked by a shrill sound suddenly piercing the dawn, I whipped about to see my sister—eyes closed, fists clenched—screaming at the sky.

"Hope Ann Wilson, shush that nonsense and come on here!" I might as well have been talking to a fence.

Ignoring me, she put all her energy in that scream until she was so funny-colored in the face and shaking that she scared me. Without thinking, I marched the distance separating us and swatted her fanny.

"Quit showing your behind and acting like an uncivilized Philistine." Papa's saying rolled off my lips as if it was mine.

"I'm telling Mama you spanked me!"

"Go ahead, Hope, but you'll have to find her first. In fact, do that. Find Mama and Papa for me. Find Noah. Find Charity." I turned about as if vainly looking for something. "No, wait! Charity's gone and can't come back."

"Yes, she can."

"She can't, Hope! Get it through your baby head. Charity. Is. *Dead.*"

Her tears were instant. "Go eat dinner with the devil, you fat-face liar!" She flung her words like poison darts while letting loose her fists, pounding on me wherever she could reach.

Rage made her stronger than I would have expected, leaving me wrestling to subdue my little sister.

"What's going on?" Clearly, we were too involved with ourselves and missed a car entering the parking area. Bent-over Pete from last night was exiting the driver's side, face scrunched up, not liking what he saw. "What're you two doing out here? We're not open yet." He shuffled toward us as if his feet hurt with every awkward step. "Were you tryna break into my building?"

I didn't care for his suspiciousness and might have felt indignant except Hope was still resisting me and our struggle resulted in the pockets of Old Aunt Spinster's antiquated dress ripping open and apples raining at our feet.

Mister Pete stared slack-jawed at the ruby-red evidence of our sins. "You little thieves! You *did* break into my building. *Police! Police!*"

His hollering scared the cotton out of me. Gripping Hope with one hand and hiking up the heavy hem of that dress with the other, I took off running, trying to escape the possibility of my sister and me winding up in somebody's work field, sledge-hammers in hand, slamming rocks, singing Negro spirituals, our ankles chained to fellow convicts in striped prison gear. We rounded corners, crossed streets, putting distance between us and Old Hollering Pete only to stop when seeing a policeman ahead, buttons shining in the morning sun, uniform starched and pressed.

I did an about-face, whirling Hope and me back the way we came, praying he hadn't heard Old Pete's caterwauling.

"Halt!"

We hadn't been in California three whole days and were about to be arrested for eating fruit from the president?

Feeling defeated, I turned to face my punishment like Papa taught me to. Surprisingly, the officer wasn't coming for us but had crossed the street, blowing his whistle, in pursuit of three youths. Why they were out alone at that time of morning was a mystery. *Maybe they're like us, looking for their family*, I thought as they scattered in various directions. Only the smallest was left behind, separated from the pack: a little, dark-haired boy who couldn't have been more than ten.

"Why aren't you in school?"

Even with the street separating us I could see the child's fear. I wanted to yell at that officer to leave him be. It was barely past seven, and unless California schools started at the crack of dawn, that little boy wasn't hardly in the wrong. Instead, I pulled my sister with me, hiding in a doorway, peeking out as the boy tried his best to communicate in what sounded like Spanish.

"Tell it to the truancy officer, you stupid Spic." Cuffing the little boy by the ear, that policeman marched him up the street to a paddy wagon and, ignoring his wails of distress, opened the rear doors and pushed him in.

Shocked, I moved us deeper into the shadows as the officer started the engine and held my breath—afraid we'd be next— until I heard the sounds of the wagon fade in the distance. I dared to peek only to see that ominous vehicle rolling in the opposite direction. Sighing with relief, I knew Henry was right in saying race hate didn't stay down south. That "Spic" was obviously an epithet and I knew race ugliness when I saw it. I prayed the good Lord would give that little boy all the help he needed and the dress-down that officer deserved.

"That child wasn't hurting nothing or nobody. Stupid California Cracker."

"I'm sorry, Faye-Faye."

I redirected my attention to my sister, wondering why she felt responsible for lawlessness only to see she had wet herself. Again.

"It was an accident." Her voice was tiny, tremulous. "Is that gonna happen to us? Do we gotta get in a wagon and go somewhere?"

Moving her away from the puddle at her feet, I squatted so

we were face to face and put on some bravery, feeling small for the way I'd treated her. "Wilsons don't have time for rolling around in police buggies."

She laughed when I tickled her tummy.

"We're spending this day getting to our family. Okay?" When she nodded, I kissed her head. "But you can't keep wetting yourself."

She tucked her chin against her chest. "I never did . . . before that . . . that . . ." Sudden tears prevented her from finishing.

I wrapped my arms around her, ignoring the smelliness of her release, and rocked her gently as she sobbed against me. "I know, Baby Girl. That black blizzard was enough to scare the piss outta Christmas." I smiled when she giggled. "Next time something frightens you, scream at it the way you screamed at me."

She pulled away, wiping her face. "I'm sorry for yelling like a big, fat diaper baby."

"And I'm sorry for acting ornery and hurting your feelings. How 'bout I forgive you and you forgive me? Deal?"

"Done."

We sealed our agreement and forgiveness with a hug.

"Faye-Faye?"

"Yes?"

"Charity's gone for good, huh?"

"No. She's right here." I placed a hand over her heart. "Can you feel her?"

She closed her eyes, smiling and nodding. "I can even hear her."

"What's she saying?"

"She doesn't like your dress."

Laughing, I took her hand. "That makes two of us. Let's go take care of some stuff." We cautiously moved from our hiding place in the building's doorway, my mind on bathing Hope and somehow securing sundries for my monthly.

Wish I'd grabbed some coins from that Central Station fountain.

Unfortunately for me, I was already in enough trouble with heaven and didn't need to increase God's displeasure by pilfering pennies. And even if I did backtrack, thanks to our fleeing Old Pete, I wasn't exactly sure where we were or how to find the station. More importantly, I couldn't go back. Not after Henry haunting my dream with his snake minions and fleshly needs. Shivering with dread, I forgot about pennies in fountains when I saw a phone booth ahead.

"Lord, it's real need not greed." I glanced around to make sure there were no early morning watchers before slipping into the booth, hoping to find a coin or two. Sadly, the return slot had the same coin-less condition I'd come to California with; the ground was equally empty. I exited that tight space feeling helpless, pathetic, so far removed from plenty and good that the pretty-in-pink woman giving us a nickel yesterday seemed like ancient history.

Los Angeles didn't stretch awake the way we farm folks did. It was simply quiet one moment, bubbling the next. A good hour had to have passed with Hope and me looking out for truancy officers while hunting for solutions to our predicament. My baby sister's soiled, cheesecloth makeshift underwear had been discarded; my womanly situation wasn't so simple.

Mama, now what to do?

After running from Mister Pete and hiding from that truancy officer, I felt on edge, infantile, and uncertain. My mother wasn't there providing clean packets like she normally did for me and Charity. Now, I had to think for myself and my only option was borrowing.

Borrowing's better than stealing.

I felt terrible biding my time until that corner drug store had sufficient customers to cover my presence and intent, but I couldn't think of any other way and solaced myself with the notion that I'd pay it back as soon as I could.

I moved quietly, quickly. Too ashamed to involve my sister, I stationed her at the end of the aisle with instructions to alert me if anyone came near. I busied myself scouring shelves swimming with options. Modess. Sanitary step-ins, or bloomers. Pad-N-Alls, pad and belts. "Lord, what's a Kotex?" More importantly, at nineteen, twenty, twenty-five cents, I couldn't begin to pay for any of them. Still, I grabbed the goods nearest me, intent on stuffing the box beneath my dress when the wrath of God descended.

"Are you buying that?" The question was harmless, his tone suspicious.

I whirled to see a glaring store employee, eyes narrowed with accusation and knowing. "I . . . yes, sir . . . No, sir . . . I mean . . . How much is it, please?"

"Show me what money you have and I'll tell you if it's enough."

I was stuck in a rut and we both knew it. "I just need to know the price, sir."

He stepped toward me, menacingly. "You must think I'm stupid. You don't have a penny or a purpose other than thievery. Stay put while I get the manager."

"Honey, why're you back here?" We both swung our attention to the woman approaching, her voice musical despite wearing the look of a mother irritated with her children. "Didn't I ask you to wait for me up front?"

I'd never met an earth angel until *she* appeared, walking quickly, confidently toward me, looking like salvation with all of her grace and ease, smelling sweet, like strawberries and cream. My eyes stretched wide as she effortlessly slid past the store clerk, positioning herself in front of me. Removing the box from my hand, she replaced it on the shelf, laughing lightly.

"Honey, no, not these. Decent women use *these*. Sir, don't you agree?"

Turning red in the face, he avoided looking at the box of woman's needs she held up for his viewing. "Yes . . . I suppose . . ."

"Would you kindly ring this up for us? My husband is waiting . . ." She took Hope's hand and motioned me while sashaying to the front of the store like somebody's queen. Within moments, transaction complete, we were outdoors and down the street.

I had to walk twice as fast to keep up with the giver of nickels that allowed hot, juicy Louisiana Dogs; the musically voiced butterfly of a woman. Only today her dress was baby blue, not pink. I had no idea where she'd come from or how she'd spotted us at the rear of that store. I simply stared at her profile, my mind whirling as if in a dream, thanking God for divine intervention.

"Stop staring and keep walking. He's probably still looking."

She was correct. A glance over my shoulder showed that store clerk standing on the sidewalk tracking our steps. I faced forward as instructed, stupefied by the miracle of her appearance. Once we'd crossed several streets and rounded a corner, she lit into me.

"I knew it couldn't have been two of you with this same sad dress in the city. You better thank God I saw you through that window and followed you indoors when curiosity got the best of me. Are you out of your mind? I don't care how badly you needed these." She shook the bag at me. "Don't you know Colored kids younger than you are jailed for less? Explain yourself."

"I'm sorry, Missus . . ."

"Miss. I'm not married. That was a white lie. Vivian Shaw. But you can call me Viv."

"I apologize, Miss Viv—"

"I heard that already. Out here about to steal in front of this cutie." Her vexation softened as she smiled down at Hope who stood quietly, watching our interaction. "Would your parents approve of what you were up to? I have a mind to march you both home and tell them."

Just like that, something broke in me and I wound up bawling unexpectedly.

"Sweet Jesus, honey, what is *wrong* with you?"

I was so busy crying Hope answered instead. "We ain't got no home no more, and still ain't found Papa or Mama."

Hope's grammar sounded bad, but so did my sobbing out everything that had happened since leaving home except that ceremony with Henry. Admitting that kind of ignorance was entirely too embarrassing. When I finished dumping our tale of woes on an ocean of tears, I felt drained. Limp.

"*My Lord*. You're out here by *yourselves*? I figured something wasn't right when I saw you on that corner yesterday."

Hope shook her head. "No, ma'am. We ain't alone. I have Faith, and she has me."

"So, I see." Miss Viv stroked my sister's cheek before opening her arms to me. "Come here, Little Miss Faith. You look like you could use a hug and some love."

My crying escalated when I sank into her warmth. "I had . . . plenty of both . . . before black blizzards."

"I'm sure you did. What're you looking at? You've never seen Colored girls in distress?" she snapped at a passerby, before grabbing our hands and hurrying off. "Heaven knows I have enough going on and don't have time for this but I don't ignore little ones in crisis." She continued as if thinking aloud. "Viv, you're crazy for considering this when you *know* Madame dislikes children." She looked back and forth between us before stopping abruptly and exhaling loudly. "You're going to have to do exactly as I say. No backtalk. No acting up. And don't even *think* about stealing nothing, nowhere. Bailing kids outta jail is not my ministry. Understand?"

Hope and I sounded like parrots, chirping, "Yes, ma'am."

"I can't promise you anything beyond today. For now, let's get you something to eat and a bath."

"I'm sorry I stink," Hope apologized, causing Miss Viv to laugh.

"Honey, hush." She glanced at me. "Truthfully? Neither of you smells too sweet. And what is that ... *thing*?"

Hope proudly held Miss Rainy Day up for viewing. "My doll! Faye-Faye made it."

Miss Viv fell quiet before murmuring, "Let's pray it doesn't have rabies."

SIXTEEN

ZOE

"Daddy, what do you think?" I sat in a park beside my father the afternoon after my LA trip, wanting the benefit of his wisdom.

My time with Gregory Owenslee had gifted me Faith Joy's name and the unexpected bombshell of her union with his grandfather, Henry. I never would have linked them together romantically, not based on that photograph in which their posture, positioning, and facial expressions hadn't indicated love, affection, or even friendship. Their captured likenesses read as strangers thrown together for the purpose of a picture. I'd left Los Angeles mystified and intrigued, yet dispirited at not having Faith Miss Me's maiden name to further my search for her. Micah Owenslee, the one person who might provide answers, was in another state out of reach.

"Am I doing the right thing by waiting until I have all the pieces of the puzzle in hand before saying anything to Mama?"

I watched my father watching my mother in the distance, surrounded by loved ones at a family function. My cousin and his wife had christened their beautiful newborn this morning. Now, we were gathered for the after-church celebration and I felt inexplicably heavy. As if underneath a weighted secret I could no longer keep or carry. I was frustrated, tired of walking in the unknown, and needed a second wind to continue this journey. Natasha and Shaun were the only persons privy to my ancestral search. Now, I craved the viewpoint of the first man I'd ever loved.

"Daddy?" I'd pulled my father aside, confiding in him everything that had occurred since encountering photos of Faith Miss Me. I loved my mother to life but, as close as we were, my father knew her best. "Your thoughts?"

Seated on a lawn chair beside me, my father slowly raked a hand down his face before readjusting the hat on his head. "I've watched your mother go through more heartache than a little bit trying to track down her birth parents." He turned to look at me. "Babydoll, you don't know the nights I held her while she cried herself to sleep trying to come to grips with this thing, or became disillusioned when a lead led nowhere. I'm not letting her suffer any more disappointment if I can help it. I'm biased but, yes, Zoe Noelle, you're doing right in waiting for something concrete before telling your mama anything." The loving care he had for my mother was evident in his expression. "Sit on this until you have something solid. If anyone can get to the bottom of this, it's you."

I nodded in agreement, relieved that his perspective aligned with mine. "I appreciate that vote of confidence and I'm glad we're on the same page. I promise you, I'm approaching this with Mama's best interests at heart. Do you know where she keeps the information she's gathered so far?"

"No, little girl, I don't and if you're about to ask me to go snooping through your mama's things save your breath 'cause I'm not doing that."

"Snooping sounds so underhanded, Daddy. I prefer examine. Or investigate."

"Use whatever synonym you want. The results'll be the same if your mama finds my nose where it doesn't belong." He tilted his chin to his chest as if peering over the top of nonexistent glasses. "I'm getting cracked upside the head."

I laughed and leaned over to kiss his cheek. "Mama wouldn't do that to her only boyfriend but if she does, I'll come to your rescue. Please, Daddy." I gave him my best puppy dog eyes and pouted, trying to sway him to my side.

My father laughed, stretched his legs. "I'm as good as dead. Let me see this picture that has you all cold-hearted and unconcerned about your father's welfare."

"Don't be a drama king," I teased, pulling my phone from my pocket only to stop when seeing my mother walking up on us.

"What're you two doing over here?"

"Nothing," Daddy and I answered in unison.

Mama eyed us suspiciously. "You're all huddled up. You must be up to something."

Daddy hopped out of his chair and wrapped Mama in a tight hug, kissing her neck and acting naughty. "I'll show you what I'm up to when we get home behind closed doors."

"Can I get a down payment on that promise?" Mama cooed, batting her lashes.

"I'm good for it, and you know this, Miss Gladys." Whatever Daddy whispered in her ear left my mother's mouth hanging open.

Grabbing Daddy's hand, Mama smiled coyly at me. "Honey, we might be leaving early."

I laughed at her as she pulled him toward the food table, advising him, "Come get some more to eat. You're gonna need sustenance."

I sat there, amused, shaking my head. "Those two're a mess." I watched them, a smile on my face, blessed by their example of a healthy marriage.

Granny, is your marriage with Granddad perfect?

Taking in the scene of relatives spread out, eating, celebrating, I had a flashback of being in my grandparents' kitchen, interviewing my grandmother for a family unit assignment when I was in the fourth grade. Granny had laughed at my question.

Baby, the only perfect person to walk this earth was Jesus Himself, and His name ain't on our marriage certificate. So, no, our relationship ain't nowhere near perfect. Your grandfather and I are two normal people doing our best to show each other love and kindness. Most times that's enough.

Observing my family, I was struck by the number of couples. Young. Old. Heterosexual. One same-sex. Most were married. Some were dating. A couple were long-lived unions joined by commitment, not vows and ceremony. Regardless of the makeup, I was surrounded by dynamic Black-on-Black love.

"We didn't do our best, Vince." I dragged in a deep breath, knowing my failing marriage didn't fit among them.

It's not "failing," Zoe. It's finished.

I wasn't splitting hairs. There was a definitive difference, and I owed myself that truth. As well as freedom.

When're you taking next steps?

I reflected on those divorce papers in my suitcase, knowing the woman in me was ready. It was my unfulfilled mother space wanting to cling to Vince Edwards—ensconced in the past, dreading the future.

A loud burst of carefree laughter intruded on my thoughts. Looking up, I saw a large group of children clustered around my father. He held a huge platter of cookies and sweets overhead, denying little ones' access. They were squealing, pleading, giggling. The whole rambunctious scene brought me joy until a searing pain sped through me at the thought of what a magnificent grandfather Daddy would have been. I scanned the crowd until I found Mama, only to feel that same pain when seeing her holding my cousin's newly christened infant.

They'll never be grandparents.

My mother had flown to Boston to be with me when my son died. She'd stayed a month, putting aside her grief at losing her grandchild in order to care for me. My father had called regularly while Mama was there, demonstrating his brand of concern for us both. Now, where did they fit in amid this prolific family, five-generations deep? Children were everywhere, kissing the day with their innocence and adorableness. Just like I wasn't part of our married-and-making-it pool, I couldn't contribute to my family's continuance or Mama and Daddy's grandparent status. I repositioned my sunglasses over my eyes to hide a bevy of sudden emotions as my heavily pregnant cousin, Layla, waddled over.

"Hey, Zo-Zo, I wanted to ask you something." She plopped onto the chair Daddy had vacated, exhaling loudly, and rubbing her distended belly. She was ten years my junior and I tended to spoil her like a little sister. Seeing her married with a baby on the way brought a tender smile to my face. "I know I should've said something before now and I hope this isn't insensitive"— she took my hand—"but I love the definition of Azizi. I mean . . . particularly since this is my first full-term pregnancy." She'd lost two pregnancies to miscarriage in the first trimester. "Would it be wrong of me to use it for the baby?"

Azizi was Swahili and meant "precious." I knew this because it was Jaelen's middle name.

Her voice was soft, hesitant. "No disrespect intended and I completely understand if you prefer I don't. I can—"

"Layla. It's okay. Do you mind giving me a little time to think about it?"

"Of course! While you're considering that . . . can you also think about being the baby's godmother?" She placed my hand on her stomach, positioning it atop a flurry of motion.

"The baby's kicking?" My voice trembled in awe.

Her smile showcased deep, enviable dimples. "All that fat

mama food I just ate has him on hype." Grimacing, she pressed her belly, manipulating it. "Now he's dancing on my bladder. Let me get to the bathroom before I have an accident." She hugged me and waddled off with my promise to respond to her requests as soon as I could.

I hate that I have to.

I hated that my son wasn't here to rightfully bear his middle name, and—Layla's love of the name "Azizi" aside—that this felt like some kind of morbid tribute to the dead, and that the closest I'd ever get to mothering was as a godparent. That hit hard somewhere between the ribs, leaving me winded and staunching tears.

Just . . . damn!

SEVENTEEN

FAITH

"I'm your aunt. You're my cousin's children, but she was like my sister. She died birthing a baby last week, and you two just got off a train from Oklahoma. Your father's unaccounted for, but we're trying to find him or other relatives. Until then I'm your last chance. Understand?"

"Yes, Miss . . . I mean *Aunt* Viv," I answered, testing the lie in my mouth and sealing her plan.

"What about you, Little Bit? Who am I?"

We both looked at Hope and were rewarded with her, "Auntie Viv."

"Good. Let's get this over with." Our new "relative" grabbed our hands, leading us down front stairs that were far nicer than the rear staircase we'd used earlier when sneaking in. According to Miss Viv, Madame, the establishment's owner, had a "no children on the premises" policy. She'd toyed with the idea of our staying hidden but there were two of us and that couldn't be easily done. "Honesty's best," Miss Viv reassured herself.

Nervousness made me uncertain. Or maybe it was the winding staircase, unfamiliar noises coming from behind the doors of strangers, and this huge, unfamiliar edifice stubbornly clutching onto an opulence fading into better days.

It's still ten million times better than a back porch or sleeping on that FSRC floor.

I reminded myself of that as Miss Viv knocked on the parlor door.

"Who's there?"

"It's Vivian, Madame."

"You may enter." The cultured voice on the opposite side was that of a woman accustomed to the obedience of others.

"Wait here and do not move until I come for you."

Miss Viv slipped into the room and was gone several minutes, leaving Hope and me standing there, alternating between peeking about at our surroundings and pressing our ears against the door, eavesdropping until Miss Viv returned, yanking that door open. Exiting the room, she did her best to finesse our appearance—grooming my eyebrows with her tongue-dampened thumb before vigorously patting Hope's wild hair then mine, eventually giving up. "You two better be glad you're cute. Come with me and don't say one word unless spoken to."

Miss Viv escorted us into a parlor that could only be described as grand. As if magically kept from aging, the room was a splendid oasis. Patterned wallpaper gleamed like pale, pink satin featuring velvet damask; crystal vases bloomed with fragrant white roses. The sun caught the chandelier's glass teardrops, casting prisms of color onto the ebony gleam of a baby grand piano that made me think of Charity and Mama. There was glorious artwork, thick rugs cushioning the spotless hardwood floors, and furniture that looked as if no one had ever been allowed to sit on it. Except perhaps one woman. She sat on the opposite side of the room dressed in a floor-length gown as if waiting for an invitation to some fancy ball or coronation. A Colored woman slightly lighter than Mama, stiffly erect with threads of gray in her silky hair, she brought to mind some far-off ruler, impervious, majestic.

"It's rude to stand and stare. Come here."

I didn't want to go anywhere near that woman looking and smelling like I did, but Miss Viv was already pushing us forward.

"They just got off the train and, other than a quick sponge bath, haven't had a chance to bathe," she explained, only for the woman to make a silencing gesture before searching the small table beside her.

"Where are my spectacles? My eyes are useless without them."

"They're right there." My baby sister, who didn't take to strangers, surprised me by pointing out the eyeglasses dangling from a bejeweled chain about the woman's neck.

"And so, they are." As she slipped them into place, either those glasses made her look like an owl, or her eyes grew huge as she sat back and spent far too much time taking us in. Truthfully, she barely glanced at me before giving Hope what felt like an eternity of her attention. "You look like her." Her voice was thick, soft.

I didn't like that lady's looking at my sister as if seeing some other someone she loved and maybe missed, and wanted to grab Hope and keep her near me when Madame invited her closer. You would've thought Hope smelled like perfume and peaches instead of pee as that woman sat admiring her, running her fingers over Hope's face, smoothing her hair. "I once had a little girl as lovely as you. What is your name?"

"Hope Ann Wilson, and I'm the baby. I'm five. That's my big middle sister, Faith."

"Hope Ann," the woman repeated, ignoring me altogether. "You have other sisters?"

"Just Charity. Some ugly ol' snake sent her to heaven, but I have a brother named Noah like that man with the big boat in the Bible."

The woman smiled as if the muscles in her face were unaccustomed to happiness. "I imagine you're hungry after traveling. Would you like something to eat?"

"Yes, ma'am. My sister would, too."

Madame looked at Miss Viv instead of me. "Ask Nance if there're any leftovers from breakfast. If not, have her prepare something. While they eat, you and I will discuss this rule violation."

"Yes, ma'am." Miss Viv had us out of that salon in a heartbeat, down the hall, and into a large kitchen dominated by a tall, sizable Colored woman in a flowered apron. "Miss Nance, sorry to trouble you but is there any breakfast left?"

"No."

"That's okay. You can make us something."

I wanted to whack Hope's bottom for talking out of turn and telling grown folks what to do.

Miss Nance simply laughed. "And who're you?"

"Hope Ann Wilson. That's Faith Joy, my sister."

"Well, listen here, Little Miss Big, children aren't allowed in this house and we sure don't feed 'em."

"I'm tempted to let 'em starve for getting me in trouble, but Madame gave them permission to eat," Miss Viv inserted.

"*Since when?*" The cook looked us up and down like we stank; and we did. "No, indeed! I don't serve dusty creatures in my kitchen. You wanna eat? Go have a little talk with Jesus and some soap, and come back clean."

Grabbing oranges from a bowl, Miss Viv made us follow her to a space behind the kitchen that might have been a pretty sunroom once upon a when. "Eat these and wait here." She left, muttering, "Lord, this is why I never want kids."

I tried not to let that make me feel bad, but it did. I didn't want to be anybody's burden. Not Miss Viv's, certainly not

Madame's. For all her cooing over Hope, that cranky lady had barely glanced at me, only enough to give me goosebumps. Peeling that orange, I was clear that, whatever her reasons, Madame didn't care for Faith Wilson. Which was fine, seeing as how my pressing business remained getting us to La Grande Station and finding my family, not making friends with a fake queen. I was grateful that Miss Viv had found us in that store when she did, but I couldn't let myself get sidetracked or give up on getting where I was going.

Plus, there's only one kind of house that has a madame and I don't wanna be in it.

My real aunt, Aunt Leola—the one my big sister claimed was fathered by a Native—had solved a mystery for Charity and me after Fanny Hollins came up missing. Fanny was only a year older than Charity, and way too unmarried to have babies. But she did. Two, in fact. That must've been Mister and Missus Hollins's limit because two babies in, Fanny disappeared, leaving her children in the care of her parents. Folks talked Fanny up one wall and down the next, but Aunt Leola explained she hadn't run off and abandoned her babies. The Hollins put Fanny out, naming her unredeemable, set on wicked ways, and "too dumb to make 'em pay."

So that's what she did. Went and worked in a cathouse in Texas to prove her daddy underestimated her intelligence.

I popped an orange slice in my mouth, recalling my aunt's words and wishing I hadn't. I didn't want to wind up like Fanny, caught in a cathouse of customers and immoral traps. Before I could fall into full-blown worry, Miss Viv appeared, instructing us to follow her up the back stairs. Once in her room, she closed the door and leaned against it, eyes closed, exhaling dramatically. "I thought you two were gonna cost me."

I held onto Hope as Miss Viv explained what would be.

"Madame's allowing you to stay the week or until we find your *other relatives*, whichever comes first."

"But she doesn't want children here," I contradicted.

"We have a lucky charm to thank. Madame took a liking to Little Bit." She tickled Hope beneath the chin before heading for a chifforobe in a corner of the small room. "Which is a miracle considering how Madame is fastidiously clean and you both need purifying. Take this." She handed me a simple sheath dress. "You're a little slimmer than me in the hips, but you already got me beat in the breasts. Hopefully it fits. I don't have a thing small enough for you, Little Bit. Oh, well, we'll figure it out." Grabbing towels, soap, and feminine products from a shelf, she herded us to a bathroom at the end of a long hall. "We usually schedule our bath time. Thankfully, most of the day workers are already out, and the night workers are still asleep, but make this quick. Wash yourselves and that scary hair. When you finish come back to my room and we'll see what's next."

Clean, fed, and wrapped in an old chemise from Miss Viv, Hope lay asleep on a floor pallet, cuddling Miss Rainy Day, nearly snoring.

"I'd be exhausted too, if I'd lived a week in your shoes," Miss Viv commented while braiding my hair.

I was capable of doing it myself but back home hair-braiding was a task Charity and I exchanged. She braided mine; I did hers. It allowed a break from chores and gave us a chance to gossip. Miss Viv's braiding let me feel close to my big sister.

"This 'adventure' has been interesting, but we can't quit until finding our family."

"I certainly wish you the best, and I'll help you get to La Grande on my day off. I saw you eyeing Madame's piano. Do you play, Faith?"

I shook my head. "No, ma'am. Only Mama and Charity. Noah was learning, but our piano was sold before he got good."

Miss Viv made a sympathetic sound. "I still can't believe you two made it to California by yourselves."

While eating the sandwiches Miss Nance had prepared, Hope and I had shared more about our lives, carefully omitting that foolishness about marrying Henry, leaving Miss Viv tongue-tied.

"We had the Owenslees." I might not've felt charitable toward them, but I wouldn't discount the help they'd given us.

Miss Viv sucked her teeth. "Honey, please. Those folks were about to make you a modern-day slave." She tilted my head back so we could see each other before adding, "In *every* way."

Thoughts of being touched by Henry had me nauseous as did thinking about the house I was sitting in. I was afraid to ask, but I did. "Miss Viv?"

"Mmm-hmm?"

"What kinda work do you do?"

"I entertain."

"Men?"

"Men. Women. Why?"

I hid my surprise. "Do you . . . like it?"

"I *love* it. It's what I've wanted to do since I was a kid."

I shuddered. "Working in a cathouse's a weird dream for a little girl to have."

"*Cathouse?*" She stopped braiding my hair to stand in front of me. "I don't work in nobody's cathouse. What're you talking about?"

"But you said you entertain, and that there're day workers and night workers and Madame's here."

She stared at me a moment before laughing so loudly that Hope turned over in her sleep. That didn't stop Miss Viv. She kept right on, holding her stomach as if her laughter was too big. "Ooo Faith, honey, you gonna make me wet my pants. In *this* case, 'madame' and 'missus' are the same. It's just some fancy French. Madame's so hoity-toity she doesn't want us calling her 'missus.' Her French foolishness is her way of holding onto her Black bourgeois days when she was rich and 'better than,' and her hotel was splendid enough to give the Dunbar competition." She resumed braiding. "This place went down after her husband died, the stock market crash of twenty-nine, and Colored folks stopped traveling as much, and fleeing the south fell off. That's when Madame turned her hotel into a boarding house. *Not* a brothel." She giggled again. "I entertain . . . I *sing*, at the Dunbar hotel." That explained the musicality of her voice, but not her being out on the street when we met.

"Oh. I heard California's cathouse ladies are taught their trade at special schools." I swallowed hard, remembering Henry's threat to find one so I could learn to please him. "Is that true?"

"Faith, you and your questions're gonna keep me giggling. Who told you that?"

"Henry."

"Who's he?"

My husband, I almost blurted, the notion lovely as chewing glass or sand. "Just somebody."

"Well . . . houses of ill repute exist, but I've never heard of any," she whispered, "sex college."

If I was Charity and Hope's complexion, I would've turned red with embarrassment. I barrelled on instead. "Why were you with the rest of those women looking for work yesterday when you already have a job?"

"That story I told about a cousin-sister dying in childbirth really happened. Except, it was my mother birthing me. I was raised by my grandparents after my daddy's grief sent him off remarrying a woman with six kids disinterested in me, a seventh. My Dunbar pay is pretty decent, but I pick up extra work to send back home to my grandparents. That's why I was out there yesterday: to help my grandparents and to make rent. Now, you know my business."

"Oh. And you still gave me your last nickel?"

"You needed it more than I did." Finished with one half of my hair, she began brushing the other. "And don't you say nothing to Madame about my singing. She despises entertainers and musicians, and thinks I work the night shift cleaning at the Colored hospital. Girl, you have a thick head of hair. Doesn't your mother ever hot comb it?"

"Only for Easter and Christmas."

"When I meet Mae Wilson, I'll ask her to rethink that."

I genuinely smiled for what felt like the first time in forever. "Mama'll like you."

"I'm sure I'll like her, too. Why didn't Miss Mae teach you to play the piano?"

"She tried, but I prefer singing."

"*Really?* Sing something for me."

"No, thanks. I'm not professional like you."

"That's neither here nor there." She moved to the gramophone tucked in the same corner as the chifforobe, put on a record, and hummed a lovely tune. "Do you know this?"

"Only a little."

"It's easy enough. Repeat after me. You'll get it . . ."

Doing as instructed, I tried lyrics that felt at home on my tongue with their bittersweet quality. That business about wanting a man to call my own felt foreign, still I sang every word after Miss Viv without tiring of her stopping and starting the record repeatedly until we sang our way through it.

"You have a beautiful voice, Miss Viv!"

"Thanks, hun. Now, do it alone." She sat on her narrow bed, making me sing with the music, then a cappella.

When I finished, I stared at Miss Viv sitting and saying nothing.

"That was pretty, Faye-Faye," Hope mumbled, half-asleep.

"*Pretty?*" Miss Viv's voice was hushed yet intense. "That was sublime. Your voice is a masterpiece." She put her hands on her hips. "Child, you sing like a woman twice your age with four husbands and thirteen babies. I'm serious," she insisted when I laughed. "Your voice is . . . velvet seduction. Shake your head in denial all you want, but I'ma keep teaching you songs, and you'll rehearse them until I figure out what to do with you and that magical gift."

The hurt of not finding Mama, Papa, and Noah waiting for us at La Grande was tempered only by Miss Viv's compassion. "We can get the word out to some churches in the area as well as folks I know. Don't give up. God works miracles."

Madame was proof. Four days after arriving in her hotel-turned–boarding house, Miss Viv and Hope were summoned to the salon. I was left to sit on the pallet where we slept across from Miss Viv's narrow bed, counting—telling myself I was going downstairs to get my baby sister if she wasn't back before I reached two hundred.

One hundred and sixty-three—

Hope burst into the room, yelling, "Faye-Faye, looka what Madame gave me!"

She ignored the rule about not running and raced to flop onto our pallet, dumping a large gift box in my lap as Miss Viv walked in looking dumbfounded, arms loaded with more glittery packages.

There were children's books. A pearl-handled comb and brush set. Hair ribbons. A yellow-haired, blue-eyed doll Charity and I would've laughed at, and that left Miss Rainy Day forgotten. Lacy socks. Undergarments. Brand-new shoes. And beautiful dresses.

"What's all this?"

Hope could've floated with her giddiness. "Madame needed a new princess."

I looked to Miss Viv for enlightenment.

"Hope reminds her of her dead daughter," she said.

"We can't accept any of it." I was my father's child and too proud to take anything from a high-toned woman. "Don't unbox another thing, Hope Ann. We're giving it back."

"No, Faye-Faye! There's something for you, too."

Miss Viv handed me a boring brown-paper bag with a folded note attached. Opening both, I was treated to a domestic's uniform and the following missive:

You may remain in exchange for your service.

It was Miz Lucy and Henry all over again, telling me my debt and how to settle it. I wasn't having it and stuffed both items into the bag.

"There's nothing wrong with honest work, Faith—"

"No, ma'am, but Madame dislikes me and this is her way of showing it. I already know she won't treat me well if I work for her."

Miss Viv sat on the edge of her bed and watched Hope, so enthralled by her gifts she didn't notice my predicament. "I don't think you have a choice, Faith. Wait, let me finish." She raised her hands to silence my objections. "We're making the best of it, but when I rented this room, it was only big enough for one person and it hasn't grown any since. We can ask for a room for you and Little Bit if you work here. For all we know, your duties may be dusting and mopping, or helping Miss Nance in the kitchen. You're certainly capable of doing that easily."

"What about my schooling?"

"Find a way to fit your chores in before and after."

"I'll be so tired I'll wind up falling asleep in class and getting in trouble with my teacher."

"Faith, think of Madame's offer as something reasonable to occupy your mind and time until reconnecting with your parents. Plus, I don't make enough to support the three of us and much as I like you and Little Bit, I can't do this long term."

I lowered my head, ashamed for acting ungrateful. Miss Viv wasn't but twenty-eight and didn't deserve to be suddenly saddled with two children. "I'm sorry. I'll work for Madame." We sat quietly, watching Hope's happiness until I added, "But I don't wanna clean those rooms at the end of the hall."

"Why not?"

Getting up from the floor, I sat next to Miss Viv and whispered, "They're haunted."

"*Haunted?*"

I described the noises I sometimes heard at night while in the restroom.

Miss Viv laughed lightly. "Honey, this place isn't in prime condition like when it was first built. That's nothing but a symphony of the wind, old pipes, and loud radiators."

I held my thoughts as Hope brought her yellow-haired doll over for Miss Viv to see. I respected what she'd said, but in my opinion those creepy noises sounded less like wind and radiators, and more like weeping women.

EIGHTEEN

ZOE

You have a dynamic support network who love you. Choose at least one of them to share this with. You've put the work in, Zoe. You're ready and more than capable of doing this.

I left the family function at the park that day, citing a sudden headache—which wasn't a lie—only to do something I hadn't in a while. I called my therapist as if in crisis.

A wonderful human with an aura of transcendent peace that I found alluring, she hadn't objected to my intruding on her Sunday, offering instead a listening ear and those words of encouragement that I was ready to do what I hadn't. By the time we disconnected I was at my lodging, seated on the side of the bed, ready to phone Natasha.

She's probably still at the park.

I knew my cousin enough to know that even if she was, she'd make time for this conversation without feeling intruded upon.

"Hey, Siri, call Tasha." I gave my smartphone the command before fear or shame could interfere.

The call went to voicemail.

"Hey, Cuz, call me. It's important."

I tossed the phone on the bed and lay back, staring at the ceiling and reminding myself I was human and there was no playbook on grief or a hard, fast way it "should" happen. Despite commonalties in the core and spirit of every being, grief was experienced differently. It was unique, showing up when, where, and how it wanted. Sometimes with a trigger, or without clear rhyme or reason.

I kneaded my forehead, acknowledging that I'd been triggered by the sweetest of things. Layla. Being engulfed by children at the family function. Even that little guy in the airport waiting area whose car crashed harmlessly against my foot. These moments seemingly stockpiled themselves in the center of my chest, leaving me on the verge of imploding. I'd promptly left the family picnic, telling myself I was drained from the exhibition, managing work back home in Boston, and the ongoing, unsolved mystery of Faith Miss Me. Those were honest, contributing factors, but the hard truth was that avoidance had caught up with me.

"To everything there is a season." Clearly, this was mine.

Pushing up off the bed, I padded to the bathroom and turned on the shower, telling myself I'd lived through the worst and could do this. I'd survived the hits to my sense of worth and femininity caused by Vince's adultery, but this was different. My failure to reproduce again was a blow to my womanhood. Still, I'd experienced that and much more after losing my son. Fatigue. Depression. Sleeplessness. Frequent crying jags that were like menopausal hot flashes in their surprise attack. The pity shown me when returning to work after Jaelen, my co-workers' eggshell treatment. As if anything they did could topple me at any moment. I'd tackled exclusion when girlfriends corralled their children together for playdates, and dealt with jealousy at seeing their fantastic pics from amusement parks and family vacations posted on social media. I couldn't join their conversations about breastfeeding, what diapers were best, remedies for teething, and the challenges of parenting. My son's death had interrupted those experiences, and I'd been immersed in a different world that—in some ways—miscolored my identity if only temporarily. Yet I stood beneath the soothing flow of warm shower water telling myself that what I was choosing to share with Natasha was a fact, not the sum total of who I was or what I could or couldn't be.

"Zo-Zo, I wish you'd told me." The hurt in Natasha's voice transmitted across the phone. "Why'd you carry this by yourself?"

"Because I couldn't speak it." We shared a belief in the power of words so I knew my cousin got it even if my selective silence didn't make sense to some. "I buried more than carried it because I wasn't ready to deal with it yet." I shrugged as if she could see me. "I am now, so thank you for being a safe place for my truth."

"Honey, please." She sniffled as if dealing with residual tears from the sob-fest we'd just had. "We're here for each other. You *know* this. Do you want me to come over? We can watch idiot TV and eat everything sinful that we have no business eating. Calories won't count since we just burned ten thousand of 'em crying."

With my eyes nearly swollen shut from all the sobbing we'd done, it felt good to laugh. "Thanks, Tasha, but I'm exhausted and have big plans with Mother Pillow and Bishop Bedspread."

"Girl, forget sleep. What you need is some therapeutic time with Doctor Dildo."

"And on that note, I'm done."

"Okay. How about Vice Chancellor Vibrator?"

"Bye, Tasha. Your straightjacket awaits." A slight smile tickling my lips, I disconnected, utterly wiped out, recalling my therapist stating during our first session that there would be times when working through grief would feel like strenuous weightlifting. My having just confided in Natasha certainly qualified.

I'm headed to the restroom and then bed.

I'd barely graced the commode with my rear end when the doorbell rang.

"Dammit."

It rang again before I could finish washing my hands. I hurried downstairs, wondering if someone had the wrong address and hoping it wasn't an evening-shift porch evangelist dedicated to saving my soul from hell or bombarding me with proselytizing pamphlets.

I snatched the door open just as the bell chimed a third time only to be greeted by a lovely bouquet of hydrangeas and a delectable individual. The divine mix of man and soft scents from my favorite blooms created a heady elixir that sent my thoughts to Natasha's quips about my need for some "me time" with intimate gadgets.

"Shaun?"

Dressed in jeans and a sport coat with a creamy white button-down open at the neck that complemented his deep, luscious skin, Shaun Halsey stood on the doorstep looking like sweet sin. His locs had been refreshed and styled in intricate rows on his head, but the man bun was gone. Instead, twisted hair fell about his wide shoulders like a soft, black waterfall.

This man is sexilicious.

"What're you doing here?" The moment the words left my lips I remembered the dinner I owed him and that we'd scheduled for the evening. "Oh God . . ."

"Are you okay?"

"Yes, but I completely forgot about dinner."

"Dinner can wait, Zoe. Something's wrong." Concern etched his face as his eyes bored into mine.

I escaped his intense scrutiny by sliding behind the door,

using it as a shield while inviting him in, mindful that dinner plans hadn't factored into my wardrobe choice after showering. I'd barely put anything on, including undergarments. "Make yourself comfortable over there." I indicated the living room and dashed for the stairs when he hesitantly headed in its direction, telling myself I was too grown to be embarrassed until meeting my reflection in the closet door mirror. My eyes were red and puffy. My hair was smashed and disheveled from lying on the bed while talking to my cousin, and my face was washed clean of makeup. In nothing except an oversized, faded T-shirt, and socks that didn't match—one of which had decided to make a hole for my toe—I was a braless, half-dressed hot mess.

"What to wear?"

I'd planned to drag Natasha to the mall and treat myself to a new outfit for the opening night of my exhibition. That hadn't happened yet which left me standing in the closet staring at clothes I'd brought from home as if they could miraculously morph from functional and work-appropriate to nice enough for a night out with Shaun.

"You know what? I choose not to do this."

I was emotionally drained and decided not to falsify that fact. As much as I'd love spending a night in Shaun's company, conversing and further bonding over fabulous food, I needed a raincheck. Exchanging my misshapen shirt and busted-toe socks for lounge pants, underwear, and a tee tapered at the waist with "Melanin Magic" in gold foil letters, I finger-combed my hair after slipping on fuzzy slipper socks, ignoring the urge to pop into the bathroom to apply mascara and lip gloss. Tonight, my real was raw.

I headed downstairs to my guest. He'd removed his jacket and placed it, folded, atop the arm of the sofa where he sat flipping through a magazine. "Shaun, I know I owe you dinner." He stood as I approached. "I apologize, but . . . I can't."

His gaze was intense as he slowly moved toward me, stopping mere inches away. The subtle seduction of his cologne enveloped me as did the warmth of his body in such close proximity. But his gently cradling my hands in his nearly did me in.

"Talk to me, Zoe."

I'd already emptied myself of tears with Natasha, yet I avoided eye contact, afraid that his tenderness would tap my reservoir and cause a resurgence. I studied the living room behind him, focusing on nothing and everything just to avoid looking at Shaun.

"I'm here." It was a sweet, simple reassurance accompanied by his tilting my chin upward so that our eyes met.

Something elusive surged through me. It fluttered about the perimeter of my heart and spirit like gossamer light. It was brilliant. Welcoming. "I . . ." Shaking my head, it was the only word I could offer.

Showing no irritation at my inability to articulate, he asked a question that left me breathless. "May I hug you?" His request held such care and respect. It left me wide open.

You don't know him enough.

Not as deeply as I suddenly wanted to, but his spirit spoke to mine. It enticed me to dive deep, reminded me that sometimes healing required vulnerability. Before my shower, I'd called my mother, electing her as the person I was ready to divulge my truth to in addition to Natasha. But Mama hadn't answered, and I'd left a message. Now, this incredible human being whom I hadn't known long enough to merit the strong sense of connection that I was experiencing had invited me to lay my burdens on him.

He was already aware of Jaelen, so I took a deep breath before slowly confiding in him. "My soon-to-be ex is expecting a baby with his latest female situationship."

He studied me before asking, "What bothers you more? His moving on?" His voice softened. "Or that they're expecting?"

I recalled that day at Natasha's when she'd shown me the

social media post congratulating Vince and Jillian, and my pain being attached to Jillian, not him. She was pregnant, giving Vince what he wanted. What *I* wanted. Vince could move on while I couldn't. My problems and I were left behind. I was forgotten.

I conveyed those sentiments to Shaun, finding myself spilling more than I'd intended, blaming the fact that he'd somehow touched me inside and left me open. "I'm a few months from forty. In today's climate that's not too old to conceive and have a healthy baby. But I can't. Not because of age, but because the sexually transmitted disease my husband gifted me caused infertility." I inhaled until it hurt. "Jaelen was my first and last. I can't have more children."

I appreciated his silent compassion, his not offering platitudes or trite expressions. Instead, he held my hands tightly until releasing one to catch a lone tear rolling down my cheek with the pad of his thumb before inclining his forehead against mine.

"You didn't answer my earlier question, so I'll ask again." His whispered words were warm against my skin. "May I hold you?"

I stepped into his embrace without hesitation. "Please do."

NINETEEN
FAITH

Four months in Madame's service felt like fifty years on a chain gang. She was meticulous, relentless, and ruled with an iron fist. No matter how hard I worked nothing was ever to her satisfaction and, unlike my baby sister, I never earned her smile or pleasure. When not treating me as if I was mentally deficient or didn't understand English, she harped that I was a disappointment, or flat out acted as if I didn't exist. I'd stopped trying to please her, silently doing as commanded in exchange for a roof over Hope's and my heads.

"Miss Viv, look at my hands!" My skin was raw and cracked like some old washerwoman's from scouring countless surfaces with lye and scalding water. Some places even bled, and my knees were stiff from scrubbing floors with a brush. Mops were off limits. "I feel like somebody's sad, black Cinderella."

"Hold on, honey. Maybe your prince is coming?"

I stared at Miss Viv without laughing. Those stupid story books Madame had given Hope were for white girls, not us. "I can't do this. *God,* I want my parents."

Despite regular visits to the train stations and constant inquiries at churches and within the community, I had yet to find them. That failure left me viciously resisting the possibility that my parents had died and we'd become that terrifying thing Mister Owenslee had named us: *orphans*.

"Wherever they are, your parents miss you too, Faith. But they raised you stronger than this, and you *cannot* disappoint them by giving in. I'll talk to Madame."

"No, thanks. The last time you did she added more work and took away my Saturdays off." It was like Moses asking Pharaoh's mercy for the Israelites only for them to wind up having to make bricks without straw. "If you ask her for anything else, she'll have me working Sunday through Sunday and sleeping upright in a corner with my uniform on so I'm ready whenever she rings that daggone bell from hell."

Miss Viv's laugh turned into a cough. "Stop before you make my throat hurt worse than it does."

"Sip your tea."

Seated on the edge of her bed, she obeyed my instructions, cautiously sipping the honey-and-ginger-laced tea I'd brought her, grimacing every time she swallowed.

"When're you gonna visit the doctor?"

"When I can afford to pay an arm and two legs."

"That's not funny, Miss Viv. You've had this summer cold too long and singing six nights a week isn't letting your throat heal."

She waved me away. "I'm fine, Faith. Go'n out of here so I can take a nap and be ready for this evening."

I wanted to protest, but the resistance on her face wouldn't allow that. "Yes, ma'am. Do you want me to bring you anything?"

"Sure. A rich man and some diamonds."

That made me smile despite my fatigue and worries. "I'll check in on you later."

"No need. Just wake me in time to get ready for the Dunbar."

"Yes, ma'am. And by the way, I'm not going back to school when the new term starts next month." I scurried from the room before she could respond.

"Faith!"

Her hollering was followed by a fit of coughing that left me feeling bad but I wasn't going back. Not to Miss Viv's room so she could talk some sense into me, or to that schoolhouse where I didn't belong. Nobody was rich, but most of the other kids arrived every day clean and pressed, with fancy California manners and book smarts that seemed miles ahead of what I'd learned in Wellston. It didn't help matters that RaeLouise was my only friend, and that my clothes came from community welfare bins or were hand-me-downs from Miss Viv that required altering. My sewing skills weren't as good as Mama's and I wound up looking a mighty mess. I was sick of feeling countrified and being laughed at, or going to class so tired from working before dawn and past midnight that I was too fuzzy-headed to focus. Further schooling wasn't in the cards for me. I was licked and accepted that.

But Mama always said for you to attend Colored college.

"Ain't no Colored colleges in California. Plus, what's the point in going just to be an educated maid for somebody like Madame?" I wanted to cry when holding up my rough, dry hands and thinking of the tasks I had yet to tackle that day. Cleaning fireplaces. Washing windows. Hanging laundry. Reorganizing the pantry. Polishing silver that wouldn't be used anytime soon. Helping Miss Nance with dinner for fifteen boarders before rearranging Madame's wardrobe—switching summer clothes with those appropriate for autumn. No school might mean I'd have a minute to breathe and, perhaps, feel more like myself and less like a servant. "Working the farm was a picnic in comparison," I fussed as I entered my favorite room.

Soft yellow walls, gleaming hardwood floors, a four-poster canopy bed, and all the finery one expected in the room of a child with well-to-do parents beautified Hope's domain. The room was pristine because I kept it that way. If left to Hope, the dolls and stuffed animals who'd become her best friends would be tossed here, there, wherever she dropped them. I'd swatted Hope's behind more than once for leaving toys on the floor and getting saucy-mouthed when asked to pick them up. She was so doted on by Madame that she'd started putting on airs, and I'd had to remind Hope that I was Madame's housekeeper not hers and that *she* was a Wilson, not nobody's snooty princess.

"This child has too much."

Picking up a stuffed rabbit, I placed it in the menagerie of fuzzy, inanimate animals on the window seat. Miss Rainy Day had long ago been relegated to a trash bin at Madame's insistence. When she wasn't looking, I'd fished it out long enough to detach that sleeve from the crumbling corn husk, determined to keep a piece of something Mama had once touched.

Glad Madame had taken Hope to the park, I sat on her bed, smoothing her soft, fine linens that felt too luxurious. I wasn't envious, just suspicious. How could an evil person like Madame give good gifts to one sister while treating another with brutal indifference?

I'd be on a pallet in the attic if my sister hadn't insisted.

The room had been gifted to Hope only. My presence was never intended. My baby sister cried and pitched such a fit, not wanting to be by herself, especially at night, that Madame relented. I was allowed to sleep beside my sister's bed on a pitiful cot, but my belongings were forbidden, left in Miss Viv's room as if contaminated. What Madame didn't know was that Hope couldn't fall asleep unless I lay in bed with her, or she crawled onto the cot with me.

Faye-Faye, sing me something or tell me a story.

I'd make anything up on the spot or sing a song from back home, and weave stories of The Wonderful Wilsons whose children bore stark resemblances to me and my siblings. Some nights I opted on reciting family facts, drilling names and dates into Hope's memory. It was my way of—considering Madame's increased influence over her—making sure Hope didn't forget her origins. After she was fast asleep, I'd slip from bed and finish whatever chores required my attention.

"Oh, Lord!"

The thought of chores reminded me I'd stopped to see to Miss Viv without hanging Mister Orville's laundry. Laundering for other tenants put a little change in my pocket periodically. I wouldn't get paid if Mister Orville came home from work tonight and his clothes were still wet. That sent me hurrying for the back stairs that Madame insisted I use.

Leaving the third floor behind me—the female-tenant-only floor—I raced downstairs without pausing on the second-floor landing. The second floor was designated for male boarders, and last month a couple had been evicted for kissing in its stairwell. I couldn't afford that and kept moving until I reached the bottom landing where a low, mournful sound slowed my progress.

The weeping women.

I'd told Miss Viv about the ongoing noises she attributed to an old hotel, wind, and radiators. It was a hot August day with no breeze or need for artificial heat, and still I heard the sound of women weeping.

"Miss Viv's never around when it happens." I'd frustrated myself trying to get her to hear what I heard. By the time I got to her the crying ceased, or it occurred when Miss Viv was at work. Today was another such instance. I was downstairs and Miss Viv was in bed sick as the walls wept. Accustomed to the phenomenon, I stopped in the stairwell and pressed my ear against the wall housing the pain of phantoms only to realize the sun was still out. That messed with my courage, knowing it was daytime, because I'd only heard the crying at night prior to this.

Spookiness belongs in the dark, not the day.

I rushed out the back door to the laundry basket waiting on the grass, humming to myself in order to suppress the eerie sense that the walls wailed for attention.

"Come on now, Faith, and help me do this."

"Miss Viv, you need to stay in bed." I didn't like how she looked. Her skin was clammy, her breathing was funny, and her face and neck seemed puffy. "You might have an infection."

"I don't have time for infections. I need to get to work and earn some dollar bills."

Ignoring her, I gently touched the side of her neck. She tried hiding her reaction, but she winced, and her pain was clear. "I can call the Dunbar and tell your boss you're ill, Miss Viv, but you can't go in."

"Who made you the adult and me the half-woman?"

"That cough and fever."

Ignoring me, she forced herself up and stumbled trying to take a step. Thankfully, I caught her before she collapsed. "Hard heads makes soft behinds," I mumbled, helping her back into bed.

"I heard that."

"Yes, ma'am. Who do I ask for at the Dunbar?"

"It's not so simple, Faith. This isn't theater. I don't have an understudy."

"Even if you made it there, your voice is so raspy you can't sing nothing."

"Did you hear what I just said? If I don't show up, if the band doesn't play, I lose a night's pay. Or worse, my job. Plain and simple, Faith, baby."

Her ragged cough was so loud I had to wait for it to end before daring, "I can be your understudy."

We stared at each other a moment before a smile tickled her lips. "Lord, I *love* a thinking woman."

"I'm not a half-woman anymore?" I teased.

"Not after that brilliant suggestion."

Next thing I knew, I was in motion, following instructions, pulling items from her chifforobe until a complete outfit was assembled.

"It might prove tight in the bust, but it should fit the hips." Miss Viv eyed the rose-colored dress with spaghetti straps and layered, 1920s flapper-style fringe. "Ooo, I'm excited to see you in it. Go wash up and we'll do something with your hair."

Bathed and back in Miss Viv's room, reality hit me across the head. "I can't do this."

"Absolutely, you can," Miss Viv insisted, looking weaker than when I'd left, yet excited. "You know practically every song on our roster, and can sing them as good, if not better, than me."

The knowing part was true. Music was medicine to my soul and I loved playing Miss Viv's gramophone in stolen moments, or being her audience when she rehearsed. She might've been humoring me, but she often took my suggestions on inflection and phrasing. On one of my Sundays off, she'd taken me to band practice after church and I'd sat in a corner of the room humming along, knowing the lyrics to every tune. Her claiming I sang them better than she did remained to be seen.

"Miss Viv, I can't go in the Dunbar's nightclub. I'm only sixteen."

"Nobody'll know unless you tell 'em cause that figure reads *full* grown woman. I'll write you a note. Give it to Smitty. He'll know what to do and he'll definitely take care of you."

I'd met Mister Smitty, the bandleader, at that rehearsal that seemed ages ago. He was a jokester, but nice enough. "What if Madame looks for me?"

We had to wait out another coughing jag. Her voice was

further strained, breathless. "She won't. Not after a day at the park with Little Bit."

Any outing with Hope guaranteed Madame's sequestering in her room and not appearing until well after noon the next day. "And what about Hope?"

"Ask Miss Nance to stay with her until you get back."

"What about my hands?" I displayed hands dry and cracked from drudgery.

"Put on some salve and my elbow-length black satin gloves."

"But I—"

"Faith, it was your idea but if you've changed your mind, it's no problem." She pushed the covers off her legs as if ready to get up.

"No! I'll ... do it."

She smiled weakly. "Honey, you got good sense. Get dressed."

When finished, I sat on the bed so Miss Viv could fix my hair and paint my face with her cosmetics. "Don't make me look like no harlot."

"It's only a hint of color, Faith. I don't want men looking at you too hard or getting ideas."

"Am I gonna be safe?"

"Smitty and the boys'll be there." She chewed her lip as if thinking. "Hand me that cigar box at the bottom of my chiffo-robe. And be careful with it."

I stood wide-eyed when the box was opened.

"Faith, meet Bertha and Beulah. Which is your pleasure?"

"Miss Viv, I can't be walking around with no gun or some switchblade!"

"You're not leaving this house without one. The Dunbar is reputable, but I've performed in places where Beulah and Bertha were my necessary friends. Better to be safe than sorry, so pick."

"Beulah ... I guess." Feeling too grown up, I strapped the

switchblade to my thigh with Miss Viv's garter belt while she issued additional instructions.

"Don't go anywhere. Don't speak to anyone. Straight to the Dunbar and back."

"Yes, ma'am, but I don't think I'm right for this."

"Honey, your voice is exquisite—"

"Miss Viv, I ain't fancy like Ethel Waters or Fredi Washington. This is LA. Not Wellston." I couldn't possibly sing for California audiences dripping with jewels and swaddled in furs. I was an Oklahoma girl. My gift was suited for small, clapboard churches filled with hardworking, humble folks earning a living with their hands, herding livestock or tilling soil; who caught the Holy Ghost on Sundays and shared meals on outdoor picnic tables when service concluded. "I ain't like you. I ain't glamorous or polished."

"Use 'ain't' again and see what happens," Miss Viv threatened. "My throat is bothering me too much to keep fussing with you. Do it or don't, Faith. It's your choice, just know you won't be the first person to take the stage scared, and you won't be the last."

"Were you afraid the first time you did?"

"Honey, hush! I was so petrified I threw up. But I went back the second night and tried again. That was six years ago and I haven't looked back since."

"And you never wanted to do anything else?"

"It was either hair or music. Music won. Now, hand me my book so I can read in bed."

I had to pass the looking glass to get the book and caught a stranger's reflection. She was pretty, older than me, and worldly. She seemed confident. Bold and ready. My heart raced, realizing it was Faith Joy Wilson looking back at me. *"Miss Viv!"*

"Told you you're gorgeous. Dab a little of my smell good on your wrists and behind your ears. Take my black clutch. There's a dollar tucked in the zipper pocket. Use it if you need it. Here's the note for Smitty. Oh, and I wanna hear all about the new trumpeter. I haven't met him yet, but he's Smitty's godson so the band's giving him a try tonight."

"Thought you said your throat hurt too much for further discussion."

"It does. Pop in when you get home so I know you made it back safely." She hugged me briefly. "You can do this, Faith. Just close your eyes and let the music take you on a journey."

That journey to the Dunbar felt perilous; still, I forced myself forward on shaky legs despite wanting to turn around and hightail it back home. Some stranger's whistling and calling me "sweet thang" had me wishing it was winter and that I had a coat to hide underneath. I felt too womanish with that dress kissing my hips and its low-cut cleavage exposing my business. I followed the burly man who monitored the entertainers' entrance deep into the bowels of LA's premier Black-owned hotel until reaching a back room where the band was assembled.

"Smitty, you know her? She says Viv sent her." Male voices filling the room fell silent as the burly man introduced me.

Mister Smitty seemed confused. "Can't say I do and I never forget a pretty lady."

"It's me, Mister Smitty. Faith Wilson. I sat in on a rehearsal with Miss Viv." Pulling the note from my borrowed clutch, I hurried to the bandleader seated on the edge of a table, a cigarette dangling from his lips, a beer in one hand. "She told me to give you this."

He glanced at the note then back at me before smashing his cigarette in an ashtray and whistling. "Well, I'll say. Last time I saw you, you looked like somebody's country cousin in a cabbage patch. What hoodoo did Viv put on you?"

I ignored the band's snickers and thrust the note toward him. "Read this. Please."

He stared at me a moment before doing as requested only to burst out laughing. "Viv might be all woman, but she has a bodacious set of balls if she thinks I'm letting a little girl take the stage."

"Mister Smitty, I know every song on your line-up. I promise I can sing them."

"I'm sure you can. In the bath."

I didn't like his comment, or how it caused the others to laugh uproariously. My shoulders tightened, my chin lifted, and I was ready to tell Mister Smitty how wrong he was when there was a knock on the door.

"Five minutes. Take your places," a disembodied voice yelled.

Band members grabbed instruments or headed for the door, grinning at my expense as Mister Smitty consulted his wrist-watch with annoyance. "That damn pea-headed boy and his trumpet best hurry up and get here." He took a final swig of beer. "Tell Viv I'm sorry she's sick, but if she's not back tomorrow I'll have to find a replacement. It's nothing personal. It's the nature of the business." Passing me, he tossed behind him, "Go home and ditch the dress. It's too grown up."

That said, he would've exited if I hadn't opened my mouth to challenge his dismissiveness. I didn't waste breath arguing. I let music speak instead.

"St. Louis Blues" flowed like an untamed, muddy river swirling with low-down grit and guttural insistence as I closed my eyes and put myself back in that cellar to borrow its darkness as lyrics danced across my lips.

Mama would pitch a fit and ground me till Christmas. Up here singing about lovesick women running after men, and me dressed all scandalous.

I was there. My beautiful mama wasn't. And I had to do

what I could to help Miss Viv. Plus, Mama had taught me and Charity that sometimes you did on a hard Monday what you never would on a soft Sunday. This was my Monday, and I couldn't silence myself no matter what that bandleader thought of me or my abilities. I simply sang.

Barely through the second stanza, I stopped when snatched forward by the arm. My eyes flew open to see gaping musicians crowding the doorway as Mister Smitty pulled me toward the exit. "I'll be damned! I don't know whose throat you stole, but those pipes just took you from the cabbage patch to high cotton." He rattled off the list of songs for the first set prior to intermission while hurrying us down a tight corridor. "I'll be at the piano. If you get stuck, just look at me. At intermission stay with the band and away from the bar. No drinking. No fraternizing."

"Yes, sir."

"How old're you?"

"Sixteen."

"Tonight, you're twenty-three."

I survived black blizzards and a host of other foolishness. I can do this.

The lights were low. I stood, center stage, gripping the microphone stand, praying to God my knees would stop shaking as the drummer counted us down before a waiting audience. I jumped when the band struck those first notes and a spotlight came up, bathing me in silvery brilliance that required rapid blinking to adjust my vision. Everything felt foreign, as if I was in the wrong place and nothing but a counterfeit.

"Get off the stage."

That complaint floated up from the audience, somewhere to my left. I'd missed my cue, and suddenly couldn't remember what I was doing or why I was there.

"Baby, either piss or get off the pot," someone else suggested, generating snickers and outright laughter.

I looked in their direction wishing I could unlock my tongue and challenge that rudeness only to find a vision of loveliness seated at a table—a crown of braids circling her head, a cascade of pink flowers floating down the left side of her white dress.

Faith, why're you standing there not singing? You'd better open your mouth and treat these folks to some good ol' Oklahoma grown.

"Charity?"

"I'm feeling less than charitable here," Mister Smitty hissed. "Get with it."

Go'n and sing, sweet sister. They don't even know what's waiting on 'em.

I wanted to fly off that stage and wrap my sister in my arms but knew if I did, her ethereal self would disappear. Fighting back tears, I took a deep breath and let words tumble from my mouth just to keep her near. I poured my whole body and soul into every note, but the more I sang, the more Charity's beautiful self faded until the place where she'd sat was empty and I was left to sing for Faith.

By the time intermission rolled around, sweat was running between my breasts from all the heat that music was generating. I'd gotten caught up and felt myself moving in rhythm, shoulders rocking, hips swaying in ways that would have landed me on the church altar back in Wellston.

"That's intermission, ladies and gentlemen. See you in fifteen!" Mister Smitty hollered into the mic to be heard above the cheering crowd—whistling, applauding, stomping their feet.

"Baby, can I buy you a drink?" yelled a man seated near the stage.

Mister Smitty answered for me. "No, but feel free to send *me* something." Grabbing my hand, he hustled us away, waiting until we were in the corridor before stopping. "Miss Faith

Wilson, I don't know who you are or where you've been hiding, but you're out now and can't go back. *Damn*, girl, you sang the ass off that music!"

Band members crowded around, seconding Mister Smitty's opinion.

"If that damn trumpeter godson of mine ever shows up, between the two of you we'll blow this roof off."

"Uncle Smitty!"

All heads turned toward a young man bursting through the back entrance, running in our direction, instrument case in hand. He bent over halfway, out of breath, one hand securing the hat on his head.

Mister Smitty marched toward him. "Godson, if I don't kick your Black ass it's only 'cause your father's my best friend."

"I took the wrong bus—"

"You won't keep a gig in this town being late, son."

"I know, Unc, and I'm sorry, but these California busses ain't no joke. They're enough to make me wanna walk back to Oklahoma."

At the mention of home, I tried peeking past Mister Smitty to see the young man enduring a scolding but he was still bent at the waist catching his breath.

"Get your ass up and get some water before you fall out. Wait . . . come meet the guys first." When the bandleader moved aside, proudly gripping the young man's shoulder, I sucked in air so sharply the sound filled the corridor.

"You all right, songbird?"

I couldn't answer Mister Smitty for staring at his godson, Dallas Dorsey, the one-time object of my affection.

I silently inhaled the sight of him as he exchanged greetings with the band. He'd grown taller and more like a man since the last time I'd seen him, but he still boasted that pretty smile, magical eyes, and smooth brown skin. He was dressed better than Sunday and I felt that dip in my belly that I'd only ever experienced with him as his godfather steered him toward me, all Southern charm and smiling.

"Godson, meet—"

"*Faith?*" My name erupted from his lips. "Is that you?"

"Hello, Dallas."

"What the hell? They said you died in that blizzard!"

"Who said that?" I felt indignant at being buried before I was dead.

"Folks back home." He rushed me like lightning, picking me up and twirling around, whooping loudly. "Hallelujah, they were damn wrong!"

TWENTY

ZOE

Laying one's soul bare can be a catalyst for accelerated intimacy. That's what occurred between Shaun and me after I confided my inability to ever reproduce again. His care had been genuine. Compassionate and complete. His sensitivity was a much-needed balm and we found ourselves posted up at one end of the couch talking quietly, effortlessly bonding.

We'd sipped wine while enjoying the artificial flames and real heat produced by the electric fireplace—him relaxed, long legs stretched out; me curled against him as if he'd been made for my comfort. I was careful not to put more on it than belonged, but it felt right. *We* felt good. Like we'd found our way home after wandering life's roads. There were moments when our conversation flowed nonstop; others, where silence was a golden blanket wrapping us together as smooth jazz provided a backdrop for our thoughts. I'd lived too much to believe in fairy tales, but calling our time magical wouldn't be a stretch.

That was days ago and my soul still felt full, rich.

Soul-sweet satisfaction accompanied me while I worked on

the exhibition. Opening night was next Saturday, slightly more than a week away, and I was pouring more and more energy into the final prep phase—poring over the program, reconfirming details with vendors and participating artists, ensuring installments were displayed to perfection, and all the other countless minutiae required for a dynamic experience. I left the museum each evening exhausted but confident in my output. I gave it my all, held nothing back. Even to the detriment of self.

"I bet your fridge is empty and you haven't had a real dinner all week."

On the phone with Shaun, I laughed at his accuracy. "Must you sound so accusatory?"

"I'm an artist. I know what it's like for the world to fade away because you're caught up in your passion, Miss Edwards. Game recognizes game. So . . . is your fridge empty?"

I stood in front of the refrigerator with the door wide open looking at next to nothing. "Maybe."

"Maybe nothing, baby. Tell me what you're eating."

I was too old to be acting like a goggle-eyed teenager. Still, I shivered as if warm fingers skimmed my spine as the sexy depths of his voice wrapped around "baby," his now frequent term of endearment that was music to my ears. "Stay outta my Kool-Aid, JeShaun Halsey," I bantered, frowning at a rancid carton of takeout, the contents of which were no longer edible, barely identifiable.

"Your deflection is an admission of guilt. You're dinner-less. Can I order you something and have it delivered?"

"You're kind, but you can't." I tossed the carton in the garbage and opened a cupboard, thankful that the rental of my soror's bayside cottage had included one complimentary grocery delivery, preventing me from eating air and drinking invisible tea. I felt triumphant pulling my box of cereal from the cupboard and pouring a bowl. "Dinner is served. Quick and easy," I bragged, only to note my pint of milk was close to its expiration date. I sniffed it and considered it borderline suspect, but good enough. *It is what it is.* I poured it on my cereal, refusing to let Shaun win. "Sorry for crunching in your ear."

"I'll manage. How's the search coming? Heard anything from Greg Owenslee yet?"

I took my sketchy meal onto the patio to dine beneath the twilight of a soft evening sky. "No, unfortunately, I'm still waiting." I felt so close, one person away from learning Faith Miss Me's last name and being able to take the next steps in the process of ancestry discovery. "I wish I had her birth date, or birth place, or something else to go on besides her first and middle name."

"I wish my grandmother was able to offer more."

"Miss Samuella's help was priceless and led me in a good direction. It's just a matter of patience, which is hard for someone like me."

"Controlling?"

"The shade!" I laughed as an incoming call beeped in. Checking caller ID, I frowned, wondering what my cookie-and-candy confectioner neighbor back in Boston needed. "Hold that slight. I'll be right back." I clicked over, praying there hadn't been a fire or break-in. "Hi, Twila."

"Hey, Zoe, sorry to call you so late."

"We're three hours behind on the West Coast, so no worries."

"I forgot about that. Still, I'll make this quick. I wanted to ask about your house. My sister's *really* interested and wants to know if you've accepted an offer yet?"

"Pardon?" I could've choked on my own spit hearing her talking about a "For Sale by Owner" sign in my yard and the lock box on my front door. "Can you do me a favor and text me a pic?" She did and I did my best not to lose it, knowing the cretin behind the shenanigans.

Vince!

I texted Shaun that I'd get back to him.

"Twila, there's been a mistake. My townhouse isn't for sale." It took a minute convincing her of the error. Her disappointment was thick. I was sympathetic but unable to remedy it. I disconnected and did my best to focus on deep-breathing exercises. Sixty seconds in, I quit. "Forget this." I called my best friend-sister-cousin. "Tasha, girl, this fool has lost his whole rabid mind for real this time." I filled her in on Vince's latest.

She was outdone and wanted to cut him twelve ways to Sunday. That didn't keep my cousin from laughing hysterically. "Zo-Zo, it takes a special kind of insane in the brain to be this brand of ignorant. He really did that?"

"Huntee, yes." I texted her the pictures as proof of his certifiability. "Thank God my neighbor reached out about her sister being interested in making an offer, or I'd be in the dark. I need to call my lawyer."

"The deed's in both of your names so we know he can't legally sell without you signing on the dotted line but, yes, contact your lawyer 'cause that nut is on a whole other level."

"That part. He's exhausting my reserve nerve."

"Yours and mine. He's obviously trying to push your buttons. He's after something. What does he *really* want, Zoe?"

"A divorce."

"It's about damn time."

I felt a foot high and wide for failing to correct my cousin's long-standing assumption that Vince was the party dragging his feet in dissolving us when I was the one guilty of hanging onto a cadaverous marriage. I'd learned in therapy that giving audible voice to a thing could decrease mental monkey chatter, freeing space in the mind while allowing relentless thoughts to be released. I inhaled deeply before confessing that I was the one who'd been holding onto this unhealthy, toxic relationship. "Some folks have support animals. I had him. He was my only link. Releasing Vince felt like letting go of Jaelen."

Right or wrong, he was the last, living connection to my child.

"It's like my holding onto these thirty pounds I gained during pregnancy because they're the only physical proof of my baby."

"Wow, Z., that's some heavy ish, but I can't fault you at all." She was quiet a moment before blurting, "You're obviously improving. You lost ten pounds recently."

"Seven."

"I consider that an indicator of your healing, and I'm proud of you for coming to terms with things. Speaking of. Why're you so calm about this 'For Sale' silliness? Back in the day you would've been blowing a gasket. Hell, a few weeks ago we'd be booking flights to Boston, ready to give your ex-clown a beat down. Mister Dark Room must be good for you."

I laughed at her nickname for Shaun. "I guess."

"Have you given him some of that good-good yet?"

"Zoe's sex life is Zoe's business," I quipped, withholding the fact that it had taken the angels in heaven to keep me from pulling Shaun upstairs and making love to him that night he'd shown up for dinner. At some point in the evening, later, when the vibe was sensual and chill, I'd wound up on his lap exchanging kisses that were sweet, deep, intoxicating. I was nobody's prim-n-prude, hadn't seen virginity since twenty, and knew every woman had a right to satisfy her wants and needs. Still, I'd had to check myself and some out-of-pocket boldness that left me feeling like—as Granny would say—a hot hussy melting ice between her legs. Us butt naked in bed would've been a logical, lusty next step, and based on the solidness in Shaun's pants as I sat on his lap, I didn't think he'd object. But somewhere in my fog of horniness, an alter ego with better sense than Hot Hussy Me intervened. What should have been a one-and-done with Vince had morphed into a pitiful marriage thanks to mind-blowing sex. I'd ignored red flags, letting myself fall in love with a wrong man for less than right reasons. I'd grown from my mistakes but—after what felt like centuries of celibacy—abstaining wasn't easy with Shaun's luscious kisses and sexilicious company. I didn't need a marriage proposal before physical intimacy, but I wasn't random and knew better than to use him simply to satisfy the flesh. Plus, it had been an emotional evening, and I refused to cheapen its sacredness. I would explore and develop my intimate, spiritual connection with Shaun *before* sexing him.

Honey, trust! We're gonna get it in.

But that was for me to know. Not my cousin. "It's after hours on the East Coast, but lemme call my lawyer so we can handle this twistedness. I'll keep you posted. Love you."

"Love you too, Boo."

The rest of the night was an outrageous tennis match with all the back and forth between my lawyer and Vince's. It seemed to take forever before my almost-ex agreed he would remove the bogus "for sale" sign and lock box provided the divorce papers were signed and submitted. I had seven days. After that, I'd be faced with an injunction.

"Honey, he doesn't even know. I plan to overnight this mess," I told my empty room, dragging my suitcase from the closet. I snatched open an internal compartment, removed the folder holding the papers and reread them. Other than the issue of the brownstone, there was little to contest. The more I considered it, the easier it was to conclude that my freedom and sanity meant more than prolonging a feud.

But he owes you!

I suppose that was Miss Exacting Ego making one last effort to get her way. I'd been wounded and as a wounded woman I deserved atonement, but I chose not to be a victim of vindictiveness. Or bitterness. "None of that can bring my baby back."

Nothing could or would.

I was ready to stop wallowing in defeatist anger. I didn't want to walk around like Scrooge's Jacob Marley, a specter of myself dragging chains, wrapped up in the stench of death and misery versus fully embracing the present. Being tied to Vince sucked life from me, as well as limited my possibilities.

"Do it for you and Jaelen, not Vince."

Finding an ink pen before Petty Ego Me could rebel, I signed, waited to feel whatever I'd feel. And simply breathed.

Seated on the edge of the bed, a warm sensation fluttered softly through me. It was quiet, gentle. Serene. And so pure it made me wish I'd surrendered way back when. Even so, I accepted the fact that resistance had been a self-protective stance. Surrender allowed openness.

You did it, girl, and you're good.

"Damn straight, I am!"

I felt so light after signing those divorce papers that I slept deeper than I had in a long time, and went to the museum the next day with extra pep in my step. I was so focused that the morning flew by. It was after one p.m. before I started wrapping up for a late lunch just as a call came in. I answered immediately seeing Gregory Owenslee on my cell's caller ID.

"Hi, Gregory."

"Hi, Zoe. Do you have a moment?"

"Absolutely."

"Perfect. Hold on a quick minute."

I hopped up to close the door to my office and sat waiting for Gregory to return, which he promptly did.

"Thanks for holding. I was able to contact my cousin, my great-uncle's daughter in Arizona—"

"Oh God, that's wonderful!" I interrupted in my excitement. "Have you spoken to him yet?"

"He's on the line, Zoe. I just three-wayed him in. Uncle Micah, are you there?"

"Yes, Nephew, I am."

I'm not sure what I expected. Maybe the quavering, age-reflective voice of the elderly. Instead, I inhaled sharply when treated to a quiet but steady voice that somehow transmitted depth and kindness.

"Good. I've merged the calls successfully for a change. I consider myself an intelligent person, but technology isn't always my friend."

Too nervous to join the men's laughter, I sat in silence, praying Micah Owenslee would offer answers to unlock the mystery of Faith Miss Me.

"Uncle Micah, Zoe Edwards is on the line with us."

"Good afternoon, Miss Edwards. I'm pleased to make your acquaintance. I understand you may be related to my old friend, Faith Wilson, and have questions for me."

"Yes . . . and thank you, Mister Owenslee . . ." My mind and heart were racing so fast I couldn't form further words except, "Faith Joy *Wilson* . . . ?" Tremors raced through me and I felt her presence so strongly when stating her name that I glanced about the office as if expecting her to manifest.

"Yes, ma'am. My great nephew here says you look like Faith's twin." His voice seemed to quiver with emotion, and it felt as if a lifetime transpired before he spoke again. "And you sound exactly like Faith, Miss Edwards."

I sat trembling, unable to speak, knowing I'd been divinely graced despite my missteps. I'd been caught up, perhaps confused, consumed by work, and wishing so badly to gift my mother a link to herself that I'd suppressed the obvious.

Since embarking on this journey of familial discovery, I'd approached Faith Miss Me as an unknown pertaining to Mama's ancestry, but now I understood what appeared to be a partial "V" on Faith and Henry's marriage certificate was actually what remained of a "W." Phenotypically? I was Daddy's mini-me. My looking so like Faith Miss Me stemmed from the fact that we were linked via *Daddy,* not Mama's lineage. Wilson was my father's family surname. Faith and I were paternally connected.

TWENTY-ONE

FAITH

That first night at the Dunbar was one I'll never forget. I fell into the hot, thrilling arms of music and was so seduced by its embrace—as well as the excitement of finding a hometown friend—that after intermission we did like Mister Smitty predicted and tore the roof off the place.

"Songbird, Godson, y'all served these high-tone, champagne folks some down-home pot liquor and neck bones."

Mister Smitty was so pleased with my performance that he paid me cash on the spot, and invited me to fill in for Miss Viv anytime she was out. I might've floated home if Dallas hadn't been alongside me, anchoring. The band had stayed for drinks, but Mister Smitty jokingly advised him to treat me to something tame like a milkshake. Which he did, and I loved every sip. Afterward, Dallas walked me home—our steps leisurely despite it being past one a.m.

"And you haven't seen them since?"

I gripped the suit jacket he'd draped over my shoulders, needing strength. "No, and sometimes I'm scared I never will. It was hard enough losing Charity. Now, my whole family's gone. All I have is Hope."

We proceeded in silence until he quietly offered, "Don't give up, Faith. For all you know, they might be a day away."

Tired of old sorrow, I changed the subject back to the magical, musical evening we'd shared as we sauntered toward my home that was once a hotel. "Are you returning to Oakland?"

He'd come to California on his own to find work in the Bay Area shipyards three months ago. "I'm not against hard work, but that dock life ain't my cup of joe. I'm interested in taking Uncle Smitty up on his offer to join the band and stay in LA . . . especially now that I've met up with an old but new temptation."

I ignored the thrill of his words and his looking pointedly at me. Dallas had always seemed sweet on Charity; not to mention he was three years my senior. I might've looked the part, but I wasn't sophisticated like the California girls he'd likely encountered. Whatever he thought he was feeling right then was probably nothing but leftover magic from our music.

"What do you think, Miss Faith? Should I relocate to LA?"

I shrugged nonchalantly despite my heart racing. "Do what you feel is best."

He smiled the smooth smile that made my belly feel like it caged a mess of butterflies. His facing me and softly trailing a finger down my cheek didn't help any. "Trust me, Songbird, I will."

I wanted to touch the moonlight illuminating his beautiful brown skin, to know what those lips that blew music into existence would feel like if I reached up and kissed him. But that kind of boldness was for LA girls, not me. "Thank you for making sure I got home safely."

He glanced at my residence as if just now aware of it. "Any woman who sings like you deserves to be escorted home by the finest trumpeter Oklahoma ever produced."

Smiling, I returned his jacket and headed for the rear entrance, choosing not to comment that I wasn't a woman.

"Faith?"

"Yes..."

He mounted the steps and kissed my cheek. "Don't stop singing."

"I won't if you don't stop playing. Good night, Dallas." My cheek warm with the soft imprint of his lips, I slipped inside and up the steps, stopping to check on Miss Viv. Relieved to find her sleeping deeply, I eased down the hall to the room I shared with Hope only to find her curled up on my cot. I quietly and quickly undressed and lay beside my sister, too tired to wash up. Sweet thoughts of the evening's performance and Dallas's unexpected appearance filled me with long-lost contentment.

I lay smiling in the dark when Hope's drowsy voice startled me. "I missed you, Faye-Faye. Where were you?"

Madame considered entertainers other than the classically trained "lowlife degenerates reflecting badly on the race." And she was famous for milking information from Hope. The less my baby sister knew, the better. Madame hated me enough and didn't need more ammunition. I kissed Hope's forehead. "I had to do something for Miss Viv. She's sick."

"I saw them," she mumbled through a yawn.

"Who?"

"The ghosts."

"What ghosts?"

"The ones that're always crying."

I'd never mentioned the wall of wailing women to Hope, to avoid scaring her. Now, her words left me chilled. "You hear them, too?"

"Only when I'm in Madame's room. But tonight, I saw one of 'em. I think." Hope yawned again and snuggled against me. "It was real dark, but she was in the cubby behind Madame's wall."

"What cubby, Hope?"

"Madame's gonna buy me a pony for my birthday." Her words were heavy. Lazy.

According to Miss Nance, Madame was no longer rich-rich and afloat only because of her boarders. A pony was out of the question, but I let my sister fall asleep with that fanciful dream, wondering what she'd actually seen.

I'd considered it strange that Madame's first-floor room was off limits to me, seeing as how she found perverse pleasure watching me sweat through arduous tasks. She relished critiquing my work, even undoing it to watch me try again to her impossible satisfaction. Shifting onto my back and gazing at the shadowed ceiling, I wondered what she was hiding.

"Maybe it's like Miss Nance said . . ."

I'd dismissed her whispering of Madame's reforming "misguided young ladies" by imprisoning them in a secret chamber with nothing but bread and water as what it was: Miss Nance's teasing way of keeping me on the straight and narrow.

Go take a peek.

I declined the invitation to acquaint myself with any of Madame's evil-doings. I chose, instead, to fill my mind with good things.

I'd fallen asleep, humming tunes from the night, my thoughts on Dallas Dorsey, when a quiet knock on the door woke me.

"Yes?"

Miss Viv's silhouette appeared in shadows when the door opened. "Why didn't you wake me when you got in?"

I matched her whisper. "I didn't want to disturb your rest."

"Only disturbing thing is me not knowing." She motioned me to follow as she eased backward into the hall. She grabbed my hand when I did, hurrying us down the corridor like two naughty children. She'd barely closed her door behind us before tossing questions. "How was it? How'd Smitty and the guys react? Did they treat you okay? Leave nothing out. I want every detail of your first night on stage."

I assured her I'd been treated well before providing an animated play-by-play of the evening as she reclined against her headboard, clearly tired and still not her best, but peppering me with questions and squealing with joy at my responses.

"Wait . . ." I stood suddenly, nearing the end. "I forgot your money in my room."

"What money?"

"The pay Mister Smitty gave me for singing."

"If you don't get out of here, Faith Wilson!" She pulled me back down onto the bed. "That's *your* money, honey. You earned it, and we're going shopping to get you something nice soon as I feel better. How'd the new horn player work out?"

I wanted to protest at her letting me keep money that should've been hers but was too giddy at the notion of buying myself something, and the matter of Dallas Dorsey. "He was good! Dallas plays even better now than he did back in Wellston—"

"He's from Oklahoma?" she interrupted.

I nodded, explaining our old connection.

Her tired voice held new brightness. "That must've been nice, seeing someone from home. Has he changed much?"

I shrugged. "He's taller. Broader. But in a nice way. Like his muscles grew. Or something . . ."

When my voice trailed off, Miss Viv tucked a hand beneath my chin. "You like him." It was a statement, not a question. I wanted to hide from its accuracy, but she wouldn't let me. "Faith, there's nothing wrong with you liking a young man. Especially one who's already a friend."

I shook my head. "I can't like Dallas."

"Because?"

"He used to like Charity. Plus"—I took a deep breath before blurting—"I'm already married."

"*Say what?*" Her loud shrieking triggered her cough. She waved me away when I patted her back, leaving me to sit as she recovered.

"You okay, Miss Viv?"

She ignored my concern. "We've been sharing life under this roof for what? Four months? Why am I just now hearing this?"

My voice was meek, apologetic. "It was best forgotten. There was no reason to mention it." I hadn't liked any boys at my new school and they returned the sentiment, so there'd been no need for this discussion. It might've been immature, but keeping that Henry fiasco to myself let me pretend it had never happened. Besides, I was no longer worried about encountering the Owenslees. We were from separate communities, and even if they did show up, Madame was too proud to let white folks dictate anything on her property, despite her dislike of me. But, it being a night of confidences, I poured out the whole sad saga to Miss Viv. When finished, I sat, fearing her opinion of me had changed.

Her sudden howl of laughter wasn't soothing.

"Go'n and laugh, Miss Viv. I know I'm stupid."

She sobered instantly. "Don't ever say that again. You're not stupid, Faith, but you were misled if you think that marriage was legitimate."

"Ma'am?"

"In some regards, this is a softer place for Colored folks, but don't think these California whites have lost their minds. It's the same here as down South: mixed-race marriages are against the law." She nodded when my jaw dropped. "What kind of crazy minister would even perform that ceremony?"

"Henry's drunk uncle! He even made us sign a certificate."

"Which you left behind, correct? I'm not judging you, Faith," she quickly assured me when I remained silent. "Like I said, mixed-race unions are illegal here, so that bogus certificate isn't worth spit." She suddenly straightened. "Did you . . . have relations?"

"No, ma'am!"

"Good." She sat back as if suddenly tired and tucked the covers about her legs before taking my hand. "I know most folks won't agree with what I'm about to say, but when you do engage, make sure you're with a man you love and who loves you in return . . . *with or without marriage.* That mutual love will go a long way in making sure it's one of the sweetest things you ever experience."

Henry and I ain't married.

I slept so peacefully that night, and floated through the house doing chores the following day, humming and giving God praise. I was angry, wondering if Henry knew mixed unions were illegal and went through the process just to get what he wanted but I decided not to let it drain my spirit and focused on the blessing that I wasn't legally tied to him. That had me dusting, smiling, and daydreaming about using some of last night's earnings to do something nice for myself.

Unlike Hope, who looked like a princess on a daily basis courtesy of Madame's endless indulgences, my wardrobe consisted of hand-me-downs from Miss Viv and the church charity bin. I kept my clothing clean and neat, but I was functional, never fashionable. I wasn't paid for the work I did for Madame: I received room, board, and hygiene needs in exchange. Other than what I earned doing chores for boarders, last night's pay was the first money I'd received since arriving in this state. Visions of a new dress or a pair of patent leather shoes danced in front of me, intoxicatingly.

"If I have enough left, I can do like Miss Viv suggested and have my hair pressed."

Most girls my age wore the latest hairstyles. Me? I sported

thick braids in their natural state gathered in a bun at the back of my neck in what Madame considered "a disorganized mess." She was always saying something hateful, hurtful. When I told Miss Viv about it her response was usually in the avenue of, "Who cares what she thinks? She's an uppity snob pissing in a cracked pot."

Grinning at Miss Viv's colorfulness, I made my way to the first floor just as the doorbell rang. I hurried to answer it and found a delivery boy on the doorstep. Giving him a nickel tip from the coin purse Madame kept in a drawer for that purpose, I accepted the package. I wasn't in the habit of opening Madame's deliveries, and blamed Hope's ghost stories for piquing my curiosity. Ensuring no one was near, I peeked at the brown bottle inside the bag but closed it quickly when hearing a noise near the salon. Looking up and finding Madame in the doorway, I hurried the bag to her before rushing to the kitchen to help Miss Nance with the breakfast dishes.

I was midway through my task before asking, "Miss Nance, what's laudanum?"

"Something you'd best not ever touch," she fussed. "That's some strong stuff with all that opium. You'll be acting out your mind like a phantom."

"Maybe it can help Madame's gout," I wondered aloud, thinking perhaps that was why it had been delivered.

She stopped to frown at me. "No, indeed. That stuff is addictive. She and that gout are just fine with aspirin."

I was still curious about the laudanum delivery and why Madame needed it, but left it at that and went about my business until the mid-day break when I could lunch with Hope and read her a story from one of her books before she napped. I'd stuck to my word and not returned to school. It was the only time Madame and I shared an opinion. She felt furthering my education was a waste for someone who would never rise above my position. I, however, didn't doubt my intelligence. I disliked her hold on my sister and didn't want to stay at Madame's much longer, but I knew Hope's and my future depended on my employable skills. When we left, I prayed it would be with a good reference.

You can sing for a living.

That thought tortured me throughout the day, seemed to holler at me as I helped Miss Viv dress. She wasn't fully recovered, but good enough to get back on stage. I hated feeling envious, yet part of me did when she left for the Dunbar that night only to wake up the next morning feverish, nearly delirious, and far sicker than she had been. She was so bad off I ran the two blocks to get the doctor, and used the money I'd made singing to pay the bill when Miss Viv was taken to the Colored hospital by ambulance where she underwent a minor emergency procedure that evening. I stayed in the waiting room, praying, until receiving the news she'd be okay. Saving her life was worth every penny.

"It was some sort of abscess or throat lesion that got terribly infected."

"*Damn.* How long she gonna be out?" Mister Smitty asked when I stopped by the Dunbar that night to inform him.

"A week or two?"

Cigarette smoke spiraled from his nostrils as he replied. "I need you to fill in until Viv gets back."

"Yes, sir, but I can't tonight." I was exhausted, improperly dressed, and needed to get home to Hope. Promising to return the following evening, I accepted Dallas's encouraging hug before leaving.

Madame treated me with typical iciness when informed the next day of Miss Viv's condition and that I would be filling in for her, cleaning the Colored hospital at night. She sniffed as if smelling the lie, but dismissed me after declaring she still expected me to perform my daily duties.

Miss Nance was warmer, sympathetic. She had a soft spot

for my sister and me, and offered to help with my chores when possible and to sit with Hope at night until she fell asleep.

"It's only until Miss Viv feels better and can go back to work." I reassured my sister with a long hug, multiple kisses, and a promise that I'd be there every morning when she woke up.

I borrowed from Miss Viv's closet, had my only friend, RaeLouise, press my hair since Miss Viv couldn't, and stepped onstage that night suited for the limelight. The audience's response was as wonderful as it had been during my maiden performance, and I felt myself, night after night, getting addicted to the praise—and Dallas—as if it were *my* laudanum.

"Miss Viv, are you sure you should do this?"

"It's been three weeks since my surgery." Her voice was thin, scratchy. "I'm sick of bedrest, and tired of you treating me like an invalid. I want to see you perform. That's that."

"Fine, but we're leaving if you start feeling bad."

"Yes, mother," she teased, promising to meet me at the Dunbar as I kissed her cheek then hurried to check on Hope before heading out, proudly carrying the box containing my new dress purchased with singing money. Since filling in for Miss Viv, I'd been squirreling away half of every dollar I made in a stocking beneath my baby sister's mattress. I was determined to leave Madame's as soon as I had enough for Hope and me to be on our own, despite being frightened by the notion. But I'd fallen in love with the silver gown showcased in the window of a small dress shop owned by a nice Colored woman, and intentionally walked past it every day en route to work just to see it until the day the shop owner caught my attention. I recognized her as a regular audience member at the Dunbar, Miz Bailey. Her seeing me through the window and waving so friendly gave me the courage to go inside and ask to try it on.

"Miss Faith, if you don't get this dress, I'll spank you myself," she playfully threatened as I stood before a mirror marveling at the way that dress kissed my frame. It felt intimate, better suited for a woman of experience; but something bold flared up inside of me and, with the shop owner's encouragement, I left with that dress in a pretty box.

Now, I stood onstage, hugged by its butter-soft caress, no longer a country girl playing in Los Angeles. I felt transformed. Provocative. Gripping the microphone stand as if a magic wand casting a spell, I lured the audience in with sophisticated lyrics dripping from my lips only to glance back at the band when Dallas's trumpet held a note longer than expected. Our eyes connected, and I felt a surge of something foreign. His gaze was so deeply intense it seemed as if the velvety notes he was creating were meant for me. The idea that only music and I were on his mind sent warm, sweet heat throughout my body. It scared me so badly I swung toward the audience and let the music take my confusion until I felt balanced.

I gave the audience the heat Dallas meant for me. I'd learned the faces of many who came for repeat performances and always put a little extra love in the lyrics for them. I was sending love toward a table at the back when an odd group walked in.

There wasn't anything unusual about white patrons in attendance, but the tallest two caught my attention. They were in the shadows, not clearly seen. One escorted a woman on his arm. Both men seemed familiar. Dismissing the notion, I focused on sending love to Miss Viv seated a few rows from the stage, glad that intermission was a song away.

"Cute shoes ain't built for comfort." I yanked off the pointy-toed pumps the moment I was off stage, heading for the tiny space Dallas jokingly called my dressing room but which was little more than a glorified utility closet.

"Hey, Songbird, there's a note on your door."

"Who from?" I asked Boolie, our burly doorman who kept miscreants away.

"No idea. Must've been left when I was in the john."

Thanking him, I headed for my "dressing room," critiquing my performance, toying with the idea of different nuances and trying to forget the thing that had transpired between me and Dallas. Finding the note Boolie mentioned, I unfolded it and completely forgot music.

I have news of your brother and parents, and will stop by later.

The earth seemed to rotate backward at lightning speed as I sank onto the chair situated at a wobbly desk that doubled as a dressing table. Shaking, crying, I read and reread that note, wondering who'd sent it, thanking God for hearing my prayers until a knock interrupted me. I jumped from my chair and snatched the door open, anticipating the note-writer, only to stumble back as a man bulldozed his way in.

"Hello, *Missus* Owenslee." Shock stole my breath away at the sight of Henry grinning that deceptive grin and looking me over in a way that left me feeling unclean. "Pa wouldn't approve of your song choices or the way you were moving those hips, but you sounded good up there. How've you been?"

"That was you I saw at the back of the room . . . with a woman on your arm." I was immediately on guard. "What do you want? Why're you here?"

His laugh was the same: slick, disingenuous. "I love music. Why else would I step foot in a coon club?"

I ignored the insult while studying him, deciding he was in far better condition than when we first met. Decently dressed or not, his snake eyes gave me chills. "Did you need something, Henry?"

"I need plenty." He closed the door and crowded the tight space. "Looks like you're doing well for yourself. Are you making decent money?"

I wanted him to leave enough to lie. "It's nice seeing you, but I need to get back."

He moved, blocking me. "You and that horn player doing things?"

"What?"

"Don't play innocent, Faye-Faye. I saw the way you two was lusting after each other. Like y'all can't wait for the show to end so y'all can get back to fornicating in whatever bed y'all sharing."

"You're ridiculous, and that's none of your business." I moved to pass him.

"Like hell it ain't!" With little room to move, he easily blocked my exit. "You giving that boy what belongs to your husband?"

I stepped back, bumping into the chair when he touched my chin. Hemmed in, I was so outdone a vein pulsed angrily in my temple. "I need you to leave, Henry."

"The only thing you need is to settle the debt you left when you ran off like some ungrateful heathen."

"I appreciate all your family did for me and my sister. Come 'round at the end of tonight's set and I'll have the money I owe Miz Lucy."

"I ain't here for Ma." His motions were so quick that I was pinned on that table, my brand-new dress ripped up the front before I could react. "I'm here for me!"

"Stop it, Henry! Get off me."

He stuffed a handkerchief in my mouth, muting my protests and screams. Pinning my arms overhead with one hand, he snatched at my underwear with the other. We were wrestling ferociously, him trying to get what I wasn't willing to give, that rickety dressing table thrashing about and threatening to break as I fought like my life depended on it. Fear twisted my insides as Henry's strength outdid mine. Somehow, I managed to free an arm to reach the garter belt beneath my dress. I yanked Beulah loose just as he undid his pants. I brought Beulah down hard across his arm, slashing him twice before he could even react.

Blood spurted, sprinkling the side of my face.

"Gottdamn nigger bitch! I have rights. *I'm your husband.*"

His fist against my jaw felt like concrete. Beulah flew free. I snatched the rag from my mouth, using my voice like a weapon, screaming, fighting as he slammed me onto that dressing table again, shoving my legs open.

Please, God, please!

It was the only prayer I could pray while swinging, kicking, warring to keep me.

Neither of us heard the door open amid our commotion. Only the soft click of a gun hammer fully registered. Henry spun around right into Bertha and Miss Viv.

"I've never been to jail, but *gottdamnit* if I'm not ready right now," she growled, pressing Bertha to Henry's forehead. She pushed me behind her while backing Henry against a wall, his hands up in surrender. "Is this him?"

"*You were never my husband!*" Those words coated my mouth with sourness as we heard the sound of running feet approach.

"What the hell!"

"I've got it under control, Smitty. Send someone to get the law," Miss Viv commanded, her gun hand steady. "You have half a second to pull your damn pants up before I shoot you where you piss. Somebody get Faith out of here."

Crying angrily, I felt myself being guided from the room as chaos broke loose.

Henry was trying to exit only to be crowded by band members who'd become my big brothers. Next thing I knew he'd been yanked from the room and was on the corridor floor, Dallas beating the sin out of him.

"Get off my brother!" Micah came out of nowhere, running into the melee as two musicians pulled Dallas away.

Mister Smitty did his best to separate the feuding factions as an officer burst through the back door. Voices were raised as sides were told, and even with the evidence of my swelling jaw and ripped dress the law was ready to let Henry leave. He was a white man and his lies were believed.

"I got lost looking for the bathroom and these niggers tried to rob me. I don't know this gal and I certainly never touched her. My brother was with me the whole time. He saw everything. Ask him!"

Micah stared at the floor, shame draping his face as Henry waited for him to corroborate his innocence. "My brother left the table long enough ago for what Miss Wilson says happened to have happened."

"Shut your mouth, Micah!" Henry yelled.

Micah ignored his brother's wrath and looked my way. "I'm sorry, Faith. He said y'all had unfinished business . . . but I never thought he'd try . . . *this*."

"You're siding with niggers over your own flesh and blood?" Henry's struggling to free himself from the officer's firm grip was useless.

"You're wrong, Henry. Ain't no way around it." The sorrow on Micah's face was so raw, it hurt to see it.

"You nigger-loving traitor! You're no longer my brother. *You're dead to me, Micah Owenslee!* And there ain't no news of your family, bitch. I wrote that note. How you like that?" Henry spat at me before being escorted from the Dunbar, screaming obscenities.

In the ensuing silence, Micah started to speak only to think better of it. He took his leave without another word, steps slow, posture dejected.

"Godson, take Songbird and Miss Viv home. We'll finish the set—"

"No." I rejected Mister Smitty's instructions as restless sounds filtered backstage from the crowd waiting for intermission to end. My jaw was on fire. My makeup was ruined and my beautiful silver gown was a shambles fit for the rubbish bin. Worst of all, my heart broke knowing my family hadn't been found. It was evil of Henry to do what he did, and I refused to bow to his deviltry. "I'm singing."

I left Mister Smitty arguing with Miss Viv about the rightness of my decision, fixed my hair and put on the plain dress I'd worn to the hotel, my hands shaking all the while. When I exited the dressing room, they fell silent. "Miss Viv, if you don't mind waiting in the wings in case I need you, I'd appreciate it." I headed for the stage, willing them to follow.

We took our places. The lights went up and the audience rumbled at the change in my appearance. Ignoring their shock, I nodded at Mister Smitty that I was ready. With the opening notes of "Nobody Knows the Trouble I've Seen" I signaled the band to modify the tempo, allowing me to lean into it with the swag and sway of slow, mournful Blues while ignoring the pain in my jaw and singing my soul's agonizing truth.

I didn't utter a sound on the way home. Huddled in a taxi between Dallas and Miss Viv, I wanted to tell Dallas everything about Henry, but I was too drained. And ashamed. Instead, I mentally arranged to repay Lucy Owenslee with interest.

No one's holding another damn thing over me or acting like they have rights to my being. And it's time to leave.

I stared at Madame's house as we arrived, seeing it as the site of oppression it was. I worked tirelessly six days a week without her acknowledgment or thanks. She tolerated me for Hope's sake, but clearly the woman hated me for breathing. I couldn't subject myself to her poison any longer and chose to find a way for Hope and me to survive elsewhere until we found our parents, even if it meant singing seven days a week in a cabaret or speakeasy.

"Do you mind waiting?"

"The meter'll be running," the driver informed Dallas as he helped us from the back of the cab. He'd been equally silent during the ride but the fury expressed when pummeling Henry lurked behind his eyes. Just the same, he was gentle with me while escorting us toward the back door.

"Faith . . ."

Miss Viv intentionally moved on.

He touched my face. "I will never let another man treat you . . . like . . . *Damn!*"

I wanted to wipe the hard anguish from his face as well as explain Henry's part in my past so that Dallas understood Henry had nothing to do with my present. Instead, I hugged him and whispered my thanks for his intervention only to jerk free when hearing my sister's screams. "Oh, Lord. *Hope?*" Racing away, I followed the chilling sounds through the house into Madame's off-limits sanctuary.

"You silly little beast! After everything I've sacrificed for you, how could you betray me?" She had Hope by the shoulders, shaking her violently. She raised a hand to strike her.

I got there first, knocking Madame backward and grabbing my baby sister, who was crying uncontrollably.

"I didn't mean to break it, Faye-Faye." The stinging imprint of an open-handed slap marred her face. "*I'm sorry.*"

I hugged her tightly to keep from attacking Madame. "No matter what she broke, she didn't deserve to be hit."

"You dirty Black bastards deserve that and worse." Madame's roiling venom was shocking to even me. Her evil tongue was a fist and I was finished with being hit.

I pushed Hope into Miss Viv's arms and confronted our landlord, every lesson about respecting my elders forgotten. "What did you call us?"

"Only what you are. Dirty. Black. Ill-bred bastards."

"Don't, Faith." Dallas intercepted me before I could sin against my parents by striking an aging lady. He planted himself between us. Hands at my waist, he backed me away. "Let's go."

"No. Not before I pay this person for whatever's so precious that she had a need to lay hands on my little sister," I screamed, reaching into my brassiere despite mixed company and pulling out dollar bills. "How much do we owe? What did you break, Hope?"

She whined pitifully. "The cubby door won't shut no more. I didn't mean to break the lock, Faye-Faye, but Madame left the wall open. I only wanted to see."

Her words were wind to fog, clearing, directing me to notice a portion of the wall that was open as if on hidden hinges. My nostrils flared with a putrid smell like rotting meat that, in my war with Madame, I'd clearly missed as my ears hummed with the diminished wail of wounded women. Their low moans made my skin crawl. "Oh, *God*."

Madame tried preventing us from rushing toward the dirge drifting through the open wall, but Dallas pushed past her. "Stay here, Faith."

Positioning myself like a sentinel, I plucked Beulah from my dress pocket when Madame tried to follow. My defiance left her screaming madly. I remembered Miss Nance's teasing about Madame imprisoning misguided ladies.

Miss Nance rushed in as if conjured up. "What's all this ruckus?"

Dallas burst into the room before anyone responded, carrying a naked, shrunken being. "I need a blanket!"

Miss Nance snatched the cover from Madame's bed and draped it over the bedraggled woman Dallas held. Her moans were eerie, signaling distress no human should ever experience as Madame lunged at Dallas, beating him with her fists.

"Put my daughter back where she was!"

Miss Nance managed to move Madame away as I rushed to help Dallas.

"We gotta get her to a doctor, Faith."

I couldn't signal my agreement. I could only stare at the withered figure with matted hair and healed-over cuts on her arms who smelled of her own waste and was nearly emaciated. Her head lolled back and I saw her face. It was bruised from abuse, but I only saw the beauty I'd missed and craved.

The world stood still as Hope and I whispered in unison. *"Mama . . .?"*

A scream shredding my throat, I tried to take her from Dallas, to cradle my frail mother as Hope wrapped herself about my legs and we both sobbed.

Miss Viv's voice was gentle. "Faith, let go so we can get her out of here."

I clutched Mama's hand as Miss Viv herded us toward the door.

"Where's the laudanum? She needs her medicine." Madame freed herself from Miss Nance and rushed about, knocking over her precious objects, trying to find the opiate she served my mother.

My hate for her was so thick I wished Madame a leisurely, excruciating death.

"Go! Get out. You never were a good daughter. You could've been a world-renowned concert pianist and uplifted the race and this family, Mae Princessa. Instead, you lowered yourself by marrying that dirty, dark farmer and giving away all my dreams. I might've forgiven you if he wasn't so disgustingly *black*. You wasted the light of your complexion."

Ignoring her raving, we moved through the crowd of gaping boarders gathered in their bedclothes, watching the spectacle.

"I'll grab some of our things, but we can't stay here," Miss Viv advised, heading for the stairs.

"Leave it, Miss Viv. I don't want a thing from this house except my mother and sister."

I clutched Mama's hand as Dallas carried her down the rear steps toward the waiting cab.

"I hated you, girl, because you look just like that damn Tomas Wilson!"

I whirled around, screaming, "Where's my father and my brother? How'd you get ahold of my mother?"

Miss Viv grabbed me about the waist, preventing me from rushing back and doing that woman physical damage.

Deranged as she was, Madame merely laughed. "Just like your pappy. Ignorant. Dark. Nappy-headed. Nothing!"

I followed Miss Viv's prompting and turned toward the cab, letting Madame's vitriol land against my back. I never wanted to lay eyes on her again, however long she lived, and left her spewing vileness into the night like a madwoman.

TWENTY-TWO

ZOE

I was beyond tempted to book a flight to Arizona to meet Micah Owenslee face to face—to see, touch, speak to someone who'd actually known Faith Joy Wilson. Only the exhibition being so close kept me from doing so. My time with Mister Owenslee was relegated to the phone.

I took an extended lunch the day Gregory connected us via conference call and sat outdoors behind the museum's atrium taking a walk back into the past to greet this ancestor who'd honored me by claiming my face as her canvas.

"How're you and Faith related?"

I smiled at Micah Owenslee's direct dive into the crux of my quest. "I wasn't even aware of Faith's existence until recently. I've assumed we were linked via my maternal lineage. Now, I see we're paternally connected. My father is a Wilson, which makes Wilson my maiden name as well. How and where we precisely link is what I'd like to determine." Granddad's side of the family was slim-pickings; he'd been orphaned, essentially. I still recalled asking questions as a child about the mysteries surrounding my grandfather's youth only for Granny to quietly caution, "Leave it be."

"I hear her in your voice," he softly commented, before asking, "Is your father able to assist?"

"I hope so." I planned on phoning Daddy as soon as this conversation ended. But, again, because of limited knowledge, and no extended branches on the Wilson family tree of which I was aware, I didn't anticipate some grand revelation. "Any information you can provide may go a long way in making sure we don't wind up searching for needles in haystacks."

"Family trees can be tricky," he commented, "so I'm glad to oblige. But could I ask a favor first? Can you possibly mail me a copy of that photograph?"

"Uncle Micah, Milani has a cell phone, right?" Gregory interjected.

"Greg, my daughter can't function without that thing. It's always hanging off her hip like a child."

We laughed briefly.

"Zoe, by chance, do you have the photo on your phone? If so, would you mind texting it to Uncle Micah's daughter Milani?"

"Absolutely." I punched in the number Gregory provided and forwarded a side-by-side composite I'd made of Faith Joy and a pic of myself, as well as the photograph of four young people from a world ago. "You should have it momentarily, Mister Owenslee."

"Thank you. Lemme check with my daughter. *Lani,*" he hollered, "did your phone get something for me?"

Momentarily, a woman was heard in the background, confirming receipt. Her voice grew closer. "Is this it?"

"Lemme see . . ." Micah Owenslee's voice trailed to silence and it was several minutes before he spoke again in a tone thick with emotion. "My dear God . . . would you look at this." He choked on his words, voice weighted with memories. Gregory and I were silent as he recovered. "I haven't laid eyes on my brother in decades. We were so young. This picture makes me feel fifteen all over again. How'd you come by this, Miss Edwards?"

I explained, as I had for Gregory, Samuella Halsey's photography.

"*I remember that!* On our trip here, there was a young Colored lady snapping pictures outside a filling station. My brother didn't much appreciate it. If I recall correctly, he threw a pop bottle at her." His tone was apologetic. "Henry wasn't always the nicest person on the planet. Sometimes that temper made him downright nasty. I'm sorry if hearing that bothers you, great-nephew."

Gregory dismissed the apology. "I knew my grandfather, Uncle Micah. No need to whitewash anything."

"No need," the elder gentleman quietly echoed before continuing. "There's so much I'd do over if given the opportunity, but I can't undo time. Still, I wish I'da stayed close to my brother despite everything. Maybe we coulda helped each other be better." He spoke as if to himself. "Best to use what time you have wisely to minimize regrets. Enough of me wishing after yesterday." He coughed and cleared his throat, perhaps making room for more pleasant sentiment. "Well, these two are a lovely sight for sore eyes. Baby Girl and Faith 'Faye-Faye' Wilson," he murmured fondly, clearly taking in the remainder of the picture.

I experienced calm satisfaction at his confirmation of their identities.

He chuckled lightly. "Of course, Baby Girl was just a nickname. Her real name was Hope. Wait, I see you sent more than one photo. Oh my . . . is this your picture here next to Faith, Miss Edwards?"

"Yes, sir."

"Good *Lord,* you *are* her twin. Just as lovely as she is."

"Thank you, sir. What can you tell me about Hope and

Faith? Do you know how old they were in the photograph, or where they're from?" I launched the note app on my phone to capture any insight he might offer. "Were you family friends? Neighbors?"

"That's a whole lot of questions for an old man like me."

"I apologize. You're the first person I've encountered who knows Miss Faith and I'm desperate to learn all I can."

He chuckled good-naturedly. "I understand. Lemme think . . . Faith was a month or two older than me so she must've been fifteen. Hope was maybe five or six. Lord, what was the name of that place where we met? It was one of those what we used to call 'blink-n-miss-it' towns it was so small. Oklahoma had plenty of 'em."

My reverse search wasn't so backward after all, I thought, recalling how I'd mistakenly searched for the name Faye Owensbey in Oklahoma at the start of this quest. I cut my self-congratulations short and focused as Mister Owenslee continued.

"I haven't been back home in a long time and those tiny places tend to slip my mind, but it was Well-something-or-other."

I opened Google and typed Well, Oklahoma without pressing enter. A dropdown list populated. One hit in particular caught my eye: *Route 66 bypasses Wellston, Oklahoma.* "Was it Wellston?"

"That's it! Wellston. That's where we found 'em."

"What do you mean by 'found' them?" I questioned while firing a text to my father when a thought tickled the back of my mind.

Where was Granddad born?

Maybe he was a gifted storyteller, or maybe I was overly fascinated with the subject. Either way, it felt as if the hairs at the back of my neck stood to attention as Gregory's great-uncle recounted his family's leaving Oklahoma only to encounter the aftermath of what was deemed the wickedest dust storm the state had ever experienced, and finding Faith and Hope alone in an underground root cellar.

"They were just two scared little girls out in the middle of nowhere." He had my undivided attention. "Thank God for leading us to them. Sometimes I think about that night and wonder what might've happened except for that spirit."

"What spirit?" Gregory asked before I could.

Chills skittered up and down my arms at the mention of an ethereal figure that ultimately led the Owenslees to that underground containment; but my heart skipped erratically at his description of the otherworldly being. The dress, the braids wrapped about the head. It threw me backward into the grip of my farmhouse dream where my beautiful Jaelen lay cradled in the arms of a young woman, who favored Hope, seated on a farmhouse porch.

"I never said nothing to my brother about it, but I saw her clear as day. God's my witness. I remember Faith asking how we found them and when I told her what I just told you, she seemed shocked but in a good way, like she actually believed me. That was Faith. She was rather reserved when we first met, but I learned she had a grit and resolution that made her different." He said this so tenderly that I wondered if he'd ever had feelings for her that weren't strictly platonic. "As for being family friends or neighbors? We weren't. We were strangers."

I sat amazed, unable to wrap my mind around Faith's predicament as he relayed a story of her being separated from kin, alone with her baby sister, traveling cross-country in a time of Jim Crow racial tension with white people she didn't know. I tried imagining myself in her shoes, surviving what must've been a harrowing experience, and couldn't.

"Our journey to California wasn't nothing to Faith but a means of finding her family. Wasn't nothing or nobody gonna keep her from them. Not even that midnight marriage to my brother."

"So, they *were* truly married," Gregory stated almost reluctantly. "This certificate is real?"

"Yes and no," his great-uncle confirmed, a touch of sadness in his tone that left me, again, wondering about his level of affection for Faith. "I mean, they had a ceremony but wasn't nothing legitimate about it," he quickly explained before Gregory or I could jump in. "It was officiated by my father's unofficial, sauced-up uncle whose license wasn't active on account of complaints other couples had made and his drinking problem. That didn't keep him from conducting ceremonies illegally. But whatever marriage certificate you have for Faith and Henry ain't good for nothing but starting a fire with."

I felt like I'd stepped into some pig-ear-eating, cross-breeding, hillbilly foolery. "I assume Faith knew nothing about this."

"I doubt it. I only found out months afterward when Henry told me . . . back when we were still speaking. If by some act of God Faith learned the truth, it was probably a relief."

I watched the airborne dance of two beautifully colored butterflies. "You say that because . . . ?"

"She didn't love him." His words held sharp edges and angles. "Truth is, she didn't even like my brother."

"So why did she marry him?" I wanted to understand her entering an illegitimate, interracial relationship in a politically incorrect, hostile climate with someone for whom she had no affection.

"Might sound calculated to some, but I believe Faith married Henry for her sister's sake. To keep them both safe. She was young. Female. Colored. Alone. Options were limited." He quieted a moment. "As for my brother? You have to understand that my parents were dogmatically religious. Henry was attracted to Faith. I think he did it to avoid feeling amoral. But his meanness got the best of him and Faith left the day after their wedding."

"Oh wow. It was really that bad?" I asked.

"It was. She and Hope were a bit of sunshine for me. Especially with my brother's orneriness and mood swings. So, I wasn't none too happy about their leaving. But in the end, I admired her and her refusal to give in. Life wasn't easy. She did what she had to and I don't blame her for it. To this day, I thank heaven we crossed that racial divide to become friends. If only temporarily. It changed me. My wife's Italian," he stated, seemingly changing gears. "Nathalia, that's my wife, passed last year. Nattie was the best thing to happen to me, but if I hadn't learned friendship with Faith, I never would've had Nathalia. So, I'm indebted. Hold on real quick. *Yes?*"

Milani was in the background, reminding him of a scheduled outing.

He returned to the phone almost immediately. "I apologize, but we're headed out to celebrate my great-great grandson's first birthday. How about we pick this up another time?"

"Sounds good, Uncle Micah, and thank you." Gregory sounded contemplative, subdued.

"Yes, thank you, sir, but may I ask three quick questions? Did Faith and Henry have children? Was she in search of just her parents, or other siblings as well? And is she still living?"

He chuckled lightly. "You definitely have Faith's persistence. I'm sorry to say we lost contact long ago so I don't know if she's still with us but, yes, she had other siblings. One died back in Oklahoma. The other was a brother who may or may not have made it to California. As for children"—he cleared his throat—"I can't say if their marriage was even consummated."

That blew me away, left me slightly tongue-tied while thanking Micah Owenslee for his time. "Enjoy the birthday celebration." After he disconnected, I spoke with Gregory a few minutes before ending the call and sitting there wondering what kind of strength it had required for Faith to escape the, perhaps, unwanted physical demands of an undesirable marriage. "I've *got* to find her." Feeling even more anxious to make her acquaintance, I consulted the notes on my phone.

Faith Joy Wilson: Wellston, OK
Younger sibling: Hope
Three siblings: at least one deceased
Brief, illegal marriage: Henry Owenslee
Offspring: unknown

"To find the present start at the beginning."

I typed "Wellston, OK" into a search engine, quickly clicked on Images, and laughed. "Either these photos are old or there's nothing in Wellston but dust and dandruff." I scrolled the pics, wondering what kind of life Faith had lived, particularly with an unkind man like Henry Owenslee only to realize my existence with Vince was equally unpleasant. "At least she got out before I did. Oh God, speaking of . . ."

I groaned, seeing an incoming call from him. I kept my voice neutral when answering. "The papers are signed and should be at your lawyer's by—"

"Screw the papers, Zoe. I need your help. *Please.*"

I pulled the phone away from my face and stared at it as if I'd fallen into some psychedelic black-hole experiment when that creature begged me to talk to his pregnant fiancée, to assure her that his receiving "oral transactions" at a strip club last night was little more than a blip on his radar of righteousness.

"Z., you can have the brownstone. Free and clear. And anything else you want in the settlement. Just do this for me."

I wanted to ask what made Jillian Masters so damn special that he was ready to cry like a little bitch at the notion of her leaving him. Why did he care about *her* pain and sensibilities after utterly decimating me with his multiple infidelities?

Simple: because she was pregnant. Vince's ability to spawn was a self-congratulatory, beat-his-chest-like-a-Neanderthal event for him, as if he alone was responsible for reproduction, and offspring confirmed his virility and manhood. If I wasn't aware before, it was crystal clear right then: Vince Edwards was a small, narcissistic, insensitive and insecure, sorry ass excuse for a human.

I forgive myself for ever being with him.

"Come on, Z., you know I've changed and that this was just a slip-up."

I knew no such thing and breathed in freely, happily reminding myself I wasn't a slave to his pain. Through therapy, meditation, and mindful living, I'd worked hard to reclaim balance and my sense of self. My keys of freedom included truth and integrity, and I chose to never again compromise either for him. "You're a ho, Vince, and I wish Jillian the best. Now, lose my number like I'm about to lose yours."

I hung up and blocked Vince's number before deleting him from my contacts. That felt so good my shoulders did a happy shimmy dance just as a text from my father chimed.

It was his response to my earlier inquiry about Granddad's birthplace.

Dad was born in Wellston, OK. Why?

"Oh my God, yessss!"

I never believed in coincidence. Rather, divine manipulation and intervention.

I wasn't certain of the exact dates of my grandfather's migration from Oklahoma to California, but if anyone knew them it would be him. Granddad's short-term memory played hazy games on him every now and then, but that long-term memory was rock solid. Perhaps that resulted from his hoarding his past so fiercely that he forgot very little. Regardless, I needed access to his memory vault and for him to trust me with his yesterdays. I had no concrete proof, but everything in me shimmered confidently. His siblings were deceased; perhaps, she was a cousin. Regardless of her exact placement, I felt it deep in my spirit: Faith Joy Wilson was Granddad's kin.

TWENTY-THREE

FAITH

Finding Mama was a divine blessing, made bitter only by her condition. She was bathed in bruises, caked in her own excrement, and lost in a laudanum fog that prevented her from being fully present. She required medical care for nearly a month thanks to malnourishment and purging That Demon's drugs.

I hated That Demon with every ounce of my being, and praised heaven when she was imprisoned.

"Faith, you need to forgive to live."

Miss Viv was right but, laying out my evening attire and glancing at Mama seated by the window as Hope read to her, I didn't feel like hearing holy advice. "She nearly killed my mother."

"But she *didn't.*"

"She would've if Hope wasn't curious."

When Hope heard the wailing that night, she wanted to prove herself a big girl, that she was unafraid, by asking Madame about it. Only, Madame wasn't in her room when Hope entered and found that retractable wall slightly open.

I tried to unlock the cubby door with Madame's letter opener. I broke it, but I was real brave, Faye-Faye.

What Hope called a "cubby" I called a cage, a locked space behind that wall where my mother had been cruelly contained, her mournful moans permeating the walls of that house as if the sad, heartbreaking song of countless women.

At times, I blamed myself for not recognizing the being who'd birthed my mother; but Mama's parents had thoroughly evicted her from their lives with only the clothes on her back. The matter wasn't a welcome topic and we never even saw a photo of the people who didn't deserve to be our grandparents. Not to mention, I was frustrated at other boarders claiming afterward that they'd heard the moaning too, and ignored it as the house being haunted, and that one man had even moved out because of it.

"And why would that disgusting hospital woman sell Mama to That Demon?"

"She didn't sell your mother, Faith."

"Like hell she didn't!" Clearly, I'd been around my band brothers too much and had to apologize for my foul language. Still, nothing made sense and without Miss Nance we never would've known of That Demon being contacted by some woman employed at a Bakersfield sanatorium who'd confessed like a sinner when confronted by the law. According to her, she'd provided governess care in younger years and instantly recognized Mama when she was admitted by my father. She'd contacted That Demon that should've never been a mother and was compensated for quietly "releasing" Mama into her care.

"Papa would've never left her there if he'd known what would happen." I soothed myself, deciding Mama must've declined drastically after leaving Oklahoma and Charity, then losing Hope and me. Maybe she needed more care than Papa and Noah could give, and the sanatorium was meant as a temporary fix. Whatever the case, it resulted in the evils of fate. Mama couldn't remember being admitted and, unfortunately for us, the place kept such poor records that there were no helpful links leading us to Papa. "And why'd a Colored girl even have a governess? Isn't that some British nonsense?"

"That was Madame being extreme bourgeois, honey."

"And the laudanum?" I held up a hand, anticipating Miss Viv's response, we'd hashed and rehashed the subject so much. "Cruelty. Control. I know." I sank onto the bed and looked at my mother, wondering how she could be That Demon's daughter. Mama was beautiful, gracious, generous. Compassionate. She hadn't deserved punishment for loving a man despised by class-conscious, color-struck parents.

Hate never makes sense.

"Faye-Faye, what's p-u-r-p-l-e?"

"Baby Girl, try your best to sound it out like Miss Bullocks taught us."

"Purrr . . . pul. *Purple?*"

"See! That's why you're gonna be the smartest girl in your class."

She smiled broadly when I praised her accuracy and intelligence. Hope loved proving her reading skills, and I chose to believe that Mama—improved but still too silent and sunken for me—found Hope's voice soothing. Hope had started first grade last month at a school close to the hotel; but living in the Dunbar was only good for now, not long term. Mama needed her own room, and Hope was a child who needed to run and play like we'd always done back home. That required the outdoors, not hotel living.

I lay on my back and stared at the ceiling, feeling incapable of making miracles occur, exhausted from the day job I was working to pay the bills from Mama's month-long medical care. "I have to find my brother and father."

Even if California didn't have farmland to offer him, Papa was smarter than the average man and would find a new way to support us. Even if it wasn't enough, with my day job and tips earned singing added to whatever Papa made, the two of us could take care of the Wilsons.

"You'll find them, honey, but for now rejoice that a miracle gave you your mother. Now, hurry up. Smitty'll dock your pay if you're late."

I pushed myself into an upright position. "Thankfully I'm only going downstairs, and I don't get paid anyway."

Mister Smitty and his wife were kind enough to put us up the night we escaped That Demon's house of horrors. Not wanting to impose on them or wear out our welcome, I'd approached the Dunbar's manager the next day and arranged for a room and meals in lieu of my portion of the band's fee. The only cash I'd walk away with after our gigs were tips if and when left by the audience, but I'd be grateful for them. Our room was a tight fit with four people and two beds. Miss Viv took one. Not wanting her out of our sight, Hope and I shared the other with Mama. Sometimes she woke up moaning, screaming. When she did, we simply held her and I sang her back to sleep.

Thank You, God, for letting us find her when we did.

Pushing out a gust of breath, I got up from the bed and started dressing so I wouldn't be late, despite having nothing but a three-hour nap after returning from my day job at the corner diner. Dallas had made a habit of taking me there after our gigs because I was too young to socialize at the hotel bar with the band. We'd become such frequent patrons, sipping milkshakes and enjoying burgers, that the owner liked me enough to give me a job serving tables and cleaning despite my lack of restaurant experience.

"What did Doc Reed say?" Miss Viv's prolonged pause wasn't lost on me as I slipped into my dress for the evening. "Miss Viv?"

Her recovery hadn't gone as expected. Her throat stayed bothersome, she hadn't returned to the stage, and she seemed to be concealing something. She busied herself, fingering my pin curls. "Doc can't tell the extent until the swelling's completely dissipated but . . . there's evidence of heavy scarring that might interfere with . . ." She blinked away tears. "*Voilà!* Your hair's perfect. Now get downstairs and sing their wigs off."

"Yes, ma'am, as soon as you answer one question. Can you take the stage again?"

She swallowed a sob. "It's a little iffy right now, Faith, but most likely not." She put on her usual cheer. "If I can't, I can always do hair. Guess this means you're taking my place in the band. Permanently." She pushed me toward the door. "Go. That dress is wicked and Dallas is waiting."

Ignoring her teasing, I hugged her hard. "Don't you ever worry about nothing, Miss Viv. If you sing again, praise God. If you don't, as long as anyone in the Wilson family is breathing you have a roof over your head." I kissed her cheek before hurrying to do the same with Mama and Hope. "Baby Girl, be sure to help Miss Viv with Mama and I'll bring everyone a pecan roll."

When my mother softly smiled at the mention of her favorite treat, I thanked heaven for restorative miracles.

"Mister Smitty, what's this?" I frowned at the envelope he thrust into my hands at the end of the evening. I'd arrived tired, but music did its magic, gracing me new energy so that I laid it all out on the table, giving the audience more than what they'd paid for.

"Tonight's earnings." He exited the band room, his voice trailing behind him. "Nice work, everyone. Go home, be good, and don't do nothing I would."

I rushed into the corridor after him. "Mister Smitty, this is a mistake. I get meals and a room in exchange—"

"The fellas want you to have it."

"Thank you kindly, but no sir—"

"Leave me alone, Songbird."

"Mister Smitty, I can't take everybody's pay!"

"Dallas, come get your woman." He walked out the back entrance whistling, leaving my band brothers laughing and dodging me and that envelope.

"Dallas, they can't do this," I complained as he draped his jacket over my shoulders.

"Looks like they can and they did."

"But they have families to feed."

He took my hand and steered us toward the exit. "*You're* family. And don't let Uncle Smitty fool you; his pay's in there as well."

"Is yours?"

He held the door open to the night, allowing me to proceed. "Maybe."

"Dallas Dorsey!"

He kissed my cheek. "Hush, Faith Wilson, and accept the gift. Wanna eat?"

Overwhelmed by the band's kindness, I slipped the envelope in my pocketbook and nodded before leaving the building with him. The night sky was soft, soothing. "Why don't you ever go for drinks with the boys?"

"I prefer eating with a pretty woman."

"Guess we'd better go find one for you to eat with."

He stopped walking, perturbed about the face. "Why do you do that, Faith?"

"Do what?" I stopped and stared up at him.

"Dismiss my compliments."

"Because they're a dime a dozen. You're always calling me pretty when you used to like Charity."

A deep frown creased his brow. "Where'd you buy that wrong notion?"

The night's performance had been excellent, Mama was

improving, and I had an envelope full of blessings. Maybe I was sad about Miss Viv, or tired from singing six nights a week and working at the diner by day, but something sour was sitting on me. "Y'all were always laughing. Chatting."

"We were church musicians who played together. That was our common denominator."

"You saying you didn't like Charity?"

"As a friend and fellow musician, yes, and that's it."

"Well, you're stupid. Charity would've made you a fine wife."

His jaw twitched. Fire lit his eyes. "I may be slow on the upswing but you're ignorant for not knowing *you* hold my interest." Tilting his hat brim at me, he stuffed his hands in his pockets and resumed walking.

"Maybe I don't wanna hold your interest. Ever consider that?" I tossed at his broad back.

"Good night, Faith. Go home and stop acting childish."

I planted my hands on my hips. "If I'm so childish why're you always taking me out and feeding me, or bringing me sweet treats and flowers? And watching me when I sing, or playing your trumpet and staring at me like the audience ain't even there? And why's Mister Smitty always calling me your woman?"

He swung in my direction. "Because maybe I love you, Faith Wilson. *Damn!*"

Sourness disappeared as the sweetness of his words washed over me, leaving me frozen and staring. All the infatuation I'd held back home for him melted into a warm pool in my stomach. It was soothing. Exhilarating. Frightening. My voice trembled when asking, "Do you or don't you?"

"What?" Confusion clouded his handsome face.

"You said 'maybe'..."

He kneaded the bridge of his nose before exhaling at the night sky. "Lord, I don't know why You're testing me with this woman." He snickered briefly before looking at me, smile fading. "I love you, Faith. There's no maybe."

My heart pounded as I slowly went to him, and found the courage to do something I'd always wanted to do. I stroked his full lips that blew magic into a trumpet before offering what I'd been too afraid to admit. "I love you, too, Dallas. Forgive me for calling you stupid?"

I felt pure tenderness when he cradled my face and kissed me for all of nighttime LA to see. I kissed him back without shame, losing myself in the splendor of loving and being loved by a beautiful being.

I did as Mister Smitty asked and wore my best and sang "the pants off those lyrics" three weeks later. That was easy enough, seeing as how loving Dallas put new flare and fire in my renditions.

We'd been steady, sharing our time and learning our love since our sidewalk admissions. He was patient, supportive. His down-home accent was thick as mine, but he had more polish. Still, with him I felt less country and isolated, and I slowly started feeling as if Los Angeles could offer me good things. Miss Viv and Hope adored him. Mama smiled big whenever he visited. He was kind to them all, but particularly gentle with Mama. I think she considered him her hero for carrying her from that cage in the wall. If she did, she wasn't wrong. Dallas was the hero of my heart. Bold. Beautiful. Strong.

"Stop looking at me like I'm new money," he quietly teased, squeezing my hand as we sat in the band room waiting on Mister Smitty and some mysterious guest who wanted to meet us after the night's last set.

"Don't blame me. Blame yourself for being so good-looking." I sealed my words with a kiss that quickly ended when

Boolie, our burly doorman, entered the room, his scowl deeper than usual.

"Songbird, you got a visitor."

Audience members, friends of the band, often stopped by with hellos or appreciation after a performance. "Invite 'em in, Boolie."

He shook his head. "It's that white cat that was here the night of that ruckus."

Dallas jumped up and was out the room before I could react. I ran after him, not wanting a repeat of Henry's unpleasant appearance, but found his brother in the hallway instead.

"Micah?"

Cap in hand, he looked uncomfortable but determined. "Hello, Faith, is it okay if we talk somewhere?"

"She's not moving. Say whatever you need to right here." Dallas's protective wariness was palpable. Dangerous.

I nodded at Micah, okaying his speaking in front of him.

"I apologize . . . for Henry's wrongdoing, and whatever else my family did that made you leave. Pa and Ma had to borrow the bail money and are upset with me for not co-signing Henry's cockamamie story to the police, but what he did was . . ." Micah looked away, ashamed. Putting his cap on, he looked at me, eyes welling with kindness and sincerity. "I wish you God's best. That's all I wanted."

Watching him walk toward the exit, I asked Dallas to wait when he took my hand to steer us back where we'd been. "Micah, hold on." I rushed toward him. "I thank your family for bringing me and Hope to California. Truly. But that never gave them rights to my freedom. I left because my life belongs to me. I'll repay Miz Lucy—"

"How much you owe?" Dallas interrupted, approaching.

"Fifteen and some cents, but I'll handle it."

"Here's a twenty. Keep the change." Dallas stuffed the bill

in Micah's shirt pocket when we both simply stared at the money he extended.

"Dallas Dorsey, don't handle my business!"

"Finish up, Faith. Uncle Smitty's waiting." He moved toward the band room, giving me some semblance of privacy, but still distrustful and watching.

"Is he okay?"

I smiled at Micah. "He will be. I appreciate you coming and saying what you said. Have you replaced your guitar yet?"

He smiled shyly. "I just about saved up enough."

"When you get that guitar, come back and we'll do a tune. Just us two," I added when he glanced at Dallas.

"Sounds good. Give Hope my regards . . . and I'm glad you have him." He nodded in Dallas's direction.

"Me, too, Micah. Thank you for being my friend." I hugged him quickly and returned to Dallas.

"You all right?"

Assuring him I was, I took his hand and hustled back into the room just ahead of Mister Smitty and the stranger in his presence.

"Band, this is the gentleman I mentioned yesterday. Monsieur Marceaux. Give him your attention."

He was a skinny, dark-haired white man with a funny accent. "I've watched all of your performances this week and loved each better than the last. Mademoiselle, you are a *force de la nature*. I invite you to France."

I stared at Dallas, then at Mister Smitty who frowned at Mister Marceaux, barking, "Hold up! I thought you said you wanted the entire band."

"*Mais bien sûr*, but of course! My country is enamored with your culture. Many Colored Americans have become expatriates there. Artists. Authors. Musicians. And many are brilliant. But this young lady is your *pièce de résistance*. She's your difference that will attract the crowds. *Vous appelez-vous,* Faith? *Oui?* That is your name?"

"Yes, sir."

He shook his head. "Sounds too much like a church singer. Do you have another?"

"My middle name is Joy."

He smiled brightly. "*La Joie.* Fitting for someone who brings such pleasure to others. Do you mind being Joie?"

"Lemme make sure I'm hearing correctly," Dallas interrupted. "You not only wanna take Faith to France, you wanna change her name in the process."

"Not solely her," the Frenchman corrected. "All of you, on a three-month tour that could be repeated, extended depending on its success. As for mademoiselle: not change, embellish. Add her name to the group's title and make her stand out as your divine vocalist."

Until then we'd been "Smitty Hughes and Company." I looked at our bandleader, gauging his reaction. He sat twirling an unlit cigarette, letting a long silence coat the room before smiling. " 'The Hughes Company featuring Joie' sounds good to me."

"Joie *Wilson,*" I corrected. I had no idea what kind of notoriety we'd gain, but if we were a hit overseas; that could filter back to the States. If it did, I wanted my last name included on the off-chance of Papa or Noah hearing about us, or even seeing me photographed with the band. Happiness filled me at the thought that music could be the vessel that brought us back together.

Mister Marceaux scanned our gathering. "So, is it settled?"

"Let's see the terms and numbers," one of the band demanded.

The Frenchman pulled a folded document from his inner jacket pocket, laid it flat on the table, and moved away while we huddled about it, whispering.

Mister Smitty shushed us and focused on our visitor. "You'll have our answer by the end of the show tomorrow."

"*Â demain*. Until tomorrow." When he kissed my hand with an "*Enchantée*," I felt Dallas stiffen.

I poked him in the side after the man left. "Stop acting jealous."

"Got his Frenchy-ass nerves, putting his French lips on my woman."

"So, are we accepting?" our drummer questioned as I giggled.

"You saw the pay. Divide that by the five of us and it's still three times what we're currently pulling in. Go home and discuss it with your wives and girlfriends, but my answer is *hell, yeah*," Mister Smitty yelled.

Cheers erupted. Dallas swooped me up and twirled me around. I was breathless when he put me down.

"As the leader, your pay should be higher than ours, Mister Smitty," I offered giddily.

He chuckled lightly. "That's why I like you, Songbird. Let's go celebrate."

It was my first time sitting at the bar in the hotel with the guys, and my first taste of champagne. I liked the bubbles tickling my nose, but not so much the taste. Still, I drank my share in celebration until we said our good nights.

"What time is it?" I asked Dallas.

"After two," he supplied while directing me toward the Dunbar's stairs.

Mounting the first, I stopped and shook my head. "I don't want to go up yet. Is Joe still gone up north?" It was a loaded question. Joe was Dallas's flat mate who was visiting family in the Bay Area.

He shook his head and cupped my elbow as he joined me on the stairs. "I'm taking you up to your mother and Miss Viv—"

"They'll be there when I get in." When he opened his

mouth in protest, I descended the stairs and walked toward the exit, boldness and freedom cushioning every step.

He had to clear a space for me to sit; his flat was such a mess.

"Is this how men live without a female's touch?"

"That's why you're here," Dallas teased, dropping onto the chair across from me in the tiny room that served as a parlor. He fiddled with his tie, nervously.

I smiled, seeing a side of him I hadn't witnessed. He always seemed so confident and put together. His strength reminded me of Papa, but the music in him made Dallas passionate, sensitive. His kindness toward Miss Viv, Mama, and Hope increased my love for him. He'd treated us to a day at the Ink Well, Santa Monica's Colored beach. We'd splashed in the ocean while he sat with Mama drawing in the sand, helped Hope collect seashells; then bought us so many hot dogs and pop we were all nearly sick. He took me to the picture shows, immersing me in that wonderful world of movies my parents couldn't afford. As much as I liked moving pictures, I liked the Jujy Fruits Dallas bought for me the best. That was Dallas. Generous. Thoughtful. Protective. Fascinated by the world around us. He was three years my senior with a seasoned soul that earned the admiration of older men; and he made love to his horn so thoroughly that if it was a woman, I would've been livid. He spoke of marriage, never compromised me. He showed me respect, and didn't bring me to his flat if Joe wasn't there. Now, I wanted us to be alone here, to perhaps test and taste what we'd carefully evaded.

"Play something for me."

He leaned toward me, face suddenly serious. "Baby, you shouldn't be here."

"But I am. So . . . play. Please. But quietly, so we don't wake the neighbors."

He hesitated, watching me a long while before rolling up his shirtsleeves and pulling his trumpet from its case almost reluctantly. "What do you want to hear?"

"I'm not sure . . ." I thought about it, but no tune came to mind so I made a suggestion. "Follow me."

I closed my eyes and hummed a bit. He mirrored my notes and added his own. We went back and forth, leading, following, allowing melodies to flow freely. Lyrics eventually replaced humming, and I sang from a place in my heart that had endured magnificent loss. Charity. Papa. Noah. Yet, it was a place that dared to believe. In love. And possibility. In minutes, we gave birth to a full song, but it was the final refrain that I sang and sang.

Let the world turn,
Let seasons change,
I'll hold onto hope always,
That I'll be finding you,
And you'll be finding me,
Yes, I'll be finding you,
And you'll be finding me.

When the final notes of Dallas's horn faded into the night, a sob slipped from my lips and I felt myself shaking.

I waved him away when Dallas put his horn aside to close the space between us.

I wanted air and to let whatever was trapped in me finally be free.

He complied, allowing me to empty an ocean of pain that had filled itself beyond capacity since losing Charity. Being nearly consumed by a black blizzard. Separation from my family. That ordeal with the Owenslees that culminated in marrying Henry. Feeling like a fish out of water in a big city. That Demon that abused Mama and treated me like a disease.

Working around the clock to care for my family. It poured out and I let it. When finished, I felt clean.

"You all right, baby?"

I took a deep breath and simply looked at him, this man on the verge of twenty who loved me with the depth of someone who'd walked this earth before. My love matched his in its bigness, but I wasn't sure its expressions did and suddenly craved a bigger language. I wiped my tears on the hem of my dress before slowly moving across the floor to him, humming the song we'd just created while stroking his face as if love spoke through my fingertips.

He shivered. "Faith . . ." His voice was deep, thick with heat and need. "We can't do this."

"What if this is what I want, Dallas?"

"Is it?"

I whispered my, "Yes."

He chewed the corner of his mouth before shaking his head. "Nawww, baby, I wanna marry you first."

"Tomorrow's not promised." I'd buried my sister, lost my brother and father. If I never saw another sunrise, I wanted to know what loving him felt like. Boldness had me in its clutches, as I breathed deeply, reaching back and unzipping my dress. I did so slowly, not like some sort of teasing burlesque but to give myself a chance to decide differently if need be. The fascination and ravenousness that claimed his face as I lowered my garment gobbled up any leftover hesitation. I felt enchanted. Liberated. Still, as my dress pooled at my feet, I stood there in my underwear and half-slip, unsure what to do next.

"Baby, there's no shame in not being ready. I promise you I can wait." His words were sincere, but the look on his face was pure fascination and want.

My words came out shy, hesitant. "Have you done this with other women?"

"Yes . . . two."

I thought a moment before reaching back and unhooking my brassiere. "You're my first, but I wanna be your third." I slid out of my half-slip, adding it and my brassiere to the pool at my feet before folding my arms across my bare breasts. In nothing save my panties, my bravado wavered a bit.

"It's okay, Faith. Come here."

When Dallas took my hands and led me onto his lap, thrills shimmied through me as his gaze latched onto my breasts. He stared at their fullness while licking his lower lip before cradling my face. "I love you, baby."

"I love *you*, Dallas."

He kissed me so deeply, held me so tightly that my chest hurt with intoxication. I returned his kiss the way he gave it and found nectar. It was so heady I could barely breathe as his strong hands roamed over me, touching my hips, my breasts with a gentleness that sent shockwaves through my being.

I didn't question my boldness when helping him undress; or the unexpected loveliness I experienced as he removed my undies. I embraced love's gentle lead as Dallas repositioned me on his lap so that I faced him. His lips were on my neck, his whispered words in my ear, offering me a final opportunity to walk away. As if the world beyond could ever match what he gave. I wrapped a possessive hand about that part of him that was powerful, unyielding. "I choose you, Dallas."

He hissed an expletive and blew air through clenched teeth. Gripping my hips, he positioned me so that I could take him in as I wrapped my legs about his waist. "We won't rush," he promised. "You control this."

I nodded, biting my lower lip as I began a slow, delicious descent. I was careful; even so, the pain was so piercing as he widened me that I yelped and buried my head in the crook of his neck.

He was my comfort. Rubbing my back. Stroking my hair. He whispered soothing love that let me relax. Gradually, raw pain subsided. Other sensations introduced themselves despite the remaining ache. Wanting to explore those sweet sensations, I moved slowly. Carefully. I liked what I was feeling. Warm. Heady.

"You're beautiful, baby."

I accepted his love-filled compliment as well as his touches, his kisses that branded my lips, my throat, my breasts—treating me to shocking feelings that pulled odd sounds from me, increasing my joy and the rhythm of our bodies. It was a fountain, a symphony, those indescribable sensations that permeated my center and skyrocketed, exploding outward with a force that left me screaming, my body quaking. I was breathless, unable to think, falling against my love as he continued thrusting into me until christening my ears with the sounds of his immense pleasure that I found intoxicating.

We clung together until our breathing normalized and our hearts no longer pounded like bass drums. We kissed tenderly, whispered words of devotion and love. He grabbed the blanket from the arm of an empty chair and wrapped it around me, allowing my modesty as I padded to the restroom to refresh myself before glancing in the mirror at a new woman. Bold. In love. Nearly fearless.

When I returned to the parlor, Dallas was whistling along with the tiny transistor radio he'd turned on. I accepted the hand he held out to me, feeling oddly shy yet serene as I sat on his lap and cradled against his chest as he draped the blanket over us both. I fell asleep hearing his heartbeat, feeling safe, cherished, and far from lost.

TWENTY-FOUR

ZOE

I was weary of records and certificates. Birth. Marriage. Divorce. Death. I'd exhausted every search I could think of since that conversation with Micah Owenslee to no avail. I'd decided to contact an investigator like Natasha suggested, but wanted to discuss the matter with Granddad first. Daddy, however, vetoed the idea. His father was private, proud, and might view an outsider's "poking in his business" as some sort of violation or intrusion. I'd honored my father's asking me to hold off a bit, to allow him to poke around "the family vault" in the hopes that some overlooked or obscure connection miraculously turned up.

"I feel no closer to finding Miss Cousin Faith than I was two weeks ago." I was convinced of her kinship. Confirmation was a mere necessary formality.

"Actually, you are closer," Shaun contradicted as we relaxed on the patio overlooking the marina, enjoying the unusual warmth of the March evening, and the smooth jazz floating from my phone as citronella candles warded off insects. A full moon sprinkled silver confetti atop the bay as we sipped wine and indulged in our multicultural feast. Unable to decide between Chinese, Italian, or Mexican, we'd ordered some of each. "She has a place in your family tree."

"True. At least that's what my heart says, but we'd still need a DNA test. I *have* to speak with her to clarify these links before going to Granddad." A need for solid proof aside, I was more fascinated with her now after speaking with Micah Owenslee. It was no longer merely about filling in missing faces in the family tree. My quest was personal. The information I'd gathered formed mere sketches. I wanted to fill them in with broad strokes of color, to hear her life story from her lips, experience the power of Faith Miss Me's presence. "If Daddy doesn't uncover something by the end of the week, I may have to go ahead with that private investigator. Better yet, I'ma have to disobey my father and go to Granddad directly."

"Do what you do, Miss Edwards," he teased, leaning toward me. "I like a woman who obliterates obstacles to get what she needs."

I met him in the middle. "Oh really? What if I told you this table's in the way of what I want?"

"It can be moved, madame."

I grabbed his arm, laughing, when he moved as if to hop up. "There's no need to reposition offending furniture." I abandoned my chair and eased onto his lap. "How's this?"

"Excellent."

I massaged his shoulders, appreciating the feel of firm muscle beneath my fingertips. I loved art and beauty. Smiling into his eyes, he was the epitome of both. I kissed his nose, his jaw, as if discovering the taste of a masterpiece.

"You missed a spot." His voice was dark coffee, smooth chocolate. He pointed to his lips which I gladly kissed. Gently. Deeply. Unlatching vast hunger within me.

The exchange was so thorough, intense, that my insides melted into a pool of massive want and I was on the verge of inviting him to take next lusty steps when the doorbell interrupted. I whispered an unladylike expletive.

"Expecting someone?" The huskiness in his tone was proof of his pleasure and passion.

"No. And if it's Natasha, she's fired." I planted one last kiss on his lips before heading for the front door and snatching it open only to find my mother, not my cousin. "Mama? What's wrong? And where's Daddy?" I stuck my head outside and looked toward the parking area.

"Nothing's wrong, and your father's not far. Can you let your mother in?"

"Sorry." Laughing, I pulled her indoors and hugged her tightly. "What's going on?"

"This." She took my hand and led me into the kitchen, placing a manila folder on the counter. "It represents a risk, so I need you to not divulge how you got this."

I frowned as she explained some genome project headed by a renowned professor of biology and genetics who'd once worked in her department. She'd moved on to spearhead a nearby lab, but they'd maintained contact. "Your daddy gave a saliva swab and a blood sample—"

"Daddy doesn't do needles."

"It was a thumb prick, Zoe, and he did it gladly. For you. And Granddad." She opened the folder holding a single sheet of paper.

"What is it?"

"Babe, you were finished, right?"

We looked up as Shaun entered the kitchen, bringing dinner dishes with him.

"Oh . . . hello. You must be Missus Wilson." He put the dishes in the sink and approached with hand outstretched.

"I am. You must be Shaun. Zoe speaks highly of you. And I don't do handshakes, I hug."

After hugging and exchanging pleasantries, my mother put

her back to him while mouthing "Babe?" at me, her eyebrows wiggling. I ignored her silliness and focused on the folder.

"So . . . what is this?" I extracted that single sheet of paper.

"A lead to two women who appear to be your grandfather's sisters and your great aunts. Faith Joy Wilson and Hope Ann Wilson Mabrey, complete with last known contact information on the back."

My mouth hung open. *"Wait! What?"*

"Babe, I'll say good night and allow you and your mother—"

"No. Stay. Please." I gripped Shaun's hand while slowly scanning the document. "Didn't Granddad's siblings die when he was a child?"

Mama shrugged. "So we thought."

"Then how can these women be my great aunts? Oh. My. *God . . .*" My voice faded as I greedily scoured the data in front of me.

I didn't fully absorb my mother's long, technical explanation of the genome project and Daddy's DNA samples producing links in its massive database and countless other details. I was too consumed with a graph similar to a family tree, connecting pieces of our puzzle and providing definitive proof that linked Faith and Hope Wilson directly to my grandfather. If the data was to be believed, they were siblings.

"This doesn't make sense. Granddad's mother and siblings died when he was a kid," I repeated, trying to make sense of what little I knew about his past. "Where's Daddy, and what's the accuracy rate of these results?"

"I told your father to meet me here. I came straight from work," Mama explained while pointing at the accuracy rate printed in the bottom right corner. "Ninety-nine-point-nine percent."

I stood there speechless, my hands shaking with nervous excitement.

I'd known in my gut that we were connected, but I'd

compartmentalized Faith Miss Me and Hope as possible distant cousins. This closer, implausible connection felt mind-bending. Miraculous.

I'd prayed, but God had surpassed my deepest requests.

My scream was enough to make my mother cover her ears. I did a happy dance before hugging Shaun. Then Mama. Embracing her, my joy took a bittersweet hit that she hadn't experienced similar outcomes.

Her mother senses kicked in. "Don't worry about me. I had the same test. Unfortunately, the results were spotty and inconclusive. If it's meant for me to find my bio family, I will. If not, I'm loved by two incredible parents. When your daddy told me what you were doing, I felt this might help. I'm ecstatic for Granddad."

I hugged her again, whispering in her ear. "I always knew my mother was a boss."

She hugged me back. "And don't you forget it."

"Our God is *so* good." Granny sat at the kitchen table, that folder in front of her, rocking gently from side to side, tears in her eyes. Daddy sat beside her, a supportive hand at her back. "I can't count the times I've asked the Lord to lift your grandfather's hurt. Looks like He's using modern-day technology to do it."

"And a little spit," Daddy added.

"Get on away from here." Granny slapped his arm playfully before sobering. "Son, I told your daddy he needed to tell you kids his whole story. He just couldn't. It was too much." She sighed heavily, and folded her hands atop the table. "I met your daddy here in California, but I think us both being from Oklahoma is what let him open up to me. My mama told stories of those black blizzards so I knew he wasn't exaggerating *nothing*.

Hearing that he'd lost his sisters to a dust storm broke my heart."

I listened as Granny shared memories of the early days of their marriage when my grandfather had nightmares of that dust storm that took nearly everything from him. His memories were so vivid and violent that he'd wake up screaming, fighting off horrors that only he could see.

"It was kinda like what those soldiers get . . . PTSD." Granny wiped a falling tear before looking at me. "They've just about faded over the years, but sometimes those nightmares were so terrible, your granddaddy would drink pots of coffee just to stay awake and avoid sleeping." She shook her head, sorrowfully. "Lord, that man's been through some things. So . . . what's next? Do we wait for your granddad to get back before doing anything?"

Once monthly, Granddad went to dinner with his surviving quartet buddies. According to Granny, he'd only been gone a few minutes and wasn't expected home for several hours.

"I think I should call now while Granddad's out." Despite the test's near-perfect results, I considered caution best. Science wasn't flawless. If a fluke was involved, I couldn't stomach the idea of raising my grandfather's expectations only to crush them.

"I agree." Daddy added his stamp of approval before giving the questions I'd written a last go-over. "Looks good. See how many of these details they can confirm. If it's sufficient, we can go from there."

I looked at the paper listing Granddad's birthplace, date, and other details Granny provided, feeling as if I'd been welcomed into a precious family vault previously sealed.

"Don't get caught by emotions or try to make things fit. We want truth, so be objective. And if these ladies *aren't them?*" Daddy shrugged. "At least you followed your instincts. Do you want to make the call with all of us here?"

"Thanks, Daddy, but I should probably make the first call alone so they don't feel overwhelmed. I'll take notes."

"Don't you leave out one detail."

I kissed Granny's forehead. "I won't, nosey woman."

I chose the family room and my grandfather's favorite chair, needing his essence when calling the women I genuinely believed were his sisters. Inhaling deeply, I dialed the number for Faith Wilson. While the report provided evidence of DNA matches, the contact information had been Mama's gift obtained via a highly advanced database used for her family research. There was no address and I didn't recognize the area code, but hoped I wouldn't be waking her.

My spine straightened when my call was answered only to sag upon hearing that irritating message: "The number you have dialed is not in service." I tried again in case I'd misdialed but received the same results. My heart started pounding. "Relax, Zoe. You have Miss Hope's contact. She can connect you to Faith."

I held my breath while calling, exhaling audibly when she answered on the fourth ring.

"Hope Wilson Mabrey speaking." Her voice was tinged with sleep, yet strong, direct.

"Good evening, Missus Mabrey. I apologize for waking you. My name is Zoe Edwards."

"Yes? How may I help you?" she added when I sat in silence, too nervous to continue.

Get it together, Z., you prayed for this opportunity.

"Ma'am, I know this may sound strange, but it's highly possible that we're related. Your sister, Faith—"

She was suddenly no-nonsense. "My sister, Faith, is gone. I'm the only one left."

I'd cautioned myself of the possibility that she was no longer here based on her age; even so, being denied the chance to meet my look-alike on this side of life knocked the wind out of me, leaving me with an immense sense of loss that left me speechless, my heart in knots.

"Are you still there, Miss Edwards?"

I rapidly shook my head to recollect myself. "Yes . . . ma'am." I wiped an unexpected tear.

"Wait one moment." Muffled voices were heard on her end. "I'm going to move this call into my office so my husband can sleep. Stay with me."

I sat, wounded by Faith's passing, a sinking feeling in my stomach that perhaps—like Henry Owenslee—she'd recently died and I'd been deprived of her by something as simple as poor timing.

"Now, what's this about our being related?" Hope Wilson Mabrey questioned once settled in her home office.

"I'm so sorry to hear about Aunt Faith." The title slipped from my lips without effort.

"*Aunt* Faith? Who are you, Miss Edwards? And how're we related?"

"My maiden name is Wilson." I explained Daddy's recent DNA test and the photograph that led me here. "My father's father is Noah—"

Her ear-shattering scream cut me short, left my heart pounding, my pulse in overdrive.

"*Missus Mabrey!*" My own scream received no response. "Oh God!" I flew to my feet and was pacing, scared witless, when Daddy burst into the den.

"What's going on?"

Granny entered behind him, praying, as I explained what occurred. I put my phone in speaker mode so they could hear, afraid I'd caused horrific damage to the party on the other end. Words were indiscernible, but intense sobbing and jagged breathing were crystal clear. *"Missus Mabrey..."* When she didn't answer, I felt desperate. "Aunt Hope!"

Sounds of someone fumbling with the phone filled the air and a man spoke. "This is Emery Mabrey, Hope's husband. Who's this?"

"Zoe Edwards, sir. Is she okay?"

He'd barely begun replying when the phone was obviously removed from his grip and his wife returned on the line, her sobs somewhat quieted.

"Missus Mabrey, I'm so sorry for causing you such distress—"

"No! If this is legitimate, it's an answer to the prayers Faith and I prayed for decades." Her voice was thick, intense. "We lost our brother, Noah, a *long* time ago. And you're claiming to be related to him? Is he still living?"

"Yes, ma'am, to both questions."

"Thank You, Jesus! Thank You, Lord!" Her praise was louder than her scream had been. *"You heard our prayers. Oh God. Oh God. Oh God."*

I sank onto Granddad's chair, goosebumps decorating my skin, feeling the presence of the Creator as if in a Sunday service. Daddy sat on the sofa opposite me appearing equally moved as Granny took my phone.

"Hello, Hope, this is Noah's wife, Bertine... or Teenie... Can you tell us anything that might help confirm your identity?"

"Hello, Teenie. What do you wish to know?"

"Where was my husband born?"

"My brother, Noah Riley Wilson, was born the ninth of September to Tomas and Mae Princessa Wilson right here in tiny Wellston, Oklahoma."

I was so shaken Daddy had to take my fact-check list and cross off *birthdate, location,* and *parents.*

"How large was his immediate family?" Granny continued, sitting next to her son.

"Besides Mama and Papa? It was just us three girls and Noah. He was the only boy." Her tone brightened. "And oh, how we never let him forget that. He used to complain about being surrounded by 'girly, frilly-ness,' but I think he liked having all sisters and being the sole prince. We all worked the fields, including Charity, Faith, and me. But being the only boy meant Noah often got more of Papa's time and attention."

Now abideth faith, hope, charity, these three . . .

I shivered, remembering the early part of this voyage of discovery and reading that verse after my farmhouse dream. Aunt Faith and Spirit had led me to it, offering me truth that I mistakenly interpreted as mere encouragement to continue. I was ecstatic that I had.

I sat quietly, awed as my great Aunt Hope answered every query beyond our satisfaction, even offering details that brought illumination to dark places and granted a broader view of my grandfather's childhood and history.

"Aunt Hope"—again the title was effortless—"we cannot thank you enough for indulging us our ten thousand questions."

"I have eleven thousand of my own, but before we get into them, my brother nearly lost his left foot sustaining an injury the day our big sister, Charity, was bit. Did it ever heal?"

Granddad had walked with a limp all of my life due to a partial amputation resulting from an old injury, the details of which were cloaked in that impenetrable cloud of the past that he shrouded himself in. I exchanged looks with Granny and Daddy as if, despite the accurate answers she'd already provided and the DNA links, this intimate detail alone solidified the fact that Hope Ann Wilson Mabrey was truly Granddad's last remaining sibling.

Despite the time difference putting Aunt Hope two hours ahead, we stayed on the phone another hour talking. Rejoicing. Crying.

"That's so tragic." My tears flowed in abundance, hearing of the death of their oldest sister, Charity, and the family's exodus that resulted in their separation. "Why would Granddad keep all these secrets?"

"Zoe, honey, my brother was raised in a time when men prided themselves on the care they provided their families," Aunt Hope offered. "Our father was fiercely protective. My brother wasn't the oldest, but as the only boy, Papa drilled into him that he was responsible for us girls. When Charity was bit, Noah blamed himself. Faith tried to soothe him, reminding him Charity had gone to get that saw Mama sent *her* to get. That didn't matter to my brother. He felt that if he'd come home from the Dorseys' when he should have, Charity wouldn't have been there and never would've encountered those rattlers. That was bad enough. Add to that whatever torment he went through after Faith and I were swallowed by that black blizzard and you may understand his silence."

"But both of those horrors were acts of nature, Aunt Hope. There's no shame in that."

"No, Zoe, there isn't. But in a matter of days your granddad lost half his foot, not just one but *all* of his sisters; and our mother wasn't in the best state mentally after Charity so you can only imagine how being separated from me and Faith affected her. My brother's a sensitive soul and would've misinterpreted those crushing losses as some perverse proof of his failure or fault. His not telling what little he did to anyone but Teenie makes sense. He was proud, wounded, *and* devastated."

"Not to mention traumatized," Granny added.

"Yes, ma'am," Aunt Hope agreed. "Hold on a moment . . ."

I allowed those truths to sink in as Aunt Hope spoke to her

husband. "I'm back. Emery's asking, can you FaceTime on your phone?"

"Yes, ma'am. We can switch to that mode if you'd like."

"Let's. That way we can all see each other while we talk."

Granny looked at her watch. "We better hurry up before your grandfather gets back."

We'd elected to speak to Granddad and fill him in on everything that had transpired and allow him to decide next steps.

"Yes, ma'am." I quickly switched to FaceTime mode and sat back, my heart pounding excitedly as the face of a woman who, as her adult self, looked so like my grandfather that they couldn't deny each other populated the screen. "Hello, Aunt Hope."

She sat silently, hands over her mouth, rocking slowly back and forth, tears streaming, her voice a strangled whisper when she spoke. "Not long before she passed, my sister started having dreams of an angel knocking on doors, calling her name while ringing Christmas bells. That last bit didn't make sense, but I told Faith it meant someone was or would be looking for her."

Here comes Zoe Noelle with her magical bells and angel tails.

Granddad's ditty rang in my ears as Aunt Hope dried her tears.

"Your dreams were on the money, Faye-Faye. Your look-alike angel found us." She paused momentarily. "My sister died five years ago today. I woke up missing her something terrible this morning, but here you are, letting me see her face again. That's a gift from heaven."

"She's agreed to a DNA test for verification purposes, but everything else aligns enough for us to believe it's her, Granddad."

Granny, Daddy, my uncles, and I sat silently waiting for a

reaction from my grandfather the next morning. Seated in his favorite chair, he stared at the far wall. Stoic. Unmoving.

"Noah . . . baby . . . what're you thinking?" Granny touched his arm, gently.

He tucked his lips in and made chewing motions, his sure sign of deep contemplation. "I'm telling you, Teenie, my sisters got swallowed up, buried in that black blizzard. Now, y'all telling *me* my baby sister's still living? This feels like somebody's sadistic idea of a joke. Like we're opening some ol' box best left shut, like it's too damn much."

"We understand, honey, but we really believe it's Hope. You'd never forgive yourself for not doing this."

He massaged his brow as if soothing his consternation. "Miracles happen, but Lord knows I couldn't stand it if it's not her."

It was risky, and the possibility of causing my grandfather additional pain weighed on me as I vacated my seat and knelt in front of him. "We're here with you, Granddad." I reminded him of Daddy's DNA leading us to Aunt Hope, and banked on science. Unfortunately, in my excitement I'd left everything—photos, laptop, *and* my phone—on the kitchen counter when running out the door this morning and was unable to provide the pictures as proof of his sisters' survival. "Whatever way it goes, we got you. Okay?"

He looked at me long and hard before sighing heavily. "You said you can get her on this here thing big enough for me to see her clearly?"

"Yes, sir." My cousins and I had gifted our grandparents a laptop several Christmases ago. They'd barely used it, except to play Spider Solitaire and other games. I opened it and launched Zoom while explaining video-conferencing. "But it's your choice . . ."

Inwardly, I did a happy dance when my grandfather nodded his consent. His agreement brought joy to my heart and soothed the hurt I'd felt at the news of my great aunt's death. Based on her guesstimated age alone, I had known there was a chance Aunt Faith was no longer with us. That didn't lessen the gut punch of grief in hearing she'd passed. Now, we'd never meet face to face, we two women of the same family, divinely connected phenotypically. Despite never knowing her, I'd cried for my loss, as well as Granddad's, and felt the heavy disappointment of a failed quest.

But Aunt Hope is here.

Reminding myself of that divine blessing, I video-conferenced her in.

"Here, baby, put on your glasses." Granny situated Granddad's trifocals on his face.

"I can put on my spectacles, Teenie. I ain't no invalid."

"No, you're not, with your double negatives."

I laughed at Granny's quip but quieted as Aunt Hope, Uncle Emery, two of her five children, and a granddaughter, Camille—who looked so much like Natasha that it was scary—came into view.

"Good morning! Give me one moment to reposition everything." Thanking Daddy for situating a TV tray in front of his father, I placed the laptop on it before scooting behind Granddad's chair and brought Aunt Hope full-screen. I smiled into the camera, my hands on Granddad's shoulders. "Thank you so much for allowing this. Aunt Hope, this is—"

"My big brother, Noah Riley Wilson," she finished before I could. Her voice was clouded with emotion. "We had Faith and Charity. Both have gone to heaven. But we're here, the last two. Mama used to sing us a little song she made up with all of our names in it. Do you remember?"

Chills sped down my arms when she began singing a tune I'd often heard my grandfather hum.

There's Faith, there's Hope, there's Charity,
My angels from above,

I couldn't hold back tears as Granddad joined Aunt Hope in finishing the refrain.

But Brother Noah built a boat,
And saved them from a flood.

When Granddad pressed a hand against the computer screen, saying tearfully, "That's my baby sister," and Aunt Hope returned the gesture with, "Lord, thank You for keeping my big brother," I didn't cry. I sobbed as if a deceased beloved had been brought back to life.

TWENTY-FIVE

FAITH

"Who's gonna walk Hope to school when I'm not here?"

"I will." Mama's answer was quiet but authoritative. With each passing day, Mama was emerging and present, her beautiful self. My pending departure to France seemed to have chipped away at the fog she'd been lost in. She was more lucid, smiled easily, and even slept without haunting dreams. Seeing her returning to herself was a gift, constantly opening.

"What if the boat sinks like that *Titanic*?"

Mama and Miss Viv laughed.

"Faith, honey, you're clutching at straws and being ridiculous," Miss Viv admonished while trimming my hair.

"It can happen." My insistence was complicated. I'd never been so far away from home before. I didn't know a lick of French and, despite what Monsieur Marceaux said, wondered if I was headed to just another country that treated Colored folks like the plague. Plus, I couldn't look for Papa and Noah from overseas. I was torn between leaving and earning good money my family could use, or staying put, making sure Mama and Hope were okay while continuing our search for our lost beloveds.

Mama stopped folding laundry and placed herself in front of me. Miss Viv's trimming scissors stopped as Mama lifted my chin. "Many things can and do happen, Faith. Good. And ugly. We know this because we've lived it; but if life doesn't quit on us, we don't quit on it." Looking in Mama's eyes, I saw hesitation and maybe some misgiving. More than that, I glimpsed the soft fire of determination that I would have opportunity. "So, you go on over there and knock those French folks off their seats with your gorgeous singing. We'll be fine. You hear me?"

"Yes, ma'am." I watched her return to the laundry, telling myself she was stronger than I'd ever be, only to remember my journey and how Papa had always told us never to compare our experiences with someone else's. Our lives were what *we* were supposed to live. It hadn't been easy, and Mama couldn't seem to say enough how proud she was of me for getting Hope and me safely to California. She never faulted me for that debacle with Henry, telling me I'd done what I had to in the moment. She called me tenacious, resilient. Her warrior.

I'm going to France. And if I like it enough, I'm going back. With Papa, Noah, Mama, Hope, and *Miss Viv!*

I inhaled a deep breath to capture the scents of familiar comforts. I wanted to take them with me like a warm, soothing blanket. My nostrils filled with hair pomade, the pressing comb on Miss Viv's hot plate, and Mama's powdery scent. I'd take these and all my precious memories with me to a new country, knowing I had people to come home to. Family. "Mama, I'ma wire back most of what I make. I want you to save it for me, please."

"I will. You just make sure you keep enough for yourself. Your funds will be here when you get back to do whatever you need with it."

Mama had been so lost in sorrow and herself, that she didn't recall a thing about that sanatorium. Plus, that laudanum had messed with parts of her memory, leaving her with no clue where Papa could be, or even the whereabouts of his sisters. Wherever Papa was, I was sure he still had the deed to our land. When we found each other and things got better, we'd likely head back to Wellston. Until then, we needed to have something of our own however long we stayed on the Gold Coast. "We're buying a house with that money."

Mama swung around to look at me. "What?"

"Papa always said, 'Own what you have,' so that's what we're doing. I don't mind sharing a room with Baby Girl, but we'll find something big enough for Noah to have his own room. And a yard. With a big tree so Noah and Hope can have a tire swing."

Mama stared at me a moment before smiling. "I named you what I did for a reason, so you'd always have plenty of conviction and happiness."

I returned Mama's smile, imagining a house in my mind, thankful when realizing I was dreaming, anticipating good things like I hadn't in a long while.

"Well don't you look fancy, Miss Faith!"

I felt sophisticated with my new hairdo and the makeup Mama agreed I could wear, and that Miss Viv had shown me how to apply so I'd look naturally enhanced and not like some painted lady or circus clown.

"My baby looks like twenty million bucks." Kissing my cheek, Dallas co-signed Miz Bailey's opinion, looking at me like he'd never seen a prettier woman.

After what we'd shared, I often felt shy at his attention. Other times, I craved it. And him. We were together twice after our first loving but since his flat mate came back, we'd been unable to be together again. It was probably for the best, seeing as how I didn't like lying to Mama about my whereabouts, or having her looking at me like she was trying to see something hidden beneath my skin. Music was so intimate that it hadn't been easy climbing on stage with Dallas, knowing what I really wanted was us alone and unclothed, touching, sharing. Today was one of those crave days and I was glad to have Miz Bailey and her entire dress shop in between us to keep me from acting disorderly and prying that man's pants off.

"Thank you both for your compliments. Miz Bailey, can you help me find a few things for this trip?"

"You're gonna wear my things in Paris?" She clapped her hands excitedly. "Ooo, yes!"

"Do you have time to make a replica of my silver dress?" I hated that the first performance gown I'd ever purchased had been destroyed in that fracas with Henry and wished I still had it.

"I'm sorry but I'm scrambling enough as it is. I got orders to fill and my seamstress up and quit to move back to Arkansas. Now, I gotta find a seamstress *and* my tenant left. I tell you; when it rains, it pours."

Miz Bailey owned her shop as well as the apartment above. I stared at the ceiling, wanting to see through it. "How big is your apartment?"

"It runs the width and length of the shop, and has two bedrooms and its own private bath. None of that sharing like you have to do in rooming houses."

"How much are you asking for rent, and do you mind my seeing it?"

"Lawd, that light in her eyes tells me she's up to something."

I pinched Dallas for his teasing before turning back to Miz Bailey. "I'm thankful, but the Dunbar's a little tight for the four of us. Your shop's close to Hope's school, and it'd be nice having somewhere better to stay before we leave in two weeks." I smiled big, thinking on something else, gushing the rest in one huge breath. "I might be able to help you as well. My mother's not a professional seamstress, but she sews better than good enough if you'd like to consider her services. If you can show me the apartment and I like it, would you consider renting to us?"

"Girl, you got gumption. Lemme get the keys." Miz Bailey locked the shop door and turned the sign to *Closed* before leading us out the back upstairs to her tenantless apartment.

I didn't like it—I *loved* it and paid the first month's rent from my share of the band's contract advance. That left me with very little to use on my purchase, but I exited the shop with peace of mind which was far more important. "With what I send back home and what Miss Viv makes doing hair, we'll be okay. Right?"

Strolling away from Miz Bailey's, Dallas kissed my temple. "It's gonna work out fine."

"You promise?"

"Yep."

I looked up at him. "Dallas Dorsey, you're a good man."

"That's why I have a good woman. You want ice cream?"

"Yes, but can we do something else first?" I laughed when his eyes narrowed and he licked his lips. "Not that. Can we go by the station?" I hadn't been since taking on that diner job which, incidentally, I'd let go of two weeks back in order to get ready for France. Before then, I went on a weekly basis. Sometimes it felt useless, like life was a trickster keeping Papa and Noah somewhere out there. But finding Mama was proof that miracles happened. I couldn't give up. Not yet. Probably not until my last breath. I headed for the station with Dallas, hoping it never came to that, but if it did, my family and I would find each other in heaven.

The Dunbar staff surprised us with a going-away celebration on the night of our final performance. There was cake, balloons, and champagne that even Mama indulged in. Hope was ecstatic that she'd been allowed to stay up late and ate more cake than a little bit. I was concerned Miss Viv might feel sad that I was going instead of her but every time I looked around, she seemed happy, chatting with Boolie the doorman.

"Chick Webb. Dizzy Gillespie. *Duke Ellington?*" Mama was giddy reading our schedule and the acts that we'd open for. Eventually we'd headline, but this was Monsieur Marceaux's way of cleverly introducing us to our new audience by having our band open for well-established artists. "That's one piano-playing maestro," Mama commented. "And he dresses like the duke he is."

"There's also some new singing sensation named Ella that Monsieur Marceaux's gonna try to get me a duet with. Mama, do you miss playing the piano?"

She nodded. "Every day. But not as much as I miss your daddy and Noah. And Charity. I'm going to miss you something fierce, baby."

"I can stay—"

"No, you can't. And no, you won't. Go'n out there and make your musical mark on the world. Before you leave here, I want you to come to the drug store with me to get some things so you and Dallas don't create something before you're ready."

Blushing, I looked away, shocked that my intimate relationship with Dallas hadn't escaped her notice.

She turned my face toward her. "I know a woman in love when I see one, Faith. I also know what change looks like when a woman has tasted what you've tasted. And praise God again for the apartment," she moved on quickly. "I like Miz Bailey and I think I'll enjoy working for her."

I watched my mother enjoying the evening, only to realize she was still a young woman. Her soul had been bruised, but she was beautiful, and I desperately needed Papa there to take care of her and Hope.

But she's strong.

I reached over and hugged her suddenly, knowing I'd do

whatever I could to ensure our well-being. Including, making my way to the newspaper office before leaving for France to place a missing persons ad. My prayer was that Papa, Noah, my aunts, or someone who knew them would see it and help bring us together. I trusted God to help make that happen.

Two weeks later, I was a ball of nerves approaching that gang-plank, and prayed my stomach wouldn't act up the way it had been lately once we'd pushed out to sea. I swallowed my nerves and watched the band cart our luggage onboard before turning back to my family of three.

"I'm *not* crying."

Laughing at Miss Viv's insistence, I wiped tears from her face. "We'll just call this rain." I hugged her, thanking her yet again for all she'd done for us. "Don't forget, you're always family."

"I sure am. Now, bring me something nice from Paris."

Releasing her, I hugged my mother. She held me fiercely, neither of us speaking. We'd been separated from each other for months that felt like infinity and were reluctant to let go. But this time there were no black blizzards. Or venom. Just magnificence and a new future. "I love you, Mama. When you find Papa and Noah, tell them I'll be back soon."

She merely nodded, choked by emotions as I hugged her again and kissed her before kneeling to embrace my baby sister. My heart constricted so tightly, thinking on our journey. Just the two of us Wilsons, alone. I thanked God yet again for allowing us to safely arrive here, and for giving us the strength and good sense to stay together no matter what. "I love you with every fiber of my being, Hope Ann Wilson." She was my light in darkness.

"I love you the same way, Faye-Faye. Guess what?"

"What?"

"I think you're my best friend."

I laughed and picked her up, twirling her around before setting her down. "Make sure you write me so I can see all that pretty penmanship. And don't forget to tell me all the new things you're learning in school and about those friends your own age."

She giggled when I tickled her tummy while kissing the top of her head as the ship's horn sounded.

"Faith? We gotta get onboard, baby."

I glanced back to see Dallas striding down the gangplank. Watching his easy gait and brown-skinned deliciousness, I knew he'd spend more time in my ship cabin than his. And that's the way I wanted it.

"You take good care of my baby, Dallas Dorsey!"

"Yes, ma'am, Miz Wilson." He exchanged quick hugs with everyone before taking my hand and leading me toward the ship. "You okay?"

I nodded, despite the tears streaming down my face. "I'm more than okay. I'm full of hope and faith."

Once onboard, we wiggled our way through the crowd of sailing passengers to find the band positioned at the rail, waving to those not taking the journey. Unwrapping the satin scarf keeping my curls in place and tied beneath my chin, I waved it in the autumn breeze while tossing kisses at my family only for the breeze to gust suddenly, snatching the scarf from my grip. "Oh, Jesus . . ."

I leaned forward trying to snatch it, only to see it drift like a colorful cloud toward the dock.

"I'll get it!" Hope released Mama's hand to run alongside the ship.

"Hope Ann, come back here."

"Yes, ma'am." Hope looked crestfallen when the scarf fell out of reach, only to smile when a gentleman plucked it up from where it landed near his feet and extended it in her direction.

Thanking him, she took it and waved it back at me. "You can't leave this, Faye-Faye!"

I grabbed Dallas's hand when the boat jerked into motion, knowing that months would pass before seeing my beloveds, yet thrilled with excitement for what lay ahead. "You keep it for me. Drape it around your neck like a Hollywood queen."

She giggled merrily. "Faye-Faye, can you bring me back a new Miss Rainy Day?"

"I can, and I will. Love you till forever, Baby Girl."

"Love you till forever plus seventy-eight days, Faye-Faye!"

I laughed and leaned against Dallas, letting him wrap me in his arms and his love as we waved farewell until my family faded into the day, and only the horizon and the future in front of us remained.

TWENTY-SIX

ZOE

That first conversation between Granddad and Aunt Hope wound up being an impromptu family reunion of sorts. Not only was it amazing meeting relatives, but there was abundant laughter, tears, and awed reverence as we listened to our elders share stories from their past and reconnect. An hour in, Granny tactfully suggested we allow Granddad and his sister some time with just the two of them.

That was days ago. Since then, Granddad and Aunt Hope spent so much time catching up that Granny teasingly called her newly discovered sister-in-law "Noah's other woman." As for my grandfather, he moved with greater purpose and energy, exhibited newfound peace, and was plotting a face-to-face reunion with his baby sister.

"I haven't stepped foot in Oklahoma in years." Now, he counted down the days until returning to the old homestead where Aunt Hope lived.

That the land was yet in the family was a miracle and testament to the strength of Aunt Faith, and her fierce belief that one day her beloveds would be reunited there in her final resting place.

"She fought those folks tooth and nail over their 'squatters' rights' and taking our property." Apparently, a long-standing dispute between our family and the Native American tribe that had enslaved my great-great grandfather resurrected itself when the Dust Bowl sent our family further west, leaving our land unprotected. "It was more than bad blood. My grandmother had a . . . What do you young folks call those problematic sexual situations?"

"An entanglement, Aunt Hope?"

She laughed brightly. "*Entanglement!* Yes. Our grandfather killed one of them for trying to take the plot of land the government distributed to slaves of Natives, and had to sneak out of Oklahoma under the cover of night to avoid execution. That left Granny fending for herself and six children, and winding up in a compromising entanglement that resulted in my Aunt Leola when she was threatened with eviction and was desperate to save the homestead. Wilsons never would've left that land except for black blizzards. It held too much of us. No way on earth was Faith *not* going to fight for it." Her voice grew reverent. "My big middle sister cussed those folks in beautiful French and got a team of lawyers to reverse that mess. It took years, but she did it. When I pass, my family knows to intern my body here on the land where I took my first breath. Did you get my package?"

"I haven't checked the mail. I'll do it as soon as we finish." My great aunt and I were nearly as bad as she and Granddad, enjoying our developing relationship and communicating almost daily, usually via video-conferencing. Each time we did, she needed a moment to collect herself because of my resemblance to Aunt Faith. But she was careful to assure me that her tears held joy, not pain.

"I sent that package via express mail so if it doesn't arrive by today let me know and I'll cuss out those post office folks."

That left me laughing. "Aunt Hope, I can't exactly see you

cussing anybody." A retired geologist, Granddad's sister was an elegant woman who looked a decade younger than her age, with a genteel disposition and charm that stamped her as Southern bred.

"Zoe, baby, don't let this smooth face fool you. I can cuss like a sailor if I need to, ask God's forgiveness, then sit somewhere with my ankles crossed, fanning myself and sipping mint juleps."

Our shared laughter was like a gentle heart hug. "Duly noted."

"Before I forget, I received *your* gift via email last night. It's so generous, sweetheart. You didn't have to do that."

"I'm honored that you accept."

"I most certainly do. Thank you. Now, stop letting an old lady infringe on your time. You have an exhibition needing your attention. Call me if your package doesn't arrive so I can raise dignified Cain."

Still smiling after our goodbyes, I grabbed my keys and headed for the communal mailboxes just as Natasha drove up. I waved and watched her park. "Hey, Tasha!"

"Hey, chick." She exited her car, waving a grease-stained takeout bag. "Look what we're eating!"

I groaned, recognizing the bag's logo, knowing the contents. "Why would you bring those loaded fries up in here?"

"Girl, hush. This ain't nothing but a little love."

"All this edible love y'all keep feeding me wants to take up permanent residence on my rear end."

"Is Shaun complaining?" She wiggled her eyebrows and grinned.

"I'll let you ask him." I switched my high and wide behind to the mailbox, delighted to find the package from Aunt Hope inside.

"What's that?"

"Something from Aunt Hope."

"Open it already," my bossy cousin demanded.

"I will as soon as we're inside and I find the scissors."

We'd barely cleared the entrance before Natasha was fussing. "Hurry up and open the damn thing, Zoe!"

"Stuff some fries in your mouth and quit rushing me." Unable to locate scissors, I grabbed a knife and headed for the patio where we could enjoy the sunset. Once seated, our hip-spreading loaded fries were pushed aside as I sliced through the tape sealing the box and gently removed its contents. "Oh. My. *God.*"

"What is it?" Natasha pulled her chair close to mine.

"Some kind of portfolio." My heart skipped several beats as I opened it to xeroxed fliers announcing Aunt Faith's performances. They were meticulously, chronologically arranged, granting us a journey through history and her career. "*Ohmigawd!* She performed on the same bill as Duke Ellington and Chick Webb!"

"And Dizzy Gillespie," my cousin added. "And *the* Ella Fitzgerald!"

We squealed and stomped our feet in full fan-girl mode while listing the other, numerous famed entertainers with whom our great aunt had performed.

"Tasha, this is incredible."

"Right! Why wasn't she ever known? Why didn't she go solo?"

"Aunt Hope said she tried but backers and promoters wanted male-led bands, and those who were open to female leads thought Faith Wilson sounded too much like a gospel singer. That's why they made a play on her middle name and she headlined as Joie Wilson when she went to France."

"Even with all that patriarchal BS, she had an amazing career."

"That she did," I commented, reaching the back of the portfolio and feeling breathless when seeing the program from her funeral. I traced the lovely outline of her photograph on its cover as Natasha read her sunrise and sunset dates aloud. "Hold up. Look at her birthdate!"

"April twentieth," Natasha read only to fall silent.

We stared at each other as I barely whispered, "Jaelen passed away on her birthday," before closing my eyes, not in sorrow, but with a reaffirming sense of divine interconnection.

"Dang, Cuzzo, the connection between you two is crazy beautiful."

"I know." I considered my farmhouse dream, realizing it was Aunt Charity holding Jaelen as Aunt Faith sang behind them. It was her way of letting me know my baby was safe, that they were his guardian angels. Filled with splendid peace, I opened the small photo album Aunt Hope sent containing pictures of her big middle sister in various stages of her life. "She was damn gorgeous."

"That part! And she looks like she didn't put up with too much stuff."

I laughed. "Aunt Hope said she was a firecracker. What's this?" Opening a tiny case, I found a thumb drive inside.

"Get your laptop and let's see what's on it."

I did, only to sit with chills flooding my entire being as Aunt Faith's voice filled the air. The recording was old, scratchy. That didn't prevent us from being arrested by its majesty. The instrumentation seemed to fade for me as I focused on the velvety tones of Joie Wilson singing the song from my dream that I often found myself humming.

I was instantly submerged in the tale of a young woman who'd lost the greatest of loves, and was willing to move heaven and earth in the name of restoration. It was beautiful, gut-wrenching; yet the final phrasing left me feeling that she'd made peace with the weight of her want and possessed unshakable assurance.

Let the world turn,
Let seasons change,
I'll hold onto hope always,
That I'll be finding you,
And you'll be finding me,
Yes, I'll be finding you,
And you'll be finding me.

Our arms intertwined, Natasha and I listened to that song until the sun bowed gracefully and gave the moon the sky.

"Did the car pick them up?"

"Of course, it did, Zo-Zo. Sit your behind down and relax."

"I can't." Opening nights were always dizzying for me, but this exhibition was as personal as the breath I breathed. I'd arranged for my grandparents to be chauffeured to tonight's opening reception, and they hadn't arrived yet. I wanted to phone Granny for their exact location, but my grandmother didn't tolerate crazy. I checked my makeup a final time, instead, thankful that Natasha had arrived early in a show of support. "God, Creator, Universe please bless all things to go smoothly this evening."

"And don't let me have to throat-choke this chick in the process," Natasha added. "Amen."

A knock on the conference door punctuated our laughter. "Yes?"

The administrative assistant poked her head into the room. "Zoe, your grandparents are here."

"Thanks. I'll be right there."

"Looka God! I didn't have to resort to violence. I'm telling you, Zoe, there's power in my prayers."

I exited the conference room where I'd set up shop for the evening with Natasha on my heels and headed toward the entrance to greet our grandparents and escort them to the atrium, thankful for Estelle's support and flexibility. My last-minute idea for a private reception on opening night, before the big wigs and patrons arrived, hadn't fazed her in the least. Her "let's make it happen" demonstrated, yet again, her leadership skills—how she could pivot on a dime, was forward-thinking, and believed in me.

"What a pretty room."

I smiled at my grandmother's gushing as we entered the small atrium I'd had transformed into a private salon. My parents and other relatives were already assembled as well as Granddad's quartet members and close friends. White floral arrangements decorated a table offering hors d'oeuvres as the Alexander Morgan trio's live rendition of 1930s big band sounds created a nostalgic atmosphere.

"Baby, you shouldn't have gone through all this trouble for us."

"Anything for my duke and duchess." I kissed my grandmother's cheek and squeezed my grandfather's hand while quelling the nervous flutters I felt at Shaun's absence.

He'll be here. Relax.

I took my advice and mingled with guests until Estelle slipped through the side door, signaling that the intimate ceremony could begin.

I positioned myself behind the podium.

"Good evening, and welcome to the private pre-opening of *Black Life in a Distressed West*. I'm glad you're not shy and have already helped yourselves to refreshments." Good-natured laughter rippled warmly. I acknowledged Estelle before continuing. "I'm honored that you've chosen to share the evening with us. This exhibition was conceived as a tribute to bold people who dared to come West, pursuing dreams. But it's also become a treasure to me personally." I paused, allowing my emotions to settle. "My grandparents, perhaps like some of you, came to

California during the Dust Bowl. Unfortunately, *our* mass arrival isn't included in much of the visual narrative. We are erased. Forgotten. This exhibition reinserts *us*, and I'm delighted to share it with you." I subtly cued the administrative assistant stationed in the rear to have my first surprise brought in. "Before we proceed, I'd like to invite Mister Noah Wilson, my grandfather, to join me at the front of the room."

"What? No, thank you, granddaughter. I'm good sitting right here."

"You don't have a choice, Noah. Get on up there."

Smiling at Granny's whispered advice that proved louder than intended, I walked to where they sat, offered my grandfather my hand, and escorted him up front as a huge, covered frame was positioned on an easel.

Holding his hands, I felt emotional.

"Granddad, your voyage and its aftermath were far from easy, but I thank you and Granny for surviving that westward migration that changed your lives and offered choice and opportunity to our family. I offer you this gift in appreciation."

I stood aside as Granddad removed the cloth from the oversized collage celebrating his lost past.

"My. Dear. God . . ."

One of the first things Faith did after reclaiming our land was locate our sister's grave. That's how we found Mama's old tin of family photos, in the ground with Charity.

My great aunts had had the photographs restored, and Aunt Hope had graciously sent digital copies to me when learning my intentions for the evening. I'd had them enlarged on canvas so that they showed like a sepia-toned work of art. An image of my great grandparents with their four children inhabited the center and was flanked by two single images on either side: Charity, Faith, Noah, and Hope in chronological order. My grandfather stood speechless, tears bathing his face as he basked in the oversized, beautifully arranged images of his beloveds.

Sounds of admiration drifted from the guests as I focused on him. "Are you okay, Granddad?"

He patted his tears with a handkerchief before hugging me fiercely. "Every time I looked at you, I saw my big middle sister. Now, I can look on us all again. Thank you, my precious Zoe Noelle, with the silver bells and angel tails, for gifting me another glimpse of my origins."

I lay my head against his chest and shared his tears until seeing Shaun enter at the back of the room. I smiled my pleasure and gave a signal for my second surprise before releasing my grandfather. "Would you like to have words, Granddad?"

He shook his head. "What can an old man like me say in a time and place like this except 'God is good?'" He stared at the canvas. "I never thought I'd see us all together again."

It took all of my unproven acting abilities not to react when Shaun entered the side door with a special guest. Admiring his gift, Granddad's back was to them when he suddenly stopped speaking and straightened his shoulders as if sensing a presence. I watched him slowly turn in Shaun's direction, and placed a steadying hand at his back as he wobbled at the sight of Aunt Faith's "Baby Girl" and Miss Viv's "Little Bit."

Video-conferencing did my Aunt Hope no justice. She was regal, beautiful, and her voice wavered with boundless emotion. "Is that my big brother?"

Unable to move, Granddad stood transfixed as odd, inarticulate sounds escaped his mouth and his baby sister approached him, escorted by Shaun.

Her hands shook as she cupped his face. "Noah. Riley. Wilson. Where've you been?"

Granddad's crushing embrace was Aunt Hope's only answer.

"They're too cute."

My grandfather and his sister hadn't left each other's side the entire night. When they weren't holding hands, her arm was tucked around his as he, Aunt Hope, and Granny sauntered through the museum enjoying the exhibition. All three had been photographed as living legends, positioned beside pieces from the exhibition, and I couldn't wait to see the finished photographs. Uncle Emery had been unable to travel due to a medical condition but Aunt Hope's granddaughter, my cousin Camille, had accompanied her instead.

"I agree they're cute, Miss Edwards, but so are you."

I laughed at Shaun's compliment. " 'Cute' is not what I want to be at nearly forty. Can I get 'attractive,' 'delicious,' or 'sexy'?"

"You're all of those things, Zoe."

"Watch out, JeShaun Halsey. That slick tongue might up your access."

Seated, surrounded by portraits of the past and enjoying the live band, we both laughed.

"Were you pleased with the evening, Mademoiselle Curator?"

The evening's festivities had been well-attended and the exhibition well-received. The local news sent a crew for coverage, and a journalist was in attendance, feverishly typing notes on her iPad for a write-up. A brief lecture by a premier art historian had proven engaging; and the trio's live music from the era added to the ambience. Observing our surroundings, I confirmed my pleasure.

"I don't think one thing could've been better. I'm just sorry Nana Sam was unable to attend." I'd invited Shaun's grandmother as well as Micah Owenslee. Miss Samuella hadn't felt well enough to travel, and Mister Owenslee had declined, gracefully, saying it was a night for my family.

"It would've been incredible for Nana to have seen her photographs in a museum."

I grinned at Shaun, knowing he was unaware of the special

portrait book I'd ordered for his grandmother as a "thank you" for providing the precious portal that reconnected my family, imagining her pleasure when seeing her photography between its covers.

"Why're you cheesing like you won something, baby?"

"Because I did." I leaned up to kiss his cheek. "Thank you."

"For?"

"Seeing me in those photos of Aunt Faith and bringing us together. She obviously meant for me to find her."

Shaun studied me a moment before standing and extending a hand.

I simply looked at it. "Yes?"

"Let's dance."

Accepting his offer, I wrapped my arms about his neck and slowly swayed to the sounds of Alana D., a Bay Area vocalist, whose surprise appearance with tonight's trio had been a joy for many. Now the night was winding down and her voice was a perfect, sultry background.

"Perhaps your aunt intended for us to find each other as well, Zoe."

"Absolutely. So . . . do you want a situationship? You. Me. Us?"

He chuckled deeply. "I'm down with that, but here's to hoping it leads to permanence."

I met him halfway when he bent to kiss me, losing myself in the taste and feel of his lips as that sultry guest chanteuse segued into a song that needed no introduction. Aunt Faith's "Finding You" flowed effortlessly as if from an open vessel. Forgetting my surroundings, I pressed into Shaun and his kiss, thankful for the gift of family and the power of unforgotten portraits.

EPILOGUE
ZOE

One Year Later
Wellston, Oklahoma

We gathered about our ancestors' final resting place, listening as Granddad recounted their youth with laughter and tears, impressing on us the importance of togetherness, love, and preserving our history with acts of remembrance such as this. When he finished, Aunt Hope, seated beside him beneath a towering shade tree, honored the woman who'd enabled our assembly.

"My sister Faith used to say to me, 'Baby Girl, we're gonna be together again. Watch and see.' And so, we're here today. Celebrating. Family, please bow your heads as Reverend Coulter III blesses this monument."

I bowed my head and my thoughts immediately latched onto my great aunt with whom I'd fallen deeply in love. Faith Joy Wilson had been ahead of her time in many of the choices she had made, and I found her life story amazing. I often tried imagining myself fifteen and leaving home without my beloveds, in the company of hostile strangers and couldn't see myself succeeding. I admired her courage and fierce devotion to family, and was livid at the ill-treatment she'd encountered, not solely inflicted by external adversaries, but namely one who should have helped, not hindered: my great-great grandmother. Madame, as she was known, was a bitter and bent woman best left unremembered.

When we left that place, Faith took care of us all. Me. Mama. Miss Viv. And never complained about it.

Aunt Hope regaled me with so many tales of Aunt Faith's sacrifices that I was challenged to do more with what I had and, as soon as Reverend Coulter finished, I'd reveal the newly established Faith Joy Wilson scholarship for students of color majoring in music.

"And, dear Lord, we thank You for bringing this fine family here to honor *all* of their ancestors even before Tomas and Mae Wilson..."

I grinned as Reverend Coulter ramped into the next gear of a long-winded prayer that allowed my thoughts to further drift to Aunt Faith's thriving, not simply surviving, in an era not designed for the success of Black women. My precious doppelgänger created space for herself and lived according to her strengths and passions. I'd cried when learning we shared similar heartbreak, but was empowered by her tenaciousness. She'd stared down opposition with grit and determination, and let her wounds weave themselves into music that healed. Her voice was sweet magic that brought listeners under her spell. She was never a household name in the States, but that 1935 trip to France wasn't her last. She returned annually, had a devoted following, and established dual citizenship there.

She was a renaissance woman. A boss!

My great aunt lived without apology. Even in loving Dallas Dorsey.

We have that in common, Aunt Faith, being boo'ed up with good men.

Shaun squeezed my hand when I nearly laughed. I covered it with a fake cough and refocused on Reverend Coulter's prayer, and maybe said "amen" a little too loudly at the end.

"Bae, are you okay?"

I smiled at JeShaun Halsey, world-class photographer and the exceptional man I had the pleasure of loving. Our bicoastal relationship required work, but we gave it one hundred. Thankfully we were both in control of our own calendars since I became a full-fledged independent curator five months after my *Black Life in a Distressed West* exhibition ended. I was scared as hell, but found strength in Aunt Faith's daring to live differently. I might've taken that courage too far in proposing to Shaun last week. He declined, outdone that I'd stolen his shine.

Baby, how was I supposed to know you had an engagement ring waiting on me?

I accepted *his* proposal when he got over himself and went down on bended knee.

Now, beneath that huge tree, I leaned against him as his arm slid about my waist, experiencing a happiness that, to others, may have seemed strange there on family land dedicated to our deceased. Yet, as the covering was removed and the sun shone on the marble of the newly installed monument, I felt it clearly. Joy. Peace.

Serenity enveloped me as we, the reunited descendants, admired the exquisite engravings of our forbears' names. Similar to the collage I'd gifted to Granddad, the enormous stone was dominated at the center by my great grandparents Tomas and Mae Princessa Wilson, with their children's names—two on the left, two on the right—in ascending order from youngest to oldest. Natasha considered it semi-morbid to include Granddad and Aunt Hope's names when they were yet living. I understood wanting to be connected with beloveds, and the settling of life on this side. Or as Granddad said, *When I lay down for good, my eternal bed is already made. Only detail missing is the date.*

I was thankful that whatever time remained for my grandfather and Aunt Hope, they'd spend it together, brother and sister, divinely reconnected.

"Zoe Noelle, I understand you have something to present."

"Yes, sir," I answered my grandfather while moving through family to stand beside this brand-new stone of remembrance marking the graves of our beloveds. I looked at our gathering, marveling at the power of genetics. Until last year many of us hadn't met, yet we bore amazing resemblances. Some of our mannerisms were even the same, making us a study in nature versus nurture. My heart swelled as I revealed the news of the scholarship I'd created and others increased the award amount by offering additional contributions. I closed my eyes in gratitude and bowed in thanks as my heels sank into the green grass beneath my feet, a lush contrast to those long-ago dusty conditions that forced my family's exodus. Opening my eyes, I found the curious sight of two cousins carrying gigantic blue and silver balloon arrangements, and moved aside to allow them to stand where I had.

"Everyone, take one," Aunt Hope instructed, waiting until we did. "Today, April twentieth, is a day that only the good Lord could make so special in countless ways. It's my middle big sister's birthday, as well as my great-great nephew's sunset. Little Faith"—Aunt Hope addressed me by my new nickname—"these balloons are for my Faye-Faye *and* Jaelen. We love you both. Until we meet again..."

I was so moved I couldn't speak and simply hugged Shaun as love enveloped me. Blinking away tears, I blinked again when seeing her manifesting near the monument ensconced in radiance.

Aunt Faith's appearing no longer freaked the ish out of me like when it first happened. I'd been listening to "Finding You," humming in my pitiful pitch and washing dishes when I caught a flash of silver to my left. Seeing the hazy outline of her form and face, I dropped the plate and flew out my townhouse. I called Mama and when she finished laughing at my antics, she advised me to welcome her if it ever happened again. It did. Only when listening to her music.

"Probably to tell you to stop butchering her melodies with your off-key singing," Natasha had teased.

Whenever I wanted to sense her presence, I played her songs. Sometimes Aunt Faith appeared. Others, she didn't. But when she did, our connection was like warm, soothing liquid. I'd come to realize that my initially thinking she was tied to Mama, that there was something similar in their eyes, was simply a universal sorrow, the loss of family connections. Now, she stood smiling brilliantly, holding the hand of a beautiful toddler I instinctively knew was Jaelen.

One of the hardest things I did when I returned to Boston after my exhibition was packing the room that had become a sacred shrine: my son's nursery. I kept a few mementos and a cute teddy bear, but shipped the majority to Layla's new baby, donated the balance to charity. It was a bittersweet act, but very necessary.

We can adopt if you want.

Shaun's suggestion had touched my heart. And I would definitely consider it. I loved his daughter to life and would be her bonus mom when I married her dad. That was enough for now. I was content, blessed.

Standing there, seeing my son near that tombstone with my Aunt Faith, my soul knew joy in abundance. His smile was sweet as he waved at me. As blue and silver balloons—tokens of oneness—floated toward heaven, I blew him a kiss and watched the two walk away, leaving me with the bliss of knowing my beautiful baby was in the company of our ancestors. Loved. Safe.

· · ·

FAITH

I don't know why life lets me come back sometimes. Maybe to grant my dream of seeing my tribe enjoying the fruit of our labors and restored unity. Watching my beloveds gathered here on land my grandfather was given when freed from slavery is astounding and rewarding after too many years of legal wars and wrangling. At times, Mama and Baby Girl suggested I let it go, the battle got so intense. But I couldn't. My grandfather killed someone in self-defense. My grandmother was compromised and conceived Aunt Leola. My father held on so tightly we lost Charity. All in the name of preserving this homestead. I had to honor that. Not to mention I couldn't leave Charity alone here, or let black blizzards win. This belonged to us. I refused to give up.

Now, look at us Wilsons. Together. Again.

I'm proud of Noah and Hope for reuniting our clan, sharing memories that bind us together, defying separation.

I don't fault my baby brother for being unable to tell his story until finding Baby Girl again. He was ten when rattlesnakes and a black blizzard took part of his foot, and all of his sisters and mother from him. Mama went out of her head and started cutting her arms, hurting herself, after her girls were lost, so that Papa and Noah had to put her in that Bakersfield sanatorium, not knowing how to rescue Mama from herself. I can't imagine the helplessness they must've felt. Especially a proud man like Papa who'd lost everything and couldn't cover his family.

It's only for a minute, Mae. Until I can set us up. I promise, I'll be back.

Unfortunately, when Papa returned, That Demon had already squirreled Mama away. Papa was told Mama simply walked off. He never forgave himself for losing "all his girls," and buried himself in physical labor every weekday, pouring his sorrow into California soil as a ranch hand, resorting to liquid comfort come weekends. Papa was that kind of disciplined while working, resorting to taming his pain with liquor Friday through Sunday. Noah was there through it all, dosing Papa with raw eggs and tabasco sauce or scalding black coffee Sunday nights so he'd be ready for work come Monday. That didn't make life easy for my baby brother. He became quiet, withdrawn and might've been utterly lost but for the kindness of two elderly widowed sisters, the Milbreys, who lived in the farming community and took a liking to him. They made sure he was fed, helped whenever Papa's weekend drinking got out of hand. Even with their help, it was my brother who lived with the daily evidence of our father's demise and a loss of family that left Noah wrapped, trapped in silent misery. He never went to college like Mama wanted, staying on and helping Papa work the land for others until he was grown and had enough to buy his own small farm and was able to care for Papa until he passed. Thank God, Noah found Teenie. Loving her was healing. So was music, and singing in his quartet. Still, he buried the bulk of his past deep inside himself as if speaking it—or even our names—might snatch happiness away. Finally, he's free to talk about it, now that he has Baby Girl.

Look at them. Sitting there like two kids, licking homemade ice cream cones made with Mama's recipe, so good it has them humming. That's the magic of Mama.

After everything she went through, Mama was less talkative, but her smile and disposition remained gentle. Sometimes she had nightmares and would be terrified for me or Hope to be out of her sight. We'd hold her, sing to her, and Miss Viv—who'd left *that* house when we did and never looked back—would massage her scalp and comb her hair, telling wild stories that made Mama laugh. Those two became close as sisters and helped each other heal.

We all cried when Doc Reed confirmed Miss Viv couldn't sing anymore; but being the woman she was, she picked herself up and pursued her second love. She became a hairstylist, pressing, curling hair in our kitchen. When business was low and slow and she doubted herself, we'd cheer her on and I simply paid the bills.

Singing let me do that.

Life changed after France. For me, Mister Smitty, Dallas, and the band. Theirs wasn't some white fixation—walking on the wild side or indulging in taboo sensations—like here. Those French folks savored our music and treated us like humans. We were a hit and I did like I promised: sent home most of every dollar I earned for Mama, Hope, and Miss Viv until we had enough for a down payment on a precious three-bedroom bungalow. Monsieur Marceaux wanted to extend our contract after that first three-month visit, but I had to get home to my small tribe. I needed to see them for myself despite their claiming they were fine. Thank God it wasn't a lie.

Hope did excellent in school. Miss Viv was doing hair. Mama stayed on sewing for Miz Bailey and our little bungalow became her queendom. I loved that we had something of our own again and gave all I could to sustain it including spending four months in France, six months home. Then back again. Eventually I was even able to treat my three ladies to a summer month there every other year.

I sang so frequently, earning a living and taking care of my family, that sometimes I'd be so hoarse I could barely talk the next morning. Mama would make ginger-and-honey tea, wrap my throat in warm cloths and poultices. It always worked, and I took Mama's magic—and sometimes Mama and Hope—on the road.

Whenever I hit the road Stateside, it was with the prayer of finding Papa and Noah in whatever city or town we performed. Despite missing persons ads in the paper and hiring the best detectives my money could afford, that never happened. It was as if the earth had swallowed my father, brother, and even Papa's sisters whole, erasing their existence, mocking my efforts to find them. But every year, like a pilgrimage, I sat at Central Station hoping for a divine appearance. Dallas always offered to go with me, but that was one time I didn't want his presence and preferred sitting alone. Still, I appreciated the support of good love.

And he was that. Through all of life's challenges.

When we boarded that ship on our first trip to France four weeks after Dallas and I wrote "Finding You" and first made love in his flat, I was expecting, without knowing it. I'd had stomach aches before leaving, and all the discomfort I experienced during the voyage I attributed to seasickness. Two weeks after our first gig in Paris, the bleeding started, I miscarried and—though we didn't try future prevention like Mama suggested because we both wanted a baby—I never conceived again. It hurt us something bad, but in time we healed and when Hope married and had children, we spoiled them rotten.

Are you not marrying me because we haven't gotten pregnant since losing the baby?

Dallas proposed in front of the Eiffel Tower the year after our first tour. I loved that man with every breath and felt so miserable declining him, but loss shifted something in me, was too scarring. I worked overtime to assure Dallas I wasn't rejecting *him*. I was embracing my right not to lose love again, as well as learning my life could be bigger than back home where I'd lived with love, but without dreams. He thought it was because I was too young and vowed to propose until I accepted. We had problems like anyone else, and even broke up twice before getting ourselves fully settled, but we savored the fullest forms of love for nearly six decades. But, despite Dallas proposing annually, we never married. Not until I proposed to him on his eightieth birthday.

We had a quiet civil ceremony the following day. Three weeks later, my Dallas was dead.

Baby, seeing as how marrying you had those results, I'm glad we waited until I was old.

He still teases me, claiming I shocked him to a three-week-long death by saying "I Do."

After that first voyage to France, he fell in love with the ocean and made me promise to cremate him and sprinkle his ashes on the waters if he passed before me. So, I honored that. Now my darling's ashes are sparkling somewhere in the ocean, but his spirit is right here beside me. We're together forever and I'm overjoyed to be here in this eternal place even though I treasured earthly living. I recorded music. Sang around the world. Visited many countries. Spoke fluent French. And no matter how hard Dallas and Mister Smitty fussed, on opening night of every one of our performances, I wore that 1920s rose-colored fringe dress Miss Viv loaned me the first time I ever performed to honor her. When it wore out, I had a replica made. That kind of humility kept my feet on the floor when my music soared.

My career wasn't flawless and singing never made me rich-rich, but I always had more than what I needed. I was expansive, a Colored woman with freedom. Freedom sent me back for my high school diploma in my sixties; earned me a Bachelor in Music in my seventies when I retired from singing. Having plenty let me send Baby Girl to college where her long-ago love of rock collecting came in handy and she earned her doctorate in geology. Miss Viv stayed with us until falling in love with and marrying ol' burly Boolie; and Mama lived into her mid-seventies. With her support, I'd hired that team of lawyers to get back our land. It must've been providence because six years after winning, Mama passed and we were able to lay her to rest beside her firstborn. But now, it's not only Mama and Charity, but Papa. Dallas in spirit. Me.

We're not merely asleep. We're the sparkle in sunlight, the ripple in a brook, the cool of a sweet breeze. Through such wonders, we laugh. We speak. That's how Papa—his words floating on butterfly wings—let me know he fought that black blizzard for me. He stayed in Wellston two whole weeks looking for us until admitting to himself we were gone. Irony of ironies, Hope and I arrived in California looking for them, while he was searching for us in Wellston. But as they say, all's well that ends that way. And it's well, thanks to my Little Faith, Zoe Noelle, living with me stamped all over her face.

Her face. Her spirit. That shared stubbornness. I knew she wouldn't quit until solving the mystery of her visage in my picture. Before that picture, I summoned her with a whisper. The first time heaven let me visit her was when she was reading that write-up celebrating Steinbeck's *Grapes of Wrath*. I whispered a little indignation in her ear and got her to thinking about us folks missing from the narrative. I counted on her displeasure and perseverance ultimately bringing us Wilsons back together. She didn't let me down one bit. When Noah led her to Papa's grave, she helped my baby brother exhume and relocate Papa's remains from California back home last year so that he could rest alongside his beloved, Mae.

Papa, Mama, Charity, so many others, and me: we're the tribe. Guiding our descendants and watching over the innocent beloveds like precious Jaelen. Dallas's ashes might be sparkling in the ocean, but that's nothing but dust of the flesh. Like I said, our true selves are here. All of us who've crossed over to join the ancestors. We're vibrant. Shimmering. The earthly separation this tribe endured was temporary. We're never orphaned. We're joined eternally.

Reading Group Guide

Discussion Questions

1. How does the theme of sisterhood present itself in *The Dust Bowl Orphans,* and what impact does sisterhood have on Faith, as well as Zoe?

2. Prior to reading this book, what was your knowledge of this natural phenomenon, the Dust Bowl? Had you previously considered its impact on African Americans?

3. Charity Wilson dies early in the story. How does she continue to be present in Faith's life even after her tragic demise?

4. Zoe admits to being her father's "mini-me," yet she goes on a quest to discover the identity of the young girl in the picture with the hope that the unknown ancestor is connected to her mother's lineage. Why didn't she immediately make the connection that Faith was a paternal relative?

5. Faith reconnects with Dallas in Los Angeles. How would you describe their romance?

6. What did you admire most about Faith? Zoe? Hope? Or any other character?

7. How do race and religion intersect in *The Dust Bowl Orphans*?

8. *The Dust Bowl Orphans* is a dual timeline narrative, alternating between historical and contemporary characters. Did you find yourself favoring one storyline over the other? Or did you enjoy both equally?

9. When we first meet Zoe, she is separated from Vince, has survived the devastating loss of her newborn son, and is experiencing some professional stagnation. In what ways does the past (e.g., Faith, Charity) help Zoe heal in the present?

10. How would you describe Faith's relationship with Micah? With Henry?

11. Describe Faith's relationship with Mr. Smitty and the band. Does Zoe have any relationships that are similar in nature?

12. How did you feel when Hope and Noah are reunited at the end?

Author Q&A

What inspired you to write *The Dust Bowl Orphans*?

My grandfather was born in the tiny town of Wellston, Oklahoma—the same town in which *The Dust Bowl Orphans* begins. For me the story is a tribute to my great-grandparents who, in the 1930s, dared to pull up stakes and leave Wellston and migrate to California in search of better life opportunities for themselves and their six children.

How much research went into writing this book?

Much! I scoured articles, journals, even videos, and was blessed to interview a professor of art history, which was crucial for our contemporary character, Zoe. As a writer of historical fiction, accuracy is extremely important to me. I want to transport readers back in time by painting and providing images of the era in which my story is set, not an anachronistic view of history. I want readers to see, taste, sense, and experience whatever the historical time frame in a genuine, authentic manner, to feel as if they've been dropped into a tableau of yesterday. I want them to be involved yet viewing the past from a safe distance. Research is key to accomplishing this.

What do you mean by readers can view the past "from a safe distance"?

The collective, historical experiences of African Americans and many other diverse cultures isn't necessarily something that we wish to repeat or revisit. It is often pain filled and fraught with injustices and atrocities. Historical fiction allows us to encounter such incidents from the safe space of a reader. Memories may be triggered. We might even recount stories our ancestors told, ones our grandparents or parents shared. That creates resonance (good or bad), but we're able to close the book or stop reading and disconnect or take a break from a story when necessary.

Much of your work, including *The Dust Bowl Orphans*, is female-centered. Is that intentional?

I write what I know. (And sometimes, what I don't.) I'm a woman, so of course that naturally informs the worlds and characters I create. I'm fascinated by African American female characters and the cosmos in which they move and live. I'm interested in my characters' hopes, dreams, motivations, and concepts of themselves and others. And as a Black woman writer, I approach my work as an opportunity to celebrate my fellow Black females, past or present. Does this mean I am restricted to female-focused fiction? No. There's a story in the treasure chest of my creativity that features a male character who keeps reaching out to me. In due time, I'll tell his story.

1 Corinthians 13 references faith, hope, and charity. This also happens to be the names of the Wilson sisters. Is this what inspired their names?

Yes, as well as a little song I remember singing as a child in church: *"Faith, Hope, and Charity, that's the way to live successfully ..."* I started with the names of our main protagonist, Faith, and her baby sister, Hope. Naming the oldest sister Charity seemed a natural fit. The meanings of their names are crucial to the story and the characters' journeys, even imperative. We all need faith (trust), hope (daring), and love (affection) in life.

Music and art factor greatly into the story. Why is this?

I come from a musical family. I played piano as a child and into my young adult years, and according to my mother I sang before I could talk. I have cousins who are musicians, and my family consists of many singers. But it wasn't until I was an adult that I learned my great-grandfather, Papa (to whom the book is dedicated), sang in a quartet. Greater shock still was the fact that Papa also performed with his sons in church—that is, my great-uncle and my grandfather! How I wish I could've been a fly on the wall seeing and hearing their musical renditions. Additionally, as a child I was very artistic and forever drawing something. I suppose my gifting Faith and her family with musicality and Zoe with artistic gifts was an intentional/unintentional means of honoring my family talents.

The theme of sisterhood is one that seems to possess center stage of *The Dust Bowl Orphans*. Was that intentional?

Again, my novels are predominantly female-focused, so sisterhood is a logical outcome or response. I suppose you could call it intentional, in that I am the middle of three daughters who were raised by our divorced mother. My sisters, and loving, non-antagonistic female relationships, are highly important to me.

Why did you choose to write this story as a dual timeline narrative?

Doing so allowed me to view two sides of history, and how today is connected to yesterday. Sometimes we live as if the present is fully disconnected from our historical pasts. I love seeing how the past positively affects or impacts the present. We walk through Faith's life—her trials and triumphs—in the 1930s, only to see how her experiences are salient and relevant to Zoe, our contemporary heroine. The past inspires the present, and the present isn't created in a vacuum or isolated vortex. There is always a touch place and overlap. We can glean wisdom and gather strength if we take the time to acknowledge and appreciate those who've gone before us. I can never know all of my ancestors on this side of heaven, but I thank, honor, and reverence them just the same.

Author Essay

I love the sound of fallen leaves crunching beneath my feet in fall. I adore the sight and sound of ocean waves crashing against the shore or rushing gently toward me. And the smell and lulling rhythm of rain beyond my windowpanes is hypnotizing. Soothing.

But storms? They're not my thing.

Years ago, when my college-age children were cherub-faced wee people, my family visited my mother in Texas. It was our first trip to the Southwest after my mother's relocation there, made all the more sweet because we didn't tell her we were coming in advance. We simply showed up on her doorstep, wearing huge smiles and surprising the daylights out of her. It was a wonderful visit that seemingly ended too quickly with the onset of a vicious storm that I still remember.

The storm blew in the day before we left, complete with ferocious rain and hail that turned the gutters into rivers. Sirens blared at the local school. News reports of the storm's impact seemed laced and ladened with doom and gloom. Or perhaps that was my vivid imagination on hyperdrive. What was clear and indisputable were the high winds that whipped the rain sideways and blue skies that turned the color of midnight. Needless to say, my husband and I were more than a little leery about flying home the next day and could only pray.

Thank heavens, the storm lessened to a manageable degree that allowed us to flee (okay, leave) the longhorn state the day after that horrific storm made an appearance. Despite minimal inconveniences, our flight was not delayed. We returned home to the sunny west coast, very grateful and intact. More than a decade has passed since then, yet "surviving" that storm is an experience I won't forget.

Perhaps I'm a west coast wimp who dislikes torrential Texas rain that's blown sideways by gale-force winds, hail the size of golf balls, and black skies that were blue mere moments before. Maybe something in my DNA objects, imagining that such were the storms my maternal great-grandparents endured. At some point in life, my great-grandfather resided in Texas, but relocated to the neighboring state of Oklahoma and the tiny town of my grandfather's birth—Wellston. It wasn't until the mid-1930s that my great-grandparents packed up their hearth and home to relocate to California . . . right around the time of the Dust Bowl.

Many of us are familiar with the Dust Bowl and how it swept through Oklahoma and the Midwest thanks to John Steinbeck's *The Grapes of Wrath*. Whether we turned the pages of the book or watched the Joad family's saga play out on television, *The Grapes of Wrath* proved a window into this natural phenomenon and time period. That is, for those of us who didn't personally experience it. We witnessed the agony and outcome of storms of black dust so fierce and frequent that crops failed, livestock perished, and economies were devastated. And *that*, on the heels of the Great Depression. What I, personally, didn't see was the impact of the Dust Bowl on persons who look like me.

That, in part, is why I penned *The Dust Bowl Orphans*.

A dual timeline told from twin, varying perspectives, *The Dust Bowl Orphans* is two novels in one. It is the harrowing story of our historical heroine, Faith Wilson, and her contemporary counterpart, Zoe Edwards. Described as "beautifully written," this novel examines themes of migration, racism, religiosity, feminine power, faith, and family. Which leads me to the other, more personal reason for my penning this story: *my* family. The Kelleys.

We were there. We, meaning African Americans.

We succumbed. We survived. We battled those horrendous storms that buried homes and inked the skies. Loss and decimation were equal opportunity disasters that did not spare persons with brown skin despite our being omitted from the narrative. *The Dust Bowl Orphans* is a celebration offering a differing perspective. It is my shifting the gaze and honoring those who went before me, who enabled the possibility of future generations. Posterity. It is my tribute to my ancestors who picked up stakes and left Oklahoma in search of better. It is a story of journey, uncertainty, but the steadfastness of family and community.

As I sit in my kitchen writing this, I can't help glancing out the window and experiencing thankfulness. It's a bright morning here in California, the state that received my great-grandparents when they fled Oklahoma. My lemon tree is bearing fruit, and I am safe in a place where storms are possible but infrequent. I've felt rain, as well as pain. Yet, as I consider the Dust Bowl and my ancestors, even my Texas rain experience seems minuscule in comparison. They are the root. I am the fruit. And *The Dust Bowl Orphans* is my tribute.

A LETTER FROM SUZETTE

Dear Reader,

Thank you for choosing *The Dust Bowl Orphans*. I hope you thoroughly enjoyed it! If you did and would like to keep up to date with all my latest releases, sign up at the following link. Your email address will never be shared, and you can unsubscribe at any time.

Also, if you enjoyed Faith and Zoe's journey I'd be grateful if you wrote a review. I'd love to hear what you think, and it makes such a difference helping new readers to discover my work as well. If you're using an e-reader, the app lets you post a review when finishing the book. How convenient is that? Your review can be as brief as a sentence, but it has tremendous impact. And by all means, please tell a friend!

I love hearing from my readers—you can get in touch on my Facebook page, Goodreads, or my website.

Blessings until next time,

Suzette

www.sdhbooks.com

facebook.com/sdhbooks
instagram.com/suzetteharrison2200

ACKNOWLEDGMENTS

I could never be creative without the Creator. It is to the Divine One that I give all praise and glory. Thank you for choosing me.

I thank my beloved husband and children for believing steadfastly in me. I cherish your support, and your ability to ground me with humility.

I also acknowledge my extended family and fellow authors—particularly those women writers whom I affectionately call "Lit Sis." You help me hold it down and not give in.

I'd also like to extend an extra special thank you to Dr. Bridget R. Cooks, Ph.D., Associate Professor in the Department of African American Studies and the Department of Art History at the University of California Irvine. Your phenomenal knowledge and expertise aided me in rounding my character Zoe Edwards—specifically, Zoe's life as an art curator. Thank you for answering my countless questions about art, museums, and exhibitions with grace, generosity, and enthusiasm.

Thank you to the wonderful staff at Bookouture, particularly my editor, Emily Gowers, for your constant support. Emily, I love our chats and laughter, and am beyond grateful that you believe in me and for this literary journey that brought us together.

And last, but never least, to my newsletter subscribers, every reader, book club, book blogger, or interviewer who has allowed me time and space, as well as embraced my writing gift, thank you!